Stephen Dixon Late Stories

TRNSFR BOOKS

PUBLISHED BY TRNSFR BOOKS,
AN IMPRINT OF CURBSIDE SPLENDOR PUBLISHING,
CHICAGO, ILLINOIS

TRNSFRMAG.COM
CURBSIDESPLENDOR.COM

LIBRARY OF CONGRESS CONTROL NUMBER: 2016949233
ISBN 978-1-940430-87-4

EDITED AND DESIGNED BY ALBAN FISCHER

PRINTED IN THE UNITED STATES OF AMERICA

FIRST EDITION
TRNSFR BOOKS 001

Praise f

"Mr. Dixon wields a stubbornly plain-spoken style; he loves all sorts of tricky narrative effects. And he loves even more the tribulations of the fantasizing mind, ticklish in their comedy, alarming in their immediacy."

—*The New York Times*

"Some writers are able, in a mere 200 pages or so, to rewire your circuitry in a way that makes you unfit for your own life. Stephen Dixon is such a writer, and he can do it in a short story as well."

—*The Los Angeles Times*

"Stephen Dixon is one of the great secret masters—too secret. I return again and again to his stories for writerly inspiration, moral support and comic relief at moments of personal misery, and, several times, in a spirit of outright plagiaristic necessity: borrowing a jumpstart from a few lines of Dixon has been a real problem-solver in my own short fiction. Please read him, you."

—Jonathan Lethem, author of *Dissident Gardens*

"There is no better chronicler of our antic and anxious age than Stephen Dixon."

—Daniel Handler (aka Lemony Snicket)

"You have to go into a Dixon book the way you'd go into a game of strip poker: ready to end up naked. He gives it to you straight, and means every word. He is the least pretentious living writer."

—J. Robert Lennon, author of *Familiar*

"A hip Saul Bellow."

—*Publishers Weekly*

Late Stories

Wife in Reverse

His wife dies, mouth slightly parted and one eye open. He knocks on his younger daughter's bedroom door and says "You better come. Mom seems to be expiring." His wife slips into a coma three days after she comes home and stays in it for eleven days. They have a little party second day she's home: Nova Scotia salmon, chocolates, a risotto he made, brie cheese, strawberries, champagne. An ambulette brings his wife home. She says to him "Wheel me around the garden before I go to bed for the last time." His wife refuses the feeding tube the doctors want to put in her and insists she wants to die at home. She says "I don't want any more life support, medicines, fluid or food." He calls 911 for the fourth time in two years and tells the dispatcher "My wife; I'm sure she has pneumonia again." His wife has a trach put in. "When will it come out?" she says, and the doctor says "To be honest? Never." "Your wife has a very bad case of pneumonia," the doctor in ICU tells him and his daughters the first time, "and has a one to two percent chance of surviving." His wife now uses a wheelchair. His wife now uses a motor cart. His wife now uses a walker with wheels. His wife now uses a walker. His wife has to use a cane. His wife's diagnosed with MS. His wife has trouble walking. His wife gives birth to their second daughter. "This time you didn't cry," she says, and he says "I'm just as happy, though." His wife says to him "Something seems wrong with my eyes." His wife gives birth to their daughter. The obstetrician says "I've never seen a father cry in the birthing room." The rabbi pronounces them husband and wife, and just be-

9

fore he kisses her, he bursts out crying. "Let's get married," he says to her, and she says "It's all right with me," and he says "It is?" and starts crying. "What a reaction," she says, and he says "I'm so happy, so happy," and she hugs him and says "So am I." She calls and says "How are you? Do you want to meet and talk?" She drops him off in front of his building and says "It's just not working." They go to a restaurant on their first real date and he says "The reason I'm being so picky as to what to eat is that I'm a vegetarian, something I was a little reluctant to tell you so soon," and she says "Why? It's not peculiar. It just means we won't share our entrees except for the vegetables." He meets a woman at a party. They talk for a long time. She has to leave the party and go to a concert. He gets her phone number and says "I'll call you," and she says "I'd like that." He says goodbye to her at the door and shakes her hand. After she leaves he thinks "That woman's going to be my wife."

Another Sad Story

He gets a call. It's a sheriff in California. He has some very bad news for him. His daughter's been involved in a serious automobile accident. It was on a narrow two-lane road by the ocean. She apparently overcorrected her steering too much to avoid hitting an oncoming car in her lane and went over an embankment. "Yes, yes, is she alive?" "I don't know how to put it. I've never had to tell this to a parent. She died in the ambulance taking her to the hospital." He puts down the receiver. What to do? He has to call his other daughter. He should tell his wife first. But his wife's dead, so what's he thinking? His sisters. One of them, who can tell the other. He'll do nothing. He'll lie on his bed and go to sleep. First he should put the cover over his typewriter. No, don't even do that. He pushes the cover off his bed and lies down and closes his eyes. The phone rings and he gets up to answer it. Probably his older daughter saying she got back to L.A. okay and something about the interview she had in Berkeley. It's the sheriff. "You hung up before I could finish. I wanted to tell you how to reach me, where we are, what hospital your daughter's at and some of the things you or someone you designate to represent you need to know and do." "I'm to fly out there. I haven't been on a plane in almost fifteen years. I understand flying is much different today. The preparations at the airport and long waits and so forth. I'll get a pencil. A pen, I mean. I always have one on me. I'm a writer. What's a writer without a pen? But for some reason I have none in my pants pockets and one isn't on my dresser. That's where I am now.

In my bedroom. I was working here, which I also use as my study, when you called. I usually keep a pen on the dresser for messages and to doodle with while I'm on the phone. Where are you? What airport do I fly in to? I'll remember." "Better write it down, sir." He gets a pen off his work table and writes on a piece of paper on the dresser the sheriff's name and phone number and the names of the hospital and airport and city. The paper's a bookmark that came with the last book he bought at the only shop he buys his books at. They always put one in the book you buy. "I think I have everything I need now," and he gets off the phone. He lies on his bed. He should call his younger daughter in Chicago. What did he do with the bookmark? Oh, if it's lost, it's lost. But it couldn't have gone far. He should call one of his sisters. But what will either of them do but scream and cry and say this is the worst possible thing that could have happened. He wishes he could speak to his wife. He can't handle this alone, at least now. Maybe if he shut his eyes and slept a while. He shuts his eyes. He has to call his younger daughter. They were very close. But then he'll have her hysteria to deal with. Maybe he could get one of his sisters to tell her, but she'd only want to hear it from him. He gets up and goes into his older daughter's room. When was the last time she slept in it? A few weeks ago. She came for a brief visit. She had a free roundtrip because of all the flying she's done the past few years. When he dropped her off at the airport, she said she had a wonderful time. When he called her the next day in L.A., she again said she had a wonderful time. He had dinner ready for her the day she came. She said it was the best meal she's had since the last time she was here. He said he started making it a week ago and defrosted all of it yesterday. The salad, he said, he made today. They went out for dinner at a Japanese restaurant her third and last day. What did they do for dinner the second night? She gave him a drawing she did in California. She worked on it for several weeks. "We should get it framed," he said. The day after she got here they went to a framing shop. "You choose," she said. "No, you know better about these things than I. Get what you want, and I don't care the price." He left a deposit for the frame. The shop hasn't called yet to say the frame's ready. What will he do when they call? He'll say "I can't speak. I'll call you in a few weeks." They went out for lunch after they left the shop. Later that day he was going to the Y to work out and swim and asked her if she wanted to come. She said if she finds a yoga class in town, would he drop her off there? She found a yoga class on the computer in his wife's study. He dropped her off, then picked her up after he went to the Y. They got Persian takeout that night, a favorite food of his wife and daughters. He sits on her bed. She comes into the room. "What are you thinking, Daddy?" "Nothing," he says. "Just thinking." "It's got to be of something." "Your mother. It's been so lonely without her. But I don't want to make you sad by telling you how sad I am. Two years, already, and I've barely adjusted to it. All the decisions I have to make on my own now. She was so good at giving me advice and helping me to make up my mind and planning what we should do. I'm also sad that you're leaving." "I wish my visit was longer, but I've got my teaching to get back to." "We should have timed it better. Planned your coming here during your spring break. That's what Mommy would have suggested, because what was the rush? But I'm glad for even the short time you were here. It's been fun. A good change for me." She sits on the bed and holds his hand. "I'll try to come back here for spring break too." "Do it. I'll pay for the trip, and I don't care what it costs. Now I should call your sister. I don't want to but it's something I have to do. And I have to call an airline. What airline flies to Santa Barbara or the closest city to it? I don't know how to find out." "Call any airline in the phone book. They'll tell you." "Good thinking. Could you do it for me?

Then I'll call your sister. And your aunts, or one of them, who can call the other." "Now I'm the one who's not thinking," she says. "I can get all the information you need on the computer." She leaves the room. He goes into his bedroom and lies on the bed. He folds his hands on his chest and shuts his eyes. I must look like a corpse, he thinks. All I need is to be in a suit with all the buttons buttoned and to have on a dress shirt and tie. The phone rings. He's going to let it ring. But maybe it's his older daughter. He gets up and grabs the receiver off the phone on the dresser and says hello. "I found out what airline you should take," she says on the phone. "Tell me," he says. "I'll write it down. Though what am I going to do about the cat? I'll have to get someone to look after him." "Call one of your friends, or Mommy's friends. Anyone would do it for you." "That'd mean I'd have to speak to someone other than your sister and one of my sisters and you. I couldn't do that. It's not in me right now. I really don't see how I can go to California." "You have to. I'll be here. We'll have so much fun. I'll show you my favorite places. We'll go to museums. And there are so many good galleries and restaurants here." "Okay, I'm coming." He lies back on the bed and clasps his hands again on his chest. He sees he's wearing a suit and dress shirt and tie. The suit's the same one he got married in at her apartment twenty-nine years ago. His wife insisted he buy it for the wedding. He was going to wear an old sport jacket and freshly pressed slacks. The suit has a few moth holes in it but it still fits. "I am a corpse," he says. "I can't move."

Two Women

A woman calls to him from his bedroom. He's reading in an armchair in the living room and drinking some wine. "Come on," she says, "what are you waiting for? Get your penis in here." The voice sounds like his wife's. It also sounds like the woman he met three months ago at a Christmas party and whom he's very attracted to and he would like to start a serious relationship with and even thinks he'd eventually like to marry. His wife died a little more than a year ago. Today is the thirty-first anniversary of the day they met. It was at a book party for a woman they both knew. She'd come from her parents' apartment uptown. She'd stopped off there to spend a short time with them and give them a present for their wedding anniversary that day. He'd never slept with this other woman. They hadn't even kissed on the lips. Or once, but mistakenly on her part, she said. They were saying goodbye by her car after one of their weekly lunches and she put out her lips when she meant to offer him her cheek to kiss. "That was unintentional," she said. "It was nice, though," he said. "But it was an accident, caused by my momentary absentmindedness, which I admit I'm prone to, so it meant nothing, means nothing, and we should continue our friendship as if it didn't happen. In other words, don't make anything more of it than it was." They've been meeting for lunch almost every Wednesday since they met. All but once at the same restaurant. "Why go to another?" she said. "We're more interested in the conversation than the food, although the food's more than adequate there, and they leave you alone once you get it. And if you want more coffee, which we always do, you just go up to the counter and help yourself from one of the Thermoses. I like sticking with the same thing, if it's good, how about you?" and he said "The same." Two weeks ago she came to his house at night when he wasn't expecting her. Rang his doorbell. He turned on the outside lights and looked through the kitchen door and saw it was her and let her in. "I was in the neighborhood," she said. "I've been dying to see what your writing space looks like and thought now would be as good an opportunity as any." "That the only reason you came?" and she said "That's the only reason, and maybe to have a glass of wine with you after. I'm fascinated with writers' work spaces and what the whole room looks like. I'm planning to put together a photography book on the subject, even if a couple of excellent ones have been done. But mine won't have the writers in the photographs. Just where he writes and what he writes on, and if there's a cat sitting on the keyboard, that's okay too." "My writing space is ordinary," he said. "Except that I work in my bedroom and I still write on a standard manual typewriter. So there's that, and when I'm not writing, the typewriter's always covered so no dirt or dust or cat hair blows in. And lots of paper around it, of course, and I write on a long formica work table. I'll show you." He led her into his bedroom. "This is perfect," she said. She pulled out a camera from her should bag, adjusted the lens and took lots of photographs of his work table and manuscripts on it and the typewriter with the dust cover off and then with two sheets of paper in it. Then they had a glass of wine, she said she had to go, he walked her to her car, and she offered her cheek to be kissed. "See you Wednesday," she said. "Same time and place." "Where was that again?" he said. "You're so funny," she said. "I like that." Now, either she or his wife is in his bedroom. If it's his wife, then "their" bedroom. "Hey," one of them says, "what the heck's keeping you? Get in here, will you? Or just bring your penis in, leave it here, and the rest of you can go back to the living room to read and drink." He gets up from the armchair and goes into the bedroom. The curtains are closed and the room is dark. "Where are you?" he says. "Under the covers," she says. "Right side or left?" and she says "Come here and find out." There's a sound of covers moving. "Now I'm not under the covers anymore, but I'm on the same side of the bed." "Are you naked?" and she says "Not a stitch." "You know, I don't know which one you are. You sound like my dead wife, but you also sound like the woman I met at a Christmas party three months ago." "Well, if you get in bed, you'll learn which one I am. Either way, I'd say you can't lose." "You're right," he says. "If you're my wife, then it's a dream come true. There's nothing I wanted more than to hold her again, in or out of bed. And if you're this other woman, the one I think I've been falling in love with and whom I also think I'd eventually like to marry, which I shouldn't say because she told me she doesn't want me to fall in love with her and I'm sure marriage to me is the last thing on her mind and she just wants us to remain good friends, then it's also a dream come true." "'Dream come true,'" she says. "Pardon me for saying this, but what a hack phrase for a professional writer of fifty years' standing to make. But as I've said, and I don't want to say again, come to bed and find out." "Your attitude and the way you express yourself are also like my wife's: frank, succinct, and a way with words. And your voice: sweet and soft. I really couldn't tell them apart." "What of it?" she says. "For the last time...are you coming to bed? I'm getting cold with no covers over me or clothes on. But take off all your clothes first." He undresses, gets in bed and pulls the covers over them. He touches her and she touches him. "Your hands are warm like my wife's always were, except right after she washed dishes, and you touch me like she did too. Delicately and in the right places, as if you know from experience with me where I like to be touched." "I touch you the way a woman touches a man in bed; nothing more." "Your breasts feel like my wife's, too; full. And your nipples: large and hard. But that doesn't mean you're my wife. Same with the shape of your buttocks: so round. And your legs: long, a bit heavy at the thighs, but strong like hers. Also your nose and hair. Even your pubic hair. I suppose most pubic hair must feel the same, but it's the amount I'm talking about. A lot of it, which you might not want to hear, but which I like." "So, two for the price of one," she says. "My wife also used to say that, but about other things." "Did she?" she says. "Why do I think I knew that? Anyway, after we're done here—and take your time. Whether you think this is a reunion or our first time, don't rush it. We have all night." "That's what my wife used to say too and in the same way. But can we stop for a few minutes and just kiss? I want to see if your lips and the way you kiss passionately—that one quick time when I sort of stole a kiss from you wasn't enough to tell—are also like hers, and of course for the pleasure that goes with it." "I think that does it," she says. "Let's say I'll take a raincheck, but now I'm going to sleep." "I'm afraid to say it, because you might bite my head off, besides saying that the last thing I said is also a hack phrase, but that part about the raincheck is something she said plenty of times when she couldn't make love or wasn't interested, for one reason or another." "Good," she says, "but now you'll just have to wait until daybreak to find out which one I am." "I could always turn on the light." "Don't ruin it," she says.

The Dead

Bartok's dead. Britten's dead. Webern's dead. Berg's dead. Górecki's dead. Copland's dead. Messiaen's dead. Bernhard's dead. Beckett's dead. Joyce is dead. Nabokov's dead. Mann's dead. de Ghelderode's dead. Berryman's dead. Lowell's dead. Williams is dead. Roethke's dead. Who of the rest of the greats isn't dead? The past century. The start of this century. Bacon's dead. De Kooning's dead. Rothko's dead. Ensor's dead. Picasso's dead. Braque's dead. Apollinaire's dead. Maybe all the greats are dead. My last brother will be dead. My two other brothers are dead. Robert. Merrill. My last two sisters will be dead. Madeline's dead. My parents are dead. My wife's dead. Her parents are dead. Their relatives in Europe are long dead. My two best friends are dead. I lie on a hospital bed. I can't get up. I can't turn over. I'm stuck to the bed by wires and tubes. I can't get comfortable and I feel so hopeless and I'm in such pain that I almost want to be dead. I ring for the nurse. Usually someone responds. This time no one answers. I wait. I don't want to antagonize them. I ring again. What will I say? "Make me dead?" "Yes?" "Pain medication, please." "I'll tell your nurse." "I need it badly." "I'll tell your nurse." She comes. "Pain level on a grade from one to ten?" "Nine." I want to say "ten" but there's got to be a pain worse than mine. She gives me the medication through my I.V. I fall asleep. When I awake I begin to hallucinate. Too much pain medication, they've said. What can I do? It's the only way to stop the pain and sleep. The room's become a prison cell. Bars on my windows and door. Then it's an asylum cell. No bars; just extra thick glass. People pass. I hear low voices. "This," they say, and "That." I've got to get out of here. I yell for help. People keep passing my room both ways but no one seems to hear me or turns to my glass door. They all wear white doctor outfits. Gowns. Robes. Whatever they're called, but very white and clean. Lab coats, maybe. Hugging clipboards to their chests. "This," they say. "That." Then some muttering and they're gone. "Help," I yell. "I need help. I'm going to defecate in my bed." They continue to walk past. "Okay," I say, "I'm going to shit in my bed." Dummy, I think; the nurse. I ring for her. I can barely manage the little box. The summoning device. Whatever it's called. The thing that turns the TV on and off and raises and lowers the two ends of the bed. I don't know what anything's called anymore. Not even what brought me in here. Bowel interruption. Obstruction. Even if I got the right term, two operations after I got here, I don't even know what it is. "Yes?" "Thank God. Pain medication, please." "I'll tell your nurse." She comes. "It should be no more than every four hours. But we're ten minutes away, so close enough." "Thanks. And it must mean I've slept most of the last four hours. That's good. More I sleep, the better. And I think I need changing." She looks. "You're imagining it. Do you need to go now?" "No. I don't want to sit on it for the next hour. And I haven't eaten anything for days, so there's probably nothing there." I fall asleep. I dream I'm being devoured by lions. I fight to get out of the dream and wake up. So what was that all about? Literary lions? Ah, who cares for interpretations. I close my eyes and hear voices. I open my eyes and see people in white smocks walking past, all of them holding clipboards. "Build," they say. "Don't build." "Then cut." "Okay." I've got to get out of here. Dreams, awake, there's always something to be afraid of. The doctor the other day, who was just a resident making the rounds and not even my regular doctor, who said he read my x-rays and I might have to have a bag outside my stomach to collect my shit. If I'm to die, and I'd want to if I had to have one of those bags put in, let me die in my own bed with a big overdose of whatever we got there or they send me home with. And if I'm to live, I need a less frightening room. I want to call my daughters but I can't find my cell phone. They recharged it today and said they put it in a place I could easily reach, but I don't see it. I feel around me. There's the summoning device. A handkerchief. A pen. I'll say I know it's late but I'm going crazy and you have to get me another room. "It's the drugs. But without them I'm even in worse shape. I'm probably not making much sense," I'll say, "but I'm hearing voices. Other people's voices. And seeing people walk past my room who are either dead or intentionally ignoring me, but they never answer my cries for help. If I don't get another room, I'll pull all the wires and tubes out of me, even the Foley, no matter how much that might hurt, and escape." But don't scare them or wake them up. They've been so good to you, flying in from different distant cities and staying in your room eight to ten hours a day. Reading to you, though you didn't want to tell them you didn't want to be read to. Holding your hand and doing things like putting damp washcloths on your forehead, though you didn't want those either. Angels, you've called them; so let your angels sleep. And you're not in that much pain now. Comes more often than it goes. And the muttering voices have stopped and no one's walking past your room but the regular nurses and aides, who'd come if you called out for them. Try to sleep. Time will go faster. I pull the covers up to my chin. I'm warm but not too warm. I'm comfortable. My body feels normal. I fall asleep. I dream I'm in Tokyo, where I'd always wanted to go, but got there without having to take a plane. I wake up and it's the beginning of daylight. Dusk. Dawn. What's it called again? I should know. That one's so easy. Words are what I do. But I'm in pain again, which always makes me confused. I ring the call button. That's what it is. Call button, call button; remember it. "Yes?" "Pain medication, please." "I'll tell your nurse." A different one comes. "Hi. I'm Martha. Your tech's Cindy. The new shift." She erases from a white board on the wall the names and phone extensions of the previous nurse and tech and with a marker writes their own. "You slept poorly, your last nurse said. Lots of agitation and talk. Like you wanted a hot thermal bath. Sorry, fella. We don't have that here. And how dragons were out to get you and something about your arms being cut off at the elbows by a sword. And you perspired something awful. She had to wipe you off." "I don't remember any of it. Well, dreams." "Because of all that, I want to hold off giving you the pain medication as long as I can. Still hurting?" "Level nine or eight." "Think you can tolerate it for another half hour? And you could use a fresh gown." She takes off my wet one and puts a new one on. "Anything else you need?" "My cell phone." "You've been sleeping on it," and she pulls it out from under my arm. She goes. Poulenc's dead. Prokofiev's dead. Mahler's dead. Granados is dead. Did I say Bartok's dead? Pärt's not dead. Who else isn't dead? Tanizaki's dead. Solzhenitsyn's dead. Hamsun's dead. Borges is dead. Conrad's dead. Konrad's not dead. Did Lessing recently die? The Italian writer whose first name starts with a D and who in one book wrote too much like Kafka is dead. Kafka, of course, is dead. Cummings is dead. Stevens is dead. Auden's dead. Yeats is dead. Pollack's dead. Leger's dead. Kadinsky's dead. Malevich is dead. Moore, Maillol and Matisse are dead. My pain isn't dead. I shit in my head. I mean in my bed. Suddenly it came. I piss into a catheter, so there I'm okay. I want to clean myself up in the bathroom. I want to drink a glassful of icewater. I want to stand up and walk out of here. I press the call button. "Yes?" "I'm sorry, but I need serious cleaning up. And I presume new bedding and a new gown and my bed remade.

I'm lying in slime. I'm sweating like a pig. I need the thermostat lowered. Please have someone come right away." "I'll tell your tech." A young woman comes. Almost a girl. She has a new gown for me and sheets and washrags and a basin of water. "Oh, I see you already have my name on your board." "You're the tech? I'm sorry for the mess I made." "I'm actually a nurse in training but a tech today. So let's have a look. Roll over on your side." I grab the side rail and pull myself up. "I don't know where it came from. I haven't eaten for a week. Nor drunk anything. All the nourishment and liquid I get comes from ice chips and what's in those bags. And this time it's not my imagination and did I defecate?" "In abundance. Won't take a minute." She takes off my gown, wipes and washes and dries me and shakes a can of baby powder over my behind. "Smells nice, doesn't it. It's one of my favorites." "This must be awful for you. Cleaning up an old man. It made me hesitant to even call for you, but I had to. I'm locked in here." "Don't worry. I'm used to it. And when I become a full-fledged nurse in a year, I'll mostly have a tech doing it for me. You have an abscess in your anus. Has your doctor or one of your nurses spoken about it?" "Nothing." "It must hurt and you don't want the infection getting worse. Tell them." She puts a new gown on me and then changes the sheets with me in the bed. "It's a wonderful profession, nursing. Look at the good work you do. I had to go into one that helps no one." "And what's that?" "Writing." "I don't read much myself. I'm more interested in the sciences." "Good for you. Keep at it. Every man should have as a wife one who is or once was a nurse. That's not a proposal. I was just thinking. Once you get sick the way I did, it'd be so comforting to know I could be taken care of like this by my wife, but at home. My wife's dead." "I'm sorry." "Two years and a month. Greatest loss of my life." "I can imagine. There, you're as clean as new. And you smell nice too." "Thank you again. As I said, you do wonderful work. Can you give me something for my pain now?" "The nurse will have to do that. I'm not allowed. Ring for her." "If I have another accident, and you never know, I hope it's another tech who takes care of it. I'd hate for you to have to do it again. Once, at least in a short period of time, should be enough." "Honestly, I'm good with it. I'm on for twelve hours and it's one of the things I'm here to do." She goes. I ring. "Yes?" "Pain medication, please." "Your nurse is very busy with another patient, but I'll tell her." "Isn't there another nurse who can give it to me?" "It's very busy out here. Sometimes it gets like this, patients who need immediate attention all at the same time. I'll get you a nurse as soon as I can." Hemingway's dead. Faulkner's dead. Paley's dead. Sebald's dead. Lowry's dead. Camus's dead. Eliot's dead. Mandelstam's dead. Akhmatova's dead. O'Neill's dead. Williams is dead. Miller's dead. Hopper's dead. Giacometti's dead. Klee's dead. Miro's dead. Sheeler's dead. Soutine's dead. Arp's dead. Sibelius is dead. Strauss is dead. Hovhaness is dead. Vaughan Williams is dead. I have to shit again. I need a basin. Whatever that thing is to put under me in bed. It's comparable to a urinal, but for the behind. Not a chamber pot. I ring. Nobody answers. I ring and ring. "I told you, sir. All the nurses on the floor are tied up with other patients. One will attend to you soon as she can." "But this is for a bowel movement. I don't want to do it again in my bed. All I'm asking for is that thing that goes under me while I'm lying here." "A bedpan?" "A bedpan, yes. You can get a tech to do it. But not the same one; Cindy. She already did it once, and expertly, but I made a mess and I don't want her to go through that again." "You don't get a choice, sir. If she's available, I'll get her. And if not, someone else." If it wasn't for my daughters, I'd like to be dead. But I can't have them going through their other parent dying so soon after the first. A different tech comes, gets the bedpan out of the bottom drawer of my side table, "Raise yourself," and puts it under me just in time. "At least this time I'm not making a big mess in bed for you to clean up as I did with my regular tech." "There's always something that makes life look a little brighter. Think you're done?" "No." "Ring for me when you are. It's a crazy house out there today, worse for the nurses than the techs, so one of us should come." "Thanks." Bergman, Fellini, Antonini, Kurosawa, Kieślowski—all dead. And Babel. How could I have left out Babel? Babel's dead.

On or Along the Way

The announcer on the classical music radio station says the next piece will be a symphonic poem, "or what's also called a tone poem," by Rachmaninoff. The title is "The Rock," and the piece is based on a short story by Chekhov called "Along the Way." The story, she says, is about an elderly destitute man and a rich young woman who meet at an inn during a blizzard. "They're sort of thrown together in a room the innkeeper calls 'The Traveler,' since it's reserved for travelers passing through or stranded there." The man and woman talk for hours and gradually warm to each other. "There's a chance—one could even say a hope—they could become good friends or, at the very least, traveling companions for the rest of their journey. But the woman leaves the next morning in a sledge that the man, standing in the road, follows with his eyes till it disappears. He eventually begins to look like a huge rock covered by snow," she says, "hence the title." He doesn't know the story, but the ending is a familiar one for Chekhov. Two people from vastly different backgrounds or economic circumstances or both who meet for the first time and talk intimately together, often after having lived in the same district their entire lives and known about each other for years, and whose lives...Well, there's a possibility that after their first meeting they could come together...their lives could...even marry, or help each other in some way...but...Anyway, what seemed promising suddenly stops, usually because one of them doesn't say something to keep the other from going, or the weather's cleared or the wheel or axle of one of their carts has been fixed or the obstacle in the road's been removed, and they go their separate ways, with little chance they'll meet or speak to each other again. He was never good at summarizing stories, not even his own. But the ending to this story, from what the announcer said, is one Chekhov used several times in a similar way, and maybe a lot more than that, since he's read only about fifty of the 568 stories and sketches his wife said Chekhov wrote. The Rachmaninoff piece comes on. For the last minute or so there was an announcement for a free lieder concert at the music academy downtown and a recorded ad for this radio station saying sixty percent of its budget comes from listener membership contributions, "so won't you take a few minutes of your time and become a member by dialing the following phone number or pledging online?" He listens to the music for a minute, doesn't particularly like it, then doesn't like it at all and turns the radio off. Sometimes what to him is awful music can be depressing. This station plays a lot of it, most of it in the morning till around ten—oompah marches, schmaltzy waltzes—although it plays a lot of good music too. As for becoming a member, he and his wife have been one for about twenty-five years, though he now takes the senior citizen membership. But the story. If his wife were here he'd ask her about the Rachmaninoff piece. She's the Chekhov expert. His stories are what she did her master's and doctorate on: her thesis on the beginnings of his stories—about twenty of them— and her dissertation on the endings: ten. He'd say "Do you know of a Chekhov story called 'Along the Way'? I don't. And how can a symphonic tone poem, which is what I always called them, be based on a short story? Especially one with a plot like what the announcer gave, for we're not talking opera here, which seems mostly like a long conversation between a man and woman in an inn and ends with the man standing in what I assume's deep snow and looking like a rock." She might say she's read more than 300 of his stories and sketches in Russian—she once told him that—and about half the 400 or so translated into English, and the one he mentions isn't familiar to her, although the ending is like several of his. "'Along the Way'? Are you sure the announcer didn't give another title? Though there are a number of his stories that have different titles for each new translation of it. 'Grief,' for instance, which I've also seen as 'Heartache' and 'Misery,' and in one translation, 'Sadness,' though I could be wrong on the last one. I know there are at least four different titles for it in the English versions. If you want, I'll go through my notes on his short stories, and if I don't find anything I'll look at my story collections of his, both in Russian and English. If I find the story in English, do you want to read it?" He'd say "I would, and then maybe you could read it for the first or second time and we'll talk about it. That's always fun. And it won't be a waste of time. I've never read a story of his, except for some of the minor sketches, which aren't stories, right?—that wasn't anything but clear and readable and good, and twenty to thirty of them were great. I don't think I can say that about any other short story writer. Maybe Hemingway and Babel come closest." So she'd check, she might say, maybe not now but by the end of the day. She has the entire 16- or 17-, or whatever the number is—he could go into her study and find out—volume collection of all of Chekhov's stories and sketches in Russian. He'll check the collections of Chekhov's stories he has in English. He goes into the living room, pulls the three collections off a bookshelf and finds the title "On the Way" on the contents page of one of them. Has to be it. He turns to the last pages of the story. A man, standing in a snowfall "as if rooted to the spot" and gazing at the tracks left by the woman's sledge-runners, soon begins to resemble a white boulder. He then reads the first few pages of the story, flips through the rest of it and goes into her study with the book. "Hurray, hurray," he says, "I found it. In an old Modern Library edition of Chekhov's stories that I think I bought when I was in college, translated by that old reliable, Constance Garnett. Or I think it was by her. It doesn't say who the translators are, except for around five of the stories on the acknowledgments page, and she's got all of them but one. Maybe it's at the end of the book," and he looks and it isn't. "But it's almost got to be by her. The copyright is 1932." "Nothing out of the usual," she might say, although she's gone in to this before. "And other than for the top translators today, who are almost as well known as the authors, things haven't changed much since. Translators were always poorly paid and often didn't get credited in the book. But woe is me if the translation didn't read that well or the story in the original wasn't that good. Then they got the blame. 'Sloppily translated'; that type of criticism—the writer, of course, getting off free. Let me see it." He holds open the story to the first page. "Oh, yes," she might say, maybe after reading a paragraph or two, "now I remember it. Not one of my favorites, which is why I never taught it in class, but still, as you said, a good story. Two people at an inn during a tremendous snowstorm. Howling wind. He relied on that a lot. Also the storm beating on the windows and roof. If he had a weakness, it was that. The woman's supposed to be a good deal younger than the man, who's described as elderly, though he's in his forties, so maybe only old for that time and place. She's a landowner, or her brother is, whom she's traveling to by sledge. The man was once fairly prosperous—I believe he even once owned an estate, or ran one—but for a long time has been down on his luck. At first they don't seem to be a likely match. But by the end, because they're so kind and frank and helpful and even solicitous to each other, you think, if you didn't know Chekhov better, they might team up. I don't think it ever happens in Chekhov, in his fiction or plays, or it's rare when it does. He's traveling with his young daughter. A very nice little girl, but sad, like so many children in his stories—so put upon and being dragged all over the place by her father." "The synopsis of the story the announcer gave," he says, "never mentioned the daughter. She probably didn't have the time, or the program notes for the Rachmaninoff piece didn't say so." "If I remember correctly," she might say, "the woman has some money of her own and is very sympathetic to the young girl and would have made a wonderful surrogate mother to her and a good wife to the man. I forget what happened to the man's wife. I think she died or deserted him for someone else, and he was left with the daughter. That would explain his descent." "What I'd like to know is how you make a symphonic tone poem out of a story like that," he says. "An opera, as I said—a one-act one—I can see, although the snow might be a problem." "Oh," she might say, "they know how to do snow on an opera stage. *La Bohème*, for instance. But I have to confess I don't really know what a tone poem is." "I guess what Richard Strauss did in his *Don Juan* and *Till Eulenspiegel* and so on, and what Sibelius and Smetana did in theirs. A narrative in music, though I'd think it'd be a very difficult form to put across. But we'll forget the music and read the story—I've already started it and I know how it turns out—and talk about it sometime today?" "You finish it and I'll catch up," she might say. "I'll also read it in Russian, if I have the time, in case the translation misses some of it." "See you later, then," he says. He goes into their bedroom, plumps up and piles the four bed pillows, her two and his, on top of one another against the wall, and lies back on them and reads the story. After he finishes it he goes back to her study. She's not there.

Cape May

They used to go to Cape May about once every two years, mostly to observe birds at the bird observatory there. Went three times, once in the spring and twice in the fall, before she got too sick to go. It wasn't something he much liked doing: standing on the beach for a couple of hours in the morning and then in the afternoon, sometimes when it was cold, trying to find birds through the binoculars he'd bought her. Also, dragging her in her wheelchair through the sand to a spot she wanted to see the birds from, and then dragging the chair back to the paved path, sometimes with the help of a birder or two. She didn't mind the cold, or said she didn't. He'd tuck in her afghan around her chest, wrap her mohair shawl around her shoulders and neck, pull her wool cap down over her ears and put her gloves on for her. "You warm enough?" he'd say, or something like it, and she'd say "Now I am. Thank you. So let's go find a bird we've never seen." There were always lots of birders on the beach, no matter how cold it was, some with what seemed like expensive binoculars and others with elaborate telescopes on tripods. Sometimes one birder would be operating two or three telescopes, all pointed in different directions. Everyone out there was very friendly and nice and most seemed to know a lot about the birds they'd come to watch and photograph. Some would ask her if she wanted to look through their telescopes: they had them focused on a bird's nest or bird in a tree or hidden in a bush, sometimes hundreds of feet away. Maybe not that far, but a good distance, certainly far enough away where it couldn't be seen without a highpowered telescope or binoculars, which hers weren't. He doesn't think she ever saw a bird through one of these telescopes, which he did, several times. For one thing, her eyes were bad because of her MS. And because she was sitting in a wheelchair she usually couldn't get her eye close enough to the lens. A couple of the telescope birders even took the tripod off and held the telescope up to her better eye, is the way he'll put it—he forgets if that was her left or right—but they could never keep it steady enough to focus it on what they wanted her to see. He doesn't think she ever even saw a bird through her binoculars. She couldn't hold them, so he held them to her eyes but could never get them aimed or focused right for her. Still, she liked being on the beach or observation platform with all those serious bird watchers. And every so often a bird would fly near them—one they'd never see around their house or neighborhood, where they also used to take walks to observe birds, or even in Maine, where they went to every summer for two months. And someone would shout what kind of bird it was and later tell her, or someone else would, or she'd look it up in the bird book she always took to the beach with her, what its identifying marks and other things about it are so she could recognize it on her own next time. But they also in Cape May, or at least he did with her, have some of their happiest moments together. Not at the bird observatory but in a restaurant which, once they discovered it, they went to for dinner every night in their three trips to Cape May. It was a fluke or just good luck, chance, whatever it was, how they got to it. The first time they went to Cape May they weren't able to reserve a room in any of the hotels in town. All of them were booked because of a convention that week, and the bed and breakfasts, which had a few available rooms, were in old buildings with steps leading up to the front porch and more steps and staircases inside. They always brought her portable ramp with them on trips like this, but it was only good for three steps at the most. Also, the bathroom in these B&B's, the owners told him on the phone, were too small to turn around a wheelchair in. So, because it was the off-season, the closest open lodging they could get to Cape May was a four-story motel about ten miles away. It was an ugly place, with a pink façade and an enormous neon sign in front and tacky furniture inside. But it had an elevator to their floor, a kitchenette to make breakfast in and a roll-in shower in their bathroom, which surprised them—not even some of the best motels and hotels they'd been to had that—and it kept them, along with the free reserved handicapped parking space, coming back to this motel the next two times. What he's saying is that if they had been able to book a suitable room in a Cape May hotel the first time they went, they no doubt would have walked to a restaurant nearby—several were open—and not come upon this one on the outskirts of town. They were driving to Cape May from the motel their first night there to look for a restaurant to have dinner in and saw a sign for this place along the way. "Think we should check it out?" he said, and she said "What do we have to lose?" They went down a side road. The restaurant's parking lot was almost filled. If they didn't have handicapped plates, they wouldn't have found a spot. "A good sign," he said. He looked at the menu, liked what he saw, got her out of the van and they went inside. It was a huge place—probably could accommodate a hundred-fifty diners at one time—with a large lobby where they waited for their table to be called. It was crowded every time they ate there, and they always had to wait for a half hour or more, which was fine with them. The lobby had several buffet tables in it, one for shrimp cocktails and tiny crab cakes, another for several kinds of freshly shucked oysters on the half shell, and a third just for martinis and Manhattans. She loved oysters, maybe more than any other food. While he didn't know how anyone could eat them raw—fried, he liked. He got a half dozen oysters for her and a martini for him and they sat beside a small end table, it seemed, and she ate and he drank. "Sure you won't have one?" she said. "Five is plenty for me." "Positive," he said. "Like a sip of my martini? It's delicious; just right." "You know I hate the taste of them." "Thought I'd offer, though, and same with me your oysters. How are they?" "The best, ever." After swallowing each one—he'd first squeeze a lemon wedge over it and have to bring the oyster to her mouth with that little oyster fork, holding the shell beneath it till it was inside—she gave a big almost rapturous smile and said "Ummm . . . ummm . . . " and maybe after the second or third oyster "You don't know what you're missing." "I know what I'm missing and I don't miss it. Did I ever tell you of the time I ate a foul raw oyster at the fish restaurant Oscar's on Third Avenue and all evening thought I might die from being poisoned by it? Long before we met. Maybe ten years before. My father was in the hospital—Mt. Sinai—and my mother and one of my sisters and I had just come from seeing him there." "Don't go into anymore details about it. I don't want to ruin my eating these oysters. You survived, I'm thankful to say. And not because we wouldn't be here if you hadn't and I wouldn't be enjoying these oysters so much. What kind did the shucker say they were?" "Some local Indian name. Lots of syllables, half of them vowels. But okay, I won't say anything more about my one bad oyster. Eat. Enjoy. That's what we're here for." So it was that smile of total delight she always had while eating oysters at this restaurant—its name, he forgets too, but he thinks he could look it up online if he wanted to— that made the trip to Cape May for him. The ummms. The look of complete satisfaction. That she was so happy, sitting in her wheelchair in the lobby, smiling at him after being fed each oyster and he saying "I'm so glad you're enjoying this. I really am. I think I sometimes live just to have you enjoy something and be happy." "You're sweet," she said a couple of time after he said this. "And you're beautiful," he said the first time. "I know that oysters, and I can't say I subscribe to this notion, are supposed to be an aphrodisiac, but I'm the only one eating them. Sure you wouldn't like the last one?" "Wouldn't think of it. And I won't need it, if that's what you meant. Do you want it to be the last one or should I get another half dozen for you, maybe of a different kind." "Six is more than enough for me. We have a whole meal to go. And seeing what they do with oysters, I'm sure it'll be great. Tomorrow. We should probably come here tomorrow night for dinner. Hang out in this waiting area for a while before dinner, even if they say our table's ready right away, and you'll have your martini and I'll have my oysters. And next time we come to Cape May to see the birds, and we have to come back—we're having too good a time—we'll come here again and have the same things. Or I'll have three of one kind of oyster and three of another, and maybe you'll try one of their Manhattans." "Okay with me. I like both, and why go anywhere else? This place is as good as they come and I love this room and watching the other people waiting and the surroundings too. The things on the walls. Your personal shucker. Everything." "And the martini's that good too?" "I'd have another," he said, "—by my drinking it so fast and it's such a large glass too, you know how much I like it—but I want to have wine with dinner and be able to drive back to the motel." "I wish I was still able to drive. Then you could drink as much as you want." "Don't worry about it," and he held up the oyster fork and she smiled and nodded and he gave her the last oyster. Then he held her hand and drank what was left of the martini with his other hand and said "Cape May's a great place. I mean, we haven't seen much of it yet, but it certainly seems like it. Although if it wasn't for this restaurant, I don't know." "I'm glad I like looking at birds so much and suggested we come here," she said. So they came back to

Cape May two more times. She gave up on taking the binoculars the last time. They also didn't take the portable ramp. Found they didn't need it. Went to the same restaurant for dinner every time. That would make six times they waited in the lobby there. She always had a half dozen oysters on the half shell, sometimes three of two different kinds and sometimes all of the same kind. He had a Manhattan once but didn't like the way it was made. Too sweet. The other times he always had a martini, straight up with both an olive and lemon twist in it and made with the best English gin they had or a Russian or Swedish vodka. About a year after the last time they went he said "Like to go to Cape May in the next month or so for a couple of days?" She said "Maybe this time we should pass it up. We always do the same thing, go to the same place, so let's try something different or somewhere we haven't been to in a while." "Oh, but that restaurant, whose name I always forget. How I'd miss it. By now we could find it blindfolded, and we don't have to make a reservation for it because we actually like waiting in its lobby for a table." "It's a wonderful place," she said, "but we ought to go back to Chincoteague at least once, and have dinner at that fish restaurant on the water we always liked. The one connected to a seashell shop. And we can take a drive or two through the national wildlife park there and see its birds. They're probably the same ones as at the beach in Cape May; part of the same flyway, isn't it?" "Okay," he said. "Time getting there is just about as long, maybe a bit longer, but the drive's just as easy, and isn't the Blackwater bird observatory along the way? That restaurant you mentioned isn't as good as the one in Cape May and not as much fun to go to. But you're right. We haven't been to Chincoteague for a while, and we always had a good time there. Maybe, since we were last there, there's a new seafood place in town better than the one we used to go to, and which has oysters you'll find as delicious as the one in Cape May had."

"Maybe," she said. "Chincoteague oysters. They were just about my favorite at the Cape May restaurant, but no local oyster was ever in season when we went to Chincoteague." "So we'll do that, next month, for a weekend, or two days during the middle of the week, at that motel nearest the water—The Retreat, or something, I think it's called. The one with a heated indoor pool I liked and handicapped facilities almost as good as the awful-looking motel in Cape May had. But I think it's called The Refuge, not the Retreat. That would make sense for that area, the motel so close to the National Wildlife Refuge. The Refuge Inn; that's it exactly. Now I know what to look up when I make a reservation." But she got very sick the next month and then very sick a few times the next year, and they never went.

Alone

He drives back from a lunch at a couple's house. There were several other guests there. They were all couples. One woman came by herself because her husband, a doctor, had some work to do at a hospital. So he was there alone. His wife is dead. He looked at the couples and thought each person here has someone to go home with or to but him. Isn't he used to it yet? He isn't. He doesn't like going home alone. Being alone at home. Going to these lunches alone. But what's he going to do? His daughters are in other cities. The food was good at the lunch. There were turkey and ham slices on a plate. Smoked fish on another plate. A potato salad dressed with just vinegar and mustard and olive oil. A beet salad, a snow pea salad, sliced tomatoes, bread. He wanted to have a glass of wine or beer, when others were having it, but he doesn't drink alcohol in the afternoon. Makes him too tired. He had water. He stayed pretty quiet during the lunch. The conversation was lively but he didn't participate in it much. Once, he said, "Oh, I have an anecdote regarding that," and everyone at the long dining table turned to him and he said "It's about the president of the university I taught at, the fellow who you say now runs a prestigious medical research institute in Minneapolis. We had—my department—a visiting writer reading his fiction. Big crowd. This guy's very well known. And the president came into the lobby after the reading—his residence was on campus and I suppose he was just taking a walk, saw the building lit up and lots of people leaving it, because he hadn't gone to the reading, and...Jesus, what was I getting at?

Something he said to me. Then something I said to him. I know it ends with him saying 'What's a hunk?' Damn, I forget. I'm sorry. Carry on, please. I'm not very good at telling stories anymore." "Sure you are," the hostess said. "He's a very funny guy," her husband said, "or can be," and everyone laughed. After coffee and fruit, the wife of one of the couples said "We'll have to excuse ourselves. We have guests coming for dinner and I've a lot of preparations to do." "I have to go too," he said. "No guests coming, but something at home." He stood up. The couple stood up. He had nothing to do at home. He shook hands with three of the men, kissed the cheek of the hostess and a woman he'd seen at this house for dinner several times when his wife was alive, and the couple and he left together. He stopped in front of a plant outside and said "I have these around my house; but all around it. They came with the house, but mine are five to seven feet tall. Any idea its name?" and the woman said "Aucuna; that starts with an 'a' and 'u.'" "Boy, I really asked the right people. I should cut mine down to about two feet, the way the Pinskis have it." "That would be about the right height for them, two to three feet. They're great plants. Hearty; red berries. And they're not cheap if you buy them at a garden store. I love them." "Well, if you want some, I've got plenty and you can just dig them up. I've pulled a number of them up without any problem when they were taking over the place." "I'll do that, "she said. "I'm serious." "So am I," she said. "In the spring. We'll both come over. We have just the right tools and know how to do it. I'll get your phone number from Ginny and Schmuel." Then they shook hands goodbye and they got in their car and he got in his car and started to drive home. But now, he thinks, he doesn't want to get home so quickly. Too soon. He stops at a restaurant on the way, one that sells its own bread, and gets a small loaf of his favorite kind here, sunflower flax, and asks for it to be sliced. "That's all?" the woman behind the counter says, and he says "That'll have to do it. I just came from a big lunch." Then he stops at a bookstore, also along the way home and the best independent one in the city, and for about ten minutes looks for a book to buy for when he finishes the one he's currently reading, doesn't see anything that interests him, and then thinks he needs a new *American Heritage College Dictionary*. His is so old it has a photo of O.J. Simpson in the margin, and its first fifty pages or so are curled up at the ends and folded into one another and he has to flatten them out to read them. Do they have the new edition, the fifth? They have it, one copy, and he takes it off the bookshelf. And he remembers he wants to give the new hardcover editions of *The Oxford Book of American Poetry* and the one of *English Verse* to a couple that got married this September—the bride a former undergraduate student of his—and invited him to the wedding in Nyack, but he didn't go. He didn't want to be there alone. Go alone, he means, and it would have meant two days away from home. Even if it had been here, he knows he still wouldn't have gone. He would have felt too out of place. During the reception, because his former student had told him it'd be at a large rented hall and there'd be a band, people would have got up to dance, and things like that. The store doesn't have either book, so he orders them and they'll call him when the books come in. He pays for the dictionary, didn't think it'd be so expensive, and gets back in his car and continues home, but tells himself he doesn't want to get there yet. Let's face it, he tells himself, I don't want to be alone there yet. That crazy? No. He stops at the market a half mile from his house, even though he doesn't really need anything there, and gets a shopping basket and thinks of things to buy. He can always use more carrots, the way he eats them, and picks up a two-pound bag of the organic kind. And the cat likes sliced turkey from the deli department. He likes to give him a little treat of it every now and then, so he gets a quarter pound of it. It'll last a week and he'll have some too. And he thinks he's out of scallions, so he goes back to the produce section and gets that. Anything else? He should have got some gourmet chicken salad at the deli department, but it'll look odd, going back for just that and he gets the same server who gave him the sliced turkey. He gets a few cans of cat food, even though he has plenty at home, and a package of rice cakes because he thinks he has only one rice cake left. Is that it? Well, what's he going to eat tonight? He's had an open-faced tuna melt almost every other night that past two weeks, the cheese on top of tomato slices on top of the tuna salad he makes, on top of two slices of toasted bread—the sunflower flax would be perfect for it—which he puts in the oven for about fifteen minutes and then under the broiler for one. Has he tuna at home? He has, more than one can, he's almost sure. Oh, get out of here, and he starts for the checkout lanes, and then thinks just a couple more items. Maybe he'll bump into someone he knows—that happens a lot here. A neighbor, or someone from the Y he goes to every day, and they'll have a quick chat. Or get a coffee from the coffee machine here. Only a dollar and it's not bad. And the café au lait for two dollars is in fact good. He gets a regular coffee, black, puts a lid on the container and pays up for everything. "Plastic okay?" the checkout person says and he says "Usually I get paper. But I have so few items, plastic's okay, and I can always use the bag in a wastebasket." She bags his purchases, says "Have a nice rest of the day," and he says "Thanks; you too," and leaves. He drives home, puts away the food he bought—bananas, he thinks; forgot he's out of bananas. Well, next time. Actually, tomorrow, maybe before breakfast, and he'll pick up a few other things, because he always slices up a banana into his hot or cold cereal. He drinks the rest of the coffee and checks his cell phone on the sideboard in the dining room. He rarely leaves the house with it and uses it mostly to talk to his kids, who are on the same plan with him. No messages. He brings the dictionary to his bedroom and checks the regular phone there. Same thing. The cat's sleeping on the bed or resting with his eyes closed. He sits on the bed and pets him. "So how's it going, my friend? Keeping the joint free of mice and burglars?" The cat stands up, stretches and jumps off the bed. "Want to go out? Fine with me. Do it while it's still light out." He walks to the kitchen. The cat follows him. If he wants to go out he usually stays by the kitchen door and sometimes gets up on his back paws and scratches the wall next to the door or the door. He sits by his empty food plate. "Eat the kibble in your bowl. It's not dinnertime yet. Later I'll give you some more wet food." The cat looks at him, stays seated. "All right, all right." He gets a little of the turkey out of the plastic bag it's in and drops it on the plate. The cat eats it and goes to the door. "You gonna leave me all by my lonesome? Okay. See ya later," and opens the door and the cat goes outside. He goes back to the bedroom, sits at his work table and thinks should he continue writing what he started this morning? Still has a couple of hours before it gets dark. Nah. He knows where it's going. Tomorrow. After breakfast. He takes off his sneakers and lies on the bed. Room's a little cold. So what? Nah, don't get cold. He gets the wool throw off the chair near the bed. His mother gave them it when their first child was born. From Ireland, she said. Sent away for it. She also gave them one of a different plaid when their second child was born. His older daughter used this one for a long time. Then left it behind when she moved out of the house and he had it dry-cleaned and now thinks of it as his. He unfolds it and lies on the bed and pulls it over him up till his neck. His feet stick out. So what? They won't get cold. He has socks on. He cups his hands on his chest and thinks of the dream he woke up from this morning when it was just getting light out. In it, his wife was in a blue dress.

Corduroy. Opened at the neck maybe three buttons down and belt-ed at the waist. She had that dress before they first met and wore it a lot when it was cold out and they were going out for dinner or to a concert of play. It was one of the many clothes of hers he gave to Purple Heart and Amvets. The kids had first crack at everything of hers but over more than two years took almost nothing, not even a single piece of jewelry, though they didn't want him to sell or give anything of that away. Her hair was brushed back and hung over her shoulders. She seemed healthy, spirited, happy, ran back and forth through the house. "Hold up," he said, when she zipped past him again. "Where you going so fast? You're like a cat." He caught up with her in the hallway bathroom. She was looking at herself in the medicine cabinet mirror. He got up close behind her and said to her mirror image "You look beautiful again. And when you look so beautiful I don't want to leave you for a second." "I have to leave you," she said to his mirror image, and he said "No, you misunder-stood me. I was talking about myself. Oh, what of it? And maybe what I said about your being beautiful was the wrong thing to say." He put his arms around her from behind. She looked at the mirror image of his hands, then turned around in his arms till she was facing him and they kissed. The dream ended then. Wouldn't you know it. Well, at least he got to kiss her. He shut his eyes. Maybe I'll nap awhile, he thinks, and get to dream of her again. The cat's bang-ing one of the bedroom windows. There are three types of windows in this room: a long one opposite the bed, which he thinks is called a picture window, but he could be wrong; two small windows to the right of the bed, at the most two feet by three and which open and close with a crank; and a regular one, above the chair the throw was on and which the cat's banging with his paw. "Go away," he says. "Let me rest. You haven't been out that long, and it's nice out and you have your fur coat on." The cat, standing on an outside ledge about six feet off the ground, keeps banging the window with his paw. He gets up, raises the window and then the screen. The cat comes in and jumps to the floor and runs out of the room. He closes the screen and leaves the window a little open at the bottom. He gets back on the bed under the throw, cups his hands on his chest and shuts his eyes. He'll try again. It'd be nice to have another dream of her so soon after this morning's. It's happened, and maybe a continuation of that one or one where they make love. Those are the best, or equal to any deep-kissing dream with her, even if he's never come in one. He falls asleep. He doesn't dream, or doesn't remember dreaming, after he wakes up.

Go to Sleep

He wakes up and she's not there. What did he think? Of course she's not there. But he imagines she is. Or tries to. Sticks out his hand where she used to sleep. Feels along the mattress to the end of what was her side of the bed. Touches her. Her back. Runs his hand up her spine and smoothes her neck. Runs his hand down the crack of her back to her behind. Feels it. Rubs it. Circles his hand around one buttock, then the other. Can you feel me? he thinks. "Can you feel my hand?" he says. "You've been gone so long. It's good to have you back. 'Good'? There isn't a word for it. Can you turn over on your back?" She turns over. He feels her breasts under her nightshirt. Feels between her legs under her panties. The last few years she wore diapers to bed. Or "pads," they preferred calling them. He'd take them off her in the morning, even if they were dry, which they almost never were, after he got her out of bed into her wheelchair, wheeled the chair into the bathroom, and got her on the toilet. "I thought I threw out all your panties ages ago. They were in the second dresser drawer from the top, about ten of them. I asked you if it was all right. After all, you didn't wear them anymore. Hadn't for years, and we thought you never would. And they were old and no organization like Goodwill or Purple Heart would ever take them. Now you have a pair on. Did I miss one? I guess it means you think you no longer need the pad at night and maybe not even during the day. Good. I like panties on you better and I'm sure you do too. They must feel better. The pad, I think, could be a bit uncomfortable to wear and they're not easy to get on and off. We must have talked about this before." He moves nearer to her. He can't see her face in the dark. Can't see any part of her body. And she's still under the covers. It's a cold night. It must be around two or three in the morning. The quietest time outside. All the curtains in the room are closed. He drew them before he went to bed. Wanted to sleep late this morning because he hasn't been getting much sleep lately. Tosses around in bed for hours some nights, or after his first few hours of sleep. Doesn't know why. Maybe he should stop drinking an hour or two before he goes to sleep. What he does now, and has for months, longer, is drink right up to the time he goes in back, washes up, gets in bed and reads till his eyes get tired, and turns off the light. "Do you mind if I touch you down there? I know I did it before without asking, but that was just to find out what you had on." He's not touching her now and he says "I mean your crotch," and he feels her crotch. The hair around it. Then her thighs near the crotch. "I've always loved your thighs. You never did. You thought they were too large. Or 'plump,' was the word I think you used, but I always thought they were just right. Or not that large or plump. Or whatever I mean. I've also always loved your hair down there. So soft. You didn't; thought there was too much. And I know you don't like me talking about your body like this. Never did. But I did it anyway, maybe because it got me excited. Of course because it got me excited; we both know that. I loved their smoothness. Softness. Hairlessness." He feels her vagina. "I shouldn't play around like this. But I do want to touch it. Do you mind? Say you do, and I'll stop." He pulls on her pubic hair a little. "That didn't hurt, did it? If it did, I'm sorry; I'll stop. If you want me to go on, you'll say so, yes? Oh, this is getting us nowhere. Actually, I don't know what I mean by that. And I'm sounding like such a creep, which I can be, something we also both know. Okay, I'll take my hand away," and he takes it away and then tries to put it back.

She's not there. He lies on his back. Removes one of the three pillows—between them, they always had four—he'd set up against the wall so he could sit back against them while he read last night before he went to sleep. Maybe lying his head on three pillows kept him from sleep. Maybe not. But maybe now he'll be able to fall back to sleep. Just two, if they're good pillows, and his are, should be enough for anybody. He clasps his hands on his stomach and shuts his eyes. No, she's there, all right. She was before, why shouldn't she be there now? He reached out for her hand. But she must have turned back on her right side at the edge of her side of the bed, out of reach. If he stretched his hand or moved a few inches closer to her, he could reach her. What would he try to touch first? Her left shoulder under the covers. Doesn't know why. Just came into his head. And he's sure it's under the covers. Room's too cold for her shoulder to be exposed. Then he'd move the front of his body into the back of her and swing his left arm around so his hand could feel both her breasts at the same time. If she said his hand was too cold for that—it had been out of the covers awhile—he'd take it away. He'd fall asleep like that. First saying "Do you mind if I hold you like this and am squeezed into you?" If she said nothing, he'd stay where he was, holding her breasts. Maybe she would already have fallen back to sleep. Maybe she wouldn't want to speak. Maybe she'd just want to hear him. Maybe she'd like him squeezed into her from behind and holding her breasts with one hand and would think if she said anything she might ruin it. She might also like him squeezed into her back and holding her because it was making her warmer than she'd be without him doing all that. He turns over on his right side and moves closer to her or where she was. She's not there. He was going to squeeze into her and hold her breasts with his left hand. Not fondle them, because that might disturb her sleep or her going back to sleep, but just hold. Of course she's not there.

What did he think? But turn the light on to make sure. Don't be silly. No, turn it on. He turns over and with his right hand turns his bedlamp on. Are you ready to look? He thinks. He's facing the opposite way from her side of the bed. "I'm ready to look," he says. He turns around and looks. A pillow's there. The fourth pillow, where he left it last night, the one he didn't set up against the wall with the others to sit back against while he read in bed. Maybe she fell off the bed and is on the floor. That happened a couple of times. She broke her nose once falling off her side of the bed. There was a lot of bleeding; he rushed her to a hospital a few blocks away. This was in New York. They had to wait two hours for her to be examined and treated by a doctor in Emergency and by then the bleeding had stopped. She had a problem snoring at night after that. They were told it could only be corrected by an operation on some part of her nose, which he didn't want her to have. "Too risky for something so minor," he said. "And since I'm the one being kept up at night and the snoring doesn't seem to inconvenience you any, it should be my decision. What do you say?" He gets on his stomach and looks over her side of the bed to the floor. She's not there. A pillow is, he forgot it was missing, the one he removed from his side of the bed before. Maybe she got up very quietly and made it to the bathroom on her own somehow. Not the one in this room—he'd hear her and would have seen the light under the door when his bedlamp was off—but the guest bathroom in the hallway outside this room. "You in the guest bathroom?" he says, louder than he was speaking before. Listens. Nothing. Maybe she made it to the kitchen for something. Water. From the filtered water tap attached to the sink. Or maybe she was hungry and wanted something to eat. What's he talking about? Water. Food. Ridiculous. He turns off the light. Gets on his left side close to the edge of his side of the bed and reaches for the radio on his night table and turns it on. They're playing a piece he's heard on the radio several times but doesn't know what it's called. Schubert. Has to be. Chamber music. One of the quartets? He wrote fifteen of them. Fifteen. He's not familiar with them all but this one he is. He even thinks they heard it in Maine at the chamber music hall near where they used to stay. "Are you back in bed?" he says, without turning around. "Do you like this music? Will it disturb your sleep? Am I disturbing you just by talking? Do you want to snuggle again? Then do you want me to keep the radio on? If not, say so, and I'll turn it off. I should turn it off. We'll never get to sleep with it on. Schubert. One of his quartets, but which one I don't know. I'm almost sure we heard it in Maine once, lots of summers ago." He listens. Nothing. Turns the radio off and gets on his back. He reaches over to hold her hand. They often used to go to sleep that way, both on their backs. Sometimes she reached over to him to hold his hand in bed. Sometimes he raised her hand to his mouth when they were both on their backs in bed and kissed it. He'll leave her alone. He'll let her sleep or go to sleep. He'll tell her in the morning if she's still in bed that if he had snuggled with her any- more than he did last night he probably would have wanted to make love with her. She might say something like "Want to have a go at it now?" No, that's not like her. She'd say something more like "Are you interested now?" He'd say "Yes. Want me to take off your panties before we start?" "Do you mean my pad?" she might say. "Whatever you're wearing." "Sure," she'd say. "You'd have to, even- tually, wouldn't you? I don't see how there's any other way." He'd pull her panties down her legs and over her toes. No. He'd unbutton the straps on either side of her pad and slip it out from under her and drop it on the floor even if it was wet. No. She's not wearing anything there. She went to bed without anything on but a night- shirt. He pulls the nightshirt up to her neck. No. He pulls it up over one arm and then the other and then manages to get it over her head without hurting her ears and drops it on the floor. Sometimes even the bottom of her shirt would be wet but this time it's not. Now she's not wearing anything. He kisses her left shoulder, then her left breast. Her head's on two pillows. She's on her back. The covers are over both of them. No. She's on her right side. He kisses her left shoulder, kisses her back. He lifts her left leg, plays with her down there awhile, and then sticks his penis in. It feels so good, he thinks. "It feels so good," he says. "Shh," she says. "What?" he says. But don't be silly, he thinks. Maybe it was the bed making noise, or the cat. He gets on his back, pulls the covers up to his neck and shuts his eyes. Go to sleep, he thinks. "Go to sleep," he says. "Sleep. Sleep."

Cochran

A friend of mine said "Would you like to meet Cochran?"

"Sure, what writer wouldn't? But what would I say?"

"You don't have to say anything. He'll do most of the talking. If there's silence, even long silences, there's silence, but then he or I will say something or the visit will be over. Here, I'll call him. I'm sure he'd like to meet you."

"Why would he?"

"Because you're my friend and a writer."

He called Cochran from a telephone booth. Cochran said for them to meet him in the bar downstairs in the building he lives in. We went there. He wasn't there. We ordered a glass of wine each and waited.

"I'm surprised," my friend said. "He's usually so prompt."

"Maybe he meant another day or another hour."

"No, he specifically said he'll meet us in exactly twenty minutes in this bar and please don't be late. Also, he could only give us half an hour."

"That's better than nothing. Fact is, it's something I never expected, ever. I knew you knew him, but I didn't know how well and didn't want to ask because I thought you might think I was pushing for a meeting with him. Where do you know him from?"

"Oh, I get around."

Just then Cochran came into the bar, but from the street entrance, not the one to the apartment building. He put out his hand to me and said "Cochran. It's a pleasure to meet you, sir. I've been a long-time admirer of your work."

"Please, I'm sure you haven't read my work. It hardly gets around and there's so little of it."

"Take my word, son. I've read it. So, what are you boys drinking? Wine? Have another on me." He ordered a glass of white wine for himself, refills for us, and some bar food for us all. "Have some," he said. "It's delicious."

"What is it?" I said. "I don't recognize it. I only ask because if it's shrimp or anything even close in the shrimp family—langoustines, for example—I'm allergic to it."

"It's shrimp," he said. "You no doubt couldn't tell because the shells have been removed. I was also fooled the first time. I'll order something else for you."

"Really, I'm not hungry."

"I insist. You're young; you have to eat." He ordered something else. But he spoke so rapidly to the waiter that I again didn't make out what it was. "No meat in it of any kind," he said to me, "so you're safe. Now, let's talk about your work while we have one more drink. Or I'll have; you two can stay here for as long as you want and drink on me. The waiter will put it on my tab."

He went on and on about my work. What he liked, what he didn't think particularly worked but could easily be repaired, because it was too good to toss out; what he thought was original. He'd obviously read both my books, or a lot of each of them.

"May I now say what I think about your fiction?" I said. "Especially, the short prose. What I have to say is all good, believe me. And I'm not saying that because of the kind things you said about my stuff."

"*Stuff*. Oh, I love that. No, my friend, I have to go, and please don't save it for another time. I mean, we might meet again—I've enjoyed our brief conversation—but I get extremely uncomfortable when someone even alludes to my work in front of me, no matter how high the praise. No, I correct myself. Higher the praise, worse I feel. So." He drank up, shook our hands, patted my shoulder and left through the street door.

"He lives upstairs, as you know," my friend said, "and could have got to his building's lobby through that door there. But he likes leaving the bar and entering his building from the street, don't ask me why."

"Maybe he went for a walk or had an errand to do."

"That could be true too, though I know he wasn't planning to. He told me on the phone that after he leaves us he was going to take a half-hour nap, which he does daily at precisely this time."

We didn't take Cochran up on his offer for us to run up his tab. We drained our glasses, left, and I went back to my hotel and immediately sat at my tiny work table and started to write about my meeting with him. But the account was so much about me—what the great writer thought of the much younger writer's work and how it made the younger writer feel—giddy; ecstatic—that it seemed so silly and self-aggrandizing a piece that I tore it up. Maybe one day I'll write about it, I thought, although so many other writers, young and old, have written about their first and usually only meeting with him, that I doubt I could have anything new to say. Anyway, I met him. I liked him. He was the way I felt a very successful serious writer should be. Warm, personable, courteous, modest, affable, and it was generous of him to want to talk only about my work. It didn't take me long to realize he did that so he wouldn't have to talk about his own work. I don't like talking about mine either, or haven't since that meeting.

Cochran checked himself into a small simple nursing home in the city a year later. He told friends that after sixty years of writing without let-up he was finished with it for good. He refused to see any visitors at this home but his niece, lawyer and long-time publisher, and the word was that he didn't think he'd ever leave there or else didn't think he'd want to.

A few months after that I got a letter from his lawyer saying that Cochran had given me his one-room writing studio in a building a short walk from his apartment. He owned the studio outright, as he did his apartment, and the maintenance fees for it were paid up for the next five years. The only things I'd have to take care of were gas and electricity. "All Mr. Cochran asks of you," the letter said, "is that you not try to thank him by letter or telephone or visiting the nursing home."

I called my friend, who already knew about my getting the studio, and said "Why would he give me it? You know better than anyone that I had no connection to him but a half-hour's talk."

"Beats me," he said. "I saw him a couple of times since that day and he never mentioned you once, not even 'How's your friend?' I don't know if you know—it's in the recent J.T. Christophe bio of him—but it was the only place he wrote in other than his cottage in the country, and that he gave to the village it was in to be used as a public library, along with enough money to convert it. As for the studio, no one, for more than forty years, has been in there except Cochran, the housekeeper who came every other week to tidy it up, and the occasional plumber and electrician if something went awry. Not even his wife was allowed in it. Maybe he liked your work even more than he said that day and thought giving you the studio he'll never use again and with everything paid up, will be an incentive for you to continue to write. And his wife died a couple of years ago, as you probably know—not by her own hand, as your wife did, and nowhere near as young as yours, though just as ill—so maybe there's something in that too."

"I'd rather not talk about that," I said. "By the way, you ever write about him? I never saw anything and you never spoke about it."

"No, never, and not just because he wouldn't have wanted me to. He scorned writers who wrote memoirs, especially those who included him in theirs or published their personal encounters with him. He never read these accounts and cut off anyone who wrote about him. You?"

"For that one meeting? Nah. I kept it all in my head. Let me just ask you, though. What did you talk about with him those last times?"

"A variety of things. Sports, visual art, modern Italian poetry. Homer, Rabelais, Heine, Musil. The street he lives on. What he saw from his windows. The pigeons he fed on his window sill. Good scotch. How in his next life he was going to become a serious bird watcher and maybe even a park ranger or fire tower warden. A dog he had as a boy. And when he was in his cups, a lot about his sister, who also died young and whom it was obvious he adored. Did the lawyer say how you can get into the studio?"

"The concierge of the building it's in."

I got the keys from the concierge. It was an ordinary looking walk-up. The studio was on the third floor and I unlocked the door. It was a small room, about twelve by fourteen feet, with an alcove a little more than half that, which had a toilet but no door to it. The only furniture was a school desk that was just to the left of the only window, a wall lamp facing the desk, a kitchen chair and a bookcase put together out of bricks and three wood boards, with about fifteen books in it. One was by my friend, his first, probably inscribed. Another was a Spanish translation of one of Cochran's. Rabelais's two big books in one volume in French and a few other books in French by writers I never heard of except for Gide. I looked to see if it was inscribed, for it'd be worth a lot of money, but it wasn't. There wasn't anything on the walls but that one lamp. A typewriter was on the desk with no cover on it. I turned on the wall lamp and sat at the desk. The chair was uncomfortable. I'd have to get a cushion for it, I thought. The lamp didn't provide much light. I'd need a higher-wattage bulb for it and maybe even a new floor lamp. The typewriter was an old portable, the same Italian-made model my mother gave me when I graduated college and which I wrote on for five years till it seemed my fingers got too fat for the keys and I bought the Swiss-made standard model I still use today.

There was about half a ream of paper on the shelf under the top of the desk, the place a schoolboy would put his books and loose-leaf binder. I took some paper out, put it on the desk, which now left little room there for anything else, put two sheets into the typewriter and typed "Now is the time for all good men to come to the aid or something." The typewriter didn't have good keyboard action. It needed a cleaning, maybe a complete overhaul. The print was English. Anyway, I didn't feel like typing now.

I went into the alcove. Next to the toilet, which had one of those water tanks and pull-chains over it, was a tiny sink and counter. There was also what looked like a night table, with a single hot plate, saucepan and electric teakettle on it, and a cupboard with about six neatly stacked dishtowels, some cleaning supplies, an extra roll of toilet paper, two mugs, two saucers, two teaspoons and a butter knife and fork, a jar of instant expresso coffee, a box of teabags, an unopened tube of mayonnaise, three cans of tuna and one of mixed fruit.

It was a dismal place to write, I thought; depressing. The shabby furniture, old linoleum on the floor, stained walls that badly needed a paint job, and a view through that one window of an ugly much taller building about twenty feet across a yard. I didn't care if Cochran wrote here all those years, I didn't want to write in it. Though give it time, I thought; maybe I'd get used to the place. But even if I fixed it up, why would I want to write here? I have a nice apartment now, with a separate room, larger than this entire studio, just to write in. And both those rooms and the kitchenette and bathroom have a view of a small pretty park, and large double windows, except for the bathroom, you push out rather than pull up or down, as this one had.

I went downstairs. "I won't be using these keys," I said to the concierge. "I won't be coming back. It was very kind of Mr. Cochran"—I said all this in French— "to give me his studio, and with the fees for maintenance taken care of for five years. But it is not a very good place for me to do my writing. It was without doubt good for Mr. Cochran, but I'm saying here, not for me. I am also very aware of the great honor Mr. Cochran made to me to have this room for writing forever, and very generous of him. If you see Mr. Cochran, please say to him what I said to you. And please, give my best wishes and deepest thanks to him."

"He will be disappointed and sad you didn't like his room," the concierge said. "It was very special to him. He came to it almost every day and stayed in it for many hours and wrote masterpiece after masterpiece there. One could always hear his typewriter going click-click-click."

"Please don't say to him that I didn't like the room. It wasn't that. It's a good place to write. Few distractions and very quiet, which is perfect for a writer. Maybe he'll discharge himself from the nursing home he's in and return to his room upstairs to write."

"I don't think he'll be coming back to us. I also don't think I'll have the opportunity to tell him anything you've said."

"He's that sick?"

"That's what I've heard. What should I do with the room now? You own it. I've seen the legal papers. You could sell it, if you wish, and make yourself a great deal of money. This is quickly becoming a very desirable neighborhood. The price for an apartment—just a single studio room, like yours—rises every day. And he has such an enormous reputation."

"I really don't think it's mine to sell," I said. "He gave it to me to write in, not to make money from it. So do what you want with it. Give it to another writer. Or hold it for Mr. Cochran in case his health improves and he does return, which is what I hope for."

"I don't know any other writers," the concierge said.

"This city is filled with them, from many countries. Or the lawyer who handled the legal papers—he'll know what to do. Mr. Cochran's niece. She should probably get it. But I want nothing to do with it. I think that's the honorable positon for me to take."

I left the building, called my friend to see if he was interested in the studio, but his roommate said he suddenly had to fly home to Cape Town for a month. So maybe I should sell it, I thought. But it would be wrong and I didn't want to be bothered, and I was satisfied with what I had now. The lawyer and concierge and Cochran's niece will figure something out as to what to do with the studio. It wasn't my concern, and maybe it was all a mistake. Cochran only met me for half an hour. It made no sense. Who knows? I thought. He could have been drunk when he signed the place over to me, or took me for someone else.

I was going to stop someplace for coffee. But I got an idea for a short story and went back to my apartment to write it. The story had nothing to do with the studio and wasn't about my half-hour meeting with Cochran. It was mainly about how I met my wife more than ten years ago. It was in the lobby of an art movie house in New York. New Year's Day, early afternoon. Probably means she's single, I had thought, and unattached. We were waiting in line to get inside. She was in front of me, reading a book in French. She had a nice face and she looked intelligent and I liked that she was reading a thick book in French while waiting to see what's supposed to be a fairly artful complex movie. I thought of what to say and then said "*Excusez-moi, mademoiselle*—okay, I'll stop the pretending. My French is abominable. So excuse me again, I don't mean to disturb you from your reading, but what's the title of that book in English? It looks familiar." She gave me the title in English. "Sure, now I know it," I said, "and you're American. An interesting writer. He's from Scotland but has lived in France since the end of the Second World War, and is almost as well known for his short stories as he is his novels. And for many years now he only writes in French and translates all his works into English. Big in Europe but not so much in America or even Scotland." "That's right," she said. "You may go to the head of the class now." "I'm sorry. I guess I did sound a little pedantic, especially for someone who hasn't read more than five pages of one of his books." "No, no," she said. "You know a lot more about him than most people do, which is a shame. He deserves a much wider audience here." "May I ask if you're reading it for scholarly reasons or for pleasure, or maybe both." "Both," she said. "So you're going for a doctorate in French literature and Maitland Cochran's one of the writers, or maybe the main one, you're reading for your dissertation?" and she said "No, just for a course. Although for my dissertation I may end up writing about some aspect of his work. His poetry, even. More room there. And it's every bit as good as his fiction, and none of it's been published here or anyplace but France. I've time to decide yet." "From everything I've heard from people who have read his fiction, and also from those couple of peeks of mine into a book or two of his myself—in English of course. I'd never think of reading him in French, though I do have some reading understanding of the language—I felt he can be a very difficult writer and a little too cerebral for me. Intentionally difficult, I'm saying, and too abstruse. Anything to that?" "To some people, perhaps," she said, "but not to me. I find him very funny, in both languages, a great stylist, and once you get a few pages in to any of his books, easy to read and like nobody else and definitely worthwhile." "Well," I said, "the one you're reading was once recommended to me in English long ago. Do you think it's a good one to start off with?" "*Oui*," she said, and laughed.

Crazy

I have a dream. In it I'm pushing my wife in a wheelchair on a narrow street in New York. Chinatown, during the lunch hour. Four- to five-story buildings, lots of small restaurants, sidewalks very crowded and people walking fast. "Excuse me, excuse me," I say to people in front of us. "Better watch out. I don't want to run in to you." I've no idea where I'm going. I'm just pushing. My wife sits silently, looking straight ahead.

Then the scene changes to a street on the East Side of New York. In the forties; near the East River. Not a street but an avenue: First or Second or Third. The sidewalks are wide and again very crowded. Lunch hour. People walking very fast. Despite the tall office buildings on both sides of the avenue, plenty of sun. "We're in the Gravlax District," I say to my wife. "Can you hear me above all this noise? The Gravlax District. I only used to come here to go to a steakhouse or an art movie theater." I stop pushing and look around. "So many people," I say, with my back to her. "We never get crowded streets like this where we live. Nor the car traffic. It's exciting, don't you think?" When I turn back to her, she and the chair are gone. I took my hands off the chair's handles, something I almost never do when I'm outside with her and we're moving, or even when we've stopped but people are moving around us. Where could she have gone to? She wouldn't have just left without saying something to me. She must have been in a hurry, probably to pee. And stood up, told me where she was going and what for—most likely to a restaurant to use its restroom—but I didn't hear her because of the street noise, and then pushed the wheelchair there, or else wheeled the chair there while she sat in it.

I'm on a corner and see a restaurant a few doors down the sidestreet. I run to it and say to a man behind the lunch counter "Did a woman in a wheelchair come in here in the last minute or so?"

"In a wheelchair?" he says. "Couldn't have. We've three steps leading up to our door."

I run farther down the street to a park at the end of it. Jacob Riis Park? Does it come this far downtown? Anyway, a park that borders the river. Maybe she thought there'd be a public restroom here, and I look around. No Abby. She'd be easy to see, too, because she'd be in the wheelchair or pushing it. She can't walk on her own. No public building anywhere around, either. Just a playground, surrounded by grass and trees.

I run up the same sidestreet on the other side of the block. I look through the vestibule doors of all the brownstones on that side of the street, just as I did on the other side of the street when I ran down it to the park. In one dingy hallway I see at the end of it what looks like a wheelchair turned over. Oh my God; is it on top of her? I ring all the tenants' bells, am buzzed in. I run down the long hallway. It's a baby carriage turned over, nobody under it.

I run to the avenue where I last saw her, cup my hands around my mouth and shout "Abby, it's Phil; come back to the spot, Abby, it's Phil; come back to the spot." People stare at me as if I'm crazy. "I'm looking for my wife," I say. "She was here, in a wheelchair; now she's not." I shout again "Abby, it's Phil; come back to the spot." I keep shouting that while also looking in every direction for her. It's better to wait for her here than run around looking for her. If she comes to this spot and I'm not here, she might not know what to do to find me. I don't see her or anyone in a wheelchair. The street's still very noisy and crowded. And now I hear music, symphonic, coming from someplace, and which is so loud I won't be able to shout above it.

I wake up. The music's from the radio on my night table. I was listening in the dark to the classical music station when I fell asleep. I think about the dream. We were in Chinatown first and then on the East Side in the forties. I have to go there. I have to find her. This is crazy, I know.

I drive to the train station, park the car in its underground garage and buy a roundtrip ticket to New York. When I arrive, I go straight to Chinatown. I don't quite know how to get there, though. It's been five years since I've been in New York, my home city and also Abby's. The borough narrows at the southern end close to where Chinatown is, so just take any subway train south and get off at Worth Street or Canal Street or Chambers, whichever comes first. I get on the subway and get off at Houston Street—I forgot Houston—and think I'm near Chinatown, but it turns out to be a long walk. I'm hungry—I rushed out of the house so fast, I didn't have anything to eat and the train didn't have a food car. I should stop in one of the small restaurants here and sit at the counter and have a bowl of soup and plate of noodles, but I don't want to lose any time in looking for her.

I walk all around Chinatown. I think I cover every single block. This is crazy, I know, but I thought I could find her down here, or at least there was a chance. I don't want her to be lost. She'll get sad, frightened; maybe even terrified. She's become that vulnerable. She used to like going alone to places—even faraway countries—she's never been to before or hasn't been to in a while. But not since she got so sick. She needs me. She once said I keep her alive. Not said it to me but wrote it four or five years ago in one of the notebooks I found of hers. "Phil keeps me alive. What to do?" and she dated it: October 6th; I forget the exact year. I give up looking for her in

Chinatown. Only other place to go is the east forties. Maybe I'll find her there. Since it was the last place I saw her, I should have gone there first.

I take the subway to Times Square, then the one-stop train shuttle there to Lexington Avenue and 42nd Street. I go upstairs and walk on 42nd Street to First Avenue. I walk down First Avenue to 34th Street, then walk up Second Avenue to 42nd Street, then walk down Third Avenue to 34th Street. Then I walk along all the sidestreets between First and Third avenues from 34th to 50th Streets. I look in stores. I look in most of the brownstones I pass and also the lobbies of the tall apartment and office buildings and even in a few movie theaters. This is crazy, I know, but for some reason I begin to think I'll find her, that it's more than a slight chance. But no Abby or wheelchair anyplace. And no wheelchairs in the ground-floor hallways of any of the brownstones, though a few baby carriages, none turned over.

I have to go to the bathroom. I go into a coffee shop, order a coffee at the lunch counter and go to the men's room. I drink the coffee, have a buttered English muffin with it and ask the server behind the counter if she's seen a woman in a wheelchair here today, and I describe Abby and the chair and its tote bag hanging on the back. "I was pushing her in the chair, got distracted for a few seconds and let go of it, which I almost never do, and she was either wheeled away by someone or wandered off by herself."

"If she was in here I would've seen her," the woman says. "I've been on duty all day, never a work break. The door to this place is hard to open from the outside by someone in a wheelchair, so I always have to come out from behind the counter to help."

I pay and leave. I go to the corner of 40th Street and First Avenue, which is where she disappeared, and look around some more for her and then cup my hands around my mouth and shout "Abby, it's Phil; come back to the spot. Abby, it's Phil; come back to the spot."

Lots of people look at me. One man stops and says "Anything wrong, Chief?"

"Yes," I say, "I've lost my wife. She was in a wheelchair."

"If she got separated from you in a wheelchair and was able to move it by herself, she'll come back."

"That's why I'm shouting for her," I say. "The streets are crowded and she's sitting so low in the chair that she won't be able to see me from it. But she'll hear me and come back to the spot I lost her at." I cup my hands around my mouth again and shout "Abby, Abby, it's Phil. Come back to the spot."

A policeman comes over and says to me "You can't be shouting out like that, sir. Is it something I can help you out with?"

"My wife, in a wheelchair, was here with me and then vanished."

"I can take a description of her wife and have a patrol car look for her."

"No, I say, "it won't work. This is crazy, I know, to do what I'm doing, but I had to see it through. Thank you. I'll go home now. I just have to believe she'll be all right."

I hail a cab, take it to Penn Station, and get the next train back to my city. I better watch out, I tell myself. I could get arrested. Taken in. Held overnight. Locked up for I don't know how long in a nuthouse. Not something I need.

One Thing to Another

I've been writing the same story for weeks. I can't seem to get past page four. The woman's name has been Delia, Mona, Sonya, Emma, Patrice. The narrator's name has been Herman, Kenneth, Michael, Jacob, Jake. From now on I'll call her "his wife" and him "he." The locale is a Baltimore suburb. The time is today. The title has been *Liebesträume, Nothing to Read, Lists, The List, A List, The Wedding March, Wedding March, The Church Bench, Humming.* I always put the title near the top of the first manuscript page. So I always have to have the title before I start the final draft of the first page of the story, which I've done with this story about a hundred times. I think I know what I want to say in the story and where I want it to go. Maybe they're the same thing. What I'm having trouble with is how to say it and keeping the story from being boring, stodgily written and overexplanatory. In other words, a story I wouldn't want to read. It's been like a wrestling match. The story's fighting me and I'm fighting it. Sometimes I think it's got me in its hold and sometimes I think I've got it in mine. What I want to finally do is pin it to the mat rather than be pinned. I've fought like this with a story before, but never for so long, and I always won. But end of wrestling analogy. I probably used it incorrectly anyway. This is what I've got so far: the start. I want to continue writing it after what I write what I've already written down.

An Episcopal church is directly across the street from his house. (In some versions it's "…is right across the street…" and in others "…is across the street…" When I'm retyping a page, even after fifty times, I'm always changing a word or two or even a line. But I won't stop the story anymore like that till I get to the place where I left off.)

An Episcopal church is right across the street from his house. Every afternoon between five and six he takes a walk in his neighborhood and almost always ends up sitting on a bench in front of the church. There are four benches there, all in various places in front of the church and each facing a different direction. He's sat at least once on all of them and prefers the one that looks out on the street that runs parallel to the church. Not the street his house is on but the one perpendicular to it. He likes that bench best because it gets the most sun in late afternoon and there's more to see from it. He usually takes a book with him on these walks and reads for about a half hour on the bench if the weather permits it. If it's not too hot or cold and it isn't raining or snowing. He always takes his walk, though, no matter what the weather's like. Well, if it's raining hard, he doesn't take a walk. But if it's snowing or just a light rain, he'll walk but he doesn't take a book with him or end up on the bench there. It'd be too wet to sit on. All the benches would. None are protected by trees. If he knows there's not going to be enough light out to read on the bench by the time he gets there or it's already dark by the time he starts out, he also doesn't take a book with him, though he still might sit on the bench for a few minutes. But if he's tired from the walk or his lower back hurts, which happens a lot by the time he finishes his walk, he'll sit longer and just think about things—a dream from the previous night and what it might mean, a short story he's been working on—or let his mind wander. He's even nodded off a few times on the bench, but only when it was dark out.

So he's finished his walk and is sitting on what he's begun to call, in his daily phone conversations with his daughters, his bench.

"What'd I do today?"—he always speaks to them in the evening, an hour or so after his walk. "I wrote and went to the Y, of course, and took a walk and sat on my bench and read." It's early April, around six-thirty, a bit chilly. Daylight Saving Time started a week ago. The sun's out but setting. Cherry trees around the church are in full flower—a little early, but what does he know? No cars in the church's small parking lot the bench also faces, and no people around, which is usually what it's like out here at this time. He does hear children's voices from somewhere far off, and a car or pickup truck occasionally passes. But that's about it for distractions and noises. Oh, a jogger and a woman walking two dogs also went by, but that's all, or all he saw. So: a peaceful place to sit and think or read. He did bring a book with him—a short biography of Maxim Gorky, one of about two hundred books his wife had on Russian literature in her study and which are still there. But he isn't interested in reading anymore of it after reading the first thirty pages last night in bed. So why'd he take it on his walk? It was on the dryer by the kitchen door leading to the outside, where he'd left it this morning; he hadn't decided what book he was going to read next, so he just grabbed it before he left the house. He sets it beside him on the bench. When he gets home he'll stick it back in the bookcase he got it out of. So, nothing to read, really, he closes his eyes. See what comes, he thinks. Nothing does. Just letters and numbers bouncing around in his head, then a vertical line moving right to left, right to left, and then flashing, like lightning, but he doesn't know what it is. Maybe lightning. He opens his eyes and looks at the sky, then at the two houses across the street, and finds himself humming something over and over for a couple of minutes. Liszt's "Liebesträum." Just the beginning of it. He doesn't know the whole piece. Why's he humming it, and now? Well, nothing else to do. No, there's got to be a better reason than that. It doesn't just come out of nowhere.

Sure, it's a beautiful piece of music when played on the piano—not with the mouth sounds he was making—or even the cello, meaning he once heard it played on the cello at a concert, but long ago. Before he met his wife. Did she play it on the piano? Doesn't think so. Or she might have—she knew lots of pieces for piano—but she never played it while he was around. And if she played something—well, he was going to say she practiced it till she could play it without reading the music, and in that time he just about got to know it by heart too. But that doesn't make the sense he wanted it to—to explain why he would have had to have heard her play it, if she did.

Then he remembers. Esther, a concert pianist who was also her piano teacher at the time, played the entire third "Liebesträume," the one he was humming, in the living room of their New York apartment before their wedding ceremony began. As a warm-up, or to prepare the guests for the ceremony, perhaps. Then she went into her interpretation of Mendelssohn's "Wedding March," which was the signal for his wife to walk slowly out of their bedroom with her bridesmaid and stand in front of the rabbi with him for the ceremony. He burst out crying right after the rabbi pronounced them married, was told by the rabbi and several guests "Kiss the bride, kiss the bride," and he wiped his cheeks and eyes with his handkerchief, kissed her and thought this is the happiest moment in his life. And it was and continued to be so for around eight months, till the happiest moment in his life took place in the birthing room of a Baltimore hospital when his wife gave birth to their first child.

This is where I always get stuck. I know where I want to go from here but I just can't seem to get there or even much started. I thought a few times maybe I should chuck the third person and do the whole thing in first and that will help me. And then I always think no, it won't, so don't. Stick with third; it feels right, and that's what you have to rely on. I want him to explain why the moment their first child born became the happiest in his life and the moment they were declared man and wife dropped down a notch to the second happiest. And then to briefly give the third happiest moment, and maybe why it became that. And then the fourth, and so on, right up to the ninth or tenth, all of the last part taking up no more than three or four pages, and that would be it unless something else came to end it between now and then.

What I had in mind was something like this: The birth of their first child became the happiest moment in his life for a number of reasons, and by "moment" he means moments, hours, even the day. He'd wanted a child for about fifteen years. Impregnated three women in that time but none of them wanted to marry him or have the baby. They all thought he'd make a good father but that he'd never earn enough money to keep a family going, and had abortions. More important was that his wife was going through a difficult delivery in the hospital. It had been more than thirty hours since she went into labor and it had become extremely uncomfortable, exhausting and painful for her. Most important of all, her obstetrician—"Dr. Martha" she wanted to be called—said the baby's breathing was at risk after so long a delivery and the position in the birth canal she was frozen in—her head or maybe it was a shoulder was caught on something there—and she'll give a natural birth one last try with forceps and if that doesn't work, she'll have to do a cesarean. Fortunately, she was an expert with forceps and turned the baby over inside the birth canal and eased her out. So it was the relief after so many hours that the baby had come out alive and healthy and his wife was all right and had been able to avoid surgery and that he finally had a child, that made it the happiest moment in his life, and which it still is after nearly thirty years.

His third happiest moment was when their second child was born. He's not sure why it's not his second happiest moment, but it isn't. It's just a feeling he has. There wasn't any anxiety or relief involved in the birth because there wasn't any difficulty in the delivery. She felt something at home, calmly said to him "I think it's started," they drove calmly to the hospital, thinking they had plenty of time, and she had the baby in less than a total of two hours from the time she felt it starting till the head and shoulders emerged. "That's about as quick a delivery as you can get," Dr. Martha said, "unless there's no labor and the sac's already broken without anyone noticing and the mother gives birth while she's cooking dinner at home or being driven to the hospital."

His fourth happiest moment came during the first day of their two-day honeymoon at an inn in Connecticut, when the pregnancy kit they brought with them tested positive. She screamed and shrieked and then said "Sorry, this is so unlike me, and what will the other guests think? But aren't you as happy?" "Sure, what do you think?" and they hugged and kissed and danced around their room and then went downstairs and at the bar there shared a split of champagne. "My last drink till the little sweetie comes," she said, and he said "Why? You can have a little for a couple of months." "After two miscarriages with my first husband? No. I'm going to be extra overcautious. In the future you can drink my glass if anyone pours me one."

His fifth happiest moment was in January, 1965, when *The Atlantic Monthly* took a short story of his, almost twenty years to the month before their second child was born. He was on a writing fellowship in California, had just come back from a month's stay with his family in New York. Lots of mail was waiting for him. He'd only had two stories published before then, or one published and the other accepted, both with little magazines. Rejection, rejection, rejection, he saw, by the bulge in each of the nine-by-twelve-inch manila envelopes he'd sent with the stories. He opened the regular letter envelope from *The Atlantic Monthly*, assuming they didn't bother to send back his story with their rejection slip in the stamped return envelope as the others had. In it was the acceptance letter from an editor, with an apology for keeping the story so long. He shouted "Oh my gosh; I can't believe it. They took my story," and he knocked on the door of the political science graduate student who lived in the room next to his. "I'm sorry; did I wake you? But I got to tell you this. *The Atlantic Monthly* took a story of mine and is giving me six-hundred bucks for it. We have to go out and celebrate, on me."

The sixth happiest moment was nine years later. He was walking upstairs to his New York apartment with a woman he'd recently met. By that time—fifteen years after he'd started writing—he had eight stories published, about a hundred-fifty written, no book yet. "Another rejection from *Harper's*," he said. She was in front of him and said "I'm not a writer, but I guess that's what you have to expect." "Let's see what they have to say. It's always good for a laugh." He opened the envelope he'd sent with the story. "What's this?" he said. He pulled out the galleys to his story and a letter from the editor he'd sent it to and a check for a thousand dollars. The editor wrote "I realize this must be unusual for you, receiving the galleys to your story along with the acceptance letter. But we want to get your story in print as soon as possible and there's space for it in the issue after next. We tried calling you, but you're either unlisted or one of the few writers in New York who doesn't have a phone." That was true. He didn't. Too costly. And the sudden phone rings in his small studio apartment, when he was deep into his writing, always startled him, so he had the phone removed. "This is crazy," he said. "*Harper's* took instead of rejected. And for more money than I've ever made from my writing," and he waved the check. They were on the top-floor landing now and she said "Let me shake your hand, mister," and tweaked his nose.

The seventh happiest moment? Probably in 1961, when a woman, who had dumped him two years before and then three months after they'd started seeing each other again, said she'd come to a decision regarding his marriage proposal. They were in the laundry room of his parents' apartment building. Had gone down there to get their laundry out of one of the washing machines and into a dryer. "So?" he said, and she said "Okay, I'll marry you." "You will?" "That is, if you still want to go through with it." "Do I? Look at me. I'm deliriously ecstatic. Ecstatically delirious. I don't know what I am except giddy with happiness. I love you," and he kissed her and they got their laundry into a dryer and took the elevator back to his parents' floor and told them and his sister and brother they had just gotten engaged. She broke it off half a year later, a few weeks before they were to be married in her parents' summer home on Fire Island. A big old house, right on the ocean. Her father was a playwright, her mother an actress, as was his fiancée.

The eighth? Maybe when a publisher called to say she was taking his first book. That was in '76. He was happy but not ecstatic. He'd been trying to get a story collection or one of his novels published for around fifteen years. But it was a very small publishing house, no advance, a first printing of five hundred copies, and probably little chance of getting any book reviews or attention. So maybe that was his ninth happiest moment, and the eighth was when a major publisher took his next novel and for enough of an advance for him to live on for a year if he lived frugally. But again, not a great happiness when the editor called him with the news, since the novel was accepted based on the first sixty-seven pages he'd sent them and the rest of it still had to be written.

The tenth also happened while he was living in New York and had no phone. 1974. Same year *Harper's* took, but months later. He'd come downstairs from his apartment to go for a run in Central Park. The mailman, whom he knew by name—Jeff—was in the building's vestibule, slotting mail into the tenants' mailboxes. He dug a letter out of his mailbox and gave it to him. It was from the National Endowment for the Arts. He'd been rejected two years in a row by them for a writing fellowship, so expected to be rejected again. He opened the envelope. "Jesus Christ," he said. "I won an NEA fellowship." "What's that?" Jeff said. He told him. "But it says for five hundred dollars." "So, five hundred isn't anything to sniff at," Jeff said. "But I thought all their fellowships are for five thousand." "Now, five thousand would really be something, landing in your lap like that. Do I get a cut for delivering the news?" He ran down the street to the candy store at the corner, got lots of change and dialed the NEA number from a phone booth there. The person he finally got to speak to who he was told would know how to deal with the matter said "That is strange. We don't have any five-hundred-dollar fellowships. Let me look into it and call you back." "I don't have a phone," he said. "Then you'll have to hold the line while I check." She came back about ten minutes later and said "Are you still there? You were right. Your notification letter was missing a zero." "So the fellowship is for five thousand?" "In a week you should be receiving a duplicate letter to the one you got today, the only difference being the corrected figure written in." "When can I start getting the money?" and she said "You'll receive another letter after the duplicate one with some forms to fill out." "Can I get the money in one lump sum, or do you spread it out over a year?" and she said "Everything will be explained in the instructions accompanying the forms. But to answer your question, yes." "One lump sum?" "If you want." "Whoopee," he said, slapping the metal shelf under the telephone. "Boy, am I ever going to write up a storm the next year." "That's what we like to hear," she said.

The eleventh or twelfth happiest moment in his life? He forgets what number he left off at. It could have been when he was living in a cheap hotel in Paris and was called downstairs by the own-er to answer a phone call from *"les États-Unis,"* she said. He ran downstairs. Something awful about one of his parents, he was sure. This was in April, 1964. He'd been in Paris for three months, learn-ing French at the Alliance Française; his ultimate aim was to get a writing job in the city with some American or British company. It was his younger sister. "Dad's not too thrilled with my making this call," she said. "Too expensive. A telegram would be cheaper, he said, if I kept it short. But I explained the urgency behind my calling you. Prepare yourself, my lucky and talented brother. I have something terrific to tell you." "Come on," he said, "what is it? The *madame* here doesn't like me hogging the one phone." "You got a telephone call from someone at Stanford University. You won a creative writing fellowship there for three thousand dollars, this September." "Oh my god," he said. "I forgot all about it, which tells you how much I thought I'd get it." "Listen, though. This woman said because they took so long to select the four fellows, they want your decision right away. If it's a no, they need to choose someone else in a hurry. I told her I'm sure you'll take it, but I'll call you and then call her with your answer." "I don't know what to do," he said. "I mean, I'm grateful, and I should be overjoyed, but I'm just beginning to really like it here and I'm learning the language and making friends. Think they'd let me defer the fellowship for a year?" "I already asked her about that possibility," she said. "She told me you have to accept it now for this year or reapply with com-pletely different supporting material for the next year, though you wouldn't need to get new references. That's their policy." "The *ma-dame*'s staring at me. I have to hang up. I guess I'll take it, then. My feelings are mixed, as you can see, but it's too good an opportunity to pass up. And California should be fun." "Monsieur?" the owner said. "Sometimes," his sister said, "you have to give up something good to get something better or even comparable. And I'll fly out to California to see you, which will be a nice break for me."

And his next happiest moment? Can't think of one now, or where he was just as happy or even happier than he was in some of the last ones he mentioned. Maybe, going very far back, when he won the All Around Camper Award at the sleepaway camp he went to with his sisters and his brother Robert in the summer of 1948. So when he was told he won it by the head counselor. Or when the principal of his elementary school—this was in 1949, a couple of months before he graduated—called him and several other eighth-grade students into his office to tell them they'd each gotten into one of New York's elite public high schools, and one of them got into two and would have to choose, and which schools. His was Brooklyn Tech. He was happy but at the same time a bit disappointed because he wanted to go to Stuyvesant, where Robert was a sophomore at, but he obviously didn't do well enough on its admissions test to get in. Odd, because he thought the Stuyvesant test was a breeze compared to the one for Brooklyn Tech.

Any other time? Oh, how could he forget? They were in a little hill town in Southern France, looking at a Giacometti drawing on the wall of a small museum, when he turned to his wife half a year before she became his wife, and said "Let's get married." She said "Are you joking?" and he said "I'm dead serious. Here, or in Nice by a rabbi if they have one there or some justice of the peace," and she said "If I got married again it would have to be in New York so my folks and relatives and friends could come. And I'd think you'd want your family there too. But let's talk about it in a few months." "So you'll consider it then as a possibility?" and she said "Let's say I'm not rejecting the idea outright, as preposterously as it was presented," and he said "You don't know how happy you've just made me. All right. I'll shut up about it for a few months." Of course, he hugged and kissed her and then he took her hand in his and led her to the next Giacometti drawing.

And the saddest moments in his life? His wife's death, of course. Next Robert's. Then his younger sister's. Then his oldest brother in a boating accident a few years ago. Then his mother's. Next his father's. After that, his two best friends dying a year apart, both from strokes. But he doesn't want to think about them. Actually, the second saddest moment of his life had to be when his wife, two years before she died, was in the hospital for pneumonia and her doctors told him she'd have to be intubated and that there was still only a slight chance she'd survive. "One to three percent," they said, or was it "three to five"? He can't say, when he was told by them several days later that she'll survive, that it was one of the happiest moments in his life. He was too sad at the time. He'd just seen her in her ICU room—in fact, he remembers at that moment looking at her on her bed—struggling with the ventilating tube inside her. "Get this thing out of me...*please, please,*" her painful look seemed to say. No, he knew her look; that's what it was saying. But if he was going to list the saddest moments in his life, those would probably be it, plus a few he missed. His wife first, his wife second, then the rest in the order he gave.

And, to end it, something like this: He gets off the bench and walks the rest of the way to his house. The cat's waiting for him by the kitchen door. He wants to be let in and fed. He'll want to be let out after, but he won't let him. It's already getting dark. He gets the opened can of cat food out of the refrigerator, gets the cat's empty plate off the floor, washes it and spoons the rest of the food in the can on it and puts it back on the floor. The cat starts eating. He's about to make himself a drink—something with rum tonight, he thinks; he's been drinking vodka every night for a week—when he realizes he forgot the Gorky book on the bench. Leave it till tomorrow. No, it'll be gone, or if it rains, wet. Get it now.

He goes back to the bench. The book's gone. Who'd want to take it? Nobody was around; no cars were in the lot, so nobody was in the church. And really, no one but a Russian literary scholar or maybe a serious fiction writer would be interested in it. Maybe someone who lives around here was out for a walk and saw it. He wants to look at the good side of things. So it's possible a passerby got it and will bring it to the church office tomorrow and say he or she found it on one of the benches outside and thought it might belong to someone connected to the church. Ah, just forget it, he thinks. He's never going to read anymore of it. If his wife were alive, he'd go to the church the next day—midafternoon, though; he'd give the person who might have taken it time to bring it to the church—and ask if anyone turned in a book about the Russian writer, Maxim Gorky. He goes home, carefully opens the kitchen door so the cat doesn't run out, and gets some ice out of the freezer and puts it in his glass. Rum it is, with a sliver of lime.

The Girl

Summer, 1952. He'd just turned sixteen and was a waiter for two months at a co-ed sleepaway camp. He and the other waiters—there were about fifteen of them, all boys—went to another camp to play a softball game against its waiters. He was his team's best hitter. He often hit balls fifty to a hundred feet farther than anyone else on the team. He wasn't that big a kid, but for some reason—his strong arms and maybe something to do with the wrists—he could hit a ball hard and far. He also had a good eye for the ball. He rarely struck out and he got his share of walks.

Their camp was in Flatbrookville, New Jersey. He thinks the town is underwater now because of a lake that was created when a dam was built there about twenty years after he worked at the camp. The camp they were playing was also on the Delaware River, near Bushkill, Pennsylvania. They were driven there in an old World War II army truck, with an open flat bed large enough to seat the entire waiter staff and all their sports equipment. One of the camp directors and the head of the waiters sat up front with the driver. It took about an hour to get there, which was as long as it took to get to the Bushkill public landing the one time he paddled to it in a canoe with another waiter. His first time in Pennsylvania, he thought then. They didn't do much once they reached the landing. Ate the lunch they brought with them and then paddled back to camp.

This other camp had a softball diamond much better taken care of than their camp's and with real bases, not pieces of cardboard and linoleum their camp used. They were there only a couple of minutes when the camp director told the team to take batting practice and make it fast. "I want to get the game going so you kids can be back in camp to set up and serve dinner." Everyone lined up to swing at three pitches each. The camp director lobbed in balls. He hit two of them over the heads of the outfielders, who were from his camp and playing him far. "That a way to go, slugger," one of them yelled. "Show 'em where you live."

"Do that for real when you come up to bat," the camp director said. "I want to announce in the mess hall tonight that you brought pride to our camp and helped win the game."

There were about a hundred people from the other camp, kids and adults, sitting in the stands along the first- and third-base lines. One of them, on the third-base side, was a very pretty girl. She was around his age, so he assumed she was a C.I.T., or maybe they had some girl waiters in this camp. Long blond hair brushed back, slim, a good figure, and calm and collected expressions and a bright face. She had the look of some of the brainier girls he knew, but was much prettier than any of them. She was wearing shorts, cut well above her knees, and seemed to have nice strong legs. When she laughed with the girls her age she was sitting with, she laughed modestly, quietly, not loudly or uproariously as the rest of them did. And her face didn't get distorted when she laughed as theirs did. He liked her face. In fact there wasn't anything about her he didn't like. She seemed like the perfect girl for him. He had a hard time taking his eyes off her and wished he could meet her. But what were the chances of that? He wasn't the type of guy to just go over to her after the game and introduce himself and say he hasn't got much time to talk, his camp director will want to get them back on the truck soon and out of here, but can he have her name and does she think he could maybe write her? The camp director had told them before they left for this camp that it was a kosher one like theirs, though not as strictly religious, and that almost all the campers and staff came from Pennsylvania, and most of those from Philadelphia. "Just thought you should know a little history about who you'll be playing and whipping the butts off of today, and that if they offer you snacks after the game, you can eat them." Anyway: Pennsylvania. So what good would it be in getting to know her? But who knows.

After he took batting practice, he looked over to her to see if she might be looking at him. One of her friends may have told her that he had looked a lot of times at her. If she was, and she smiled to his smile, or even if she didn't smile, it might give him enough courage to make a move on her later. But she was listening, with her hand holding her chin and with a serious expression, to one of the other girls talking.

The umpire, who was some kid's father from the other camp, said "Okay, visiting team; batter up." His side went down one-two-three. The pitcher was good; hard to hit. Struck out the first two batters and got the third on a pop-up. He was on deck, batting cleanup, flexing his biceps as he swung two bats, even though she didn't seem the sort of girl to be impressed by them.

The other team got a run the first inning. Three straight singles. He played third base, and because of that fielding position and he always played close to the bag, he got a closer look at her. She was even prettier than he first thought. Beautiful, he'd say. And so mature looking and with a nice even tan on her arms and legs but not her face. Smart. For even her eyebrows were blond. If she wasn't sitting in the shade—a couple of her friends were in the sun—he was sure she'd be wearing a hat. He fielded one grounder that inning and threw a perfect peg to first. Made the play look easy. After they got the third out, he trotted to his team's bench on the third-base side and sat with his back to her. She didn't look at him when he came off the field. None of the girls she was with did. They were too busy talking and barely looking at the game, even when their waiters were up. To him that was a good sign. That she didn't have a boyfriend on the team. If she did, she'd be looking and smiling at him every now and then and maybe cheering their team on a little. So why were they there then? Maybe they were told to by their counselor or someone of authority, at least, to be there at the start of the game.

He was first up the next inning. He wanted to impress her with a solid hit and his fast base running or if possible even a home run to tie the score. For sure, one of those his first time at the plate, before she and her friends got bored with the game, as girls will, and left, if they were allowed to, because if they were all C.I.T.'s, then they could be there to be near their campers. He knew you're not supposed to swing at the first pitch, especially your first at-bat, but he was eager and the ball looked too good to pass up, coming in slow and fat, and he swung and hit it as far as he ever hit a softball, but it curved foul by about twenty feet.

"Straighten it out next time," a couple of his teammates yelled. "You can do it."

He swung at the next pitch, too—a bad one, way too low—and missed. Take it easy, he told himself. You're much too eager. Last thing you want is to strike out in front of her. Even if she had seen him hit the first pitch that far, it went foul, so meant nothing.

He stepped out of the batter's box to calm himself. The pitcher was about to throw the ball and stopped. And it was a real batter's box, chalked like the on-deck circle was and the baselines all the way to the ends of the outfield. He also wanted to give her time to look at him looking pensive and determined.

"Come on, son," the umpire said. "Get in position. You're wasting time."

Now that could be embarrassing, he thought, but he won't say anything. He saluted the umpire, then thought what a stupid move, saluting, and got back in the box. Definitely let the next pitch go past if it looks like a ball. Trust your eyes. Wait for another good one. He swung at the next pitch—it would have been a strike if the umpire called it right—and grounded to the pitcher and was thrown out.

The girl stayed around. Cheered once when her side got another run. Or pretended to cheer, really. That's what it looked like to him. Then she and the other girls cheered together "Two, four, six, eight, who do we appreciate? Na-ho-je, Na-ho-je," which was the name of their camp, "yea-a-a."

The score was still two-zip in the fourth inning when two of the players on his team got on base with walks and he came to bat. "Knock it out of the park," his teammates were shouting. "If anybody can do it, you can."

"Don't be anxious," the waiter counselor had told him. "Wait him out. Maybe we can walk around. Or just a simple hit. We need a run and that'll keep it going."

"Got ya," he said.

He swung at the first pitch, a fast one straight across the plate, and hit it over the leftfielder's head. He ran around the bases and ended up with a triple. He felt he could have stretched it into a homer, but the camp director, who was coaching at third, held him up.

"Why'd you stop me?" he said. "I could've made it. Then we'd be ahead."

"Don't be such a hero," the camp director said. "Best to play it safe. I also didn't want you sliding into home and hurting yourself and being sent to the infirmary. Who'd, then, wait your tables?"

He looked at the girl. She was looking at him. She applauded twice in his direction. Little claps. Like a seal would make. No smile, though. He took off his baseball cap and waved it to her. Good move, he thought. Dignified. She had to like it. But she quickly looked away. Anyway, she'd noticed him. He had to meet her. What would he say if he did? First of all, how would he? Like he said, he'd just go over to her and he'd say "Hi, my name is Phil. Or Philip to my friends." No. No stupid jokes. Don't even try. "I saw you in the stands. You seemed interesting. You from Pennsylvania?" This would have to be after the game, and as he thought, quick. And hopefully they'd won. Or if they didn't, then something like "Your team played a good game. I congratulate them. Are you a C.I.T. here?" And then? Well, it'd depend on what she answered. And that he didn't have much time to talk. "Uncle Abe, one of our camp directors, will be in a rush to get us back. I'd like to write you, if you wouldn't mind. Can I ask your name"—if she didn't already give it when he gave his—"and what bunk number you're in, or your address here, so I can write?" If she asked why he'd want to he'd say "Because I thought, just by looking at you, you were interesting." That ought to do it. And if they do write each other maybe once or twice while they're still at camp, what then after camp's over for both of them at the end of August? Maybe one day take a train or bus to Philadelphia, if that is where she lives, and spend the day with her. Would her parents allow it? Why not? It'd be a weekend afternoon and they're both sixteen, or she almost is, it seems. And there'd be no problem with his parents. They give him lots of freedom. And he'd have the money—he always has a job after school—to pay for the fare himself. And then go to see her a second time. Hold her hand. Visit a museum. Kiss her. Talk to her. What does she like to read? Or maybe they'd already spoken about this. So what does she like to do in the city? What is she studying at school? Her outside interests. What college does she want to go to? Lots of things. And if she lives outside Philadelphia, there must be a way of getting there, too.

The next man filed out. The score was tied for a couple of innings and then the Na-ho-je team got four more runs, almost all on walks. Since it was softball, it was a seven-inning game. He came up a third time and looked over at her. She wasn't looking at him; nor had she, when he was on the field or sitting on the bench—at least when he'd looked her—since that one time she clapped. With two strikes on him, he hit a pitch over the centerfielder's head, even though the outfielders were all playing him deep this time. The centerfielder was fast and had a good arm and threw the ball to third in time to stop him from getting another triple. He was halfway to third and felt lucky to get back to second before he was run down and tagged out. It was by far his longest hit of the day and he looked at the stands to see if she was looking at him, but she wasn't there. Where the hell she go? Standing on second base, he looked around for her. She and some of her friends were already a ways off, running—it looked like racing—to somewhere with a whole bunch of younger campers, probably the kids they were in charge of. Well, there goes that dream, he thought. Nothing he can do to meet her now, unless she comes back here before his team gets back on the truck and leaves.

The batter behind him ground out to end the inning. They didn't score another run, though he felt he did all he could to win. Two big hits, no errors or strikeouts, knocking in their only runs. Anyway, they were behind by so much with only one more turn at bat, another run or two wouldn't have helped.

After the game, they were told to shake the hands of the opposing team, take what refreshments were there—cupcakes and sugar cookies and lemonade—as they probably won't be getting back in time to have supper before they set up and serve, so they'll have it after, and then get back on the truck.

When he shook the pitcher's hand, he said "Good game. You guys played well. What can I say? The better team won. But can I ask you something? There was a girl sitting in the stands. Tall, she seemed, and very pretty, and really blond hair. Over there," and he pointed. "With some of her friends. You know which one I'm talking about?"

"Yeah, I know her."

"Does she have a boyfriend?"

"She could. I don't know. What a question to ask."

"No good? None of my business, right? She's intelligent, though. I could tell by her face—sort of the expressions—and the way she smiled and also her laugh, not like a horse. Even the subtle way she applauded me when I got that triple to tie the score."

"She applauded you?"

"Not 'subtle.' Reserved? Tempered? Is that a word? Little claps. Almost pretending. And 'subdued' is what I think I mean."

"She's a very nice girl," the pitcher said.

"Hey, I didn't say she wasn't. I was complimenting her on the way she tried to show her congratulations or whatever you want to call it to someone on the other team. She from Philadelphia?"

"She could be. I wouldn't know."

"We were told that almost everyone from your camp is supposed to be from Philadelphia."

"That could be so. I am too. Where are you from?"

"Do you know her name?"

"Sure. Are you asking for it? Because I don't know if I should give it. It might be wrong to. She might not want it handed out. Ask Sid there—the assistant head counselor—the guy in the white tennis shirt. If he thinks it's okay, he'll give it."

"Nah, I should probably forget it. It might be a nuisance, my asking, and what would be the use?"

"If you say so, pal. She's a helluva looker, I'll grant you that. And good game too. Your part, anyhow."

"Yeah, I had a good day. You, also. The score wasn't even close, and you got a couple of singles."

Going back, the camp director sat in the bed of the truck, with a cushion under and behind him. It was windy back there and he said "I have something to say. Can everyone hear me?" They all indicated they could. "I want to be honest. This won't be nice. It was an experiment, going to another camp to play, one I'm not going to repeat. You played lousy softball today. What's all you're practicing get you? You could have beat them. They didn't have a long-ball hitter and the last three innings their pitcher was throwing twice as many balls as strikes. Except you were swinging at all the bad pitches as if they were strikes. Phil did okay. Three cheers for Phil. But the rest of you? I was expecting a victory. Now what am I going to tell the campers in the mess hall tonight? We lost? We screwed up? We got creamed?"

"We did," the team's captain said, "So I guess you have to. We can take it."

"No, I want them to feel good and prideful about their camp and waiters and want to come back next summer. I'll put it in words that won't make it sound as bad as it was. That the opposing team—I won't even give out its name—had the home-field advantage and a cheering squad of girls to pump it up. I know; I know. I shouldn't be taking it so hard. Only a game, and so on, but I don't like to lose. Okay, somebody's got to. And even the great Babe himself struck out a thousand and one times in between belting Gargantuan home runs."

He thought of the girl a lot afterwards, at least the first few years. And then once every third month or so, maybe, or even less: twice a year, right up till the time he met his wife. She was the only person this happened to with him. It wasn't that she was the only girl he ever had a crush on. But for some reason her face and expressions and blond hair and way she wore it and even what she had on that day—the khaki shorts and a maroon T-shirt with her camp's name on it and leather sandals—stuck in his mind. Well, maybe the same images, once they got there, just repeated themselves over and over. He thinks that's how it usually goes.

His wife, who was eleven years younger than he, was several months pregnant with their first child when he told her about the girl. He'd kept it to himself that long—they'd been together for close to four years—because he thought she might find it a bit peculiar, his recalling for thirty years a girl he never met or talked or wrote to and who only gave him a couple of weak hand claps for having hit a triple and knocking in two runs and tying the score of an inter-camp softball game. And who didn't smile at him once and never looked his way again in the less than two hours she sat in the stands, at least so far as he saw. What prompted him to finally mention her was a nine-by-twelve-inch framed photo of his wife in the living room of her parents' apartment. The photo was taken the summer before she started college, which she did when she was sixteen and a few months. She looked in the photo so much like he remembered the girl looked at around the same age. Long blond hair, shape of her face, round cheeks, sort of almond-shaped eyes. The photo was always there, so lots of the times he saw it he thought of the girl. And one afternoon, as they were walking from her parents' building to the bus stop on Broadway to get to their apartment uptown, he said "You feel okay?" and she said "Sure, why wouldn't I?"

"We could take a cab if this is too much of a trudge for you," and she said "It's good exercise. And I don't walk enough, which I should."

"You know the photograph of you with your first cat that's always on the side table to the right of your parents' couch?"

"I look a little dumpy in it, don't I. At least my skin's clear, which it wasn't always then, and Matilda looks so pretty and slim. I'd just brushed her."

"You look beautiful in it. According to the photographs your folks have around the place, you were a beautiful baby and a beautiful toddler and a beautiful adolescent and teenager and now you're an exceptionally beautiful woman in every way."

"What are you getting at?" she said.

"I have to be getting at something? All right; I am. I never told you something. And what I'm about to say is going to be okay. Sometimes when I look at that photo I'm reminded of a very pretty girl I once saw at her summer camp when I was sixteen and she was around the same age. She was very mature looking. Didn't act like the other girls she was with. Nothing loud or exaggerated about her. Quiet; self-contained, or so it seemed. Maybe she was even older than I. Maybe by a year. I never thought of that before. That sure would have stopped anything from happening, if it had ever come to that. Because I never met her—never even approached her, though I wanted to—but I also never forgot her. She looked like you in that photo. The blond hair. Long and light and combed back. The face; shape of it. Even the eyes."

"So she also had my color eyes? They're fairly unusual, though maybe not for a Jewish blond."

"That's true. Her camp was Jewish, like mine. But I never got close enough to her to see what color they were. I was talking about their shape. Even her long graceful neck—you know, swan-like, was like yours, and her cheeks. What I'm saying is I have no idea why I never forgot that face and what I described about it and the one glance and little smile she gave me—no, she didn't smile. Not to me, anyway. She did clap at me—a little clap, twice, very fast, from the bleachers she was sitting in with these other girls while she was watching a softball game between the camper waiters of my camp in New Jersey and hers in Pennsylvania. I'd just hit a triple—a three-base hit—that I could have stretched into a home run if the camp director of my camp, who was coaching at third base, hadn't stopped me. I guess, being fair-minded, she was saying 'good show' or something. But you're not really interested. And I'm getting the details of that day all mixed up. And why am I telling you it? Maybe telling you is wrong."

"Why? It's all right. I like hearing about you when you were young. And telling me this could be you saying she set the standard for the type of woman you were physically attracted to later on."

"It wasn't just physical," he said. "It was her expressions too. She seemed smart and sweet and poised and serene. Like you are today and probably were at her age. Sixteen; seventeen. And I'd think the standard must already have been set if I was that immediately attracted to her, which never happened like that with a girl before. Though you could be right. I'm not saying you're not. Maybe it did all start with her."

"Then let's say it's possible she confirmed, or reinforced, the type of woman you were attracted to from when you were even younger than sixteen, but in a big way. You liked blondes. From what you've previously told me of your love life, you always have, though that didn't keep you from also liking brunettes. Would I be wrong in saying that most of the women you've fallen for in your adult life have been blondes?"

"About half; yes."

"Was she built like me too? You know, from what you can make out from that photograph and the one in my high school twentieth-year reunion book I've shown you, where I'm on the field hockey team."

"I don't remember," he said. "The body of a young woman wasn't as important to me then as the body of an older woman became to me later on. If she had been a lot overweight, that would have been different. But she was lithe; trim. I remember her legs. She was wearing shorts. And a T-shirt, but I remember nothing about her breasts. I wanted to meet her. I thought of ways I could, but never got the chance. She left before the game was over. We lost, by the way. I even fantasized about going over to her during the game when my team was up. Or after the game, in the short time I'd have before the whole team had to get back on this old army truck to return to our camp. And introducing myself and somehow saying, without turning her off, that I had been looking at her and don't have much time to talk and could I write her at her camp and possibly continue the correspondence after the camp season was over? We'd been told that most of the campers and staff in her camp—she was a C.I.T.—"

"What's that again?" she said.

"Counselor in training. Almost everyone there was supposed to come from Philadelphia or somewhere in Pennsylvania."

"What did you think would come from your letters to each other, if she had agreed to write you? If she lived in Pennsylvania and you were both sixteen—"

"I'd visit her," he said. "Take a bus or train. It's not that far away, Philadelphia, if that is where she lived. Pittsburgh would have been out. But for her, if it was Philadelphia or a place in Pennsylvania a lot easier to get to than Pittsburgh, to become my girlfriend. And maybe the next summer she'd be a C.I.T. again, or junior counselor, would be more like it, at the same camp, and I'd be a waiter again at mine. It's possible, I might have thought, when I was thinking this girl and I would exchange letters and I'd go to Philadelphia or such to see her and maybe she could come once to New York, that we could coordinate our days off the next summer. That's how far and fast I let my imagination take me. Or I'd try to be one of the two guest waiters at my camp, which was really what I was shooting for. You made a lot more money that way—no salary but much better tips—waiting on the visiting parents, and more days off."

By now they had reached the bus shelter on Broadway. The bench inside was filled. He said "Should I ask someone to get up so you can sit?"

"I'm fine," she said. "Standing's good for me too. So what did you end up doing the next summer?"

"I got a job as a busboy at Grossinger's. I told them I was eighteen, and being a big kid, they believed me. And I guess they weren't that choosy for such a job. The summer after that, I was legitimately eighteen and in college, and worked as a waiter and made a bundle."

"You never went back to your camp?"

"No. I guess I went where the money was and where there was more potential for work."

"So you didn't even try to be a guest waiter at your camp?"

"I don't remember. Probably not. The busboy job came up and I was told if I did well at it there'd be a good chance for a waiter's job the next summer and also during the Jewish holidays, which was when you really cleaned up."

"It seems, then, that you and this girl weren't meant to get together," she said. "I mean, if you truly wanted it to happen, you would have gone back to your camp as a guest waiter, if you could get the job—made, I would think, about as much as you would as a busboy at Grossinger's—and in some way sought out the girl."

"How? By just going to her camp and looking for her? Or playing on the softball team again against her camp's team, if there was going to be a rematch, and hoping she'd be there? I don't even know if a guest waiter was allowed to play on the camper-waiter's team."

"Then by trying to get a job at her camp as a guest waiter, if they had them."

"I never thought of that," he said. "And it's getting a bit far-fetched. Because what were the chances of her returning there? Good? Only so-so? I don't know. And by then she might have had a boyfriend, if she already didn't when I first saw her. And I'd lost some of my interest in her, which would have been natural, or had become in one year more of a realist. Something. Maybe all those. By the way, what I also never told you is that when I first saw you at the party we met at, but before I went over to introduce myself, I actually thought for a few moments you might be her."

"But you never asked me if I went to a camp in Pennsylvania when I was a girl. And she has to be considerably older than I. Ten years."

"I thought her looks might have stayed that young. It's possible. Forty could look thirty. But it was just something that flashed through my mind then, or whatever it did, and I quickly knew was impossible. But I shouldn't have brought it up."

"Sure you should have," she said. "And long before. It's interesting. And if this girl was instrumental in being the prototype for the women you were later attracted to—"

"Her expressions too. Just by her face she seemed very bright and cheerful and self-contained, as I think I said, and mature. So it wasn't just her good looks that first attracted me to her, as it wasn't with you."

"I'm glad. And what I started to say was that I'm grateful to her, if she was even remotely responsible for you being drawn to me at that party. You came over, we got to talking, found we had lots in common, started seeing each other, married, and the rest."

"So it all doesn't sound too silly to you?"

"Not at all."

He stepped out into the street and saw their bus coming. "There's our bus."

"Good," she said. "I'm getting tired."

"It looks crowded. If all the seats are taken, would it be all right with you if I ask someone to get up and give you his seat?"

"Yes, thanks. I could never ask anyone that myself."

Talk

He hasn't talked to anyone today. I haven't talked to anyone today. It's not that I haven't wanted to. It's not that he hasn't wanted to talk to someone, but he just never had the chance to. He only realized he hasn't talked to anyone today when he sat down on the bench he's sitting on now. In front of the church across the street from his house. I like to sit on it after a long or not-so-long walk around my neighborhood. I usually take the same route. Almost always end up on the same bench. One of the benches in front of the entrance to the church. It's now 6:45. Closer to 6:47. I haven't talked to anyone today since I woke up more than twelve hours ago, rested in bed awhile, exercised in bed awhile, mostly his legs, and then got out of bed and washed up and so on. Did lots of things. Brushed my teeth, brushed my hair, dressed, took my pill, let the cat out, let the cat in, gave the cat food, changed its water, let the cat out again, made myself breakfast, ate, got the newspaper from outside before I made myself breakfast and ate, same things almost every morning soon after waking up, same breakfast, coffee and hot cereal and toast, maybe blueberry jam and butter on the toast every third or fourth day instead of butter and orange marmalade, same newspaper, different news but some of it the same, same cat, same water bowl for the cat, same kibble in a different bowl for the cat, same plate for the cat's wet food and same wet food till the cat finishes the can in about three days. Then I shaved, did some exercises with two ten-pound barbells, one for each hand, curls, he thinks they're called—the exercises—and so on. No one phoned. The classical music radio station was on when I shaved and exercised and after he was done exercising he turned the radio off. Then he sat at his work table in his bedroom. I could use one of the other two bedrooms in the house to work in or the study his wife used to work in, but I prefer this room, the master bedroom they used to call it to distinguish it from the other bedrooms, the room that was once their bedroom but is now only his since his wife died. She didn't die in that room. She died in one of the other bedrooms. He had a hospital bed set up for her in that room more than a year before she died and she died in that bed. She was unconscious for twelve days in that bed before she died. Do I really want to go into all this again? Just finish it. She was lying on her back in a coma, when she opened her eyes, or her eyes opened on their own, and her head turned to where he was sitting on the right side of the bed and she died. He closed her eyes with his hand. Her eyes struggled to stay open and then, after he closed them a second and third time, they stayed permanently closed. The day after she died I had the hospital bed removed. He bought a new bed for that room a week or two later so his older daughter could sleep in that room again when she visited him. But I was thinking before about my not talking to anyone today. I haven't. He hasn't. Talked to anyone today. No opportunity to, as I said. He could have made the opportunity to, I suppose, but he didn't. I didn't go out of my way to talk to anyone today, he's saying. He likes these kinds of conversations to happen naturally. He'll be in the local food market, for instance—not to bump into people he knows from around the neighborhood or initiate small talk with employees behind the food or checkout counter or with shoppers he doesn't know—but to buy things, mostly food for himself and his cat—and he'll bump into someone he knows. Hi, hello, how are you? And so on. Maybe with someone whose hand he shakes, back or shoulder he pats, cheek, if it's a woman, he kisses. Someone who most of the time stops his or her shopping to talk to me, and whom I like to talk to too. Am I being clear? He thinks so. Anyway: that didn't happen today. It's happened plenty of times in the almost twenty years he's lived in the house and been going to that market. But I didn't go to that market today. No market, and he rarely sees anyone he knows at any other market. He did, after writing in his bedroom for about three hours, go to the Y to work out. I often see someone I know from the Y in the fitness room, or whatever that room with all the resistance machines, he thinks they are, is called. Fitness center. I should remember that by now. Fitness center. Fitness center. And sometimes he sees two or three people there he only knows from the Y and have a brief conversation with them or just say "Hi" or "Hello" or "How you doing?" to. And he has, in the local market a few times—the one he almost always goes to be-cause it's so close and the prices aren't that much higher than the big chains and they get you out fast because they have lots of working checkout counters for a store its size and just about all the checkout clerks know him—bumped into people he knows only from the Y and chatted with them. Though for the most part these chats are shorter than the ones he might have with the same people in the Y, and one or the other of them will usually say something like "Funny to see you here after seeing you so many times in the Y" or "I almost didn't recognize you out of your gym clothes." As for the weight room in the Y, which is right next to the fitness center, he has fewer conversations there than he does with people in the fitness center, since there are much fewer people working out in it. They also seem more serious and involved in their workouts. But he's still had a few conversations there when both he and the other person working out took a minute-or-so break from the weights and were standing close enough to talk to each other. Like one a few days ago. "I always see you with a book. What are you reading now?" this person asked him, or said something like it: a man; very few women work out in the weight room. Someone he'd seen several times before in both rooms but never spoke with or even said "Hi" to but might have smiled or nodded at. He held up the book so the man could see the cover. "*Gil-gamesh*?" the man mispronouncing it the same way he once did till his wife corrected him. "Never heard of it. From the cover, it looks like it could be a fantasy or horror novel." "In a way it sort of is," I said. "But it's a new or relatively new translation of an epic poem, maybe the oldest literary work, or oldest one found so far. With a long introduction as interesting as the work itself, and with great notes." "What's it about?" He gave a brief synopsis of it, based on the introduction, since he was only a third of the way into the poem. And then—"This might give you a laugh"—why he bought it. "The oldest work—a classic—and the only one in my family never to have read it? My older daughter, who graduated college eight years ago, read it when she was nine or ten and took a special humanities course in grade school. And I was in a bookshop last week, the Ivy on Falls Road, looking for something to read. I always have to have something to read—at home; if I take a walk and think I'll stop to sit and rest. Even here between sets on the sitdown resistance machines for a minute or the stationary bike if it doesn't have on its TV screen something especially good on the movie channel—and saw it. In the store, this book, and remembered I'd never read it but for many years wanted to. But I've told you more than you probably wanted to hear, and you want to get back to your weights." "No," the man said, "it's interesting. *Gilgamesh*. I'll remember," and we both resumed our workouts. That's how the conversation went, sort of. I know I went on too long. He often does most days because he gets to talk so little. But today there wasn't anyone he knew at the Y to say even a word to, which was unusual. Most times, someone at the front desk there, after he slides his key through the bar code recorder, or whatever that piece of plastic on his key ring is called, and his name and photo appear on the monitor and an automated voice says "Access granted," someone behind the desk will look at the monitor and say "Have a good workout, Mr. Seidel," and he'll say "Thank you." But the one person behind the desk—usually there are two people there—was folding clean towels for members with the more expensive plan and more elaborate locker rooms, and didn't look up. He went into his locker room. Sometimes there's someone there I know from the Y and we'll talk a little. But the room was empty when I first got there and then after my workout. Sometimes, though this doesn't happen much, he might talk with someone in the shower room after his workout, but the one guy showering there today was someone he knows doesn't want to talk. I've seen him in the locker room and shower and at the front desk checking in dozens of times. Never downstairs in the fitness center or weight room. He seems to only come to the Y to swim. And I never saw him communicate with anyone. I don't even think the people at the front desk say "Have a good day" to him, or if they do, he doesn't answer them. First thing the guy does when he gets to the locker room is put his athletic bag on a bench and go around the room closing every locker that might be even just slightly open and make sure every bench is aligned with the banks of lockers. Then he'll walk around the room again and pick up any trash he sees on the floor—tiny pieces of paper, thread, part of a broken shoelace, for instance—and drop it into a trash can there. Then he'll undress and get into his swimsuit and lock his locker and go to the pool with his towel and in his shower slippers. I said hello to him a few times, but gave up. He looked right past me as if I hadn't said anything or he hadn't heard. Today I avoided looking his way once I saw who it was. I feel he doesn't want to be looked at either. I could have gone to the small food shop at the Y and ordered a sandwich to go—chicken or tuna fish salad on rye toast with tomato and lettuce and once each a powerhouse and grilled chicken sandwich, which weren't good—and while it was being made by an employee in back, exchanged a few words with the shop's owner about a number of things. The owner just takes the orders and rings them up and serves the food if anyone's sitting at one of the two tables there, which I've never done. The owner likes to talk. A few days ago it was strawberries. He said he grows them in his garden and they're very small this year, he doesn't understand it. I told him my younger daughter put in a number of strawberry plants two years ago, I got nothing but a few tiny ones last year, but this year they're all over the place and big, "What can I say?" And he once told me, when I asked, how to get the shells off hard-boiled eggs without taking any of the white of the egg with it. "Boil them for thirty to forty minutes. Infallible, and perfect for deviled eggs." But he didn't want to order any kind of sandwich today. He still has in the refrigerator, and it's probably still good but a little soggy, half of the chicken salad wrap he got from him yesterday. What were some of the other opportunities to talk today? And by talking, I mean to someone, a human being, not the cat. He talks a lot to his cat. Actually, it's his younger daughter's, but she lives in an apartment in Brooklyn, the cat likes to run around outside, so he's taking care of it for the time being. "Hey, little guy, want something to eat?" Talk like that. "Want to go outside, Rufus?" "Go on, go on," when he's half in and half out the door. "I don't want to catch your tail, and you can come back whenever you want." "It's getting dark, Rufus. Want to come inside?" "Come inside, Rufus. Don't make me have to chase you." "You here to help me with the weeding?" Because sometimes when I'm weeding outside, he'll lay down on his stomach beside me and pull a weed out of the ground with his teeth and play with it or try to pull one out of my hand that I just got out of the ground. Also, sometimes when I talk to him it seems he talks back to me with a couple of meows. And when he's at the front door and I let him in, he always meows in a sound he uses no other time as he scoots in or walks past me, as if saying thanks to me for opening the door. He never meows, though, when I open the door to let him out. When he wants to go out he'll stand silently facing the door or stand up on his back paws and scratch the door with his front ones till I let him out. If I don't want him out, he'll walk quietly away from the door after about two minutes. But no other opportunities to talk to someone today? Can't think of any. Usually, during his late-afternoon walks, he'll see at least one person walking his dog and he'll say more than "Hi" or "Good evening" to him. He'll ask the breed of the dog, for instance, and if he asked it the last time but forgot it, he'll say "I forgot what you told me your dog's breed is" or "your dogs' breed is," since several people in the neighborhood have two dogs of the same breed, and one couple has three, and walk them together. I've also asked this person or couple what the dog was originally bred for. Not that I'm really interested, but it gives me a chance, if it was a day I hadn't talked much, to talk more. "Hunting foxes?" "Herding sheep?" "Going after moles or other burrowing animals like that in holes?" He once joked, and regretted it right after, for the guy didn't seem to find it funny, "Catching Frisbees?" But in his walk today he saw no one he's talked to or just said hello to before. Saw no one, period. Oh, people in cars, and a jogger, but she came up behind him without him hearing her and was past him before he could even wave. Maybe when he gets home he'll call his daughters and, if they're in, speak to them. Although it doesn't have to be in their homes. With their cell phones, they could be anywhere: walking on the street; having a drink in a bar. He speaks to them almost every night around seven. Seems to be a good time for them. They're done with work for the day, haven't started dinner. They call him or he calls them. But that's the kind of day it's been. Where he hasn't yet said a word to anyone. Not one, and it makes me feel kind of strange or odd. It's true. It does. Both of those. But enough of that. Maybe, really, it's better not to dwell on it. If his wife were alive and still relatively healthy, or just not as sick as she was the last five years of her life, he would have spoken to her before he left the house. That would have been nice. "I'm going out for a walk," he would have said; "like to join me?" If she didn't, or couldn't because she was still working in her study or something else, then when he got back she might say, as she did a lot, "See anything interesting?" or "Meet anyone on your walk?" Or just "Did you have a good walk?" Or he might volunteer: "I had a good walk. Farther than I usually go. Saw some beautiful and unusual flowers. Our neighbors, especially the church, really take care of their properties. But for the first time in a long time I didn't see anyone else outside except a fleet-footed jogger, who ran past me before I could even say hi to her. And of course people in the occasional passing car, but they don't count." Or if she were too weak to walk and didn't want to be pushed around the neighborhood in her wheelchair—"People stare; I don't like it"—he'd say "All right, then, if I take a brief walk by myself? And I'll make it quick. I won't stop to talk to anyone." "Why should I mind?" she said a number of times. "Get out. You need a break. And talk all you want." "So you'll be okay here alone?" and she always said "I told you. I'll be just fine." But he shouldn't think of himself as odd or strange just because he hasn't talked with anyone today. I'm not odd. He's not strange. Thirteen hours? That's not so long. Listen, this is where life has led me, to this point; something. He can't quite put it in words right now. But he's trying to say what? What am I trying to say? That it's not his fault he hasn't spoken to anyone today? No, that's not what I wanted to say. Forget it. I think if I had someone to speak to other than myself today, I'd be able to say what I want to say understandably. Coherently. Clearly. Some way. But again: enough. He opens *Gilgamesh* and turns to the page the bookmark's on. I resume reading what I stopped reading when I was on the exercise bike at the Y. Is that the best way to put it? What if it isn't? What's important is that I know what I mean. Or another way could be "He resumes reading at the place he left off when he was on the exercise bike at the Y." Any real difference? Some. Second's better. I'm reading when someone says my name. He looks up. It's my neighbor from up the hill from my house. Karen.

"I didn't want to startle you," she says, "so I called out to you as softly as I could. You seemed so absorbed in your book. Am I disturbing you?"

"Not at all."

"Nice place to read, I'd say. Quiet. Surrounded by all these lovely flowers the church has planted. Best time of day too."

"Yeah, it's a great place. I come here almost every day around this time after a long walk. And I'm thinking, I don't know if I should admit this, and it's kind of laughable, but you're the first person I've spoken to all day."

"Oh, that's so sad," she says. "You know what? Why don't you come by our house tomorrow for a drink? Jim and I have been meaning to have you over for I don't know how long. We've talked about it several times, but as you can see, we're great procrastinators."

"I don't known. Maybe another time. I've become such a hermit, which I know isn't good, although it helps my work, but—"

"Nonsense. Tomorrow. Say around six? Bring your cat. I'm only kidding. What's her name?"

"His. Rufus."

"Rufus. I see him running all around. Once up a tree. He never seems to just walk. And hiding in bushes. But it'll be wonderful talking to you over an extended period of time instead of only these quick chats or when I run in to you at the market. By the way, what's that you're reading?"

"*Gilgamesh*."

"Oh, I remember it from college. You'll have to tell us tomorrow why you're reading it. I mean, what made you, I'm sure, take it up again. Tomorrow then? Sixish?"

"Yes. Thanks."

She smiles and goes. He reopens the book. What page was I on again? He thinks. Eighty-four, I think. He turns to it. I'm right. So, today won't be a day where I can say I didn't talk to a single person, and tomorrow won't be one either. Well, it wouldn't have turned out that way today anyway. He probably would have reached one of his daughters on the phone later. Maybe both.

Remember

He puts three eggs on to boil. When they're done, he'll dump the yolks and use the egg white in the tuna fish salad he's making. Should take 'bout fifteen minutes altogether, getting the water to boil and then the boiling. He reminds himself again of the owner of the sandwich shop at the Y he goes to who said to get the shells off without them sticking to the whites, he boils the eggs for forty minutes, or was it fifty, drops them in cold water and two minutes later shells them. "Method's infallible," he said, "though it does take a lot of time." Boiling them for ten minutes will be enough to get the same results, he thinks. He goes into the living room and reads a novel while listening to some soft piano music. A while later, he smells something funny. Goddamnit, the eggs! He runs into the kitchen. They've been boiling for probably an hour. All the water's boiled out, the eggshells have split and the saucepan will have to be scrubbed and scrubbed to get rid of the eggs stuck to the bottom. He puts three more eggs into a larger saucepan, stays in the kitchen and cleans the first saucepan and reads from the novel till the eggs have boiled for eight minutes. That's enough time. He can't stay here forever. He pours the boiled water into the sink, covers the eggs in the pan with cold water and waits there a couple of minutes before he starts shelling the eggs. The shells don't come off easily, but with a lot of peeling and picking he gets most of the egg whites for his tuna fish salad.

He gets dressed and goes out around seven for his daily morning walk. Says "Hello" and "Good morning" to a few people while he walks, one jogging at a very slow pace and the others walking their dogs. Gets back home. Goes into the bathroom to pee. Sees his fly has been open all the way since he last peed. People he saw during his walk, even the jogger going the opposite way, may have noticed. Why'd he forget to zip up? Should concentrate more on it. People will think he keeps his fly open deliberately if they see it another time. Or could. Or just that something's the matter with him. That he's not thinking.

Puts the tea kettle on for drip coffee. The cat. Did he let him out? He did; hours ago. He forgets sometimes where the cat is, he lets him in and out so many times in a day. There have been foxes around. He gets worried. He goes outside to see if the cat's around. Looks; whistles for him. Calls for him a few times. Starts weeding around the blueberry bush his younger daughter put in this spring by the driveway. Likes it to stand out. Often the cat sidles up to him while he weeds. Or just quietly appears next to him, lying on his stomach. From there he weeds around the other blueberry bushes near the blueberry bush. He forgets who put them in. Maybe they came with the house. His wife was always good at knowing those things. Gets a big leaf bag out of the garden shed and puts most of what he's weeded into it. That's enough work outside today. It's gotten too hot. Heads for the house. The cat. Ah, he'll be all right. Smells burnt metal through the kitchen screen door. The tea kettle. Knows all the water must be gone and the handle will be too hot to touch. Uses a potholder to lift the kettle off the stove and put under the faucet. Steam fogs up his glasses and he has to wipe the lenses to see out of them. Kettle's probably ruined, but maybe not. Didn't he ruin a tea kettle a few months ago by letting the water boil out? Sometime, anyway, but hasn't happened since. He's been extra careful about it most times. He also has to remember to always put the whistle part down.

Makes a frittata in a frying pan on the stove. He'll have half of it for dinner and then some of it cold for lunch tomorrow. Puts it in the oven for about ten minutes and then sprinkles grated parmesan cheese on it and sticks it under the broiler to make it crisp on top and turns the oven knob to "broil." Should take no more than a minute under the high flame. Makes himself a drink. A fast one: just vodka and ice in a glass. Sips it. Puts the bottle of vodka back into a kitchen cupboard. Ice container could use more ice. He empties a tray of ice into the container, drops another ice cube into his glass, fills the tray with water and puts the container and tray into the freezer. Smells the frittata burning. Damn, there goes that. Turns the oven off and pulls the pan out. Frittata's scorched. Who knows what with the pan? And it's an expensive one, his wife's before he even met her, French—Creuset, he thinks it's called; supposed to be the best. Not going to make another frittata. There's some egg salad and Muenster cheese in the refrigerator, and with two slices of bread—don't even toast them; the way his mind's going today, don't even chance it, though he's really only kidding himself; he's not that bad off—and lettuce and cucumber slices, he'll make a sandwich.

Did he take his tamsulosin pill this morning? Thinks he did, but then maybe not. Supposed to a half an hour after breakfast. Doesn't want to take two in one day. Especially one so soon after the other, if he did take it today. So did he? Think back. Doesn't come up with anything. Let it go for today. Not taking the pill one day won't kill him. Get a pill holder that has seven compartments for each day of the week. Do it next time you're in a pharmacy. Remember to. Do it even sooner. Make a special trip to the pharmacy when you go to the market later, and start using the holder tomorrow. Three carbidopa-levodopas, one tamsulosin and one omeprazole per compartment. That should do it. Prepared a lentil rice loaf and puts it in the oven at 375 degrees. Lentils and rice are already cooked, so the whole thing should take half an hour; at most, forty minutes. He'll see when he looks at it thirty minutes from now. Has plenty of time to check his emails. Hopes his daughter answered his email about Maine this summer, a decision he has to have in the next two days if he's to put a deposit down for the cottage they rented for a month last summer. He goes to the computer in his wife's old study. Stares for a while at the photograph leaning against a window there of his wife and daughters, two and five years old or three and six. Tries to remember what they looked like at those ages and decides on two and five. Maine again. Wind blowing his wife's long hair. What a smile she had. And so beautiful. On a sailboat friends of theirs took them out on. All of them in life jackets. He no doubt had one on too. His daughter writes she can't leave her work till July 28th. He writes back and then reads three other emails. What a drag. One's a long one from an editor about a story of his coming out in a magazine, that needs an equally long response. Sure he wants to keep this? Is a word missing there? He's already mentioned the color of the jug two pages earlier, and since there's only one jug, does the color need to be given again? Her name's Lily at the top of the page, Lila at the bottom. Surely that's an error. Should the verb tense, line 9, page 14, be in the present, when the sentence starts off in the past? Around two dozen others. He checks the original manuscript. Makes the corrections or gives reasons why he doesn't go along with the suggested changes, or no reasons: he just wants this and that to stay put. He's very slow at the keyboard. Types with two fingers now, sometimes three, and is always making typing mistakes and correcting them. Then he sends it. Then thinks does he really go along with all the editor's changes he did agree to? Maybe he answered too fast just to get it out of the way. He rereads the last email he sent the editor. Makes a few changes back to what he originally had and sends them. While he's here he clicks on—that can't be the right term for it; what is the right term then? He'll remember—a twenty-eight minute dramatization, with English subtitles, of Kafka's *The Judgment*, a German writer he's been corresponding with the last few years sent him. Three minutes from the end of it he remembers his loaf baking. Turns off the computer and goes into the kitchen. It's been more than two hours. He never checked a clock. Thought he'd just know when thirty to forty minutes were up or he'd look at the time on the computer, which he didn't do, when he first sat down at it. Loaf's completely ruined. God, what an asshole he is. "You're an asshole," he says, "an asshole." What else is he going to ruin? He's not losing his mind, is he? No, just his memory, or whatever it is that reminds him to prevent things like this. Maybe if he'd kept the temperature down to 325; 300, even. Would take longer to bake but give him more of a chance to remember something's in the oven, so less chance it'd be ruined. Suppose he left something on the stove that long? Well, he thinks he would have smelled it sooner. And why didn't he smell the loaf burning? He got lost in something else, and there's less chance of smelling something burning in the oven than on the stove. From now on, pay attention, you hear? He doesn't, there'll be a real accident. He has no smoke alarm because he hates the noise it makes when just a slice of toast is getting burnt. He should think of getting one. He should really remember to. But he never will, and not because he'll forget to, unless one of his daughters insists on it. So he won't tell them of the burnt frittata and lentil rice loaf and the tea kettles he let boil out and other things. If he does, then the first one to visit him will go to the store to buy two or three of them and install them herself.

He puts two rice cakes in the toaster and presses the lever down. Shouldn't take long. The phone rings. He goes into his wife's study to answer it. It's his sister. "How are you?" "Fine." "What's doing with you?" "Nothing much, and you?" "The same," and so on, when he smells something burning. "Hold it," he says; "the rice cakes," and he puts the receiver down and goes into the kitchen. The rice cakes are on fire in the toaster. Flames coming out of the slots that reach the bottom of the cupboard above them. He pulls out the toaster plug, presses the button to pop up the rice cakes, blows on the flames till the fire's out, and then, with a potholder and dishtowel protecting his hands, holds the toaster over the sink and shakes it till the rice cakes fall out. Runs water on them till they stop smoking and are soaked, and puts them in the kitchen trash can. Now that could have been very dangerous, he thinks. Very. How stupid can he get? He goes back to the study; his sister's no longer on the line. He'll call her later, if she doesn't call him first, but he won't tell her why he suddenly had to get off the phone. She'll say didn't his smoke alarm go off? And then urge him to get one, at least for the kitchen. He looks inside the toaster. Nothing seems damaged. Cupboard seems okay, too. He puts two more rice cakes into the toaster and turns the timer knob all the way to the left. Stay here, and then when he thinks they're ready, pop them. He got the idea for toasting the rice cakes from his wife. That's how she always asked him to make them for her when she had cream cheese or butter or peanut butter put on them after they were warmed. It'd take about forty-five seconds. "Don't let it burn," she'd say. He likes them toasted more than warmed, even some of the puffy grains blackened, and it'd take a little more than a minute. Room still smells of burnt rice cakes. He turns the exhaust fan on. It makes so much noise, he won't have any trouble remembering to turn it off. And remember, never leave the rice cakes in the toaster for that long again. Maybe a better idea would be never to toast them again. Let's face it, it's getting or gotten to the point where he's beginning not to trust his memory that something's in the toaster or oven or on the stove that needs checking into every now and then.

Puts a pill into his mouth, fills half a juice glass with water, gets a large container of yogurt out of the refrigerator, lets the pill dissolve on his tongue, swallows it with water, opens the refrigerator and starts to put the glass on the shelf where the yogurt was, realizes he means for the yogurt container to go back into the refrigerator but after he has a spoonful of it, puts the glass upside down into the dish rack, has a spoonful of yogurt, puts the spoon into the sink and the yogurt container into the refrigerator. Absentminded, that's all. Not really a problem. Was doing too many things at once and too quickly; just didn't think.

He goes outside for his daily run and longer walk. He runs first, just a quarter-mile or so. He can't run like he used to not that long ago, which was about two miles every day. Then he starts walking fast. He feels his fly. It's open; forgot again. Makes him even more worried about himself. Toaster, oven, stove, forgetting his keys when he goes out to drive the car. Goes back to get them and often gets distracted and when he leaves the house again realizes he's forgotten his keys a second time. So: remember to check your fly every time before you go out. Remember, remember. Right. Check. Every time. Will do. At least solve that problem.

Goes to the market to shop, comes back, smells gas. Checks the stove. He left one of the burners on though no flame. How'd that happen? What was the last thing he did on the stove? Boiled water for coffee this morning. Turns the exhaust fan on. What's he want to do, kill himself? If not by fire, then gas? Big joke. Funny. Knows it'll never get that bad. If his wife were alive he'd tell her it. No he wouldn't. And what was the joke again? Couldn't have forgotten it that fast. If not by fire, then gas. She'd get frightened for him and her both. Concentrate more. Just concentrate on everything to do with what he does in the kitchen and his fly and what he needs to have on him when he takes the car. Though how many times has he forgotten his keys and wallet? Not much but enough. Maybe once every two months or not even that. Though maybe more. Keys aren't that big a problem. Most of the time he knows almost immediately when they're not on him. But sometimes he's gotten to the market or wherever he's gone to, felt his pocket where the wallet should have been, and had to drive back home for it, a few times from miles away.

He goes outside to get the newspaper by the mailbox. Picks it off the ground, takes the plastic sleeve off, starts reading the headlines as he walks back to the house. His fly. Why's he think it might be open? He didn't. Just checking. It's open. Didn't he tell himself to concentrate more on it? Zips it up. At least nobody was around to see it.

Turns on the light switch by the CD player to two living room lamps so he doesn't have to walk to his bedroom in the dark. Done it several times before, and even though he walked very slowly and his arms were weaving around in front of him, he bumped into things and twice cracked his forehead on a door. After he turns on his night table lamp, he'll turn the living room lights off with the light switch above the piano at the other end of the room. Both switches work for the same lights. He goes into the bedroom, undresses, exercises a little with two ten-pound weights, washes up, makes sure a handkerchief is on the bed and his watch and pen and memo book are on his night table, and gets into bed and reads. After about half an hour, he shuts off his light. A little light comes in from the living room. Forgot again. That one he does about once a week, or about every third or fourth time he makes it to the back of the house that way. He hasn't figured out a way not to forget to turn the living room lights off before he gets into bed other than to tell himself when he first switches on the lights: Don't forget to turn the other living room light switch off after you turn the night table light on.

So he's worried. Or getting to be. Or just a little alarmed. Because what else will he forget? For he's been forgetting so much the last few months. Actually, the last year, and probably more. It could even go back to sometime after his wife died, or it's become worse since then, though he has no idea why for either. Truth is, he's not sure when it began. Maybe there were inklings of it before she died, and because he was so busy with her, he never paid much attention to it. But stove, oven, toaster, lights, fly, pills, a couple of times his phone number and zip code, feeding the cat, not knowing if he let him in or out the last time he opened the outside door for him, more than usual: people's names. What words mean but usually not their spellings. Music compositions and their composers. Hearing a familiar piece on the radio but can't come up with its name or who wrote it. Well, he's always had trouble with that, one or the other or both, unless it's something like *Enigma Variations* or *Pictures at an Exhibition* or *Appalachian Spring*, which are played on the radio so often that, great works though they are, he's sick of them. Recently, authors and their most famous works. Just the other day: Ellison and his novel. Okay, read it long ago, but it's still written and talked about but he couldn't remember his name or the book's title the entire day. Tried, too. Then, when his last name suddenly popped into his head, the first name came right after and the book's title. Also the other day: gazpacho. Bought a small container of it in the local market and was about to take it out of the refrigerator and sit down and eat it, when he realized he'd forgotten what it was called. This is a test, he told himself: let's see how fast he can come up with its name. Knows it's made of chopped-up tomatoes and cucumbers and peppers and onions and is served chilled and is of Spanish origin and the traditional way it's made in Spain, or in some parts of it, and which he doesn't do when he makes it himself at home, is with chunks of bread. He gave up, and as he opened the refrigerator to take it out, it came to him: gazpacho. With an "s" or "z," he thought. Let's see. He ran the word through his head. "Z." He's almost sure. Remembers looking it up in the dictionary, maybe two or three times, when he wasn't sure of its spelling for something he was writing. Anyway: remember. What's on the stove, in the oven, how long the thing should be cooking, or thereabouts, and so on. Cat, pills, toaster, fly. To wear a cap when he's going to be outside, even when the sun's behind clouds, to prevent more scalp lesions. To check his daily calendar book every few days to see what appointments and engagements might be coming up. People's names he's not sure he'll remember next time he sees them. Use some memory device to help him remember. For instance, if the guy's name is Tom, then "Tom and Jerry" or "Tom Collins" or "Tom-Tom," but something like that. There's a former grad student of his he seems to bump into a lot at markets and the two Starbucks he goes to and certainly at departmental parties he's still invited to, whose name he always forgets. It's embarrassing for both of them when that happens and he has to work around it to get her name, without appearing he forgot it, or ask someone else for it. So what is her name? Terry? Tracy? Teresa? He's not even sure it starts with a T, but something tells him it does. T-a? T-e? T-o? T-u? Oh, he gives up. He doesn't understand why he forgets some people's names more than others and a few people's names all the time. Knows her last name, a fairly common one, is the same as a well-known contemporary British writer, but forgets it now, too. Writes people's names in the memo book he always carries with him. About a week ago during his early evening walk, he met for the first time his new neighbors from across the street. Both doctors. That came out in their brief talk. Also that they have twin sons. He saw them and introduced himself. So what are their names? They told him and he gave them his. He in fact asked for their names again just before he said goodbye and continued his walk. Might even have told them he's bad at remembering people's names, which is why he asked for theirs again. He thinks the woman said she is too and asked for his again. But are these going to be two more people whose names he always forgets? Because he's sure to be bumping into them again. Johnny and Rachel? Or Rebecca? He thinks it's Rebecca. He takes his memo book out of his back pants pocket, and pen he also always has with him, from a side pants pocket—he doesn't keep it in his back pocket, which he used to do, because he knows he'll eventually sit on it and break it and stain another pair of pants for good; he's learned that much—and writes on the first clean page he comes to: "Johnny and Rebecca or Rachel; new doctor neighbors. Rebecca at Union Memorial, Johnny in private practice: pulmonology." Last names? She has her husband's: Mathews or Mathewson, and writes these names down. He'll put on this same page the names of other people in the neighborhood he's bumped into on his walks and exchanged names with, if he can remember theirs, and also new people he might meet around here, and look at them from time to time, or maybe only when he puts a new one down, so he'll know their names next time he meets them. Let them think he has a great memory, despite what he might have told them, and don't correct them if they say he does. Take it as a compliment, or just shrug.

Gets up, brushes his teeth, washes his face, exercises, dresses, goes into the kitchen. Oops. Forgot to shave, something he likes to do daily. Takes his shirt off so he won't wet it, and shaves and then brushes his hair. Hasn't had a shower, something he also likes to do daily, in a couple of days—could it be three? Would hate to think it was—but he'll do it at the Y today after he works out, or here. Feeds the cat, changes his water, lets him out. Remember: he's out, not in. Again: good practice, to remember that. Cat out, cat out, he tells himself. Has breakfast, washes the dishes, makes sure the oven and all the stove burners are off, puts on his baseball cap and goes outside and does some needed yard work. Is out there for more than an hour. At least it feels like it. Fills up four leaf bags with weeds and twigs and sticks, gets sweaty and tired and thinks that should do it for the day. Has to pee. Came on suddenly, even though he's taking medication for it, though it's a bit better now than it used to be. He doesn't have time to go inside, so he'll do it behind a tree. Puts his hand to his pants to open his fly, but it's already open. Oh, geez. Won't he ever remember? What does he have to do? he thinks while he pees. Maybe he could make…no, there's nothing he can do. On that score, he almost seems hopeless. But he can't give up on it. Just try to catch it as many times as he can. Always, and he means always, never leave the house or a restaurant or any kind of store he's been in a while and it has a restroom for customers, without peeing first, even if he peed just ten minutes before. Got it. A set routine he's going to remember to follow, not that he hasn't thought of this before. At least he still drives without forgetting to look all around him when he backs out of a parking space or makes a turn, understands most of what he reads, or as much as he did years before; has a good visual memory for lots of things, going all the way back to when he was a kid, and is still able to write and at times even do some tricky writing stuff. By that he means…well, that he still comes up with something new to say in each piece and say it with what he thinks, though he might be all wrong in this, in a new way. It's the day-to-day things he forgets a lot. Well, writing is day-to-day, page-to-page, till he's finished the piece. But what was he getting at? Did he once again lose what he started out to say? Not important. Really, not important. What is, and maybe this is what he was getting at, is what he's going to do about all this forgetting. Maybe he should talk it over with his daughters. They're smart, practical, want the best for him. No, doesn't want to worry or burden them with his problems, which is what his mother, when she was around his age now, used to say to him. What did he say when she said that? Probably something like "Don't worry about me. It's not a burden. You can never be a burden to me. I want to do everything I can for you." So did she usually end up telling him? Forgets. If he does tell his daughters, they'll say something like, "Daddy, you have to be more careful. You can burn down the house with you in it." "I know," he'd say. But keep it to yourself with them. He really doesn't want to worry them. And there's enough, when they're here, that they can see for themselves. Then a friend. Is he really that close with anybody? Not since his wife died. He sort of pulled himself away. Even his sister? But what can a friend or his sister do to help? He knows she'll say he should take ginseng tablets. She's big on that and claims it's improved her memory by fifty percent. He remembers saying something like "I don't know how you can measure that, but if you say so, okay." So there's nobody, really. Think. Nobody. He goes into the house. Wait a minute. How about his doctor at his next annual checkup? But by that time he'll forget he wants to speak to him about it. He always seems to forget what he wants or even thinks he needs to talk to him about. Too much time between thinking about it and the appointment. What he should have done is write it down in his daily calendar book for the day of the appointment. So for now, call his office and say he wants to see him sooner than his annual checkup, which he thinks is in March. It's always in March. But it won't do him any good. His doctor will put him on another pill. Then more upset stomach and worse constipation than he already has. That's what the hell those pills mostly do. So again: just try harder to remember. Memory devices. Anything that can help. That's really all he needs. His mind is fine. For a start, he writes "remember" in marker on a piece of paper, scissors around it and tapes it to the refrigerator door. Underlines it twice. Puts an exclamation point after it. Then writes "remember!" on another piece of paper, cuts it out and tapes it to the bottom of the bathroom window frame. Any other place? No, that should do it. He pees, doesn't need to flush it—that he never seems to forget to do when he has to, nor put the toilet seat down—and is about to turn around and leave the room when he sees the "remember!" on the window frame. Zips up his fly. Later, for lunch, he puts the rest of the lasagna he made two days ago for dinner into the oven to warm up, sees the "remember!" on the refrigerator door and says to himself, "Now remember. This is important. Come back in twenty minutes to take the dish out. Twenty? Make it thirty, at 400 degrees." The lasagna's been in the refrigerator and he just turned on the oven and he likes the pasta ends crisp if not a little burned. He pours himself a mug of coffee from the thermos, goes into the living room with it, sits, looks at the clock on the fireplace mantle, moves the mug to the side table from the chair arm so there's less chance of knocking it over, reads the newspaper and then a book—a good bio of one of his favorite writers; he's really enjoying it. He listens to music while he reads, rests his head back in the easy chair and daydreams or dreams for what feels like a few minutes and then comes out of it or wakes up. Smells something burning.

Vera

He knew he'd hear from her soon, not about his wife's death but just a phone call, since she hadn't called for a long time. He answered the phone. She said "Hi, how are you? Just wanted to know how things are going." He told her. She said "Oh, I'm so sorry. And here I blundered into the phone so cheerfully and full of hope. It has to be awful for you. If there's anything I can do to help, I'm here for you." "Thank you," he said. "Right now, though, I can't talk about it—it's still too soon to—so I'll have to hang up." "I understand. Oh, my poor dear. Much love to you and your daughters."

They'd been in touch for so many years. Twenty-five, maybe. For a while she called him about once a year, usually on or near his birthday. "I know it's around this time," she said a couple of times. He never called her unless she left a message on his answering machine in his office at school, and even then most times he didn't call her back. For the next ten years or so she called him every four to six months, in his office but now a few times at home. Always to find out how he and his wife were doing. Abby said once "She's just checking to see if I've finally croaked, so she can move in on you. You're still a good catch, you know. Your looks, health, tenured position, writing, and our combined assets." He said "Not a chance. With all the infusions and new medications and stuff you're taking, you're only going to get better the next few years, and she and I are only telephone friends. For some reason I mean something to her. I'm one of her oldest friends, she said. We go back more than forty

119

years. One doesn't have too many of those, so she doesn't want to lose contact with me. Who else does she know who remembers her parents and the house she grew up in and her two Scotties? I don't care much for her calls, but by this time I don't know how to keep her from making them. But if you object, I'll find some way to stop them." "Why would I object? Anything that'll happen between you two will happen after I'm dead. And it might even be good for you, a way to take your mind off losing me. And she's still pretty and quite lively, you say." "Well, that was a while ago, but what does it matter?"

Last time he'd seen Vera was fifteen years ago when he was in her city for a new book of his. Took the train up from Baltimore, she met him at the station, took the train back. They had coffee at the cafe in the bookstore. He was giving a reading there and bought a copy of his book at full price—thought it would make him look cheap to her if he took the author's discount, which was offered to him—and inscribed it and gave it to her. *To Vera, my dear old friend.* She never mentioned later on that she'd read the book or any part of it or even started it, and he never asked.

About two years after that she called him to say she was staying overnight in Baltimore—she had an audition for a part in a play at the best theater company there—and he asked Abby, she said it was all right, and invited Vera for dinner. "But not to sleep here, okay?" Abby said. "I'd find that a little strange." He picked Vera up at her hotel and drove her back. She said in the car "Your wife is beautiful, spiritually and physically. Such magnificent skin and hair—that of a much younger woman—and a lovely voice and manner of speaking. And so intelligent. I felt ignorant compared to her. She obviously adores you. And you're so good to her, tending to all her needs and just the way you speak to her. I like seeing that, although it's nothing short of what I expected of you. What she must think of me, though, for the way I treated you in the past." "Not at all. She knows all about it and said that was long ago, when we were practically kids. Believe me, she never had a bad thought about you. That's not Abby." "Good. I didn't tell you, by the way, and you were both very discreet about it, but once again I didn't get the part. They said I was good and it was close but I was just a mite too old for the role. That's always a good excuse. I didn't think I did well." "Nonsense. I'm sure you did well. And I'm sorry—for you and also because it would've been nice to see you on stage and have you over for dinner again, and we would've taken the kids to the play too. They would have loved knowing that we knew one of the main characters."

Since that first phone call after Abby died, she called him about once a month to see how he was doing. "I'm concerned about you," she said in her last call. "Your daughters away. You living alone after so many years with Abby." "I'll be all right," he said. "I'm getting used to it—the living alone, I mean. As for my daughters—I miss them tremendously, but they come down for weekends now and then." "Have you ever thought of visiting me? It'd be a good change for you, doing something new, and I'm not that far away. Two, two and a half hours by car." "I never go anywhere. The local Y; the local food market; that's about all. Oh, for a book at a nearby bookstore about once a month. I don't think I've been out of Baltimore County since Abby died seven months ago." "That's what I'm saying. I'll show you around here, take you out to dinner, and you can spend the night. I've a guest room." He said "Maybe you're right. Let me think. No, you're right. It could be a major emotional breakthrough for me, just reaching the entrance to 95 North, and my kids will love it that I even attempted to get away from the house for a day. They'll think, next time I might even drive up to see them in New York. Okay, I'm coming. But dinner's on me. And breakfast out also, if we have that too."

He drove to her apartment near Philadelphia. During dinner he thought she's still so lively and funny and beautiful. In great shape too. Slim, very fit; tight behind. She even shows cleavage of a woman thirty years younger. Same with her skin. Hardly a wrinkle on her face and neck, and nice texture to her hair and just a few wisps of gray. "How can you look so young?" he said. "Pardon me, but we're almost the same age, and I've gotten to look like an old guy." "No you haven't," she said. "And it's not through surgery. You know I'd never do anything like that to my body. It's exercise, yoga, long walks every morning, and lots of filtered water and harmless facial oils and creams. And of course healthy organic foods, which is why I chose this restaurant and why it's a bit pricey. As for my hair, this is its natural color. What can I say?"

He slept in the guest room. "Oh, one problem," she said when she invited him to come. "I've only been here a few months and haven't a spare bed yet. I'll buy it this week. I'll need it sometime. For instance, if my son ever decides to visit me." He knew she was short of money, so he said he'd like to pay for the bed. "It'll probably cost no more than a motel room would, but so what if it costs more." She got it at Ikea, set it up. He gave her a check for it when he got there.

He didn't sleep well. The bed was uncomfortable. And it was a hot muggy night and she didn't have air conditioning because she never liked it, nor an extra fan. "Take mine," she said. "The heat doesn't particularly bother me." "Wouldn't think of it," he said. "I'll be fine." He was hoping, as he lay in bed for hours, that she'd knock on his door and say something like "Would you like to sleep in my room with me? With the fan and cross-ventilation, it's much cooler."

They had cold cereal and yogurt and coffee for breakfast. He said he wouldn't mind a slice of toast and butter if she has, and she said she was all out of bread. "I should have planned it better. But the nearest natural food market is ten miles from here and I only do one shop a week." Then they walked for more than an hour along an old restored canal. "I do the same route daily," she said, "even when it rains. It's so tranquil. I get my most inspired thoughts here. Poems; even stories, I've begun writing. And ways to bring in enough money so I can quit my awful job." His older daughter called him on his cell phone after they got back and asked how he was. He said in front of Vera "I'm having a great time. I'm so glad I came."

He said to her in her building's parking area before he left "It's already past one. I hope I haven't taken up too much of your time." She said "Why would you think that? From now on I'm going to make it my duty to see that you start thinking much better of yourself." They kissed goodbye—a friendly kiss, lasted no more than a second—and during the drive home he thought he hasn't been this happy for a long time. Things are looking good. Just that she allowed him that quick kiss on the lips.

He called her that night. Thought for about an hour whether he should do this and then thought why not? He wants to know. She said "What a surprise to hear from you so soon." "Wrong of me?" and she said "No, I like talking to you. We've a lot to say." "Listen," he said, "I want to be frank and direct with you. What else can I be at this stage in my life? Do you think something new and promising has started between us?" "It's a very distinct possibility." "You know what I mean, of course," and she said "You don't have to spell it out for me." "Oh, that makes me feel good to hear you say that. So let's do it again, but soon, and how about this time you visit me? I'll show you around. No canals. But there's a beautiful reservoir just a half hour from me, and lots of other attractive places. And Baltimore's a fairly interesting city, if we want to do a little exploring there." "All that might be nice," she said. "Let me see which of the next few weekends I'll be entirely free. I'll get back to you."

He called her three days later and she said "Was I supposed to call you? I forget. But I've been thinking. Maybe it's not such a good idea I come down. I doubt my old buggy could make it both ways, the train will be too costly, and I've a ton of work that's piled up at my job and it seems it's going to be like that for weeks." "The work you might be able to do here. I'll leave you alone. And I'll pay for the train fare. I've two spare bedrooms, but I'll put you up at a bed and breakfast if you prefer." She said "That might be better—the B and B or an inn. It's sweet of you to offer all this. Let me see. I'll get back to you."

He called her a few days later. "Tell me. Am I bothering you by being so persevering?" he said. "No, I can understand why you called, and I apologize for not calling you. I thought about it—knew what I wanted to say—but kept putting it off. I've decided we shouldn't meet again except as platonic friends." "Wow, there's a word I haven't heard in a while." "People don't use it anymore?" "I'm sure they do," he said. "And a platonic friendship is what I want with you too." "No you don't," she said. "Be honest. You want romance, love, sex, marriage, constant companionship and the like. And you should have all that, after what you've gone through, just not with me. I don't think it's the right thing for us and I don't see that it'll ever be."

He was once engaged to her. Almost fifty years ago. He was 24 and she was 23. She broke it off a month or two before the wedding. The ceremony was going to be at his mother's apartment and the reception, for the twenty or so guests, in a closed-off section of the Great Shanghai, a restaurant on a Hundred-third Street and Broadway. "I'm not ready," she said. "It's too soon after my first unfortunate marriage." Two years before that, when they'd been seeing each other almost every day for three months, she suddenly disappeared on him—couldn't be reached by phone and her parents and a couple of her friends didn't know where she was, when he called them, and she gave no indication she was home when he rang her downstairs buzzer in her apartment building and then her doorbell several days in a row. She'd started up with a much older guy she'd briefly dated and had been in love with the year before. They got married and she had the marriage annulled in less than a year. He got a job as a reporter in Washington soon after the breakup with her. Two years later he moved back to New York as a news editor. He called up friends of hers, a married couple he'd gotten to know while he was seeing her, asked the wife how they were but was really more interested in finding out what Vera was doing. She told him about the annulment and invited him over for dinner and said would he mind if she asked Vera to come too. "I'm sure she has no interest in seeing me," he said. "Not true," she said. "She's spoken about you highly several times." "Well, if she's there, she's there." She came. They had lunch the next day and were sleeping together in a week. They got engaged in a few months and a few months after that she broke it off. Three years later, he was coming back from Paris, where he'd gone to write and learn French and possibly get a news job or something in writing or editing. He got a letter from her while he was there and after that they wrote each other about once a month. She knew he was coming back but didn't know how or when. She called his mother, who'd previously given her his Paris address but wouldn't tell her the name of the ship or when it'd dock in New York. "She's trouble," she told him. "You're too blind to see that. She'll just make you sad again. I never should have told her where you were in Paris or that you were even in Paris. Bucharest, I should have told her." "Come on, I'm twenty-eight," he said. "Much better now in dealing with things like that. If it doesn't go well, and with our history, no reason why it should, *tant pis*, as the French say. Not to worry." He called her. They went out to dinner and slept together that night. Next morning, while they were having coffee in her kitchen and he was about to ask if they could spend the day together or get together again that night, she said "I have to confess something to you. It is nice seeing you again. But last night, and this morning when you pushed me into it again when I definitely didn't want to, I did what I promised myself I wouldn't. I'm not saying the first time wasn't fun. But I've done enough harm to you. It's not going to work out the way you want it to and by now you should be able to see that as well as I. You don't want to get hurt again and I don't want to hurt you and then feel guilty about it again." "You're right, I don't," he said. "And you can sure do it to me—oh, boy, can you. And I'm not going to make a big scene over it. You're safe from that, anyway. I'll just leave."

Fourteen years later he met Abby and they got married in three years. About twenty-seven years after that he visited Vera and the next day invited her to visit him. She's called him several times since—around once every four months, he'll say. And when he learned how to receive and send e-mails on Abby's computer, she's e-mailed him a few times too. Always wanting to know how he is and what he's been doing. He always says on the phone "I'm fine, keeping busy, writing something new. How are you?"

The Vestry

He was going to leave the house. Planning to, he means, around 7:40, to go to the church across the street to see a play being performed there. He felt he had to get out of the house, and it might be interesting. The whole experience of seeing the play, he means. He didn't know about the play, though. It was by a writer who held no interest for him. Hack works, he thought of them, even if one won a Pulitzer years ago and another won some other prestigious award. He hasn't read anything about the writer for years and assumes he's dead. But he had to get out, is what he's saying. He almost never does, except for the usual things: the Y, markets, post office, an occasional coffee. He had thought he'd go to a few concerts at the symphony hall downtown, but without ordering the tickets first as he used to do when his wife was alive. Just park the car in the hall's garage, go up to the ticket window and get whatever's available. Apparently, the hall is never filled. They used to go to about six concerts a year and two to three operas at another concert hall. They also, for the last ten years of her life, got season tickets, which means about six plays, to the best theater group in the city. He meant to go to those too, at least once or twice, meaning one or two plays, though preferably more if the lineup of plays was good, and at least one opera. Sometimes he even got dressed for one or the other of them—for movies too—meaning he took off his sweatpants or shorts and long- or short-sleeve polo shirt. He has no dress shirts and wouldn't wear one to one of those events if he did. But a few minutes before he was to leave the house and drive to the theater or symphony hall or place where the opera was to be performed, he said to himself, and sometimes, maybe the first part of this, out loud to himself, Does he really want to go? He does. He wants to get out, to do something different and perhaps be entertained or moved or whatever would happen. But he doesn't like driving at night, and if it's an afternoon performance or showing, especially around this time of year, then chance driving back at night. He also doesn't much like sitting in a concert hall or theater or opera house, he'll call it, for two hours and usually more. A movie theater he doesn't mind, and also movies are almost always much shorter. He also doesn't like going alone, and he doesn't know anyone to go with, not that he'd ask anyone if he did know someone who'd want to go. That wasn't always what he was like. So he went back into the house, if he was outside and got that close to getting in his car and driving to one of these places, and went back to his bedroom and changed into the clothes he took off to put on the dressier ones. Sometimes he never even got that far. He'd go into the bedroom to change his clothes, as preparation for going to one of these events, and think Why bother? He knows he's not going anywhere, so he should stop fooling himself and wasting his time getting dressed when he's just going to get back into his old clothes again. One time, he now remembers—it was to a concert that was playing one of his favorite pieces, Mahler's Third Symphony—he was in the car, had started out maybe a half hour earlier than usual because he thought for this concert—*Das Lied von der Erde* was also on the program—the hall will be filled—and said to himself, Where does he think he's going? He knows he'd rather stay home and have a drink or two and some snacks and read and listen to music on the radio or CDs than drive to the hall and go through the hassle of parking the car and standing on what he's almost sure will be a long ticket line and maybe not even be able to get a ticket, and so on. And it's getting dark, so it'll be dark when he drives back and he'll probably be tired then, since it'll be an hour or more after he usually goes to bed. And he's seen this symphony performed twice already, both times with his wife. Once here in the same hall about ten years ago and the other time almost thirty years ago at Carnegie Hall, maybe a few months after they first met. So he turned around and drove home. That was as close as he got, far as he can remember, to go to one of these things since his wife died. Or really, since she got sick—very sick; had to have a trach put in and other serious procedures done to her, and they didn't want to risk going to anything like a concert or movie again. "You go," she once said. It was about an hour before the concert was to begin. "Two late Mozart piano concertos and the Jupiter Symphony? You love them. I'll be all right by myself here." "You kidding?" he said. "No way."

But tonight he's going to a play. It's being performed by a group calling itself "The Good Shepherd Players," which could mean it's affiliated in some way with the church of the same name across the street or just calls itself that because it's being performed there. It could be, for all he knows, that if this group performs in other places, it calls itself after these other places, but he seriously doubts it. He's never heard of a theater group or opera company or music ensemble or any kind of performing troupe like that that changes its name to the place it's performing at, and he doesn't know how he could have even thought that. This group puts on, for two consecutive weekends—Friday and Saturday nights at eight, Sunday afternoons at three—a play every year, it seems, or has for the past three. Someone once told him it's a pretty good acting company, a cut above being amateur. Sort of between professional and amateur, so semiprofessional. Maybe it was his wife who told him, having heard it from someone else. He seems to remember that. He knows she never went to one of its plays. He first saw a sign advertising this year's play in front of the church about a month ago. The sign was professionally done. Tickets were fifteen dollars, it said, ten for children sixteen and under. He wrote the dates and times in his memobook when he saw the sign and transferred them to his weekly planner when he got home. Today's the first Saturday the play will be performed. He didn't want to go to the Sunday matinee. It'd break up his day, or just change it too much, though he'd be less tired after than if he went to an evening performance. But he likes to spend Sunday reading the *Times* and then writing for a few hours and then going to the Y and then after that to either one of the two markets he does most of his shopping at and then to a small restaurant he likes about two miles from his house. He goes there with a book, the only time he does anything like that during the week, and reads for about half an hour while he eats a sandwich or salad and has a medium-sized latte or Americano. So Sundays were out. And Friday he thought would be the first performance in front of a paid audience, so maybe not the best one to go to. Let them get the opening-night jitters and kinks in the production out of the way. The next night would be better. He also thought he might see someone he knows from the neighborhood at the performance. That'd be nice. Someone to talk to, however briefly. If he sees an attractive woman with an empty seat next to her, he might sit in it, first asking if it's taken. Oh, what's he talking about? Forget women. Just try to get an aisle seat, if there's a middle aisle, so he can see the stage better, though of course if nobody tall's sitting in front of him. He doubts the seats are reserved, if they're all the same price. And there'll be refreshments there, he's almost sure. In fact, he remembers now the sign saying so, the proceeds from it going to some medical research organization. No, a soup kitchen. But the point he's making is he has to get out. He means, not doing just the same things every day. No, he doesn't mean that. He means he has to stop giving himself excuses not to go to things. And the play's right across the street. What could be more convenient? A two-minute walk. Doesn't have to drive to it. No problem about coming home at night. And it'll break the ice, sort of. If he goes to this, maybe he'll go to other things like it. The theater downtown, and its Sunday matinee, if he has to. Opera, if the season isn't over. He stopped subscribing to the local newspaper months ago, so he doesn't know what's going on in town. Concerts at the symphony hall he knows will be going on another four to five months, all the way into May. So it's settled for tonight. He's going.

He looks at the time. A little past six. Plenty of time to change his clothes. He's through writing today, been to the Y. Dinner? What he calls dinner, he'll have when he comes back. He sits in the easy chair in the living room, takes the book off the side table, opens it to the bookmark and finds the place where he left off. Should he have a drink? It'll relax him for the play. But also might make him tired, which could end up being an excuse not to go to the play. Maybe around seven, seven-fifteen, a short one. Better, nothing to drink till he gets back home. Less he drinks, less chance he'll have to pee during the play, another reason for getting an aisle seat. So he reads for a while and then goes into the kitchen and prepares a salad for the next two days and puts it in separate bowls and turns the radio on and listens to music while he reads the newspaper spread out on the dryer. At seven, he pours an Irish whiskey on the rocks and sits in the easy chair and reads some more of the book and drinks and around seven-twenty he goes into the bedroom to change his clothes. He intends to get to the church about twenty to eight and buy a ticket and find a seat. He'll have the same book with him, so he'll read while he waits for the play to begin and maybe even during the intermission. And plays never start on time. He'll also look around to see who else is there. He's curious what sort of people come to something like this. Of course, friends and relatives of the people involved in the play, but others. How they're dressed and what they're saying. He hopes, though, there are a number of people going to it. He hates being just one of a few people in the audience. Feels the actors are looking at him, and it makes him want to look away from the stage. He changes his clothes, looks at his watch on the night table—7:35, so time to get moving—and he gets his wallet and keys and puts on his jacket and cap and gets his book and turns on the outside lights, leaves only the kitchen light on in the house, and locks the door and walks across the street to the church. So he's doing it. No big deal for anyone else, but for him?—something. For a while he didn't think he'd do it. That he'd give himself an excuse not to. For instance: He'll go next Friday or Saturday night, when the performances should be even better than tonight's. And after all, he'll have nothing to do those nights, just as he has nothing to do tonight but go to the play. Other excuses. He'd think of them. If there's anything he's good at, it's that. He walks through the church parking lot to the church entrance. Well, how about that, he thinks. You made it. Congratulations. You deserve a medal. Now, if only the play will be good and not too long. But the important thing is you're here.

He goes inside. A man's selling tickets at a card table in the lobby, or whatever it's called in a church. Not the "nave," though that came to mind. It has a name. "Vestibule" will do. Or just "the entrance." But what's he going on about? Three people are on line for tickets, and he gets behind them. Other people, maybe ten, stand around or are seated in chairs against the walls, probably waiting for somebody or just to go into the theater. So, already a fairly good crowd. His turn comes. A sign on the table says "Cash or check only." "One, please," he says. He gets a twenty out of his wallet. The man gives him a ticket—"No. 116," it says on it; that can't be the number sold just for tonight—and a five-dollar bill in change. "Now where do I go?" "Oh? Your first time with us?" the man says. "Wonderful. It'll be a surprise. Walk straight through the lobby, then left down the stairs to the vestry, where the play is being performed. Take any seat you want. The play started promptly last night, so I see no foreseeable reason it shouldn't start on time tonight. Enjoy." "Thank you."

He goes straight, left, down the stairs. Coat hooks line one wall of what seems to be the anteroom to a much larger room with rows of unfolded metal chairs in it, which must be the vestry. Several coats are on the hooks. He stuffs his cap into a side pocket of his jacket and hangs the jacket up on one of the hooks. A young girl hands him a program when he goes into the vestry. "Enjoy the performance," she says. "Thank you." Though maybe the vestry is both this room and the anteroom he hung his coat in. He'll want to look up "vestry" when he gets home. Will he remember? Should he jot it down on his bookmark or the program? He forgot his memobook but has a pen in his jacket. Not worth the trouble. And he'll remember. About fifteen people are already seated, most near the front. Nobody in the first row, though. Probably too close to the stage, which is only a foot or so off the floor. He takes a middle aisle seat, about halfway from the stage, no one in the seat in front of him. There are about ten rows. He counts them. Twelve. Ten seats to a row, five on each side of the middle aisle, so a total seating capacity of more than a hundred. So maybe a hundred-sixteen was the number of tickets sold, up till then, for tonight. But can't be. Play's going to start soon and more people would be here. Maybe it's the total of last night's sales and tonight's, or else they're not selling the tickets in numerical order. It also could be a lot of people bought tickets in advance for tomorrow's and next week's performances. He looks at the program. Two acts, it says, with a fifteen-minute intermission, five to six scenes in each act. "Morning." "One hour later." "Three hours later." "The next morning," and so on. In the second act: first scene is two weeks later, morning. The program has several local businesses advertised in it. Realtors, the market and liquor store he usually shops at, the flower shop he used to go to a few times a year when his wife was alive. Her birthday, their anniversary, a number of times when she was very angry at him. Flowers or a new African violet plant always seemed to make her feel better to him. An ad for the church's pastoral counseling. There's no stage curtain. Actors, he just now notices, are lying on cots and supposed to be sleeping or resting. Mosquito netting covers three of the four occupied cots. One cot is empty and has a rolled-up bare mattress on it. More people take seats in the audience. Still nobody in the row in front of his. He doesn't recognize anyone. Must be past eight now. He saw no reason to bring his watch. He opens his book and starts reading. A couple come into his row from the other end and the woman sits next to him and the man on the other side of her. Minute later the woman whispers something to the man and they each move one seat over. Could it have been something about him? There was nobody in front of them. She probably just felt more comfortable not sitting next to anyone. He puts the book down on the seat she left. More people come in. About fifty seats are taken. Music comes on. "Waltzing Matilda." It must be around ten after eight. The lights dim in the audience and brighten on stage. The door to the room is closed. The music fades out. A woman dressed like an army nurse might be dressed sixty years ago walks on stage. She raises the bamboo blinds of the one window in back, which looks onto what seems like a jungle, and then pulls the mosquito netting away from one of the cots and ties a cord around the middle of it. The men in the cots start stirring: scratching their faces, yawning, stretching their arms out. "Rise and shine, mighty warriors," she says, pulling the netting away from another cot, "rise and shine. It's a special day." The program says the play takes place in a military hospital in Burma for British, Canadian and American soldiers in World War II.

The play's terrible. Everything about it: acting, writing, characterizations, laugh lines that aren't funny, romantic and tender scenes and one tragic one—a soldier learns his brother has been killed in battle in Europe—that are cloying, boring, totally unconvincing, something, but they're awful. Fifteen minutes into the play, he wishes he hadn't come to it. He'd leave but thinks that would disturb the actors: walking up the aisle, opening the door and trying not to make a sound. If he's lucky, he thinks, it'll be a short act.

The first act lasts for about an hour and a half. Maybe it only felt that long because he was so bored by it and it was a half hour or so less. The audience applauds at the end of it. He doesn't. The actors leave the stage. Lights come on. Three teenagers immediately start rearranging the furniture on stage—letting down the blinds, removing one cot. He hurries up the aisle, gets his jacket and puts it on in the lobby. He seems to be the first one there. The girl who gave him the program is sitting behind the card table with a woman— they look like mother and daughter—selling candy bars and what seem like homemade brownies and cupcakes with pink and white frosting and fruit juice in paper cups. He was wrong. The money will go to some children's group of the church, a sign on the table says. "Would you like to buy a refreshment?" the girl says as he's putting on his cap. "No thanks, sweetheart," he says. "Maybe some other time," and he leaves the church. Outside, he thinks she looked disappointed when he said no. And that was so stupid what he said about some other time. He was in too great a rush to get out of there. He should have bought something even if he didn't eat or drink it. She probably even made the brownies and cupcakes with her mother. Well, others will buy. He can't always feel bad for everyone. There'll have to be some sales. Others might even buy just because they don't want to disappoint the girl by saying no. And it'd be silly and seem peculiar to go back and buy something, though something in him wants to.

He gets home, changes into his bathrobe, sits in the easy chair in the living room and reads the op-ed articles in the newspaper. He has a drink, then a second. Place is nice and warm. He makes himself a tuna melt with tuna salad he made the day before and sits in the easy chair and eats it. So. Was it worth it going to the play? He feels no pride, or relief, or whatever it is, that he finally got out of the house to go to a performance of some kind. Because what did it prove? He now feels even worse than before he went. Why? He just does. Oh, damn, why does it always have to be this way? He feels even less willing now to go alone to some future concert or movie or a play done by professionals in a real theater in the city. He doesn't think he'll ever get in his car to go to one if it means he has to go alone. He didn't feel good sitting by himself in the vestry, and it wasn't just the boring play. Though there were, though he only got quick looks before the room went dark, a couple of attractive women there with women friends, it seemed. Who knows? If he had stayed he might have been able to start a conversation with one of them during the intermission in the anteroom or the lobby while he had a refreshment, the fruit juice, probably; he's not much for candy or cake. But what is he thinking? From what he saw, they were too young for him. Thirty years younger than he at least. That will always be the case, it seems. Ah, don't be so down on yourself. It doesn't always have to be the case. He might meet someone somewhere accidentally, or a friend could set up something or introduce him to her, and things could start up between them. "This was fun. Like to meet for coffee someday?" That sort of thing. He doesn't have to think it's too late for him. Just stay in shape and be ready to say the right thing to get or keep things going. Someone to go to a play with and later talk about it, even the awful plays. Someone who might do the driving-home after, if she's staying at his place that night, or he at hers. All of that could happen. He has to think it can. Oh, dream on, dream on.

What They'll Find

He wakes up, washes, dresses, makes the bed, lets the cat out, and right after he puts his sneakers on for a short run, he gets a sharp pain in his stomach. He lies down on his bed, doesn't know what's causing the pain but thinks it'll go away. It gets worse and won't stop. He sits on the toilet awhile, thinking maybe it's that, but nothing comes. Three hours after he first got the pain, and when it's hurting even worse than before, he decides to drive to Emergency in the hospital about two miles away. He puts on his muffler, coat and cap, gets his wallet out of the sideboard in the dining room and his keys off the hook by the front door, but feels too weak to drive and sits down by the phone in his wife's old study and dials 911. EMU comes, checks him over, has him walk to the truck outside and lie down on the gurney in back, and takes him to Emergency. He dies two hours later. In his wallet, under a two-by-three-inch piece of transparent plastic—it's the first thing one sees when the wallet's opened—is a handwritten note that says "If I should die unexpectedly or be incapacitated, my name is Philip Seidel, SS#099-56-3324. Instructions on other side." He wrote that and inserted it in his wallet after he got out of the hospital the last time. The instructions say "Call my daughters, first one first," and gives their names and cell phone numbers. "If neither's reachable, call Aaron Henry," and gives his home, office and cell phone numbers. "If he's unreachable, call Maggie Rothman," who was his wife's best friend since they were freshmen in college together and became sort of a surrogate mother to his daughters after his wife died, and gives her phone numbers, though she lives in New York, as do his daughters. Next he gives his own address and home phone number. Underneath this folded-up slip of paper are two sterile adhesive bandages and several passport and school yearbook photos of his wife and daughters, all of them at least ten years old, which is about how long he's had the wallet, and one of them his wife's visa photo to the Soviet Union that goes back to three years before he met her.

His daughters will be called. Or one of them will, and she'll call the other. Maybe his friend and former colleague will be called by the hospital too, or one of his daughters will call him. His daughters will come to the hospital straight from the train station. They, and possibly his friend—he's sharp on things; that's why they'd want him there—will deal with whatever needs to be done after someone dies. Documents. Signing papers. Going through his wallet to find his Medicare and Blue/Cross Blue/Shield cards. Contacting, probably with the help of a social worker at the hospital, a funeral home to pick up the body later that day or sometime the next day to be cremated, something he told his daughters he wanted done with it. His daughters will go home. If his friend came to the hospital, he'll stick around and drive them, or else they'll take a cab.

This is what they'll find at home. The door will be unlocked. The cat will be outside, sitting on the doormat. They'll let him in and give him fresh water and food. Both of them will probably pick up and hold the cat till he starts squirming in their arms, which he does with everyone when he's held more than thirty seconds or so, and he'll either jump to the floor or they'll let him down.

His daughters will turn most of the lights on in the house and probably, for a while, the outside lights too. They'll probably check the thermostat in the dining room to see if the heat's on or at a temperature they want. All the rooms will be clean, other than for some tracks the EMU people made on the kitchen floor. It was still a little wet outside that morning. The cleaning woman, who comes every Tuesday for four hours and then makes herself a mug of herbal tea and a sandwich from smoked turkey and a roll he bought at the local market the day before and lettuce from the refrigerator's vegetable bin, will have been there just two days ago, and he was always cleaning and tidying up after himself in the house. He never liked to see a single thread or a leaf from one of his houseplants on the floor. There'll be some slices of turkey left in a zipper bag in the deli tray in the refrigerator. He used to give it to the cat, in small pieces, the next two to three days. He once shared what turkey was left with the cat but hadn't for months. Not since he stopped eating anything with salt in it after his doctor told him his blood pressure was getting dangerously high and he wanted to put him on a medication to lower it. He told both daughters in separate phone conversations that he didn't want to go on another pill if he could avoid it. His bowels were already too affected by the pills he's taking. That maybe a salt-free diet and a short jog in the morning and a long walk that ended with a short jog at dusk and more exercise at the Y than he's been doing will lower his blood pressure to a level where he won't have to take any new medication. His doctor didn't think so, he told his daughters, but they'll see. It can't hurt or make things worse, he said; just make eating less interesting. He was already taking a pill three times during the day at six-hour intervals for his Parkinson's and another pill once a day for an enlarged prostate. He would have taken the Parkinson's pill with his breakfast this morning after his run and the prostate pill a half hour after breakfast. The pills are in pill containers on a shelf above one of the kitchen counters. These pills and the little smoked turkey left—in fact, everything in the deli tray—and some other foods in the refrigerator they think might be too old or past their expiration dates or they just don't want to take any chance on will be the first things they'll dump into the trash can in the kitchen. If they get hungry and don't use his car to drive to a market or a restaurant for dinner, what will they find in the house to eat? When he knew they were coming for a weekend or more, he bought things they liked. Flax seed bread, bagels, almond milk, Honey Nut cereal, Greek yogurt, goat cheese, other foods he didn't eat. There's half a loaf of whole wheat bread in the refrigerator that he bought for himself a week ago, but it's salt-free. They'll find it tasteless, even toasted and with butter or jam or both. In the freezer are two of the six bagels he bought for them the last time they were here and which they didn't want to take back with them, so he froze them and they can have them this time. Also different dishes in plastic food containers in the freezer. He liked to cook and would only eat a quarter of what he made and freeze the rest and rarely ate what he froze and most of the time, a month or two after he put them in the freezer, he threw them out. They'll dump almost everything in the freezer the next few days and all the spices on the spice shelf on the kitchen wall, most of which have been there more than a year. There are cans of different kinds of salt-free beans and diced and crushed tomatoes and tomato sauce in a kitchen cabi- net. There are also several pastas and a box of rice noodles in that cabinet. So it's possible that instead of eating out in a restaurant or going to a market for food they'll make dinner from some combina- tion of what they find in the kitchen cabinets and a salad from the refrigerator's vegetable bin and fruit from the fruit bin and the bowl in the center of the dining table—bananas, clementines, a grape- fruit, ripe pears—and wine from one of the bottles in the two wine racks under the sideboard.

They'll find in the refrigerator part of what was to be today's breakfast he prepared the night before. A bowl with soy yogurt and cranberry compote he made a large batch of so he could have it every morning for one to two weeks and a sliced banana. That'll also be dumped. They'll also find in the refrigerator a small plastic container of cut-up fresh fruit. Sometimes he prepared three containers of fruit at once, usually the same fruits equally distributed in the containers, lidded them and took them out one at a time with the bowls the next three mornings.

A salad fork for the fruit and tablespoon for the bowl of cereal will be on the one placemat on the table, a folded-up cloth napkin under them. He put the utensils there the previous night before he went to bed, something he did every night if he knew he was going to have breakfast at home the next morning. The napkins and placemat will be a little stained with food, since he also used them for his last two lunches, and they'll drop them into the washing machine in the kitchen. They won't find anything in the washing machine when they open it or anything in the dryer next to it. He did a wash two mornings before and folded up everything and put it away. The spoon and fork they'll put back into the utensil drawer under a kitchen counter.

The coffeemaker on the short counter between the stove and sink will also have been prepared the night before: water, filter paper and grounds. Alongside the coffeemaker will be the mug he planned to drink the coffee out of and a thermos he was going to pour the rest of the coffee into after he filled up the mug.

He didn't pick up his newspaper by the mailbox this morning, so it'll still be there. They'll pick it up the next morning with the next day's newspaper. They knew his morning routine almost by heart now. They'd seen it when they were there and got up early enough and he talked self-mockingly about it on the phone several times. "It's crazy," he said, "but since your mother died this is what I do." If he hadn't gotten sick he would have made sure the living room door to the porch was locked, gone outside through the kitchen door and locked it, taken a short run with maybe a brief stop or two on the roads' shoulders when cars were coming his way, got the newspaper at the end of the run, unlocked the kitchen door, hung the keyring on one of the hooks by the door, turned the coffeemaker on, taken the container of fruit and bowl of soy yogurt, compote and banana out of the refrigerator, or done that before he left the house, got the jar of sodium-free granola off a kitchen shelf and spooned some of it into the bowl, set the bowl and container of fruit on the placemat on the dining table, poured out a mug of coffee and put it on a coaster on the table, poured what was left in the coffeemaker into the thermos, shut off the coffeemaker, let the cat in by now if he wanted to come in and given him a fresh bowl of water and a plate with wet food on it, which he would have got out of the refrigerator or opened a new can of cat food from the kitchen cabinet that had all his canned foods, or if there was very little food left in the can from the refrigerator, done both; brought the newspaper to the table if he hadn't already left it there when he came back into the house after his run, taken his first Parkinson's pill of the day if he hadn't already taken it, and sat down at the table and started to eat his breakfast and drink his coffee while he read the newspaper, starting with the capsule weather forecast for the Washington edition at the top right corner of the page.

They won't find any dishes or utensils or pots or pans or anything like that in the kitchen sink or dish rack. He washed the little there was last night and put them away. The paper bag of paper, plastic, metal and glass for the single-stream recycling pickup this Friday will be next to the trash can in the kitchen. On top of the dryer will be the book he was reading last night in the living room easy chair and which he put there by the door so he wouldn't forget to take it with him to the Y the next day. They'll find in the refrigerator an aluminum pie pan, covered with aluminum foil, the dinner he would have had tonight. He'd cooked two chicken breasts and some root vegetables together in the oven last night. Then, standing beside the stove and without cutting up the chicken breasts but waiting till they were no longer hot, he ate with his fingers about half of what was in the pan. The dinner was so good, and he was also a bit tired of cooking something different almost every night, that instead of freezing what was left in the pan, he'd have the same dinner tonight. They'll re-cover the pan with the same foil they found on it and throw all of it out too.

Dining room will be tidy, everything—chairs under the table, place mat, napkin, eating utensils—in its place. He rearranged the fruit in the fruit bowl the day before so it'd look neat and nice. Living room will also be tidy, except for an empty juice glass on the end table next to the easy chair, which he drank two glasses of red wine out of while he was reading the previous night. The empty wine bottle will be on top of the recycling bag. They'll think it was so unlike him to leave a dirty glass on a table overnight, and he must have forgot to bring it into the kitchen to wash it. They'll figure out, if not this week then the next, which day the garbage gets picked up and which day all the recyclable stuff, and also to put the trash cans and things on the street early that morning or the night before. They'll bring the juice glass to the kitchen and probably have to soak it awhile in soapy water to get the dried residue off the bottom of it. There's no scrub brush in the house to get in that glass, and a sponge with detergent on it never got rid of all the residue.

Their beds haven't been touched, other than for the cat taking morning and afternoon naps on them, since the cleaning woman cleaned their rooms and straightened their covers and pillows the last time she was here.

They'll have some work to do in his bedroom. He made his bed after he got up. They'll strip it and wash the linens with the two towels and washcloth from his bathroom, and in another wash the patchwork quilt Abby and he had a woman in Maine make for them about thirty years ago. They'll throw out his personal items in the medicine cabinet above the sink: comb, hairbrush, toothbrush, nailbrush, shaving soap, and maybe his shaving brush and razor and package of razor blades. Or maybe they'll include the shaving brush with the other things of his—clothes, shoes, slippers, his one tie, and so on…coats, sport jacket, belts, his one dress shirt, which he ordered from L.L. Bean several years ago and never took out of the plastic bag it came in—they'll give to organizations like Goodwill and Purple Heart. What also might go will be what remains of their mother's skirts and shirts in his bedroom closet and which they told him a number of times they didn't want. They never took any of her clothes other than two mufflers, and those only when it was very cold outside and they needed something warm around their necks, and some head scarves he never saw them wear and two knitted wool caps she brought back from the Soviet Union before he met her. For the last three years he's been gradually giving her clothes to the same organizations. There are two empty drawers in their dresser that were once filled with her belongings. His old terrycloth bathrobe, hanging on a hook on his bathroom door, is too ragged to give away, so they'll dump it. They'll also probably throw out the shopping bags of tax receipts of the three previous years that are in his bedroom closet and seemed to spill over to the floor every time the cat got in there. They'll probably keep, once they see what year it's for, or at least till they speak to his tax accountant, the bag of receipts for this year. They'll also give to Goodwill or Purple Heart the two ten-pound weights on his night table that he exercised with most mornings, and the two fifteen-pound weights they're resting on, which he stopped exercising with a year ago when he bought the ten-pound weights.

What to do with his writings, though? And his typewriters, two spare ones on a shelf in the guest closet, and the remaindered copies of his books in cartons in the basement, and all his writing supplies? Between them, they'll keep a few copies of each of his remaindered books and give away the rest. Maybe his former department will want some to give to its students, or the Baltimore County library system might be able to use them. They won't know what to do with his old manuscripts of published works they'll find in the file cabinet under his work table and the newer unpublished manuscripts and photocopies of them on the bookcase in his bedroom, and will have to ask his writer friends and former colleagues. Maybe the school library's special collections department will take both the old and new manuscripts along with whatever notebooks and letters and such they find of his and a copy of each of his books. As for his writing supplies—one of them will keep the unopened ream of paper for her copier. The other stuff—typewriter ribbons, correction film, binder clips, lots of cheap pens and two staplers and a box of staples and so on—they'll probably stash in the bags for Goodwill and Purple Heart, hoping some of it can be used. The typewriters, if no writer they speak to wants them or knows anyone who does and none of their friends want them either, they'll give away to one of those organizations. And all those photographs. Boxes of photographs, albums of photographs, drawers of photographs. He kept them without ever taking them out and looking at them, except for the memorial album his daughters made of their mother, but they'll know what to do with them.

On his writing table is the typewriter he worked on the last few years. Never broke down. "Never gave me trouble," he used to say. "I have spares that I'll probably never use." To its immediate right on the table is the first draft of the story he was working on. To its immediate left is the pile of scrap paper he took from to work on the same page of the story over and over again till he was satisfied with it and was ready to switch to the clean final-copy paper. And to the immediate right of the first draft of the story is the stack of clean paper. Behind the typewriter is the part of the story he completed—fourteen pages held together by a binder clip. All the stacks will be neat. He made them that way yesterday after he finished writing for the day and fitted the dust cover over the typewriter. It was getting dark out and the two lamps on either side of the typewriter, each with warnings on the inside of the shade not to use more than a 60-watt bulb, don't give enough light to write when it gets that dark. Besides, he was tired after writing for a total of about eight hours that day. The story in progress, the completed part and the first draft, will also probably go to the special collections department if it'll take it with his other manuscripts. The dictionary and thesaurus he kept on the table to the left of the scrap paper pile are in too bad a shape—lots of dog-eared pages, especially at the front of the books, and covers separating from the spines—to give to Goodwill or some other place or keep themselves. So they might put the books in their own shopping bag, because they'll be so heavy—maybe even double up the bag before they put the books in—and put it out with the rest of the recycled paper or throw out with the trash.

What they call the guest bathroom—the one off the hallway between their bedrooms and his—will be in the condition the cleaning woman left it the last time she worked for him, except for the kitty litter box, which might need changing. The cleaning woman, which was okay with him, never took care of that. Though the cat, even when it was raining or snowing, usually found a dry place outside to dig a hole and piss and crap, so they might not have to deal with it. The towels on the towel racks in the bathroom and the bathmat folded over the bathtub rim haven't been used since he washed them after his daughters' last visit, so they won't have to be changed either.

His wife's old study will also be neat and clean, other than for a demitasse saucer on the computer table that he used as a coaster for whatever he was drinking while answering e-mails or just seeing if he got any. If the saucer seems clean they'll probably put it in the kitchen cupboard on top of the other demitasse saucer and small plates without even rinsing it.

There are no other rooms in the house. The basement, but nothing down there but the furnace, water heater, well tank, dehumidifier, which he got when they bought the house and turned on when the weather started to get muggy and left on till around the middle of October, and a floor lamp and empty dresser. Also a few children's records and an old phonograph, that has no needle in it, on top of the dresser, and cartons of remaindered books—not only his but ones his wife translated, and for two of them, wrote introductions to—stacked one on top of another with the titles of the books written on the sides of the cartons facing out, and many stretched and rolled-up paintings his daughters did in high school and college. Up until about ten years ago they also used the basement as a playroom and later as a place to hold sleepovers.

Closets? Nothing much in them except for the one in his bedroom. By now his daughters' closets are almost empty. And the hallway closet has his two reserve typewriters and a couple of his coats and, hanging from hangers, about five of his wife's shawls friends of hers had given her once she was only able to get around outside in a wheelchair. Also a walker he was discharged from the hospital with after he got sick with a bowel obstruction two years ago and had to be operated on and a shower chair his daughters bought him after he got home. He'd been meaning to bring both to the basement and leave them there for possible future use or give to a loan closet.

They'll know where to go to start dealing with his personal matters. Everything they'll need for this is in a file folder under the computer table next to his wife's sewing machine, which they'll also probably give away. The folder has specific instructions what to do if he dies or is mentally or physically unable to handle his finances anymore or the business of the house and car and taxes and so on, and all the documents that go with them. Stapled to the folder's flap is a sheet of typing paper—he's told them this and pointed it out a number of times—saying something like, but definitely using this greeting: "My darlings. Instructions what to do in event of my death or permanent inability to conduct my own affairs are in the first sleeve of this file folder—sleeve A, and right at the front of it, first thing you'll come upon." The instructions, which are three typewritten pages, start off with the names and phone numbers of his lawyer, financial advisor and tax accountant. Each should be told of his death or incapacity as soon as possible, the instructions say, so everything he owns and things like the federal and state estimated taxes they'll have to pay and their mother's testamentary disclaimer trust can be temporarily or permanently transferred to their names. Included in the instructions are the account numbers of his portfolio with his financial advisor, the number of his TIAA-CREF account and the phone number for it, the phone numbers of all the places he pays his bills by automatic bank withdrawals—utilities, phone, secondary health insurance, E-ZPass, AAA and so forth, his Social Security number and the Social Security Administration phone number to call if he dies so it'll stop depositing a monthly check in his bank account. Everything like that. His credit card and checking account numbers and phone numbers there. Even the phone number of the funeral home that cremated their mother and should cremate him. "What to do with the ashes?" he wrote. "Your call. But I'd advise leaving them at the funeral home." Each document and contract in this folder, the instructions say, will be in the appropriate alphabetical sleeve. House deed and home insurance in the "H" sleeve, for instance. Title to the car and auto insurance in the "A" for automobile, sleeve. "You'll figure it out," the instructions say. Contract for the roof put on about ten years ago—"It's a 20-year guarantee"—in the "R" sleeve, new windows put in just a year ago, in the "W" sleeve, and so on. "Don't think of all this as being morbid," he wrote in the instructions. "I don't want you to go through the hassle and stress I did after your grandfather died. He left no instructions what to do with his estate and where his investments were and who was the insurer for his co-op and where the keys were to his safe deposit box at his bank, and dozens of small and big things like that. You know the story. He said all the important papers and contracts and monthly statements and names and phone numbers of the financial people to get in contact with and such after he died were in the top drawer of his dresser. But there was nothing there but boxes of cuff links and tie pins and watches and about 20 white handkerchiefs and the same amount of black socks, and a thorough search of his apartment also turned up nothing. He was a great person," he wrote in the instructions, "and I loved him more than I did my own father, but it took me a year and a half to sort everything out. Your dear mother, his only heir, was unable to help other than for going to the bank with me about once every two weeks to get her signature notarized on one document after another." He also wrote where to find the key to his safe deposit box at his bank, which has a lot of valuable gold coins in it—"Krugerrands, they're called, which your grandfather gave your mother a few of almost every year." Also, that behind the Beckett section in the bookcase in the living room are two small jewelry boxes with their mother's very valuable pearl necklace, which her mentor at Columbia willed to her, and the not-so-valuable, other than its sentimental value, amber bead necklace he gave her as an engagement gift. "In those boxes are also some pins and earrings and earstuds of your mother's, and our gold wedding bands and the much wider gold wedding bands of her parents, all of which—certainly the four wedding bands—ought to be worth something at Smyth Jewelers on York Road, which is where I'd go to sell them," he wrote. "But you two should keep the necklaces and wear them, as your mother did, on special occasions. Or anytime you want, really, and hand them down to your children, if you have any, when they grow up and if they're girls, or your daughters-in-law, if you only have boys, and they marry. The Krugerrands will only get increasingly valuable every year, maybe so much so that you'll be able to send your kids through college for a couple of years after you've cashed in the coins. But do what you want with everything. Don't keep anything just for my sake." At the end of the instructions he mentioned the automatic generator outside and the well in the basement and what companies to call to get both serviced twice a year. "It's important to do that if you want to keep them running smoothly. If you sell the house right away, tell the new owners this."

They'll come into the house, after they leave the hospital, and probably find the kitchen ceiling light on. It was gray and dreary out the morning he got that sharp pain that wouldn't stop and kept getting worse, and he had turned on the light when he first went into the kitchen. Usually he didn't have to.

Therapy

What's he going to tell the therapist? Or "talk about with," or whatever he's supposed to do with a therapist? He's never been to one and he has his first appointment the day after tomorrow. She asked on the phone why does he think, so late in his life, he needs to start therapy? He said the main reason is a very bad one, one he thinks she won't particularly like: his daughters urged him to go to a therapist, and more to please them than for any other reason, he's going to try it. It'll make them feel better. The younger daughter more than the older one, but both. He wants them to feel they have some control over his life—the betterment of it—and that they suggested a good thing. Other reasons are he's become almost anti-social in his self-imposed isolation and reclusiveness the last few years. And he's never gotten over—he's still grieving and suffering—his wife's death nearly four years ago. And he's getting old—or is old—and all the fears and anxieties that go with that. "Okay," she said, "that's enough. I can fit you in. Let's start, if the time and day are good for you, this Friday, 10 a.m. Or the following Friday, same time." "Let's start right away," he said. "And not to get it over with. But why should I wait any longer? I've decided to go, so let's do it." "Okay," she said. "This Friday, 10 a.m. Let me give you directions how to get here. Where do you live?"

Why's he going? he asks himself the next day, Thursday. Day before his first session, or whatever it's called when the therapist and patient meet. He should know. His wife was in therapy before he knew her. And then continued for about twenty of their thirty years together, the last ten years of it or so on the phone because it got too hard on her to get her up the steps in her wheelchair to the psychiatrist's office. She'd call him every other week at a time they arranged at her last session, he'd call back a short time later, and they'd talk for the next fifty minutes, the door to her study closed. He tried to stay away from the door. Didn't want her to think he was snooping. Her voice was always muffled. And then she'd open the door after she hung up the phone. He never asked her what she talked about with her psychiatrist and, before that in New York, with her therapist there, or not much. Maybe: "So how'd it go?" and she'd know what he was referring to and say "Good" or "Pretty good." "I'm not asking what you talked about," he said a couple of times. "Just wanted to know if it went well." And a few times in those years of phone therapy in Baltimore: "I guess I came up because of our little dispute since you last spoke to him and what I said" or "what I did," and she'd say "Yes" or "You did, but not for long. I only get to talk to him twice a month, so I have a lot on my mind." "I'm glad you have someone else to speak to other than me," he said once, and she said "I've a number of people to speak to, but it's important for me to also speak to a professional, someone I pay."

Maybe tomorrow the therapist will start it off by asking him a lot of questions about his life, and later in the session why he thinks it's necessary to do what his daughters want him to, especially if he might not have wanted to start therapy. If she does ask that he'll say he doesn't really know, but he assumes it's to make them happy, just as he thinks his seeing a therapist will eventually make him happier than he is now. They'll talk about his wife, of course. She'll ask questions, he'll give answers. But how much can they get in in fifty minutes? Well, certainly they'll get in that. That he isn't fully recovered—maybe nowhere near so, he'll say—from his wife's death. He means he's still bereaved. Tremendously so. He should have gone to the bereavement counseling the hospice center offered for free for up to a year after his wife died, but he didn't. He was crying enough. He felt he was crying too much. Any thought or mention of her set it off. He still cries sometimes when he thinks of her. He'll probably start crying during the first session because he's thinking and talking about her. Thinks about her many times a day. If he said twenty, thirty, would she believe him? he'd say. Because he's not exaggerating, he might say. And dreams about her almost every night. Even dreams of her half the times when he takes thirty-minute afternoon naps. He started a spiral notebook, which he calls "My Dream Book," of dreams just about her. It doesn't have any dreams in it that don't have her in them. Started it four days after she died. That was the first time he dreamed of her after she died, and he's filled up three dream books and is near the end of the fourth. He's already bought a new spiral notebook. And he doesn't spend an entire page on a dream. Most times he recounts them in a few lines, and then writes the next dream, with the date he's dreamt it, right under it. Has he gone back to read any of them? he might say. Very little, and always a few hours after he wrote them down, and never goes back to them again. In other words, he has a dream, wakes up—he always seems to wake up after a dream—writes it down, and reads what he wrote when he gets out of bed in the morning. So what's he writing them down for, filling up book after book of them, if he's not using them in some way to benefit him personally—some insight about himself he might get from the dream—or in his writing? Maybe for something later, but what he doesn't know. Sometimes he dreams about her two and three times a night and she was once in four different dreams of his in one night. And they're mostly good dreams. He usually feels good after he wakes up from a dream she's been in. But sometimes she's angry at him in a dream or she's started an affair with some much younger guy or she wants a divorce or she just wants to separate from him for a while, and she won't listen to him pleading for her to stay, and when he wakes up from one of these dreams he doesn't feel good. Regrets often come back after one of these bad dreams. Why he did this or that to her. He did mostly good things to her—they were never anything but faithful to each other those thirty years, he wants to point out: he certainly was and he can take her word she was too—but so many times he didn't do such good things. When he got angry at her for spilling something, for instance. Or just dropping a fork or spoon she was holding and he had to pick it up. He remembers saying, he doesn't know how many times, "Oh, not again." And the times he had to clean her up. After she made in her pants, he's saying, or on the floor because he couldn't get her on the toilet fast enough because she didn't tell him in time. And the time he slapped her hand. That was probably the worst thing he ever did to her, physically. She'd knocked over a mug of hot tea on him and it hurt like hell for a few seconds, and he reacted instinctively, he could say, and slapped her, but he only did that once. He's not blaming her. Meaning, for anything she did. Not for her bowel movements on the floor or pissing in her pants and sometimes right after he'd changed her and pissing in the bed lots of times and on the floor. How could he blame her? She was helpless. Or she became such. She had little control over her body functions, is the best way of putting it. He's blaming himself for every single bad thing he did to her. Not only after she became sick but before that when she was healthy. There wasn't any malice in her. She was a person without malice, he's saying. He means that. He's not trying to make her seem better than she was or himself worse than he was. She did nothing to intentionally hurt him. Never. She never said anything harsh or critical of him that he didn't deserve or that wasn't right. He doesn't like to think of it but occasionally he does and the bad dreams also bring it up. So he'll probably have to talk about it with the therapist. It'll come up. He's almost sure it will. How could it not? And if he cries while he's talking about it, that's probably good. No, it is good. It's good to get those things out.

What else? He's cut himself off from most of the people he and his wife were friendly with before. Rarely accepts an invitation for dinner or lunch at a restaurant or someone's home or even just for coffee someplace. Or a movie, on a Sunday afternoon, so it's not just his eyes and the problem of driving at night or that he's afraid of getting stuck in rush-hour traffic. And a couple who were maybe their best friends here has offered numerous times to pick him up for dinner at a restaurant or their house or to go to a movie or play and drive him back. That it's no inconvenience to them, even though he knows most times it's out of their way. But they'd like to do it, they've said, because they'd love to see him more often than they do. Once, he let them drive him to a movie and then wine and tapas after at a place right next to the theater. Did he have a good time? Did it make him feel he should accept more invitations than he does? No. He felt uncomfortable and he was barely intelligible when he had to talk to them, something he can't explain. He gave them excuses the other times. Excuses they and everyone else who invites him out can see through. And some people, after he turned down their lunch or dinner invitations a few times, have called to say they'll be in his neighborhood that day and would like to drop by for a chat, but he always says he's busy with something, so maybe another time. But why? And he knows they just want to see if he's okay. He used to like going to movies and eating out after or having lunch at an informal restaurant with people or having friends over for drinks or coffee or dinner, but all that when his wife was alive. He used to make the dinners, buy a special dessert he thought everyone would like—a fruit torte, a Black Forest cake—and set the table, serve the food, wash and dry the dishes after dinner. He liked doing that. Having friends over also made his wife happy. Sometimes they had two other couples for dinner, but no more than two—he thought that would be a little hard for him to manage without his wife's help. What about this? Maybe he turns these people down for whatever invitations they make to him because he really wasn't that friendly with them. His wife was—she was so much more sociable than he—even after she got sick, but not the last half year of her life or so. But he likes this couple. Likes talking to them most times. They're smart and interesting and very much involved with life. Books, music, theater, art, politics. Lots of things. Music, maybe the subject he likes talking about most. Both the husband and wife are excellent pianists and she also plays the violin and they sometimes performed duets together for their guests and they like most of the same composers he does but can talk about them and their music much more knowledgably than he, of course. Maybe, because he thinks they liked his wife way more than they liked him, they're just saying they want to see him more often than they do because they feel sorry for him. That's the kind of people they are, and sorry for his loss, he means. Or because they think it's something his wife would have wanted them to do or might even have asked them to near the end of her life. Is that another problem? That he thinks that about himself? That people only invited him to dinner and similar events, as this couple still do, out of some obligation? That they might like his writing—this couple say they like it very much; that they eagerly look forward to each of his books; that his oeuvre, as they called it, take up an entire shelf in one of their bookcases and the ones he didn't give them they bought—but don't really enjoy being with him as much as they say they do, or at least alone with him now that his wife is dead. That most people were mainly friendly with him because they liked his wife's company and he was along for the ride, if he can put it that way. He and the therapist will talk about it, he's sure. What he just thought about himself and why he's cut himself off from old friends so much, to the point where almost all of them don't call him anymore. Why would they? he could say. Would he keep inviting someone to dinner or lunch or for coffee who kept refusing him? Or he'll talk and she'll listen and, he supposes, say something every now and then. That's why he'll be going to her, isn't it? He'll find out.

Another thing is that he won't go to New York. It's where he and his wife were born and brought up. They lived together there for years. Kept an apartment there for about twenty years after they moved to Baltimore. Got married in the apartment; conceived both of their kids in it. His daughters live in Brooklyn. He could stay with one of them, but that would mean going to Brooklyn and he wants to go there even less than he wants to go to New York. His sister has an apartment on the East Side, with a spare room he can sleep in. He can stay there and it'd give him an opportunity to be with her for a day or two. He used to love New York. Walking its streets, stopping in someplace for coffee. So much to see and do. Museums. Central Park. So many art movie houses, they used to call them, and a terrific variety of good affordable restaurants. Chinese food like he never gets in Baltimore. He certainly isn't going to drive to New York alone and deal with its crazy drivers and cars cutting him off and the parking and so on and possibly getting stuck in gridlock for he doesn't know how long. But he won't even go in by train. For sure, not the bus, which his daughters like to take between New York and Baltimore. He hates long trips by bus. Feels trapped. And there's the good chance he might have to pee a lot and the bus will probably only have one toilet for sixty or more passengers. He also feels trapped and uncomfortable when he stays just for a night at someone's apartment or house, and that's everywhere, not just New York. He can stay in a hotel in New York, but he doesn't want to do that either. It's not the expense but the possibility of bedbugs, which has become a big problem in New York. Hotels are expensive there but he can afford it for one or two nights. Maybe just one, because he wouldn't want to leave his cat alone longer than that. He knows he can get someone to look in on the cat—a neighbor's kid, who lives right up the same driveway as his—but he doesn't want to take the chance the cat will scoot out the door. The cat might stay out all night. Foxes are around. One caught their previous cat and nearly killed him. Bedbugs, though—that really scares him. That's all he needs is to bring even one back to his home. The therapist might make something out of all or some of that too. He hasn't been to New York in what will soon be two years. Nor has he seen his sister in that time. She's five years older than he and in relatively good health and they get along well together, but she doesn't like to travel out of New York except for a stay in Rome for a month once a year.

So what else? Probably, plenty. He doesn't talk much with people he knows. Lets others do most of the talking. He used to be funny, sprinkle his conversation with amusing or interesting anecdotes, but he doesn't anymore. Or else he relies solely on the anecdotes to be his part of the conversation—"That reminds me," he usually says—ones he's told many times before, so they now come out sounding a bit too well-rehearsed, but he's mostly silent with people he knows: listening, smiling, laughing, nodding or shaking his head, pretending to be interested, but really bored and not saying much. What happened? He doesn't know. His wife's death changed him, that's for sure, because all this started after she died.

Also, he doesn't want to go away for even a week in the summer. They used to go to Maine with the kids for two months. They loved it there. And it got them out of the heat and humidity for most of that time. Now he's anxious about driving long distances alone. It's a twelve-hour drive and he doesn't want to stay overnight in a motel on the way. It used to be fun with his wife, and relaxing—not having to make the bed or cook dinner that night. A simple breakfast, but actually much more than he usually had, the motel would have prepared for its guests the next morning. Maybe one or both his daughters would drive to Maine with him this summer and stay a week or two in the cottage he'd rent for a month. Wouldn't seem worth the trouble to drive to New York to pick them up—drive to Brooklyn, in fact—making the trip even longer if he didn't stay the night with one of them, and who'd drive back with him? Maybe one could drive to Maine with him and stay a week or two, if she could get off work that long, although, to be honest, she might not want to spend her entire vacation time with him or in Maine, and the other would come the last week or two, if she could get off work that long and same thing about wanting to spend her entire vacation time with him and in Maine, and drive back with him. But there would still be the same problem. He'd have to pick one of them up in Brooklyn when they leave for Maine and drop the other one off when they return. And he'd want to have both with him in Maine at the same time. They always have a better time together that way. His daughters can talk to each other, when he's not talking much, and borrow his car and go someplace, when he wants to stay in the cottage and write. It's a dilemma. He doesn't see right now any way to work it out. And would he want to be alone in Maine for even two weeks, if that's what it'd end up being if his daughters came up with him or left with him but could only stay two weeks? Alone, that is, other than for the cat. He has friends in the same area he and his wife always rented a house in in Maine.

People he liked seeing a few times each summer, when he used to go with his wife and kids for two months. Maybe it's not something a therapist could help him out with or would listen to him talk about with much sympathy or interest. He should be thankful, she might think, he can be in Maine for so long, even if alone, during what is typically such a hot month at home. Or maybe therapists don't think or act like that and always come up with something to say. His daughters would know. They're familiar with therapy. For him, it's all new territory. He should ask them.

Anything else? His neurodegenerative disease, of course, which he thinks he showed small signs of his wife's last two years but was first diagnosed for it a year after she died. His doctor said he'll never be cured of the disease but he won't die of it. He got it so late in his life that it'll never get that bad. His father died of it forty years ago, but the doctor said medications and treatments for it have vastly improved since then. Still, he's scared. Sometimes his right hand shakes. Some days he feels weaker than he does other days. He never stumbles but he has lost his balance a number of times during the same period his hand shakes and he feels weaker than usual. When he tries to run, he runs clumsily. That never improves. Short jerky strides; nothing like he used to do, and he can only run a quarter of a mile at the most before he has to stop. He wouldn't even call it running anymore. It's closer to something like speed-walking, but a little more than that. So he sometimes thinks he's getting worse. Is this something to bring up to the therapist? His fear? But the doctor said he's showing fewer signs of the disease than he did in his last checkup a half year before. "It might be that I'll only need to see you once a year," the doctor said. He's also afraid he'll get sick again with the bowel obstruction he had two years ago and he had to be operated on twice in three days to turn a section of the small intestine around. He thinks that's what the surgeon did. One operation to straighten out the kink in the small intestine and the second operation to see if the first one worked. Something like that. Almost every time he's just a bit constipated or he has even a slight stomachache, he worries the obstruction has come back. He doesn't want to go back to the hospital and be operated on again. And maybe twice in three days again, the second to see if the first operation worked. He doesn't understand. They couldn't have done that with x-rays? Did he ask? He forgets. He felt he almost died in the hospital. His regular physician said he could have with what he had. And the pain before he was operated on the first time was about as bad for twelve hours as he ever had in his life, but the pain after the operations was for a while even worse. They gave him pain medication that made him crazy for almost an entire day. He hallucinated, heard voices, thought he was in hell, that he was being punished for things he did in the past but wasn't told what they were. A woman in a lab coat stopped in front of his room and held up to the window a clipboard and pointed to a long list on it without looking at him. He yelled for her to help him, or thought he did, but she quickly left. He kept yelling for someone to help him, screamed sometimes or thought he did, but nobody came to his room. His door was wide open and he heard people walking past or standing outside it, talking about obscure things—space shuttles, metallurgy, a 16th century pope—all of it in a language he understood only a few words of. It sounded more like a combination of several languages of different origins plus pig Latin. He also pressed the call button a lot, or thought he did. Nobody came into his room or asked on the intercom, as they usually did, "Yes? What is it?" Then he remembered he had a cell phone and put on his glasses and found it and called one of his daughters—this he knows he did—for them to come and take him home right away or else he's going to escape from the hospital, in his hospital gown if he has to, and make it home on his own. It was around two in the morning. They were at his house, a five-minute drive away. They'd come down for the operations. They called the hospital and he was moved to a room much closer to the nurses' station so someone could look in on him more often. The voices he'd heard turned out to be that of hospital workers on the floor, standing and chatting in front of the employees' lounge across the hallway from his room before they went inside it or after they came out of it. So how come one of them didn't check to see what was the matter when he was yelling for help, if the yelling wasn't part of his hallucinations? He's also worried he'll get very sick at home. Something he can't take care of himself. A minor stroke or a major one, or something equally as bad, and no one would be there to help him and he couldn't reach the phone or didn't have the energy to even dial 911. He'd die in his bed or on the floor. Who'd look after the cat in the time before they found him? He's serious. For how would anyone know he was dying or dead? After awhile his daughters, when he didn't answer the phone or call them back for a long time—a day, two, maybe even longer—would call a friend of his in the neighborhood who they know has a key to his house, just as he has one to his, and he'd find him, maybe alive, maybe dead. He worries about all of that. Also what it'd do to his daughters if he died that way. Aren't most of these good reasons to go to a therapist and talk about? Probably. He'd think so. He doesn't know.

One thing he doesn't need to go to a therapist for is his work. He's never had a writer's block for more than two days or three, if you could call that a block, and it only seems to happen after he's finished something he's been working on a long time and is having trouble starting a new work. But he knows something always comes, so it's never really a problem. It was more of a problem for the first ten years of his writing, which means up till about forty years ago, when he didn't know something would always come. He writes every day, always gets something done. Page a day, most times; 300 pages a year, on average, enough for a book if he was writing a short one. That publishers, for the most part—major publishers and the prestigious small ones—aren't interested in his work, also doesn't bother him. Or bother him enough to stop him from writing for even a single day or slow him down. He still has a good time writing. Finds it interesting, what he writes: the contents and different styles and so on. He likes what he's doing—always has—is what he's saying, or maybe repeating. Likes what he writes. Though maybe, because he feels so good about his work, that that's something that should be talked about with the therapist. Why? Is that a problem? He has a high opinion of his work, maybe higher than it deserves, and a fairly low opinion of the fiction of just about every living writer he's read except for a couple in Latin America and one in Europe and maybe a few from some other places, or one or two of their books, but he doesn't say so about any of that either. He never says anything good about his work to anyone, or never beyond saying something like "Maybe I did okay with that one," and rarely badmouths another writer's work, at least a living writer. But maybe he should say to the therapist what he thinks about his own work. "To be honest," he could say, "since I think that's what's expected of me in therapy—absolute honesty," he doesn't think his work is getting, or has gotten, the attention and honors it deserves. No, don't start something that might hurt his writing. That, above everything else, he wants to avoid. Skip the honors and big-time publishing. They really don't mean much to him. They once might have—thirty years ago, maybe; thirty years ago, definitely—but not now. It's enough for him just to continue writing and like what he's writing and getting published, no matter how small and little known the publishing house. The money that comes with major publishing and honors would be nice to get, but not worth getting bitter and upset over and have that affect his writing. Talking about it won't help his writing—it doesn't need help, he feels—so what would be the reason to discuss it? So some things he might have to hide from the therapist. Things he knows would hurt his writing if he brought them up, or at least not talk about them till the time comes to. What does he mean by that? He doesn't know or isn't sure. It's obvious he's confused by the whole thing—conflicted is a word that's often used in therapy—that he remembers his mother-in-law, a psychotherapist, using a lot—which also might be worth talking about eventually, his conflict over this. One thing he knows is he always feels lousy about himself after he thinks too highly of his writing. So maybe he could talk about that, why he feels that way, or something close to it. But there he goes again. Of mixed minds about it. He should probably only talk about things with the therapist that he's sure he wants to talk about.

And he has enough dough. Money isn't one of his problems. He inherited a little when his mother died and his wife inherited even more than that when her parents died, and he also has income from his pension, Social Security and investments. He's invested wisely, he could say, or chosen the right financial advisor. And he does make, on the whole, a couple of thousand a year off his writing. It's not as if nothing comes from all the writing he does and has done. So he has enough money to live modestly on for the rest of his life, he thinks it's safe to say, and also to give to his daughters from time to time to help them out. He even tells them to use his credit card, the one they share but he pays the bills for, to take a cab anytime they want to when the weather's bad or it's late at night or just dark out. For things like that, and medicines, doctors, dentists, even yoga. Really, anything they don't have the money for or that would cut too much into their budgets but they think is important. He thinks he can afford it. If he talked about that to the therapist, which he doesn't see any reason to—it would just be looking for praise from her, if therapists give praise to their patients—he'd say he's been generous to his daughters, but it's the only right and fair thing to be. Not just because he wants them to be healthy and safe, which would be reason enough, but because around half of his money came from their mother, so in a way it's theirs.

So he has enough things to talk about to the therapist, or to tell her, whatever the way it's said. More than enough for two or three sessions, he'd think. He's ready for tomorrow, though he worries that he doesn't need a therapist. That he can work out all the problems he might have on his own. He also does a lot of it in his writing. But he wants to make his daughters happy by his seeing a therapist. Not a good-enough reason to go to one, he supposes, if it were the only reason—he knows it isn't, or maybe he's wrong about that. But he can go to one at least once or twice, can't he? If it doesn't work out, if he doesn't think it's going anywhere, is useful and so on, after four to five sessions, maybe, because he has to give it some time—he'll say so to his daughters and the therapist and stop going. He doesn't want to waste the therapist's time, he'll also say. Though they might use that excuse as another reason why he should start therapy, or continue it: that he worries he might be wasting the therapist's time. Oh, just go. His daughters have already said they're proud of him for calling one of the three therapists they got from the *Psychology Today* online listing for his part of Baltimore County. When he told his sister on the phone what his daughters said about his agreeing to go to a therapist, she said "Isn't that why we do everything—to please our children?" "Not for me, it isn't," he said, "or not everything, though part of what you say is true. Yes, I want to make them happy. 'Proud of me' I don't care about." "You don't?" and he said "All right, maybe a little. I certainly don't want them to think bad of me, but by my not going to a therapist, I don't think they would." "Can you repeat that in simple language? What you said is too complicated to understand, or the way you said it is. For the therapist, you'll also have to speak more clearly. Though if you don't, though I don't know why you wouldn't, she'll see something more in it than I just did."

So he's ready, as he said. It won't be a big bust. Doesn't work, as he said, then it doesn't. At least he tried and it made his daughters happy. But something will come of it, or should. His older daughter said "I bet you'll also get a story out of it." "Now that, for sure," he said, "would be the last reason I'd start therapy. That's not how I operate. If I were to write a therapy story, and I seriously doubt I ever will, I'd use my imagination and what I know from other people who were in therapy or practiced it—group, individual, marathon, if that's still done; all of it. Your mother and her mother, for instance, and my sister, and that might be enough. If I need more, then former women friends. It seemed every one of them was in some form of therapy when I was seeing them or living with them. I never questioned anybody about their therapy, but I'm sure some stuff filtered in. Though who can say? I hardly ever know what I'm next going to write. But I certainly won't tell the therapist what you said." "Why not?" she said. "In therapy, you don't have to hold anything back." "I know. We've discussed it. Or I did with your sister. But I wouldn't want the therapist to think she was in any way being used. Her time was. You know what I mean. Anyway, too many therapy stories and novels have been written and none of them, that I read, were any good. And mine wouldn't say anything new. Like stories and novels about academia, I don't think one can be written about it. They're both too weak as subject matter to make good material for fiction. That's what I think. I'm sorry." "You're probably right. Good luck. Call me to tell me how your first session went. I hope you like it, and the therapist." "I'm sure, because you and your sister chose her and the two other names out of what must have been a long list of possible therapists for me, she's got to be good. At least for what I might need, because of her work, as you said she said in her brief bio, with artists and writers and academics and bereavement and trauma and such. Or as right as a therapist can be. After all, writer and teacher, that's me." "Another thing, while we're on it, is that you should stop saying things so much just to please us. Or work on that with the therapist, too." "Right. I'll bring it up. I didn't mean to irk or irritate you in any way by it." "Believe me, I didn't take it that way. I know you mean well. So you're definitely going? No pulling out at the last minute? Though that's all up to you." "Definitely going. I won't call it off. At least for two to three sessions. Then we'll see. I also have to see if Medicare kicks in. And if it doesn't, then my supplementary medical insurance. If neither does, then I don't know if I'd continue. Though I'd hate to have money stop me. But let's go one step at a time."

Intermezzo

've written about this before. But maybe I missed something. I don't think I did. Though maybe something small but important. Right now I can't think what that could be. Anyway, I love remembering the incident. And that's all it is, an incident, but one of my favorites with her. It was all in about five minutes. Six, seven, but short. I'd gone to her apartment building on Riverside Drive. Walked the forty blocks or so from my apartment on West 75th Street. This of course was New York. We'd been seeing each other almost every day for a few months. I said hello to the doorman in the lobby. The elevator was waiting for me, door open, and I got in and pressed the button for the seventh floor. As I rode up I took my key ring out with the key to her apartment on it, which she gave me a month after we met. I got off on her floor. Right after I got off, or maybe a second or two after the elevator stopped but before the door opened, I heard her playing the piano in her apartment. There were two apartments in the small hallway the elevator and stairway were on, one to the left of the elevator as you got off it and Abby's to the right, so I immediately knew where the music was coming from. Also, I'd never heard music of any sort from her neighbors' apartment, neither recorded nor being played by one of them on an instrument, and remember remarking about this to Abby. Arguments from that apartment—sometimes hysterical screaming from both the husband and wife—we'd heard plenty of times, mostly through the walls separating the two apartments but sometimes while we were waiting for the elevator to come. "Let's walk," I said

once. "It'll be embarrassing if they open the door and see us standing here." Once, we even heard the woman say "You despicable
filthy bastard. I feel like killing you, and one day I might." And the
man say "You kill me? Not before I kill you first," which made no
sense, but it was said with such venom that it didn't have to. We had
nothing to do with her neighbors except, whenever we saw them
alone or together, to say hello. As for Abby, I'd heard her playing or
practicing one piece or another before but never this piece and I'd
never heard her playing while I was still outside her door. Later, I
asked her what it was. "A Brahms' *Intermezzo*," she said. "So there's
more than one?" And she said "Three, all opus one-nineteen. This
one's in B Minor." Or she said "This one's in E Minor." Those are the
first two. The third one's in major, though I don't know what letter.
I know the one she said I heard was in minor, but I forget if it was
the B or E.

I didn't use the door key to get into her apartment. I'd put the
key ring back in my pants pocket while I was listening to her play.
Then she opened the door for me. Big smile, happy to see me, and
we kissed and hugged before we closed the door. I asked and she
told me what she'd been playing—"I've just begun to learn it, so
I'm not very good at it yet and probably never will be"—and what
key and opus it was. She opened the door for me because I rang
the bell. I rang it after she stopped playing—maybe a minute after,
because I thought if she was going to play more of that piece, if
there was more to it, or something else, then I wanted to hear it for
a while outside her door. It'd disturb her playing, I thought, and
probably stop her if I was inside the apartment listening to her play.
But why'd I ring her bell instead of using the key? Good question.
I hadn't asked myself that before. It meant, for one thing, that if
she was still sitting at the piano, she'd have to get up to open the
door. She might not want to, I thought, at that particular moment.

She might be resting a minute or so before resuming the piece she was playing or playing through it again or starting a new piece. So I'm really not sure why I rang. No, I don't know. The reason seems to be lost or, I'll say, escapes me. So think back. Maybe the reason will come back in my remembering the incident the second time around. Or third time. The first was when I wrote about it a few years ago.

I walked to her building from my building. It's about a two-and-a-half-mile walk. I don't remember if it was pleasant out. I do know I didn't show up in her apartment wet and cold. Certainly not wet. We wouldn't have hugged so quickly. I would have taken off my jacket or coat and cap. I went into her lobby, took the elevator to her floor. The elevator was definitely waiting for me when I walked into her building. Was its door open? If it was there on the ground floor, the door was almost always open. Whether I said hello to the doorman, I'm now not so sure. If he was there, I said hello. If he was taking a short break in the restroom in back of what we called the building's office on the ground floor, which might have been what the building's staff called it too, then of course I didn't. I would have gone straight into the elevator, pressed the button for the seventh floor, and gone up. I first heard her playing the piano that day either while I was still in the rising elevator but close to her floor or just after the elevator opened on her floor and I got off. I know there was no one in the elevator with me. I'd say most times there was, and usually more than one person. The building was seventeen stories tall. Or sixteen stories and two penthouses, or roof apartments tenants in the building called them, which were reached by getting off the elevator on the sixteenth floor—that was as far as the elevator went—and walking up a flight of stairs. And, from the second to sixteenth floor, there were four apartments to each floor—the other two and their separate hallway and stairway you got to by going through a door to the right of the elevator. So I'm saying there were lots of people using that elevator in the front of the building—the one facing the entrance and its revolving door—and that I seldom rode up in it, it seemed, without another tenant or two or a deliveryman or visitor riding with me. There were two other elevators—one for the apartments in the middle of the building and the other for the apartments in the rear. But that has nothing to do with what I'm trying to get at with this except, maybe, to show how large the building was. Nah, knowing that doesn't help anything. Why was I so sure it was Abby playing the piano in her apartment? Because who else could it be? I thought. She was taking lessons at the time—every Thursday afternoon after she finished teaching a Humanities course at Columbia—but took them in her piano teacher's cramped studio apartment in the West Eighties. "She has two Steinway Grands," she said, "which she gets tuned twice a year. Both are five times the piano my Acrosonic is, and playing the one she reserves for her students makes me feel I'm a much better pianist than I am." Her piano teacher was who suggested she learn the Brahms *Intermezzo* and she eventually became a good friend of Abby's and played at our wedding in Abby's apartment three years later: the first prelude and fugue of The Well-Tempered Clavier.

So I got off the elevator, had my key ring out probably from the time I got into the elevator and pressed the button for the seventh floor or maybe even before I went into the building and walked up to its revolving door, ready to stick the key into her door lock, when I thought Wait. Don't go in yet. Listen to her play. This is a special moment. The music's beautiful and she plays it so delicately. Stay out here for as long as the music lasts. I'd never heard her play this way, meaning with me on the other side of the door. I put the key ring back into my pants pocket. Or maybe I didn't till the playing stopped and I decided to go inside. I'll explain that in a moment. While I listened to her play I said to myself, How lucky can you get? Having a woman you love who loves you and who can play such beautiful music so beautifully? Something like that. Then I just stopped thinking, I could almost say. Just listened. Listened without thinking, I could almost say. The beautiful playing. The beautiful woman who was playing. That she loves me. That I love her. That she'll be happy to see me when I finally open the door and go inside. Then I'm going to tell her I stood outside her door for however long it was and was mesmerized, enchanted, rapt—some word or words, but not one of those—by the music and her playing. So, actually lots of thoughts. But mostly, I just listened. Then her playing stopped. The piece seemed over. As I think I said, I don't think I ever heard that piece before. Not just her playing it—that I know I'd never heard—but also the piece itself. I've heard it many times since. On the radio, and a recording of it and other Brahms' piano pieces I bought a short time later. Rudolf Serkin. And, after the first time I listened to her play it from the hallway outside her door, she played it a couple of times while I was in the apartment and also a couple of times or more in the house we bought in Baltimore fifteen years later, after we had the piano moved there from our apartment in New York. I'm sure she also played it a number of times in the apartment when she was still learning it and I wasn't around. Then, I don't know why—I'm saying, after she finished playing it that first time and I waited to see if she was going to play it again or start something else—instead of using the door key she gave me, I rang the bell. Would I have stood behind the door listening to her play the piece again or something else? I'm not sure, but I think I would have, at least for a minute or two. Some movement appeared in the peephole a few seconds later and she opened the door. She was smiling, glad to see me as I thought she'd be, said "Hiya, Sweetie," and held out her arms. We hugged and kissed. I told her I was outside her front door listening to her play for about ten minutes. "You played the piece so beautifully. I've said it before: you have a special light touch. But I never before heard you play a piece so beautifully and ethereally as you did." "Oh, I don't play well," she said. "And I was only practicing." "What are you talking about? You play exceptionally well. I was completely taken in by your playing. If you had started something else, and maybe even if you had played the same piece again and I was still in the hallway, I would have stayed out there and listened to that too. What's the name of the one you played? I want to get a recording of it. Or maybe I won't and I'll reserve the experience of hearing it for when you play it." "Get it if you want. It might be good to hear the difference of a real professional playing it and me. Brahms, an *Intermezzo*, opus one-nineteen, in—" and she gave the key it's in. "But you're only saying all this because of how you feel towards me, which is very nice; you'll not hear me complaining. But you don't have to, you know. I've no illusions about my playing." "My feelings for you, sure," I said, "though that's not why I'm saying it. Believe me, I was truly entranced. The music, your playing, my being the only person listening: everything was just right." "Oh, come on. Like some tea? I was just about to make myself some. And I bought chocolate lace cookies at Mondel's this morning, and you like them, so let's have cookies and tea." "All right," I said. And that was it. I've done this once before. I love remembering it. Those wonderful ten minutes or so. And then, of course, ringing the bell and her opening the door with a smile, because she'd looked through the peephole and saw it was me, and putting her arms out for me and me going into them and our hugging and kissing. One hug, one kiss. And then the cookies and tea and her asking, while we sat at the table, how come I rang the doorbell instead of using the key—"Did you lose it?" I said "I don't know why I rang the bell. Maybe I just didn't want to break the mood or something, and opening the door on my own might have startled you or been like barging into your apartment. Not that ringing the bell wouldn't also jar things. So I really don't know. It seemed the right thing to do at the time, and I was rewarded with your beautiful smile and outstretched arms and a kiss. Anyway, I don't think music has ever had such an effect on me before. No, I really can't think of anytime that it did. It didn't make me cry but it sure made me feel good, and I still feel good. I feel great."

The Dream and
the Photograph

He puts down the newspaper, brings the glass he's been drinking out of into the kitchen and washes it and puts it upside down in the dishrack. He makes sure the door's locked and turns off the kitchen light. He's about to go to bed. It's a little past nine, around the time he almost always goes to bed, but he needs a book to read there. He finished a book this afternoon while he was having lunch and doesn't know what he wants to read next. He sees Sebald's *The Rings of Saturn* lying flat, cover up, on a bookshelf in the living room. He read it about ten years ago, remembers liking it. He's liked all Sebald's novels, *Austerlitz* the most, but that one he loaned to someone, he forgets whom, and never got it back. So maybe he'd like reading *Saturn* again, something he doesn't do that much—reread a book—or just start it in bed and if he doesn't think he'll want to read any more of it, put it back on the shelf or in the bookcase with the other Sebald books tomorrow and look for another book to read. Or he can drive to his favorite bookshop in Baltimore, only a few miles from his house, and look for a book there. He's done that a number of times at this shop, scanned the titles on the fiction shelves starting at "A" and a couple of times at "Z" till he found a book he wanted to read or at least start.

He opens the Sebald book to read the first page or two and a photograph drops out of it to the floor. "Damn," he says, "what the fuck's going on?" because so many things he grabs or even touches these days fall to the floor, forcing him to bend down and sometimes to get on one knee to pick up. He bends down and picks it up. The back of it says "6/07." So it was taken in June, six years ago to the month. The photograph has several people in it, all facing the camera. He, Abby, two of his colleagues at school, one standing beside his wife, his arm around her waist. Also the two administrative assistants of his department at the time, and three women he doesn't recognize. They must work in the Rare Books and Special Collections unit of the school's library, because that's the room the photograph was taken in. The occasion was the first day of an exhibit, timed to coincide with his retirement from teaching at the school after twenty-six years, of his original typescripts and first editions of most of his books and photographs of him doing several things related to his writing—sitting at his typewriter at home, reading to a small audience at his favorite bookshop in Baltimore, dressed in a tux at an awards ceremony in New York when he was a finalist for a prestigious literary prize, Abby standing next to him, holding on to her walker, and so on. The exhibit was up for two months. Sometime later, he forgets where he bumped into her, he asked the librarian (she must be one of the three women he doesn't recognize in the photo) in charge of the exhibit and collecting his finished typescripts and working manuscripts and letters and such—even the unrepairable manual typewriter he must have written a dozen of his books on and which was also behind a display case in the exhibit—how many people came to it. "The usual," she said, "or maybe a bit less, as it was summer and few students and faculty were around. Nine or ten? Maybe five more who didn't sign in or were in the room for other reasons but stopped to look." In the photograph Abby's in her wheelchair and he's behind her, hands tightly gripping the handles of the chair, which he always did when he stood behind it, afraid it'd roll away. She looks as if she's trying to smile but can't quite get it out. That doesn't sound right. She was forcing herself to smile. Didn't want to spoil the photograph—everyone else in it smiling as if they meant it—by looking how she really felt. That doesn't get it either. So what is it? Photograph was taken a year and a half before she died of pneumonia. She was very sick the previous year, twice almost died of pneumonia. She was still weak when the photograph was taken. Who took it? Probably someone else who worked in Special Collections, or a professional photographer hired by the library so it could publicize the event in its newsletter and on its web page. She hadn't had the tracheotomy done on her yet—that was a half year later. He knows she never would have consented to be photographed with the inner cannula, was it?—the trach tube, or just "trach"—sticking out of her neck. She doesn't look that weak, though. Her face is full and there's some color in her cheeks. Her hair is unkempt. Maybe it was hot and humid that day—Baltimore can get like that in June—so the sticky weather could have done that to her hair—it had plenty of times before—and they might not have had the time or any place to brush it once they got to the library, and brushing her hair was something he usually did for her by then. He puts the photograph back in the book, makes sure the porch door is locked, shuts off the living room light, and brings the book with him to his bedroom. Doesn't read much of it. Two pages; less. Keeps pulling the photograph out and looking at it. Why does she look the way she does in the photograph—sad, really; dejected? Because she's in a wheelchair and everyone else is standing. Because she's sick and weak and they're all healthy and strong. Because she had to be pushed there in the wheelchair—by this time, she couldn't even move it a few feet on her own—while everyone else in the photograph is able to walk and run and so on. In other words: they get around on their own while she's dependent on other people. Because she'll probably be dead in a year or two, the way she's going, and half the people in the photograph will probably be going to her funeral or memorial or whatever they'll go to for her. Because she probably needs to go to the toilet, or will soon—it's been more than two hours since she last went—and she'll have to be wheeled there and lifted on and off the toilet seat and have her pad changed. He doesn't remember doing any of that, but he probably did and all of it so she wouldn't wet herself on their way home, or if she did, she'd have a dry pad on. Because she could already be wet and is uncomfortable and doesn't want to say anything in front of all these people or she just doesn't want to pull him away from this room right now. Because she didn't want to come to the exhibit but did because he urged her to. It won't be the same if she's not there, he told her. "They're making it into such a big deal," he said, or something like it, "that there's going to be a photographer there and I want you to be in the photos with me." Because sometimes she just wants to die and she has a look that gives the impression that's what she's thinking and maybe some of the other things. "I hate being photographed," she might be saying to herself while the photographer's photographing the entire group. "I look so awful and sick and weak and ugly and my hair's a mess, while before I got sick I was pretty and had an attractive figure because I wasn't squashed into a wheelchair most of the day and I always took care of my hair myself." He puts the book on the night table, places the photograph on it, and turns off the light.

He has a dream a few hours later. Had two or three dreams, without waking up from them, before he had this one, but this is the only one he remembers. He turns on the night table light, gets out of bed and goes to the bathroom, pees, sits on the bed, his feet on the floor, and gets the notebook he's been writing his dreams in the last four years off the night table and starts to write. "7/2/13. Dream of Abby in the hospital. She's sitting on the bed, not in it, her feet almost reaching the floor. She looks good: healthy, pretty;

she seems happy. Her face is rosy, her hair's brushed back into a ponytail. She looks to be around 40. It's her last day in the hospital. Tomorrow she's coming home. We have a son, who seems to be around 3 years old. He's blond, as Abby was when I first met her, and also blond like Randolph, the son of the woman I lived with in California from '65 to '68. I was the boy's surrogate father for 3 years. Randolph, 2½ when I moved into his mother's house, even called me 'Daddy.' I say to Abby 'I have to go.' She says 'You're leaving me with a hysterical child?' The boy's been screaming on and off for the last minute. We ask him 'What is it? What's wrong, little guy?' but he continues to scream, his eyes squeezed closed. I say to Abby over the boy's screams 'You're all right now. You can take care of him. But I'm already late for my appointment.' 'Take him with you then,' and I say 'You know I can't,' and I leave the room. The boy follows me, still screaming hysterically. 'My son,' I think. 'My poor son. Then I think 'What about this tactic? Maybe it'll work, because nothing else has.' I say to him 'You like tomatoes, don't you?' He stops screaming long enough to nod. 'Well, if I give you a few cherry tomatoes, will you stay with your mother and not make a big fuss anymore?' He nods again and this time doesn't resume screaming. I empty a few cherry tomatoes out of a bag into his hand. He eats one, smiles, and eats another. He seems fine now. 'Here, have some more,' I say. 'You deserve it. You're a great kid. I always thought that.' I go back into Abby's room. She's still sitting off the bed. I say 'I got him to stop screaming. I can leave him with you now, can't I? He won't scream again.' She says 'You can. But how'd you do it?' 'All it took were tomatoes,' I say. 'Cherry tomatoes. Not the big beefsteak kind. He seems to like the cherry ones best. Here, want some? Why not take the whole bag?' and I give her it. 'No, thanks,' she says, giving it back. 'You've done enough for me.' I kiss her, say 'See you later,' and leave the room. 'Damn,' I say.

'I should have kissed the boy too. But he won't mind that I didn't. And given him the bag of tomatoes. There weren't that many left, and what am I going to do with them?' I walk to the elevator. Elevator comes and the doors open. Nobody's inside it. 'See,' I say, as the doors close. 'When you use your brains, you get things done. Don't you feel good now? But really feel good at helping her out rather than deserting her? I do, I really do. This is how I should act from now on. Helpful. Quick-thinking. Imaginative. If only I could,'" and the dream ended.

He turns off the light and lies back in bed. Room's dark. He forgot to look at his watch, but it must be around midnight. Of course he could get the watch off the night table and press the light button on it to see the time, or even turn the table lamp back on, but why bother? It's around midnight. He's almost sure it's around midnight. He got to sleep around nine, as he usually does, and he's almost always able to sleep for about three hours before he has to get up to pee. Then he sleeps, usually, another three hours, and he always falls back to sleep easily, before he has to get up again to pee. Then another three hours, and this time it usually takes him a bit longer to get back to sleep, before he gets up around six to pee, and stays up. Makes the bed, washes up, and so on. New day; all that. That's his almost unvarying routine for sleep at night, but anyway, is there a connection between the photograph and his dream? That he wanted to leave Abby, in the sense of splitting up with her—ending their marriage—though in real life he never did or ever even thought of it, though in sort of metaphorical life, if he can put it that way, she left him, her body did…anyway, by dying. No, none of that works, or if it does, it was by accident. The boy, though—after all, he was his son in the dream, so connected to him—could be the hysterical person he was sometimes when things became overwhelming for him. Too overwhelming. The tasks, he's saying; the obligations. Things he had to do and which nobody could do for him. Or which nobody but him could do for her, is what he's saying. That's the way he sometimes felt then. He would always apologize to her for his momentary hysteria. Or hysteria that lasted a minute or two and once or twice a few minutes more. Throwing a lamp against a wall. He once did that. In front of the kids and her. Glass from the two shattered light bulbs all over the place and the lamp- shade destroyed. She always accepted his apology, and sometimes said he should apologize to the kids too, which he did, though not without her saying almost every time after the first few—it's true; he acted that way a lot the last ten years or so of her life—that he's al- ways immediately apologizing for his awful behavior, and she once called it "despicable" and another time "absolutely loony." "But all right," she said a couple of times, "and I mean this. Maybe it's good in some way that you get out your hysteria, which is mostly your anger at me for getting sick and being a drain on you, we both know that. At least it's quick." And that she looked so healthy in the dream and was coming home the next day? Why wasn't it that she was coming home that day? She seemed ready. Rosy, healthy, sitting off the bed, swinging her legs. Well, it's never explained, and it was a dream. What he would have wanted, of course, in or out of the dream. Her healthy and home, if not that day then the next, but sooner the better. So another dream of wishful thinking? What else could it be of? And that he came up with a way to stop their son's hysteria? That he used his brains for practical purposes, as he said, and not just for his writing, and was effective? He made Abby happy by doing it. The last few years of her life he did everything he could to make her happy. Made her smile and sometimes laugh with his remarks and jokes and just made her feel good, or a bit better about herself. That true? That's true. In the dream she definitely felt good that he'd helped her out. Left her with an unhysterical son. He forgot to write in the dream notebook that at the end of the dream, when he went back into her hospital room with their son, he—the boy—screamed "Mommy," and ran up to her and hugged with both arms one of her swinging legs—the right, not that it makes any difference which one—and kept his arms around it, hugging tight, her leg against his cheek, wouldn't let go even when she tried to pry his arms loose, and this made her point to what their son was doing and smile. But again, what to make of it? Well, she was happy. That's always a nice thing to see in his dreams. But here, happy because of what reason? She was over her pneumonia, for one thing, or whatever she came into the hospital for, and very soon was going home. Happy with her family too, probably. Happy that she could smile and laugh and sit off the bed and swing her legs. And if he was the boy in a way, as he said before, then he didn't want to let go and stop hugging her and everything that could mean. Who can say? Also again, where was he going when he left the room? He said he was late, but for what? Said he had to go as if there was nothing that could stop him except her suddenly becoming very sick again, showing the same signs of pneumonia she showed when she got it all those times. Disorientation, barely recognizing him, talking jibberish—external signs. The first time he saw them all at once he had no clue what they meant or what was causing them. So: probably home to write. Can't think of anything else he'd leave her for. He frequently got frustrated, but would never show it to her, when he couldn't find any time to write while she was in the hospital. And her stays there lasted two to three weeks, and with rehabilitation after, sometimes a month and a half. He spent his entire day with her and was too rushed in the morning to write before he left for the hospital and too tired when he got home at night. Got there at eight when visiting hours started. Helped her with her breakfast, once she was eating real food again and not being fed through tubes. Kept her company all day. Read to her and listened to music with her and watched a movie or PBS program with her, or part of one, on the television in her room, and didn't leave the hospital till visiting hours were over at eight that night. So now he's almost sure he was leaving her in his dream to write at home. That's what he vaguely remembers thinking in the dream. And as he said, or thinks he did—said to himself—he'd be back later for several hours. And at the end of the visiting hours he'd take their son home with him and the next morning he and the boy would come to the hospital to take her home. Or he'd leave the boy with someone the next morning and take her home alone and then get their son. Anyway, though he forgets what it was but thinks he touched on it, there was a connection between the dream and photograph, right? It's been so long since he thought of it, but seems so.

Two Parts

L et's see, how do I start this? With my father or with Lotte? My father. It's already formed more in my head, so it'll be easier getting into. I told Abby I'd been thinking about something the last two days and I'd like to talk to her about it and see what she thinks. "Sure, go ahead," she said. "First help me turn off the computer." "Why do you need help?" and she said "I don't. Not yet, anyway. I don't know why I said it." She played with the mouse for a few seconds and the computer screen went dark. "Okay," she said. "I'm ready." "It's something to do when I was around ten," I said. "I don't think younger. That would make my father around fifty-one. I must have said something to him that made him mad. Nobody else seemed to be in the apartment. It must have been a Sunday or federal holiday or important Jewish holiday, because my father was always at work every day but Sunday and those holidays. I don't think he was ever sick once and didn't go to work. In his whole life, until he got very sick... I've told you, struggled to get to work and made it every day, till he couldn't anymore and was forced to retire. Wheelchair. Operations. Complications. Everything very quick. Am I being unclear here? I'm not telling it in the right order and I'm mixing up things," and she said "You're fine." "What I'm saying, with so many kids in the family and my mother and the woman who helped her five days a week and whom we had for years—the housekeeper—not around, I don't know where everybody else could have been. And he never hit me with his hand, when he was really angry with me over something. Not once that I can remember. Just a rolled-up newspaper. And always the *New York Times*, when it was still only two sections, so both sections, because it was thicker and long—I think that's why—than the *Daily News* and *Mirror*, which we also got—and ran after me with it. Maybe I hadn't done something he wanted and expected me to without giving him any lip. Like walk the dog or take the garbage out or clear the kitchen table of dirty dishes. Or that I was snappy or sarcastic or that I even cursed. Cursing would have done it. So he came after me with the tightly rolled-up newspaper, holding it over his head like a stick. It was a large apartment—you know it—and I darted under his swing. And I might have, though this I don't think I would have done, but I just might have been stupid enough to at the time, laughed impudently or challengingly or something at his feeble swing and ran back the way I had come, as if I hoped he'd take another swing at me so I could duck under it again. No, I doubt that. But he kept chasing me, once around the long dining table, as if it were a joke, but from one end of the downstairs to the other, probably saying 'You rotten kid. You stinking rotten kid.' Which is what he used to say—I think the only one in the family he used to say it to—when he was very mad at me. 'Now you're really going to get it from me, but even worse.' Then he stopped. It seemed he had to lean one hand against the kitchen counter in order to stand, and dropped the newspaper bat on the floor and sat down at the kitchen table—and I remember this, really—all out of breath. Also, I remember him saying 'You little bastard.' Remember it because he never before cursed at me using a real curse word. I laughed, or did or said something that made him look at me as if he were looking straight through me or had never seen anybody who looked so stupid, and then just stared out the kitchen window, though there was nothing to see out there but another building's brick wall up close. I think I then said 'You okay?' Or something that showed I wasn't the insolent kid anymore. He said 'Shut up. Mind your business. Go to hell, for all I care. I'm through with you.' 'Through chasing me?' I said. He didn't answer and I just looked at him from about ten feet away. I thought it might be a trick of his, to get me to lower my defenses, as they say, and then grab me and maybe hit me good, and not with a newspaper this time, which when he had hit me with it, it never hurt. I guess that was the point. But he didn't. He eventually looked at the floor, saw the newspaper there and said 'Pick up the newspaper and put the pages back in order. Do that for me at least. I haven't finished reading it yet.' I said 'You're not going to grab me when I do it?' and he said 'No, that's over with. I'm never chasing you again. You're not worth it. I could get a stroke. Why do I have such a brat as a son?' Then he shut his eyes and just seemed to be resting. 'Can I go out after I fix your newspaper?' I said. 'Because it means I'll have to walk past you,' and he said 'You know where I said you could go. Go there. That's my advice.' I picked up the newspaper, reassembled it in order and very neatly folded it in half and put it on the kitchen table and walked past him. Cautiously. But it really seemed like it wasn't a trick of his to grab me anymore. I don't think he even looked at me when I went past him. I think I did think he was so mad at me that he wouldn't talk or even look at me again for a long time. When I got to the foyer, I yelled back 'I'm going out, Dad. You want anything before I go?' He didn't say anything. 'You still mad at me?' I said. Nothing. He kept his eyes closed. Maybe his hand holding up his head. I think that's what I saw. And his chest seemed to be heaving. Maybe I didn't see that; I just think I did. I knew he didn't look well. I left the house—that's what we called the apartment—probably to play with my friends on the street or in the park, or to see if any of them were out there. Later, when everyone was home and I was in the boys' room, we called it, where Robert and I slept and did our homework—everything—I was called down to dinner by my sister, Margie. I asked her something like 'Is Dad still mad at me?' She said 'Why, what'd you do? Because he didn't say anything, doesn't look mad. They just said for me to get you, or Mom did.' I went downstairs and sat down at my place at the table. My father looked at me—quickly, I think—and looked away. He didn't seem angry anymore. But I felt ashamed. I wanted to apologize—not in front of everybody, but later—but something stopped me or I just didn't know how to. I should have let him hit me with the newspaper when he wanted to. It wouldn't have hurt and that would have been the end of it. He would have gotten it out and I would have gotten my whacks. After that, I could never quite get the image out of my head of my father not looking well for the first time and because of me. Looking sick, really, as if he were having a heart attack or stroke. But I never apologized for it. And he never brought it up after or, I think, ever chased me again. No, he wouldn't have, and I think he never threatened me again. But for years—you know, it'd come every now and then—I wanted to tell him how sorry I was that I laughed or was sarcastic to him that time he swung at me and missed. And that I also wouldn't do at first what he asked me to, whatever it was, and it couldn't have been much. The truth is, they never expected much from me—or done it as fast as he wanted me to, if that was it. I don't know why I didn't, even ten to twenty years later, when it would have been harmless, if it was still on my mind so much. To say something—started it off with 'You probably don't remember this and God knows why it's so important to me and keeps coming back, but a long time ago, when I was still an obnoxious pipsqueak...' and so on. Probably I thought he'd definitely forgotten about it—why would he remember it?—and what good would it do going over it if we couldn't get a laugh from it, and I don't think he would. But that's enough. Enough, enough. I've exhausted you with my little story, right? But what do you think?" She said "What do I think? It would have been good for you if you could have apologized at the time, or soon after, but you didn't. All right. And you were a bit bratty—that's obvious from what you said—but you turned out okay. It also would have been nice if your father could see you today. Married, children, making a good living teaching, and having time to do what you want: writing. But he can't. So forget it. Why keep punishing yourself over it? I'm glad to hear, although you may have told me it before and I forget, that your father never hit you with his hands, or any of his kids, true?" "Far as I know. Certainly not me. And I was the brattiest of us all, so if anyone deserved it, I did." "Rubbish," she said. "Nobody deserves it. Not even with a rolled-up newspaper. Because I don't have to tell you that kids who get hit by their parents more than likely, et cetera, et cetera, with their kids. You never have," and she looked at me. "Just that one time with Freya you know about, when she was two and a half, or a little more. And she got out of the Veblen Cottage on her own and walked up the driveway to the Naskeag road where cars and these huge lobsterman vans were zipping past. And, just before I caught up with her, she was about to walk out onto it, or I thought she was, so I slapped her hand so she'd know—" "I know. But never any other time, I'm sure, either of them." "Never. That was it. One slap. Admittedly, a hard one. I had to. So she'd remember never to do it again. Was I wrong?" "I don't know," she said. "You probably could have made your point another way." "Yeah. But I still feel bad about my father. Humiliating him. Taunting him, you could say. And up till that time I never saw him look so weak and sick. He never looked weak or sick. I'm repeating myself, I know. I'm always repeating myself. And that I didn't understand at the time I was taunting him and trying to humiliate him. Or maybe I did understand. I could have been that bad. Ah, I'm confused. But as you said about it—this business with my father—nothing I can do about it now." "That's what happens," she said. "You have to face it. But you done?" "Yes," I said. She touched the mouse and the computer came back on. "You never had anything in your life like that with your father," I said. "Never," she said. "You were a much better child than I," I said. "And your father, a much better father than mine. Though your mother was great, too. I don't mean to leave her out. I envy the relationship you had with them. Well, there was only one of you. But even if there had been six kids in your family, I can't imagine your father ever so much as raising his hand to you or, if you had them, your siblings, and they were all bratty boys. And your mother never would have let him. She would have given him hell if he hit anyone. While my mother, I'm afraid—I don't know why she did. Probably thought, better someone else, since it sometimes has to be done, because she wasn't going to physically punish us. I should one day explore it. But gave my father and that housekeeper—Herta—license to hit us, Herta with her hands, my father kept to the rolled up New York Times—whenever they thought we deserved it, by not saying anything to stop them beforehand or to reprove them after. But go back to your work. I'm sorry for bothering you with this, and to take so long." "Don't be. I like it when you tell me things like that when you were a boy. Anytime. When you talk about your life. You don't tell me enough of them," and she tapped her lips and I bent down to kiss them.

And then the dream I had, two days ago? Two days ago. In it, Abby said "You should apologize to Lotte Zeeotta." "Haven't I already?" I said. She said "Only to me. Not to her directly, and it's long overdue." Just then, Lotte appeared and I said "Lotte. Good to see you, and you couldn't have come at a better time. I want to tell you how sorry I am for the rotten way I treated you over the years. Using you. Please forgive me." Lotte said "It was terrible for me too, though as a victim rather than as a doer, but I have to confess there was a little fun in there too. You were my first man." "It didn't seem like it," I said. "I went in so easily." "My first man-man. I did it with lots of little boys before you. But I'm glad we finally got it out in the open, cleared a roomful of foul air. I was a fool and you were a rat." The dream ended there. I woke up and thought about the only time I spoke to Abby about Lotte, or I think it was the only time. It was about four years before she died. She was in her study, sitting at her computer, and I said "You told me once that you like it and I don't do enough of it, when I go more deeply than usual into my life before I met you. So can I interrupt you for a few minutes, while it's on my mind? Or we can put it off till another time, to tell you something that's very much like the story I told you about not apologizing to my father for something I did to him and the affect it still continues to have on me today?" "I don't remember that," she said. "When was it?" "When I told you? A while back. It's not important to go over it again, at least not now. It was of a situation that was never resolved. This one—this reaccounting, you could say, or, no, I don't think that's a word, so just something I'm telling you about— is also about apologizing. Something, it seems, I'm always doing, or doing a lot. I suppose I think I have a lot in my life to apologize for. Sometimes I feel one hasn't grown up entirely until he's corrected or apologized for all his mistakes in the past. And look at me. I'm almost seventy. Anyway: Lotte Zeeotta. I never told you about her." "Long lost love?" "Just the opposite," I said, "or close to it. Long-time sex object. I met her in Nantucket. She was eighteen, maybe even seventeen, but looked older, and acted older too. Very smart, mature. And I was…thirty-six from sixty-one? Twenty-five. So big age difference at the time. I think she was just starting college, or taking a year off before she started. Fashion design. That's what she wanted to do. I remember she designed all her own clothes, including the bathing suit she wore. Sewed them too. I'd hitched from Truro, Nova Scotia, to Woods Hole and taken the ferry out to the island. It also stopped at Martha's Vineyard. I rented a cheap room in someone's house for a few days and went to the beach to get a suntan, which I regret now, what with my precancerous scalp lesions. She was with some little kids—she was their au pair for the summer. A dull job, she said. She was tall, pretty, solidly built, had shoulders like an Olympic swimmer, and I looked at her and she looked at me and we had lots of these looks, before I moved my towel closer to their blanket and struck up a conversation with the kids and then her. I also remember bringing to the beach a Faulkner novel I'd bought with another book right after I got off the ferry— *The Town* or *The Mansion* or the third one of that series with a title like that. *The* something. Not one of his best. I left it, mostly unread, in my room when I left the island. We made a date for that night to get an ice cream at a famous ice cream shop in town. Famous, for Nantucket. Then we went to the house I was staying at—she rode her bike and I jogged alongside her. If I'm rambling too much, cut me off. Just that everything's coming back while I'm telling you this." "No," she said. "I like the details. You don't do enough of it in your own work. So?" "So, we made love. I also had a painful sunburn from the beach that day. Was applying calamine lotion for days on my body. We saw each other for a couple of hours every night and then I had to leave for New York. Not for a job. I was out of one. The radio news show I was the editor of had gone off the air the month before and I was running out of money. My last day, she came to the ferry with me. Was very sad; I wasn't. She gave me, as a going-away present, a photograph she bought in a local art gallery of a fishing boat leaving Nantucket in the morning mist. I didn't like it. It was strictly for tourists and in my head I questioned why she'd ever think I'd want to have it. I think I dumped it soon after I got home. It was very nice of her, though—it must have cost her a few bucks and she made very little from her job—and I gave her nothing as a parting gift. But I now see, almost fifty years later—I haven't thought of that photo since then—the symbolic significance of it, which was pretty clever of her." "How so?" she said. "My leaving Nantucket. The single boat. Morning mist. Tears, which she probably knew she'd have when we said goodbye. Maybe I'm wrong and she didn't see that in the photo. I waved to her from the ferry and she stood there on the wharf waving back. I didn't think I'd ever see or speak to her again, though she gave me her phone number and address. 'Write,' she said. 'Call.' How could I? She was so young and she lived in a small college town in Massachusetts—both her parents were English professors there—and I really didn't want to see her again. New Hampshire, that's where she was from. But I'd had my fun and so did she, was the way I looked at it. Callous; awful; I know." "Did you give her your phone number and address?" "I probably did—she probably asked me for them—but she never called or wrote, and I was glad she didn't." "So that was it?" she said. "No. Now comes the worst part. I bumped into her about two years later. She was coming out of a movie theater and I was going in. She'd moved to New York and was taking courses at F.I.T. and working for a fashion magazine. She was happy to see me. I was, too, with her. She gave me her phone number and I called and continued to call whenever I wanted to have sex and nobody else was around—sometimes when I was a bit loaded but always when I was very horny. She'd take a cab—I always ended up calling her late in the evening—and I'd meet her in front of my building and pay the fare. Every time. I'd stand outside and pay the fare." "The least you could do," she said. "Of course. That's not what I'm saying. She had to call a cab service. She couldn't go out and hail a cab, as her neighborhood wasn't safe at night. I never went up there because the truth is it was much easier for her to come to my apartment—easier for me—and I was afraid of getting mugged. So we'd make love, maybe have some wine or beer before, and she'd leave in the morning, sometimes very early—six, six-thirty—so she could get home and do what she needed to do before going to school or work. This went on, I'd say, for about three years. About ten times a year. No, that sounds like too much. She wouldn't have put up with that. So probably much less. I'd call, she'd come. I think that was the only relationship I had like that. Was I beginning, after a while, to feel lousy about it? A little. But it didn't stop me. My penis came first. Then I lived in California for a few years. Or Paris first and then California, when I got that writing fellowship there, and I lost contact with her. I don't even think I told her I was leaving New York. But I must have, though I'm sure she didn't care. Sometimes when I got to New York during this time, to see my folks, I'd look up her name in the Manhattan phone book and she was still listed at the same address on West a Hundred Thirty-eighth Street. I didn't call her, mainly, I think, because I didn't have to. I was only in the city for a week or two and I was living with one woman and then another in California for most of my four years there. Then, when you and I were in the city a few weeks ago—so this brings us to today—just out of curiosity, and remember, it's been almost forty years since I last saw her, I looked up her name in the phone book, not thinking she'd be there or listed anywhere in Manhattan under her old name. But she was. Same phone number, same address. That's all. I didn't call her, of course. So I'm saying, I really feel lousy at how I used her. Just seeing her for sex whenever I felt like it. She even—and this is good, what she should have done more of—chewed me out for it a couple of times. 'You only call me when you want to fuck.' That's what she said. The first woman to ever use that word for what we were doing. You never have." "I suppose I haven't," she said. And I told her 'That's not true. I like seeing you.' Then she would say 'Do we ever go out for dinner? Lunch? For a coffee? Even to a movie, where you don't have to talk to me?' 'We'll go out now for coffee,' I said the first time she told me this. 'Breakfast, even. I'll treat you to breakfast.' What a schmuck I was. Anyway, she said no, invite her when it's my idea and not because of something she said that might have made me feel guilty. I remember saying I didn't feel guilty. So would she like to go down the block with me and have breakfast? We were in my apartment. One of the few times she hadn't left early, though I was probably hoping she would. She said 'Maybe the next time if there's a next time,' or along those lines, but she had to get home, or had to be somewhere, and she angrily got her stuff together and left. We never went out to any place together. I don't think we even walked a single city block together. That I accompanied her to the subway, for instance. Did you know I could be such a louse? That I've kept this story from you for so long probably means I didn't want you to know how bad I could be." "So," she said, "what are you saying with all this? You want to call her at this phone number you found and apologize after all these years? Is that what you're getting at?" 'Something like that," I said. "Or maybe just write an apology and send it to her." "Not a good idea," she said. "You'd be crazy to. Let it go. She won't want to read or hear it. It'll only make her recall all the times you phoned her to have sex and she whizzed over to your place and accommodated you that way for years, and in turn make her feel disgusted with herself all over again. For it's possible it's been twenty to thirty years since she last thought of you and what she allowed herself to do, and in that time had worked it out with a therapist with other things that had troubled her about herself. So don't. It's absolutely the wrong thing to do." So I didn't call or write her though might have if Abby hadn't felt so strongly about it. It felt like a real warning she was giving me, and maybe about her relationship to me too. That I…well, she'd really have serious questions about it and my common sense and self-restraint and such if I called. Then, two years after Abby died, so six years after we had this conversation, when I was in New York to see my daughters and sister, I looked up Lotte's name in the phonebook. I figured if she was in the book six years ago, there was a good chance she was in the book today. And she was. Same everything. I thought: Just call. If you're not going to do it now, you're never going to do it, and you want to do it. And not to apologize right away. Maybe not to apologize at all. But just to talk to her—to say it's Phil Seidel, from way back, and I'd like to see her, if it's possible and she can find the time. Have lunch somewhere and talk about our lives since we last saw each other so many years ago. That I was surprised to still find her name in the phone book but was glad I did. There was no other way I could have contacted her. So many things have happened in these more than forty years since we spoke, I'd say. And I'm sure the same for her. For me: marriage, two daughters, long sickness and death of my wife, which I still haven't recovered from and probably never will. It's beginning to feel like that. Teaching at the university level for twenty-seven years and now retired, living in the Baltimore area for even longer than that, though for most of that time we kept my wife's apartment in New York. Books and stuff. Or maybe nothing about my writing unless she asks, though when I knew her I only had one story published. And so on. But what about her? I'd say. Did she stay in the fashion business, and so on. I wouldn't ask if she got married or had children. It'd come out if she had. I dialed and a woman answered. "Hi," I said, "is this Lotte?" "No," the woman said, "but you dialed the right number. I'm her daughter. Who is this, please?" "An old friend of your mother. Is she around?" "My mother died three years ago." "Oh, I'm so sorry to hear that. Oh, gosh. What a nice woman. And we go so far back. When she was a student at F.I.T. and also working for a woman's magazine. She was in her young twenties and I wasn't even thirty. I even knew her when she was in her late teens. We met in 1961. Nantucket. In the summer. August, I remember. She was working for some family I never met, looking after their little kids. We haven't spoken to each other since 1968. Maybe earlier. So I thought of her today. Thought of her a lot over the years and, just a hunch, I was in the city and looked her up in the phone book. Not expecting to find her at the same address or even listed at another address under her old name. A habit I have, looking up old acquaintances and friends, or at least their names in the phone book after many years." "I kept her name in the directory when I inherited the apartment after she died. Too lazy to change it, I guess. But I also thought, she had the apartment for so long, first alone and then with my father, and then me—" "And your father?" I said. "He was out of the picture almost from the beginning. I moved in with her last year to help take care of her, and then just stayed." "That's very nice what you did. Not many children would do that." "I think most would," she said. "Especially if they had a mother like mine. It gave me as much pleasure as it did her. Possibly more." "Very nice. Very nice. As I said, your mother and I were just friends. Nothing more. We'd meet for lunch or din-ner— Am I disturbing you with these reminiscences? I should have asked you that first." "It's fine," she said. "And interesting. Please go on." "And for a while, despite the age difference, maybe even very good friends. We'd see each other for lunch and sometimes dinner and talk for hours. Movies, too, and a couple of times a play, which we'd discuss after. She was extremely perceptive and smart. I'm sorry she's gone. Sorry I lost contact with her. But I was out of the country for a long time and then moved back to the States but not to New York and, you know, got married, kids, always job elsewhere. We just lost contact." "All that's understandable. What's your name, sir? Maybe she mentioned you." "Don Wilson." "Nope, I don't remember her ever talking about you. Though it's a pretty common name, 'Don Wilson,' so I might have got it mixed up with others like it." "Also," I said, "by the time you were born, probably, Lotte and I had been out of touch for years, and then she had her whole other life. And, when it comes down to it, I doubt I was that much of a figure in her life, for the most part. Just to talk to on and off for about six years, though maybe a deeper camaraderie for one or two years. But I don't want to give the impression we saw each other that much. It was sporadic. But I better go. It's been nice talking to you, and again, I'm very sorry for your loss. And your name?" "I didn't tell you? Sybil." "Same last name as Lotte's in the phonebook, or do you have your father's, or even a married name?" "It's not important, my last name," she said. "Good speaking to you, Don. Or Donald. Mr. Wilson." "Same here," I said, and she hung up.

That First Time

How did they wind up in bed that first time? The date started off with dinner at a Middle Eastern restaurant in her neighborhood. They had arranged to meet there. She got there first and waited for him inside. It was on the west side of Broadway, between 114th and 115th Streets or 113th and 114th. The food was inexpensive. The restaurant didn't serve any wine or beer but you could bring in your own. She stayed at their table and he went to a liquor store a block or two away—she told him where it was—and bought a bottle of red wine and a cheap corkscrew in case the restaurant didn't have or couldn't find one. It was a good bottle of wine, better than he ever bought for himself. He wanted to impress her. He knew from their previous date, which was their second—the first was for coffee and a cup of soup each and an egg salad sandwich between them for lunch at a coffee shop—that she knew about wine. She once worked for a week harvesting grapes in the Champagne district in France and got paid with three bottles of very good wine and a bottle of champagne and room and board. He forgets what they ate in the Middle Eastern restaurant. Falafel—that he remembers—as an appetizer, and some dolma, also to start off with, but what about the main dishes? Important? Well, he'd like to get everything in, or as much as he can, but he'll let it pass. He walked her back to her apartment building. She asked if he'd like to come up. "Sure," he said, "that would be nice," or something like it. Did she say "for a nightcap?" No, that was at the end of their second date, after they had dinner at a Greek restaurant in her neighborhood. "I warned you the food might not be the best," she said, when he walked her back to her building that time. "So we'll cross it off our list?" he said, or something like it. "Although you did say it got new owners since you last ate there, so it might have improved." They had Spanish brandy that second time in her apartment and he asked if he could sit next to her on the couch, which was really a daybed. After she said "Any place you feel comfortable," and after he sat beside her, he made a move to her and she moved her head to his, and they kissed for the first time. They kissed a couple more times that second time and then she said it was getting late, or something like it, or she still had schoolwork to do tonight—he thinks that was it—and he said "I'll go," and they went to the front hallway closet. He said he had a great time tonight, "I hope you enjoyed it too," and she said "I did. Thank you for a nice evening," and got his coat out of the closet and handed it to him. His muffler was in one of the arm sleeves—where he always put it at someone else's house, so he wouldn't forget it—and his gloves and watch cap were in the coat's pockets. He put the muffler and coat on and said "So I'll call you," and she said "Please do," and he made a move to her—his back was to the front door, hers to the closed closet—and she moved her head toward his and they kissed, the longest and deepest of their four to five kisses that night. "Whew," she said after. "That one, honestly, took my breath away." He left the apartment and she shut the door. He thought, as he waited for the elevator, "That was quite a kiss. All of them were. She's really something."

But that third night. They had met at a party two weeks before. They were introduced by the woman who gave the party. She took him by the hand, walked him over to her and said "Abigail, I want you to meet Phil. He's also a writer, but not an academic. Now you two are on your own," and she left. They talked for a while, about what she wrote and taught, about what he wrote. He said, when she told him she had to leave in a few minutes—a ballet at Lincoln Center she had a ticket for—"Can I call you? May I, I mean?" "If you like," she said, and gave him her phone number and her last name. The first date was the coffee shop in the West Seventies—between 77th and 78th Streets, to be exact, on the west side of Broadway. The second was the Greek restaurant. She gave him the address for that one and the location—between Amsterdam and Broadway, south side of the street. She got there first, as she did at the coffee shop and Middle Eastern restaurant, although he got to all three places with a few minutes to spare. Falafel, dolma, wine he went out to get—"I didn't know they didn't have a liquor license," she said. "I've only had lunch here; stuffed pitas and Turkish coffee." He said "It's fine; it'll take me a minute. But I can't think of eating dinner without wine." How'd they pay for the lunch and dinners? She let him pick up the check at the coffee shop. Said something like "It's so small, I won't fight it." They split the check at the Greek restaurant, although he'd wanted to pick that one up too. "I'm on a very generous post-doc for two years," she said, "so don't think I can't afford it." She said she thought they should leave more of a tip than he put down. "Anything you say," he said. "One thing I'm not is cheap. And I've been a waiter—the last time just a year and a half ago—so I should make twenty percent of the bill, less the tax, standard procedure. Oh, even with the tax. What's it going to add to the tip, another five to six percent?" In the Middle Eastern restaurant he thinks he said—and he'd like to remember what main dishes they had there, but he'll give up on that—"This dinner's definitely on me." "But you paid for the wine," she said, "and it seemed like an expensive bottle. I have to contribute something to the check," and he said "Please. The wine wasn't so much, and I want to." "Then the next time it has to be on me." "Good," he said, "for that means there'll be a next time, or I hope it does." "I didn't mean it like that, but I guess it came out that way. We'll see."

So they were in her apartment on their third date. After he hung up his coat, with his muffler, gloves and cap in it—she'd hung it up the first time he was there—she said "Care for a little brandy again? Same bottle as the last time. Actually, it's cognac." "Even better. But only if you're having one," and she said "I'm not. I've had more than enough to drink tonight. But you have one without me," and he said "All right. You broke my arm. It's very good cognac," or something like that, and sat on the couch. She was standing a few feet from it. Was he being too obvious, sitting where he was? he thought. He didn't think so. There were only two places to sit in this part of the room, the couch and armchair. All the other chairs in the room were hard wooden ones around the dining table. He thought if he sat on the couch there'd be a good chance she'd sit there too when she did sit down. He just didn't see her sitting in the chair. He didn't want to first sit in the chair and have to ask again if she'd mind if he moved to the couch. She came back from the kitchen with the glass of cognac and handed it to him and sat on the couch. He didn't have to point to it or say something like "Why don't you sit here?" He wanted to start kissing her again. After a little talk and maybe holding and rubbing her hand. And from there, while they were kissing, get his hand on her back under her shirt and then around to the front and, after feeling her breasts through her bra, or just one of her breasts, get his hand on her breasts under the bra and then try to take the bra off by unhitching the hooks in back. But what was it that got them into bed about a half-hour after they sat down on the couch? Once they were in bed there was no chance, of course, they wouldn't make love. Did he say something to get them there? Did he say—somehow he thinks he did and then again he thinks he didn't—after they'd kissed a number of times and he had his hand under her shirt in back and was inching it around to her breast—her left breast, because she was sitting on his right—he thinks he got that right—"Shouldn't we just go to bed?" or "To your bedroom?" or "Would you like to make love? I mean, more than what we're doing?" Or "Why don't we…?" "Why don't we" what? Or did she say—he seems to remember this too—while he was trying to unhook the bra straps in back—"Why don't we go to the bedroom and continue there?" He's not sure about the "and continue there." But that she said the rest—"Why don't we go to the bedroom?"—seems to be—he's almost positive now it was—what got them there. Wait. Didn't she say, after one of their long kisses on the couch that time and she pulled his hand off her bra or breast or away from her back, "By the way"—he seems to recall this, or is he imagining it? No, this is what she said, after they came up for air from a kiss and she continued to hold his hand she'd pulled away— "By the way, I appreciated your not trying to push me into bed the last time you were here. I wasn't ready. Besides, I still had work to do that night and also had to get up early the next morning to prepare for my class later that day." "I knew it wasn't the right thing to do," he said, "so I didn't. I thought, if it happens, it happens, though I wouldn't mind, and I'm certainly not going to try to push you, if it happened now." And did she say "You wouldn't mind?" and look at him as if he'd said something funny or peculiar? She did, and he quickly followed it up with something like "What I mean is I'd like very much for it to happen now. But if you don't want it to, that's okay with me too." That's about when she said "Then let's go to the bedroom," and maybe "and continue it there." She stood up, let go of his hand and went into the bedroom and he followed her, his first time there. He thinks he said, after looking around, "So this is where you work," or said it as a question, and she said "Ah, you noticed. My sloppy desk, the academic books, my typewriter in dire need of a cleaning." "You looking for a typewriter repair place?" and she said "Yes, you know of one? My regular one went out of business, just as the one before that one did," and he said "I'll write down its name for you later. They do both of mine, and they're good and not expensive and they love manual typewriters." That's almost word for word what they said then. He knows; they brought it up a few times over the years. The funny incongruous things they said that first time before they went to bed. She sat on the bed and he sat next to her on her right and moved to her and she to him and they kissed. While they were kissing he put his left hand under her shirt and unclasped her bra and pulled it loose in front and with the same hand felt her right breast under the bra, but maybe he's getting the right and left business mixed up—not important, though he definitely remembers sitting to her right—and she said "Let me get ready; wash up before we get too involved in this," and did something she only did that one time with him, touch his nose with her forefinger as a parting gesture, and went to the bathroom. It was a few feet on the left down the short hallway between the bedroom and living-dining room, directly opposite the linen closet. She came out about ten minutes later, barefoot and in a bathrobe. It was pink, fluffy, given to her by her parents as a birthday gift years before he met her, in the end lots of terrycloth strings hanging off of it, especially from the sleeve cuffs, but she didn't want to get rid of it or for several years wear the new terrycloth robe he got her for her birthday. "It's so comfortable. I've grown so used to it. It's like my old cats. I'll wear yours one day," and she did, about five years later. He sat on the bed all the time she was in the bathroom. When she came out she said "Aren't you going to undress? You haven't even removed your shoes. Change of mind? Too late, you know." "I'm sorry," he said. "I was waiting for you to come out so I could go in," or something like it, just as what she said was something like it, and really, just about everything he's said and will say they said was something like it. She sat down next to him and he took off his shoes and socks and put the socks in the shoes and then the shoes under the bed on the side they were sitting on. He did this every night with his shoes or sneakers if he was still wearing them when he was undressing for bed at her place. If he didn't put them on again the next morning and switched, let's say, to the sneakers, if he had put the shoes with the socks in them under the bed the previous night, then the next morning he put them in the bedroom closet. And the socks? He sometimes wore them two days in a row, especially in their earlier days when he still had his own apartment and hadn't moved into hers. He turned to her and she was smiling and he moved his head toward hers and she kept hers where it was—he's almost sure about this—and they kissed. "Now undress," she said. "Shoes aren't enough. It's getting cold, sitting here in just a robe. I want to get under the covers with you." He probably said something like "Me too, with you," and he undressed and folded up his clothes and put them on a chair and said "All right, here?" "Anyplace," she said. She was under the covers by now—bathrobe on the floor, and the color of the robe was peach, not pink, same color of the terrycloth robe her parents gave him for one of his birthdays and which, though frayed and full of holes, he still uses—looking for a moment at his erection. He went into the bathroom, said "Excuse me" first; "some things to do." She said "If you want to brush your teeth, and I'm not saying you have to, although it's always a desirable thing to do, use my toothbrush. Only one there, in the holder. Toothpaste's in the medicine cabinet. It's okay with me. If we can kiss, we can use the same toothbrush this once." "Thanks. I will," and he went into the bathroom. He doesn't remember brushing his teeth. He had to have, though. He must have peed and then wiped the head of his penis with a towel there or tissue or a piece of toilet paper and then flushed the toilet, probably washed his hands and face too, and come out. Only one bedlamp was on, on her side, the right, the side they hadn't been sitting on, and he got under the covers and they kissed and felt each other and made love. He thinks that's how it went. Light on or off? He forgets. But he thinks the rest of it is how it happened. Third date, Middle Eastern food, cognac, kissing, her looking with no discernible expression at his erection for a couple of seconds, toothbrush, washing up, and so on. Maybe more of it will come back to him some other time. But he's thought of it a number of times over the years. Ran it through his head. Talked about it with her. "Were you lying on the right side of the bed? Were we sitting on the left? Did we make love with the light on or off? What main courses did we have for dinner that night? And it was a Middle Eastern restaurant, yes?" "Yes," she said, "but the rest I forget." "Did we make love only once that night?" She didn't remember. "How could I remember?" she said. "Once. Twice. Is there a difference? If it was twice, I was probably half asleep by then." "And the next morning. Did we do it again?" She can't help him with that, she said. "But where are you going with all this? If you're using it for something you're writing, please disguise me. Make me tall and a brunette with dark eyes and long slim legs. And don't have him marry her. Don't have them have two girls. And have her have a dog rather than two cats. Though if it has to be cats, don't make them Siamese." "Don't worry," he said. "That's not my plan." So why is it so important to get as close as he can to what actually happened? Really, just something simple, and hasn't he already said? His first time with her. And just about everything in his life changed after that, or he could say it was never the same, whatever that means. No, it's true. He can say that, or just about. And it's been almost thirty-five years. December will be thirty-five, four months from now. Sometime in December. He doesn't know the exact date. Wishes he did. Has tried several times to narrow it down to it, but never could. Asked her, but all she could say was "It was a weekend day, close to Christmas. But not after Christmas, because then I'd be on winter break, and I know I had classes the following week." He was with her for thirty years and a few days. One breakup early on that lasted a month or so, but she always said it was three. He hasn't made love with any other woman since that first time with her. And hadn't made love with another woman for two to three months before he met her. Hasn't even kissed another woman since their second date a week before their third. He means, where the kiss meant anything. Just cheek kisses. Brief lip kisses hello and goodbye. Nothing more. She was the last with the big ones. Did she get on top of him—the position he liked most—that first time? And if they did do it twice that night, did she only get on top of him the second time, a position he doesn't remember her ever complaining about, except for the two or three times she fell off, though he doesn't think it was her favorite. He doesn't know which was. Never asked, and she never said. Maybe them all, at one time or another: front, side, she on top, he from behind. No, that one she found a little difficult and not as exciting, she said a few times, but she usually let him. Or did he get on top of her, whether they did it once or twice that night, and only do it that way? Probably only him on her. Did they make love any other way but the most conventional one that time? After a bit of foreplay by both of them, he sticks it in? He thinks that's all they did. Felt each other's bodies with their hands, lots of deep kisses, and then he got on top and put it in, maybe with her help because it was the first time. But their mouths only kissed, nothing else. He thinks, mostly because he likes doing it so much and having it done to him, he might have started sliding down the front of her body, maybe reached the navel—that's what he pictures—when she put her hands under his arms and made a motion to tug him back up. It was too soon for her to let him make love to her that way and then maybe think she has to make love to him the same way, he seems to re-member her saying that night or the next morning or a day or two after that, when he again stayed overnight at her place. Did they make love the next morning after that first night? They could have. It was a free day for both of them and he doesn't see them just get-ting out of bed without doing something. Maybe they only started to—kissing, touching—and then stopped. Or maybe only he started to—it'd be like him—and she told him to stop. But not important. To him, for what he's getting at, only that first time is—that first time that first night. He wishes he'd kept a journal, but he never has. Little memo books in his back pants pockets were as close as he ever got to having one. And nothing much in them but addresses and people's names and phone numbers and words to look up and changes and brief additions to whatever fiction he was writing at the time and that came to him while he was out walking or jogging or gardening or raking leaves. And also one-sentence ideas for fu-ture possible stories, few of which he used. She left behind numer-ous journals—maybe fifteen of them; maybe twenty—filled loose-leaf and spiral notebooks and composition books, going all the way back to her first year in college. Though the first journal started the last week of high school and a little bit what she did that summer: sleepaway camp, as a counselor; a romance, though no sex, "and not because I didn't want it," with a much older counselor who was also the director of all the camp's plays, but her father made her break it off. But there were gaps in her journals, and one of the longer ones was the last two months of '78 and the first few of '79, which takes in the period he's been thinking about. Since he never looked at her journals till after she died—maybe a month after and spent three straight months reading nothing else but them—he hadn't known, but always thought there'd be, things in them—de-tails; her feelings about him when they began dating and especially that first time. But as he said—did he say it? He thinks he did—there'll be other times to think of it and maybe more will come back. For now, he's satisfied at what he's got.

Haven't a Clue

"I don't think I can make it through another day," I say. "What are you talking about?" she says. "You have to. For one good reason, think of the kids." "But it's the same old thing. Day after day. Hour after hour. I go to bed so early. Why? Because by that time I have nothing to do. I've done everything. So I read in bed awhile, which means maybe fifteen minutes, if I'm lucky, and fall asleep and wake up too early. One, three, five. The o'clocks. More like eleven, one, three, five. Two-hour intervals, usually. My damn prostate. If it isn't that, it's my lower back. Mostly the right side. It keeps me up. Can't find a comfortable position to sleep in. Maybe I need a new mattress, but I'm too lazy to go out and buy one. Listen, I'm feeling old. My gripes are just about every old guy's gripes." "Do the best you can. I wish I could help you." "Your being here would help. But I wonder how much so. Oh, a lot. What am I talking about? But also my work. That's another thing. I'm getting less inclined...how can I put it? I always like what I'm working on—oh, most of the time, and very much so. Otherwise, I wouldn't do it, right?—or I'd do much less of it. I think that's so. It's the work I don't like. By that I mean, the same thing every day. Sitting down and typing, typing, and more typing. Make a mistake, start at the top of the page again. I don't like finishing a piece—oh, finishing it is fine, but the anxiety of now not having something to work on and take up my time, and just having to photocopy each piece after it's done. To get in my car and drive several miles to the nearest photocopy place to copy it. Seems ridiculous, the effort for so small a thing, no matter how long it is, and it takes so much time." "Learn how to work on a computer. Get a copier to go with it, so also learn how to use the copier. Finish a piece, copy it out; you wouldn't have to leave the house. Though every now and then, since it runs out fast, you would have to go to a store and buy copier ink, unless you bought it in bulk twelve to twenty cartridges at a time, and then you'd probably only have to go once a year. And in time—face it; it's coming—there won't be any copy places left to copy your pages. All that kind of work for people like you will be done on copiers at home." "Then I'm finished. That's all there is to it. Done for good. Or I'd find a way. I should look at it hopefully. I'd have to find a way, if I want to continue to copy my pieces, which by then—what are we giving it here? Three years? Five?—I'm not so sure I'd want to do. But eating is another example of why I don't think I can make it through another day. I don't like to eat anymore." "That could be good. Keeps your weight down." "But I eat because I know I have to if I want to stay alive. But I eat too much, more than likely a lot of that's out of nervousness of some sort, and with no pleasure." "So you've said, and it's probably true. Find a way to work it out. It doesn't seem like the biggest of problems. So far, none of what you've said does." "You're right. But exercising too. I exercise too much. I want to have the body of a much younger man, and when I say 'much younger,' I mean by thirty to forty years. I can't have it but I work at it." "Do you know why, other than just wanting to look good, or at least not like your more typical old man?" "I don't. I'm going crazy; maybe that's it. And I know all this exercising with weights and such is what's causing my almost constant lower back pain. I go to the Y and work out for more than an hour every day of the week." "Do it less." "I can't. If I miss a day—that day I'm missing, I feel lousy. Guilty. Fat. Weak. Soft. Bloated. Old. So I have to go." "Do what you want, then. I can't help you there, either." "You can help me in everything by coming back." "You know that's silly talk." "I know. I can say it, though, can't I? What's the harm? Just so you know how I feel." "I know how you feel." "How do you feel?" "Do you mind if I remain silent?" "No, of course not. I expect it. I'm lucky enough now to get any kind of response from you." "You're not getting it from me. You know that, don't you?" "I know, I know. Don't remind me. It'll only make me feel even worse. But drinking too." "What about it?" "I drink too much. Every night. Two big shots of this or that over ice, usually one and sometimes two more. Often with a twist of lemon or squeeze of lime in them, at least the first. Then, all while reading the paper, two juice glasses of wine, red or white, doesn't matter what kind. If I don't start off with the shots, I start with a juice glass or two of dry marsala or dry sherry, and then go to the two to three juice glasses of wine. It's also what's probably causing my peeing every other hour once I get to bed, not just my enlarged prostate, or the combination of the two. But the drinking helps me get to bed and helps me be sleepy, and for the next two to three hours, probably helps keep me asleep. Then I'm up every other hour, stay up for an hour, sleep, stay up for an hour, can't sleep, sleep, and so on. I mixed that up a bit, but you get the point. Every night. Right till the morning, and usually before dawn. And the morning, what do I do?" "What?" "I get out of bed too early. Sometimes before five. When it's still dark out. Sometimes before four. And I exercise with weights. And I stretch and do other exercises. I run in place in the same spot or sort of run in place around the house. Sometimes I get back in bed after it, sweaty. That's how hard I work out that early in the morning. You've seen me. You must have. Does it help get me back to sleep? Maybe, though probably not. Eventually I might fall back to sleep. It's always the same thing. All my problems. It's from getting old, being old, being alone like I am. Isolated. Having nothing to do but my writing and reading and exercising. Is this any kind of life?" "I think I know what you're saying." "You do. I know you do. I wish I could begin seeing someone. A woman I'm attracted to and admire and like a lot. Go places with, dine out, eat in, travel, talk to, phone, be phoned. Talk about some of the same things I used to talk about with you. Books, plays, art, movies, literature, the world. What's in today's newspaper. Have sex. But I meet no one. I'm retired. Most people were friends with us because of you." "Not true." "It's true. Few friends I had here on my own have either died or moved away. The only friends I have—the Pinskis, who were friends, equally it seemed, with us both—I see once a month for lunch in a restaurant and maybe three times a year, two of them Jewish holidays, for dinner at their house. The kids, well, they come down maybe once every five weeks or so, and how long will that last? They'll get married. They'll be tied down at their jobs. They'll see me less and less, and you know me, I'll rarely go to New York to see them." "So change." "I wish I could. Or maybe I don't. New York and me? We don't go together anymore. It's too fast for me. It makes me confused. Even with one of our daughters sticking close to me the entire trip and guiding me through the city. So what do I do?" "I know." "Write, read, exercise, eat enough to live, fantasize. Every four to five days, or that's been the norm since I discovered this, I turn on the computer and Google 'Naked women and Naked Girls' and masturbate to one of its links. 'Asian Girls, Teen Sex. Amateur Porn. Blondes. Hardcore.' It's all there. And I shouldn't forget my favorite, 'College Girls,' which the last time I did it to, it had three girls on one guy and a Periodic Table of the Elements poster on the wall above the bed. You've seen me." "I don't recall." "My big pleasure of the week. I enjoy doing it, I admit, but sometimes it seems ridiculous. There I am, sitting in the dark—and it's always when it's dark out. So maybe that's also why I do it—to have something to do to stay up later than I usually do at night—and I think 'I'm an old guy and I'm masturbating to a computer screen.' But that's how I am. I still have to do it. Are you surprised?" "I don't know what to think." "Do you think something's wrong with me?" "I have no answers to that. And it's probably healthy for your prostate gland. Isn't that what you once told me?" "My mother told me. When I wasn't seeing anyone for a long time. She said she read it and, delicate as the topic was, thought I should know. Still, doing it, and I mean right while I'm doing it, which sometimes does tend to take away some of the pleasure from it but never ends up stopping me, I feel, in fact, more than ridiculous. I feel stupid and sort of sordid, doing it. To a computer screen. To people moaning and sucking and screwing and climaxing and whatnot. Three girls licking, at one time, one guy's penis. And occasionally smiling at and hamming it up for the camera while they're doing it, while you never see the face of the guy they're licking the entire time. But you've seen me at the computer doing it. Don't deny it." "Who's denying anything?" "So tell me what you think. I can take it." "What I think? If it gives you some pleasure every so often? Even a little pleasure? Even a tiny little bit of pleasure and release and is also good for your prostate?" "Come on. Out with it." "It's not so bad. You almost owe it to yourself. No, I don't know what I'm saying. Especially about your owing it to yourself. If it's what you want to do and think you need to and there's no harm to anyone by it, though maybe there is to those three misguided college girls." "One even kept her glasses on. That's all she had on. These rectangular dark frames that so many young people seem to favor today. It actually, I'll say, made her look sexier than the other two, though they were all pretty and had good bodies." "But what were they thinking, letting themselves be exposed like that? Their brothers, cousins, even their fathers and possibly even their grandfathers, might in all innocence, so to speak, Google that site and see them. Maybe if…oh, I don't know. Let me alone. I don't want to think about it. I don't want to think you're unhappy, either. I don't want to think you don't feel well. Your mind, your body. Do me a favor?" "Anything. What?" "Stop typing. Stop putting all this down. Not only pull out what you have in the typewriter but tear up what you've written so far since you started this. Get rid of it all. Then cover the typewriter. Put it to sleep for the night, as you used to say. Do something else. None of this is any good for you. I can't see where it helps." "It helps. But I'll do what you say. Tomorrow I'll look at what I've done, and maybe then I'll tear all of it up. But I warn you. If I can use any of it, I'll use it. If I can use it all, I'll use that too. You never know the next day if anything you did the previous day is good. Meaning, you don't know until you look at it. I'll see if there's anything there. If there is, I'll work on it till I finish it. I'll enjoy working on and finishing it. It'll give me something to do that I like to. I know I'm repeating myself here in a couple of things and also contradicting myself somewhat from what I said before, or think I am, but there it is; that's the way I am too. Okay, I'll stop. It's getting dark out so I'll probably get to sleep tonight an hour or so later than I usually do, which is good. As I said, I go to bed too early. You still there? Well, the next sound you hear will be me tearing the last page I've written out of the typewriter. Not tearing. I don't want to tear it, as I didn't tear the previous typewritten pages out of the typewriter. So I'll pull the page out gently so it doesn't tear. That's more like what I'll be doing. That will be what I'm doing. Listen and you shall hear. Oh, how corny of me. But as you know, that's how I can be too. Not for final drafts, where I reject corniness, but firsts, where I'll try out anything, knowing the corn will go. What else I am or can be, right now I haven't a clue. Or I'm not sure or I don't know. No, it's true, I was right the first time: I haven't a clue. Do you? I'm listening. My ear's cocked. Okay. Nothing. I listened for about twenty seconds and there was nothing. Silence. Done for the night. I must seem so irritatingly boorish to you. What can I say other than that I know that's how I can be too. What do you say? To what I just said. Nothing? Then let's just go to sleep. First, though, I'll take the paper out of the typewriter very carefully so it doesn't tear. Then I'll collect, in the order they were written, all the previous pages I wrote since I sat down at the typewriter—ten of them, I see—and paper-clip or staple them, with this one, page eleven, the last. Staple them. That way, after I cover the typewriter as you asked me to and get under the covers and turn off the light, I'll go to sleep knowing I won't lose any of the pages, which I've done in the past though after a lot of frantic searching always found them. So I can safely say—more than 'safely'; I can say unqualifiedly that in all my years of doing this I never lost one. But stapling's the best way to hold these pages together, right? Better than paper-clipping them, I'm saying, if the staple isn't bent and goes in perfectly and the stapler doesn't jam, right? I'm listening. You still there? Something's got your tongue? For the last time, you still there? No? All right. No."

The Liar

This was a while ago. Their daughters were five and eight. He told her he'd like to have another child. How does she feel about it? That when they were first married they talked about having three kids. She said she'd like to, the girls have been great and she'd love to please him with a new baby, but she wouldn't have the strength to take care of it. And with all the medications she's taking, and there's no way she could get off them, she probably couldn't breast-feed the baby either. "You don't have to," he said. "And for the rest of it, leave it to me. My teaching schedule's flexible. Both kids are now in school. I'll do most of the work from day one, even the cooking." "No, and for all we know, just getting pregnant could make my condition worse. I don't want to chance it. It's progressing fast enough on its own. Two children are enough, and I hope you'll come to think so too. You've been wonderful about taking on more than your share of the work with them. I couldn't ask you to do more." "I really want a third one," he said, "but we'll do what's good for you. So okay, whatever you say."

He already knew what he'd do if she said she didn't want another child. By this time, because she was having trouble using her hands, he was putting in the diaphragm for her. Most of the times when she was ovulating and they were going to make love, she told him to be extra careful in inserting the diaphragm, and he said he would or "I know," but intentionally put it in loose. "It doesn't quite feel secure," she sometimes said. "Are you sure it's in right?" "It's in perfectly, just the way you taught me," he always said, or something like it, "but I'll double-check if you want me to," and put his hand in her vagina, knew the diaphragm wasn't in straight, took his hand out and said "As I said, a perfect fit. Now what do you say?" and she nodded and he got on the bed next to her and they made love. He came and hoped some of his semen got through the opening and made it to the egg. Hoped the egg was receptive to one of the sperm.

Several other times he said when they were about to make love during her most fertile period "What do you say; this time, no diaphragm or messy cream? I'll pull out when I'm about to come. Don't worry. I'll be very careful." "It won't be as exciting for you, though it could be a bit more so for me. But the good thing is you won't have to deal with the diaphragm and cream. But pull out long before you come. Ten seconds at least. You'll know when that is. Maybe more than ten seconds, if you don't think you can hold it back till then, just to make sure not a drop goes in me." He ejaculated a little inside her those times—sort of let it dribble out—but made no sounds or gave any physical sign he was coming. Then he said "I'm coming," or said it a couple of times, and pulled out and pretended to groan a few seconds while he did the rest of it on her stomach, if that was the position they were making love in, or, if he was behind her, in a handkerchief or on the bottom sheet or a towel. "You didn't come in me," she usually said, "—even a small amount, did you? Because then I want to get up and clean it out fast." "No, I told you. I planned to go on your belly, and that's where it went." Or "on the towel" or "in my handkerchief" or "I came on the sheet. Unfortunately, now we'll have to change it." "It's worth the effort," she said. "Though next time, if we do it like this again without a diaphragm, spread out a thick towel under us first. Then, after you do what you do on it, just toss it into the washer."

It must have worked the last time they didn't use a diaphragm.

Because from that time on, or when she first decided she was pregnant, she always insisted she have one in, even during the so-called safe days. Anyway, about a month later, she said "I have some distressing news," and told him. "You sure?" and she said "I'd say almost positive. Yes, I'm positive." "Damn, I'm so sorry. I know it's the last thing you wanted to happen. I must've inserted the diaphragm incorrectly for the first time or it slipped while it was in you. Can that happen?" and she said "Not if it's put in right. And I would have felt it. I think I'm still able to feel things like that in there. It's my hands and feet where I've lost most of my feeling." "Then maybe there's something wrong with it. A tear or puncture, somehow, or just being stretched too far from all its use. Did we ever check it?" and she said "There was nothing wrong with it. Whenever I clean it and put it back in its case, I always inspect it. I'm no lazy fool." "I know; I'm not saying. And I'm sure you're right about being pregnant. You knew, with Freya and Miriam, a month after they were conceived. Well, you know us. The Fecund Twins. I think with both girls we hit it right the first time we tried. But that was when you wanted it. So what are we going to do? If you are right." "I'm right. Abort, of course, and sooner the better, after it's been confirmed by the doctor. I already passed the urine test." "You did? Without me? It was so much fun, watching the doughnut grow. But can't we even discuss it?" and she said "No." "Come on," he said. "Surely we can discuss it a little. It might be the perfect time for us to have a third child, and maybe that was the last time you'll be able to conceive. And I swear. I'll take care of the baby twice as much as I did the first two, and I did a lot then, you know it. So I've done it. I'll know what to do. An experienced pop. I'll work my ass off and love every minute doing it. It won't be a chore for you at all. If we have to, we'll get some help for a while, and the kids will pitch in too. And your folks. They'll love our having another child.

My mother too. But your folks more so, their losing their whole families in Europe." "Please, don't go any further," she said. "It's a blatantly bogus argument. Sham, insincere, you don't mean a word of it. You just want to change my mind by fucking with it. It's not going to work. So it's final. No more talk. It's making me very angry and driving me crazy, and that isn't good for my condition either." "Then I apologize and I'll shut up. I'm disappointed, that's obvious, but nothing I can do about it, and I respect what you say." "Oh, you're too much sometimes," she said, "but I'm glad I've heard the last of it." "I'm sorry you feel that way about me, but okay."

She had the abortion. They continued to make love three to four times a week and he always put the diaphragm in for her. He put it in loose a few times in the next two years or so, made love to her from behind those times because she once said, when they were planning to have their first child, that that was the best position, if he went in deep and stayed there for a couple of minutes after he came, to get her pregnant. One time she said to him, while they were lying in bed after having made love, "I've been thinking. Correct me if I'm wrong, and don't think that what I'm about to say is in any way critical of you. But that last time I got pregnant and had an abortion, you didn't, when you said you'd be extra careful to pull out in time after you had convinced me not to use a diaphragm, intentionally ejaculate in me to make me pregnant? You could tell me now. Enough time has gone by, so I'm not going to get upset. And you wanted a third child so much, I can almost understand why you would have resorted to such a desperate deception." "Are you being serious?" he said. "Yes. I'm asking because it's puzzled me since then how I got pregnant, and I thought that was the most likely way. And that after you pulled out, you feigned an orgasm while you were still behind me, when you actually might have got rid of some if not most or even all your seed slowly and imperceptibly while you were inside me." "Seed," he said. "I love that word for it." "Don't change the direction of the conversation. Did you?" "First of all, as for feigning an orgasm, I never did in my life. If I don't have one, I don't pretend I do. If I have one, then I make sounds, soft to whatever's natural, nothing fake, though the volume, of course, influenced if there's someone else in the house. If one of the kids is home, then absolute silence, I hope from both of us." "You're not answering my question." "I'll answer it, or do my best to, by saying I didn't do what you think there's a possibility I did." "All right. I just wanted to know." "But do you believe me?" and she said "I believe you, or think I do." "Believe me," he said. "I wouldn't lie to you on this. I wouldn't lie anytime to you. Now, if some of my seed happened to leak into you while we were making love without a diaphragm and that made you pregnant, then I didn't know. I always thought I was in control of it then, but there could have been a time or two I wasn't. When you were using a diaphragm I didn't think of it and just went for maximum release in you." "That answers my question. It must have happened that way. I won't bring it up again." "But you do believe me." "More than I did when I first asked the question." "That's good enough," he said.

A couple of years later she said her gynecologist said she's stopped ovulating, so it's all right for them to make love from now on without any kind of protection. "What a relief," he said. "It'll make our lovemaking much freer. Now we can hop straight to it without a lot of fussing around and making sure the thing's in right and washing and drying my hands and giving them some time to get warm again before touching you." "Was it that bad? We always, you know, could have inserted it hours before," and he said "I think we thought that would have entailed getting you on and off the bed before I got you on the bed again to make love, so we never did it, or not after the first time." "Anyway, I'm glad of the way you accepted the medical report," she said. "I thought you'd be disappointed, even a bit depressed, that I wasn't able to conceive anymore, which I know for the last few years you secretly wanted." "Who, me? Not on your life. You didn't want another child, then that was perfectly understandable and fine with me. And the two we have are wonderful. Never a handful, so I thought another wouldn't have been rough on us either. But two's enough, as you've said; really. I'm not making this up. So what do you say? When do you think's the first time we can take advantage of this windfall? Without any appliances or anything to stop the momentum, so to speak. We haven't been able to do that for years." "Tonight, if you like," she said. "I'm sure I'll be in the mood." "How about now? I'm good for it. No, that must seem so stupid for me to say." "You have to pick up the kids in half an hour," she said. "Ah, but I suppose we have time if we do it relatively quickly, or you do, and we can now omit the tiresome routine with the diaphragm, which will give us a few more minutes." He wheels her into the bedroom, helps her undress. "I don't have to take everything off, do I?" and he said "You can leave on the socks. We'll still have time to get everything back on." He lifted her out of the wheelchair onto the bed. "That was so good," he said, after. "I don't know if it was because of what we didn't have to do, but really nothing stopping us." "You did seem to make a little more noise than usual." "You too," he said. "I thought you were going to make it this time. I tried my hardest for you to. Your pleasure comes first with me." "Oh, please." "No, I mean that." "Then thank you," she said. "Though I doubt I'll ever be able to achieve what you do every time. It makes me sad. It's not that it isn't fun without it—don't think that—but it'd be so much better with." "You'll have it. It's got to happen again. We'll work on it together. And once we've mastered the trick to it, or whatever will do it, there'll be other times too." "I hope so," she said. "I'm certainly not blaming you. It's my wretched condition. Now, help me get dressed. If you're late, give me my bathrobe and I'll pretend to them I'm still in my robe after a shower."

Feel Good

He thinks: I'm getting worse. My hands have trouble typing. They don't feel connected to the keyboard. I make a lot of mistakes, and then make mistakes correcting the mistakes. Sometimes I can't get the Ko-Rec-Type tab underneath the ribbon to type a word or letter out. I have to retype a page ten to fifteen times now to get it right, when before it was only around five or six. Also, my fingers tighten up, and sometimes, but only a few times, though it never happened before, they curl up and get so stiff I have to pry them apart with my other hand. Though if I wait a minute or so, they usually come apart by themselves. Other signs. I can barely hold a pen sometimes. And when I can write with one, the writing's so small I can't read it, even with the magnifying glass I keep on the window ledge next to my desk. And my feet feel cold almost all the time now, when before it was just a few hours a day. I wear socks when I go to bed now, but they don't help much. I wonder how long it'll be before my right foot can't feel the gas and brake pedals of my car. I also have trouble getting out of bed in the morning. Not just the morning. It happens a lot, since I have to pee three to four times overnight. To get out of bed I have to sit up slowly, then stand. The bathroom's just two feet away from the left side of the bed, the side I mostly sleep on because it's the closest to the bathroom. It's also the side nearest the chair that has my clothes for the next day and on the floor right beside that side of the bed are my socks where I left them the previous night when I undressed for bed, thinking I might put them on in the morning. I usually change my socks every other day, but I've often gone three days without a change. I think that's because they've been stretched so much the last two days that they're easier to get on. When I stand up from the sitting position I sometimes feel a bit shaky on my feet and think I might fall. So I sit right back on the bed and try to stand up a minute or so later. That usually does it. I have fallen a couple of times, which isn't much in almost a year, and it wasn't hard to get up again. Though the last time I fell was around six months ago, so who knows how hard it would be now to stand up or get back on the bed from the floor. And of course I'd first sit on the edge of the bed, but not too close to the edge, before I'd try to stand again. Anyway, I didn't hurt myself those two, or maybe it was three times I fell. The room's carpeted—my wife's idea after we moved into the house, to cushion her falls if she fell, which she did increasingly over the years. Off the bed where she was sitting or out of her wheelchair if she wasn't strapped in, and once when she was strapped in and fell over in the chair and broke her nose. That bedroom's the only place in the house that's carpeted except for the short hallway right out-side it, which the carpet company threw in for free. Then walking. Mornings, after I put my socks on and get off the bed and do what I have to in the bathroom and dress, is probably the worst time for that. That's because, or at least is the likely cause, I haven't taken the pill for my illness, which I do three times a day, since around six the previous night. So I take the pill while I'm in the bathroom and then exercise with two ten-pound weights and stretch a lot before and after I exercise with the weights, but nothing seems to help my walking much. I'm getting worse. No question about it. If I go to my doctor and tell him what I think's happened to my body since I last saw him, around six months ago, he'll increase the dosage of my medicine, which is what he did the last time I told him I thought I was getting worse, and now I'm sure I'm worse than I was then.

My back, he thinks. The lower part. This has been going on for a year: sometimes it hurts so much I can't walk. Or I can, but only tiny steps—more like a slow shuffle—and not for long. If I fell, when my lower back hurts this much, I don't know how I'd get up. It's never happened, but I'd probably have to stay on the floor or wherever I fell till I felt strong enough and not in so much pain to get myself up. If I was home I might have to crawl to the living room couch or my bed to support me as I lifted myself up. If I was outside, and nobody was around to help, I don't know what I'd do. Stay there, that's all, till I felt better. Sometimes, and this really creates a problem, my back hurts so much that I can't get my hands far enough around me to wipe my behind. I take a healthy-back class at the Y twice a week, where I'm taught various stretches to prevent and relieve the pain in my back, but they only help for about an hour after the class is over. Same when I do these stretches at home at least once a day. These back pains could be tied to my illness, or maybe not. My doctor says "Perhaps, but it'd be unusual. It's probably just your age and that you exercise too much and too strenuously." And I keep calling what I have an illness when the right word for it is disease. And my right leg. No, my left. I don't know why it's always one and never the other, and neither does my doctor. But sometimes it hurts so much I can barely walk on it and it feels like it's going to collapse on me. So I have to sit, or stand without moving, or hold on to the top of my dresser or the dryer or washing machine in the kitchen and swing that leg back and forth, meaning forward and back. And after I do this about ten times, hold it straight out behind me or as straight as I can get it behind me while I'm holding on to one of these objects, till my leg feels better or doesn't feel it's about to collapse from under me. Is this also tied to my disease, or illness, for both are just as good, because what else could it be? And my doctor? Again he only says "Perhaps," or "Maybe," and again that it more than likely comes because I exercise too much and too strenuously. That, he says, may explain a lot of my physical ailments. Have I ever thought of reducing my exercising routine by half or even cutting it out entirely for a while to see if my back and leg pains would go away? "I can't," I said. "You yourself have said it's slowing down my main disease. And I only feel good, or let's say better and stronger when I exercise at home with weights in the morning and sometimes before I go to sleep, but mainly for an hour every day at the Y on the resistance machines and stationary bike and the weights there."

And my bowels, he thinks. The medications I take for a number of things are affecting my bowels and my sleep and my mind too. It's not as clear and sharp as it used to be before I started taking them, that's for sure. I feel I'm losing my memory. Maybe that has nothing to do with my illness or disease, and it's just age. But sometimes it takes me a week to remember something that used to come to me instantly. For instance, I was talking to my older daughter on the phone two weeks back or so. I said "Do you remember the name of the opera we all went to at the Lyric Theater in Baltimore? I'd say about fifteen years ago, before you started college. It's on the tip of my tongue and has been there for a week. It's in Russian, Tchaikovsky, and your mother's favorite of all operas." She said "I never knew its name except probably when we went to see it. I do remember a grand ball scene and lots of dancing and that the scenery was huge and pretty and the opera was very long and I wanted to go home before it ended." "Funny what one remembers," I said. "And it's not *Prince Igor*. That's Borodin, if that is an opera and not a ballet. But something with royalty in it, I think. It's not *Boris Gudunov*, either, which is about a czar, and another of your mother's favorites. I'll remember it, though it's been killing me that I can't. For some reason I feel my mind depends on it." She said "Don't be silly, Daddy. Everybody forgets." It took me another week to remember it was *Eugene Onegin*. I could have looked it up online or in the encyclopedia of music book we have, but that would have been too easy. I wanted to remember it as sort of a memory test and to prove something, but it did take me two weeks and that worries me.

Face it, he thinks, I'm getting worse in almost every possible way. I know it and I know my daughters know it, but they don't want to say. It's why they call me every night and come down from New York every two to three weeks, or why I think they do. And it's why I never go to New York. I never go anywhere. My joke is I never leave Baltimore County. That's an exaggeration. I go to Baltimore city about once a month, cross the border between the city and the county to go to a Whole Foods or the Starbucks next door to it. But that's as far as I go. I never go deep into the city unless I'm with my daughters and we go to a movie or restaurant or museum there. I feel uneasy when I'm alone and not near my home. Not near my desk and my bed to rest or take a nap on whenever I want to. Not near my typewriter, even though I don't type anywhere near as well as I used to. Oh, what's the difference? I still type, with two fingers now instead of the three a year ago and the four a year before that. So I'm getting very anxious about my health. Not my health: my sickness, my illness, my disease. What it's doing to me. What it's going to do. And there's no cure, and the medication, my doctor says, only works up to a point, was the way I think he put it. But there are other medications I can take for it, he said, if the one I'm taking stops being effective. "But one medicine at a time," he said, "at least for the same illness." So he refers to it as an illness too. I just realized that.

I used to run, he thinks. Mornings, almost always, and before I had breakfast. Up, wash, exercise, dress, and out I'd go. If my wife was still in bed, and this was after she got sick, I'd check up on her, see that she was all right, and then leave. Three to four miles a day, and I did this almost every day for about thirty years. Snow, rain, bitter cold; nothing but ice coating the streets stopped me, though they might have slowed me down, and when it was that icy outside I ran in place at home for twenty minutes or more. I was as compulsive about running as I am about writing and have been about a number of other things. Then, starting a few years ago: two to three miles a day and then just two and then one and then even less than that and then no running. My legs couldn't do it anymore. Or something couldn't. So I started to walk a couple of miles a day. Maybe just a mile. First a fast walk—what might be considered a power walk, but that didn't last long. When I couldn't do that anymore, then a normal walk for about a mile. Then half that and so on, till I could only walk about five hundred feet, and not every day. I also tried to take a second walk early evening, if it wasn't too hot, but by that time my back and leg hurt so much that I could barely make it to my mailbox and back, a total of about a hundred feet. So what am I saying? What I've been saying. I'm getting worse in almost every way but I don't want to go to the doctor to be told so. Of course I'll have to eventually go to him, but what will I do if the new medicine he prescribes for my condition—my illness, my sickness, my disease—doesn't slow it down for even a little, or does but just a little though not for long? And the medicine after that does nothing, or very little, but even for a shorter time, and so on. Till it ends up where no medicine works and I can't do very much for myself. Where my hands and feet are practically useless. Where I can't get around by myself except in the house, and there mostly by holding on to things as best as I can—grab bars, tables, chairs, walls—as I move. Where even a walker doesn't help much. I won't be able to shop for myself. Maybe not even dress myself.

Brush my teeth, hold a fork or spoon, cut my food with a knife, turn a book page, get off the toilet ten times a day, clean myself up. Where someone needs to help me with almost everything. I know what it's like from my wife. Get her in bed, out of bed, down for a nap if she didn't want to do it in her wheelchair, hold the glass or straw to her lips. She hated all of it. Seated at the computer most of the day. Same will happen to me. At my typewriter, not that I'll be able to peck anything out on it by then. Learn how to use her old computer for that, or even a new one? Oh, yeah, I can just see myself doing that. Voice-activation system, as she tried to do for her work? Took her two years of private instruction to learn how to use it where she got something done. And it still didn't work half the time, and that drove her nuts. She'd cry and cry and I'd rush into her study. Forget it. And I couldn't expect my daughters to do for me even half the things I did for her. They're my children; she was my wife. So what'll happen to me then? An assisted-living facility? A nursing home? One of those? Both, if there's a difference between them. Oh, no. Not for me. Not so long as I can do something about it. If I can't, then I think I'd go the same way she did. No food, water, nutrition or medicine or fake air through machines of any sort. But my hands. They're all right now, aren't they? No stiffness or pain? I open and close them several times and they seem fine. See how it goes when you don't think of them? Same with my legs. Feet feel a little cold, but no pain anywhere, and I stand. Back, too. Well, it never hurt all the time. And my mind? It's all right, right? It's not in that bad a shape. Quick, a test: What are the three early Stravinsky ballets, starting with the one I think was first performed in 1910? Yeah, 1910. And that one I almost always get. *The Firebird*. The other two, 1911 through 1913, I almost always forget when I try to think of them all as three. Sometimes takes me a couple of days to come up with those two, if I don't look them up. *Petrushka* and *The Rite of*

Spring. And if I need another one as proof of how well my mind's working, and I never thought of them as four: *Pulcinella*, in 1920 I'm almost sure. And even another one: *Agon*, '56 or '57—anyway, when I was still in college and saw it done several times at the City Center on West 55th Street, by the New York City Ballet. Allegra Kent, the principal dancer. I think I went to this ballet, alone or with friends, just to see her, not that I could see much from so far up in the second balcony or if I managed to sneak down to the first. She was such a beauty, and what a dancer, and she was my age—if I remember, a year younger.

So I'm okay, he thinks. More than okay. I put on my sneakers. My fingers never had trouble tying laces. Probably because I've been doing it, I'd say instinctively, since I was around three or four. I remember when I first did it. "Look at me," I said. I knew I'd done something to be proud of. And my mother saying "You have accomplished"—or some simpler word than that—"something much earlier than most children your age." When I brought it up thirty to forty years later she said she had no recollection ever telling me that or of the incident, but she believed it because that's the kind of boy I was: "Always ahead of things. You caught on quick or worked on it till you mastered it." She was always praising me. My father not at all, except when I sang "God Bless America" for his friends. He'd stand me up on a kitchen counter, and after I sung, he and his friends would give me change.

Laces tied, I take the mug out of the kitchen sink where I put it this morning, and drink what's left of the coffee in it. Now I'm ready and fortified, he thinks. So get yourself outside and run. If you can't run, walk, but walk fast. You can't let yourself just fade. I open the kitchen door to the outside. I walk to the road, check my mailbox for mail. Just an ad for a new health club that opened nearby. That's funny. Or appropriate to what I've been thinking. Appropriate and funny. But stop stalling. You gonna go or not? So get a move on. If you run well, or better than you have in a long time, you'll get better. The hell with medicine that comes in a pill. Oh, I'll take it if I have to but I won't rely on it completely. And the other things the doctor has available to me if the pills no longer work. Hell with them too. This is the way to go. At least try. I swing my arms around twenty times. I count them: twenty on each side. I put my palms flat against a tree trunk and move my feet back till I'm at a ninety-degree angle to the tree—or is it forty-five?—and stretch. I do this for a minute or two. Then I sort of do push-ups against the tree while at the same angle, ninety or forty-five, palms still flat. Ten of them.

Do more, he thinks. Make it twenty, and I do another ten. Now I'm really ready. Now I'm going to go, and I start off. It's faster than a walk, but not as fast as a power walk. Then it's as fast as that. So maybe it's just a slow jog. But jog harder, faster. I do that. Just make it to the Stuarts' mailbox. I make it there. Now make it to the Fromners' mailbox. I'm going at a good jogging pace, faster than a power walk, not as fast as a regular run, and nothing hurts. My back feels fine. I pass the Fromners' mailbox and feel I can make it at the same pace to the Philbricks' mailbox. I make it there and pass it and jog at an even faster clip all the way to Hawthorn Street. I go right at Hawthorn and jog up a slight incline to Coolidge Street, which isn't that far—the length of a typical New York City block, I'd say, twentieth of a mile—and start to run on it.

I'm running now, he thinks, a real run on Coolidge to the road that goes past my house. So I'm making the entire loop without stopping. Haven't done that in I don't know how long. A year? Two? I keep running to my mailbox, which is about ten feet from the road. Don't stop. Make it all the way to the house. I run on my driveway to it. I plop down on one of the chairs on the patio near the kitchen door. So how far have I run? Quarter of a mile? A third? A half? Even a little more? Possible. Anyway, around five times as far as I was last able to do, and most of it a fast jog or regular run, not just a fast walk. I'm breathing hard. But healthy deep breaths. The kind I used to get after a sprint, which I used to love to do and did a lot till my illness forced me to stop. So I'm not fading after all. And to keep myself from fading, I've got to keep pushing myself like I just did. Push, push some more and even more than that, and you'll be fine. Want to take another run? You can do it. You're not going to drop. Your breath has already settled. You'll make it just fine, if not as far. And anytime you want to stop, just stop, for you've done plenty today and proved what you set out to prove. I go back to the road. I jog in place for about thirty seconds and then start to run. I get tired after about a hundred feet, and stop, and start to walk back. A car approaches going the opposite way from me on the other side of the road. I wave. The driver waves. I feel so good.

Flowers

In a number of stories I've read the past fifty years or so, someone is bringing flowers to the grave of someone he or she knew. To a wife, husband, parent, lover, close friend, a child. In a couple of the stories the person is bringing the flowers to his or her own grave. In one of these stories, she's not dead. It's just a burial plot and a gravestone with her name and date of birth on it followed by a hyphen but no death date. In another story, he is dead but is bringing a bunch of flowers to the adjoining grave of his wife. I forget how the writer works this part out by the end of the story. In fact, I forget everything about the story except that a dead man brings flowers to the grave of his dead wife. I also forget the name of the writer. I know he's Latin-American and I think, though he must be very old by now, he's still alive. I don't recall seeing an obituary of him, though I think I would have since he was once famous, or hearing anyone talk about him as if he were dead. I remember the long poetic title of the story has the word "flowers" in it.

I have no one, really, to bring flowers to his or her grave. My parents and two of my siblings are buried in a cemetery on Long Island—I think in Suffolk County. I know it was way out there on the island, so it couldn't be Nassau County. And it's my sister who's buried there; my brother's gravestone is a cenotaph. He was on a freighter that sent out distress signals during a violent storm in the North Atlantic more than fifty years ago and must have sunk. I forget the cemetery's name. I know it has a "mountain" in it—maybe Sinai or Nebo. It's been almost twenty years since I've been to it. To get there I took the Long Island Expressway and drove for about an hour on it. It was for my mother's burial. I was with my wife and daughters. And shortly after I passed a huge sod farm on my right—this is what I was told to look out for—I took the next exit to a wide boulevard that had a number of cemeteries and flower stores and a diner on it. Jewish, Catholic, and two veterans cemeteries and a couple of others. I remember that all the graves in the veterans cemeteries were in neat rows and most of them had little American flags on them. It was around Memorial Day, so probably that was why. I doubt I'll ever go out there again. I'm sure I won't. I don't see the point. I'd look at the graves for a few minutes, less if it was very cold out, and leave. I don't pray and I wouldn't read from some little prayer book they'd offer me in the cemetery office when I'd go in there to get the location of the graves, and I know the burial site is taken care of. My father paid for that a long time ago and it was good, he said, for another fifty years. He was proud of the arrangement he made with the cemetery for so little money. Although it wouldn't bother me if the site isn't taken care of and the graves are grown over. I have no idea what the names of the cemeteries are where my grandparents are buried. All four of them were dead before I was born, or maybe my mother's father died a year or two after. Anyway, I never knew them. I know that both cemeteries are in Queens—close to the Queensboro Bridge, I think it is, and the East River. It must be around seventy years since I went to them. My mother took us kids by cab to the cemetery her parents were in. My father didn't want to go, I remember my mother saying years after, or maybe was too busy working that day. Another time, and this time we went by car and my father drove, the whole family went to a cemetery close to the one my mother's parents were in, to visit the graves of my father's parents and two of his brothers, who died very young of diphtheria, I think, though it also could have been of influenza during the great epidemic back then. The trip to the cemetery was also around seventy years ago. I can picture all of us kids squished into the rear seat, though that image could have come from any number of times we were in the car together. A Plymouth. We always had Plymouths. "The Jewish Chevrolet," my father called it, though I'm not really sure why. I think my father paid a lump sum for the upkeep of his parents' gravesite—"In perpetuity," I can hear him say, making it into a funny-sounding word. And the Thayer Family Circle, as my mother and her eight brothers and sisters called themselves when they and their spouses met at one of their homes twice a year to have a buffet dinner and discuss family business, paid for the upkeep of their parents' gravesite. I don't know if they got the same kind of arrangement my father did for his parents' gravesite and my family's. If they didn't and because all my aunts and uncles on my mother's side of the family are dead, I don't know who's looking after it, if anyone is.

I do visit the gravesite, I suppose I can call it, of my wife almost every day. For sure I see it every day, especially now that it's late fall and most of the leaves are down. It's right outside the house, underneath a star magnolia tree inside the circular driveway. She was cremated and some of her remains—I don't want to use the word "cremains"; it just doesn't feel right as a word—were put in a cylindrical container, about fourteen inches long, I bought for them when I arranged for the cremation at a local funeral home. The funeral director I dealt with told me only some of the cremains—that was the word he used repeatedly till he switched to "remains" and "ashes," I guess out of respect to me—would be in the container but none of the bones. I thought of asking why no bones, but it seemed like an insolent, almost smart-alecky question. Not that so much, but just wrong. This was the same day she died. Only hours after her body was picked up by the funeral home and driven away not in a hearse but in an unmarked van. He said the furnace she'd be cremated in would be swept clean—"every last particle"—as it would for the body cremated in the furnace before her. I said "You have more than one furnace?" and he said "Only one. It's enough." I asked how much of her remains would be in the container? "Certainly not all," and he said "Approximately two potting trowelfuls." "What happens to the rest of her remains and what's left of her bones—excuse me; I'm just curious," and he said "They're disposed of in the most dignified manner to the deceased." I think that's how he worded it. "We just don't throw them out." I didn't want to go any further in asking "Where? Is there a disposal area for all the remaining cremation remains?" Again, I thought to, but sensed—knew—it would sound peculiar, if not a little crazy, not that I couldn't have gotten away with that, as I was already a mess, breaking down several times in his office. How I got to even ask what I did and sign a number of documents handed to me across his desk—I really didn't read them at all. I kept saying "I'll take your word. I'll take your word"—I don't know. And I know I wanted to give him my credit card and pay up and get out of there fast as I could. There was also an awful smell in the room—and I can't describe it any better—that I'd never smelled before and which seemed to get stronger the longer I was there. I felt it had to come from the furnace that was probably, or could be near this office. That this was the cremation office we were in, where only cremation business took place. I thought of asking him that too—"What am I smelling?"—but held back. I thought he'd say something like "What smell? I don't smell anything," and maybe call in an associate and say "You smell anything unusual in here?" and this person would sniff a bit and say "Nothing. Why?" The office was also warmer than I thought an office like this would usually be. I could almost swear to it, and of course I thought this also came from the furnace being so near, but I didn't say anything about it either. As I said, I just wanted to finish up and get in my car and drive home.

So I dug a hole outside my house, even before I went back to the funeral home two days later to pick up the container of ashes—a hole deep enough to put the container in the ground vertically. I filled up the hole around and on top of it with the earth I'd dug up and patted it down with the shovel. Then I put twenty-one stones around it, no stone more than a couple of inches long, in two concentric circles—the outer one of thirteen stones, inner one of seven, and an almost perfectly round stone in the center, the smallest of the twenty-one. All the outer-circle stones are larger than the inner-circle ones. That was intentional. I thought the arrangement of stones would look better that way. But the numbers have no significance. It just came out to be thirteen and seven and twenty-one after I'd made the circles and counted all the stones. The stones were chosen from a bucket of about fifty of them collected over the years by my wife and me and my daughters. We got them from the same Maine beach almost every summer, where there were thousands of them piled on top of one another, none larger than a small fist, it seemed. Then only my daughters and I got them because my wife was in a wheelchair and couldn't get close to the beach. She'd say before we went down to it "Try to get only the smoothest stones. So take your time. I'll be fine." Later, when we'd bring a few stones each to her, she'd say, "Beautiful. Every last one of them. Now comes the hardest part. Which ones should we give back? Because we already have a lot in Baltimore. You choose. I love them all." The last time we were at this beach—just my wife and I. Our daughters couldn't start their two-week vacations yet from work and I also think it was our last summer in Maine—there were posted signs there saying something like to prevent further erosion of such and such beach—I forget its name—removing stones, driftwood and other sea matter from the shore is prohibited by law. "They're right," she said. "Lucky we got what we did when it was still acceptable, you can say, and permitted. Though now I feel guilty about all the stones we have at home. Next summer—and I'm serious; you have to remind me about this—we should bring back most of the stones we have, since they're not doing anything sitting in a bucket year to year. You can still fetch me a few today. But only to look at and feel and rub against my cheek, and then we'll throw them back. Or just stick them back in the water, since they might break on other stones if they're thrown."

So where was I in all this? Flowers. That I have no grave, really, to put them on, unless I consider the area the container's in one. And why shouldn't I? My wife's remains are buried in the ground. There's a monument of sorts above it, though not inscribed, of course, though I could probably do something like that. And I treat it like a grave. I keep weeds from growing around the stones. In the fall I brush leaves and larger accumulations of pine needles off it. In the winter I brush away the snow. I sometimes say silly things while I do this. Like: "I don't want you to be cold," when I remove the snow. "Or maybe you'll be warmer with the snow covering you. No, I'll get rid of the snow." I've never put flowers on the stones. I should do that today. Just to do something different with her grave, I'm going to settle on calling it. I'm inside the house now. Do it, I think. Just don't say you will. I put on my jacket and cap and go outside. The only flowers around—a month earlier, there were plenty—are the tea roses, I'm almost sure they're called, right outside one of the kitchen windows, the one above the sink. Pink flowers that look like miniature roses but don't seem to smell. Maybe I haven't breathed them in hard enough. I could go to the flower store in the little village shopping area about a half mile from here, but why bother, and why pay for flowers when they're right here? My

wife used to quote an Eliot poem about roses in the snow in winter.
I forget the line. I really don't remember ever remembering it and
I don't know what poem it's in. Could be in the *Four Quartets*. That
sounds right. Which quartet, though, I haven't a clue. But I know it
was by Eliot because she said it was the times she quoted it, and she
knew poetry as well as anyone, it seemed. She loved the line. Used
to smile when she said it.

So I cut several roses off the bush with the pruning shears,
hold them by their stems carefully so I don't prick myself, smell
them and I still can't get a smell out of them, and lay them out
on the stones. Again, I don't know why. Maybe because—did I say
this?—I've never put flowers there before. Never put flowers on any
grave before, and it seems I should have with this one. I think my
daughters did once or twice. And then they must have removed
them after they'd been there a long time or the dried flowers blew
away if they didn't get washed away by the rain before they dried.
So many of my actions since she died have been for no good reason.
I just think of doing it and do it and wonder why I did it. Maybe I
should have put the flowers in a bud vase. There are a couple of
them in the house, in a bottom kitchen cabinet where all the vases
of various sizes are—several of the larger ones were delivered with
flowers in them soon after she died—and stand it up in the ground
between the inner circle of stones and the stone in the center. Put
water in the vase before I put the flowers in it and stand it up in the
ground wedged between two stones. Why? Why's that better than
laying the flowers across the stones? Did I say it was better? No. I
was just wondering, that's all. I step back and look at the grave.
Looks pretty. Pink flowers and gray stems against the mostly white
and light-gray stones. So I did something now I've never done, or
don't think I have. What of it? I say "I'm going to be silly again, my
darling, and talk a little to you. It's about your grave. I put flowers

on the marker, which is made solely of stones gathered by us and the kids at Schoodic Point. Remember how we used to go there almost every summer when we were in Maine? Spend about an hour there, just looking at the water, and then go to the beach near the point where all the polished stones were, collect a few of what we thought were the best ones, and then go to the same restaurant in town closest to the point. Great fishburgers and haddock and chowder and cole slaw. Nothing better. We always looked forward to that lunch. Fried clams and French fries and lobster and crab rolls and onion rings too. 'Anybody hungry?' I'd say. 'Yeah' we all said, or the kids and I did; you usually said 'You bet.' I've mentioned this before, how one of my most repeated expressions for years became one of yours, when you'd never said it before, to the point where I stopped saying it anymore. Anyway, a cylindrically-shaped container of your remains is under the grave marker, which is solely composed of these ocean-polished beach stones. Just what you wanted to hear, I know. They're in the best container the funeral home had, or the better of the two I chose to choose from. And I'm not telling you this to show what a sport your husband was. Both choices I had were made of strong cardboard, or maybe some other paper product even stronger, though both would eventually disintegrate in the ground, the funeral director said. But the container I got will last around ten years, compared to the cheaper container, which would fall apart in a year, he said. It could be he was telling me this to jack up the cost of the cremation. I was, as I'm sure most grieving spouses are, especially on the same day their husband or wife died—vulnerable—more easily persuadable and he of course knew that and took advantage of it, although maybe he was leveling with me. I want to be fair. Just going over the choices, not pushing me. I really forget. He seemed okay, though that could be part of their act too: sympathy and sincerity. I didn't mean to get into all that. But to finish: there was also a steel container, cylindrically-shaped and same length and dimensions of the other containers. But I was just shown a photograph of it, unlike the others, and I never considered buying it, vulnerable as I said I was. When I heard the price—I'll be honest with you—I said 'No way. Not worth it.' Or just shook my head. Maybe I shouldn't have mentioned this. Because steel could have been what you wanted, though we never talked about it. All we talked about for either of us was cremation or burial, and we both went for cremation. We never talked about what we'd do with the remains, though. The steel one, by the way, came to more than a thousand dollars, while the one I got cost about two hundred. And the flimsiest container…well, price never came up. I doubt they even charge for it. It'd come with the ashes, I'd think, because they'd have to put them in something when they gave them to you. They can't just stick them in a paper bag for you to take home. I also remember thinking at the time that the stronger of the two cardboard containers was better than the steel one. Not because it was way less expensive but because it'll disintegrate and become part of the earth, like ashes will, while the steel container will probably stay steel forever, or something close to that. I wouldn't want the next owner of the house, meaning after I die and the kids sell it, since I doubt they'll want to live there or keep it. Or the owner after that owner—in other words, someone we don't know and who doesn't know about the ashes we have buried out there—digging in that area one day and coming upon the steel container and wondering what it is. Unless he's in the funeral business, I doubt he'd know. And maybe even think there could be something valuable inside— jewels, coins: who knows?—and try to open it, though I think those things are sealed for good. Even the container I got is apparently unopenable once it's sealed, unless you want to tear through it with a saw or butcher's knife. You see what I mean, though, right? But enough. Too much, in fact. I shouldn't talk like this, though I know you can't hear me. Though if you can, and of course you can't, then know that I'm now going to stop talking as if I'm talking to you and weed the few weeds on your grave marker and then go inside." I get down on one knee, weed the grave marker and a little of the area around it, and go inside the house. The pruning shears. I don't remember putting them back in the pail in the carport with the rest of the smaller gardening tools. But I don't want to go outside again today. I'll look for it tomorrow. I'd hate to have misplaced it. It was very expensive, for a clipper, and very useful, and the best of the three or four I have.

Just What Is

He sees her at a restaurant. He's with his two closest friends and she's sitting down with an older woman and a child three tables away. He says to the couple "Someone I know. My favorite grad student, ever. Haven't seen her since before Abby died. That's how I divide things in my life. B.A. and A.A. Excuse me," and he gets up and goes over to her. "Oh my goodness," she says, and stands up and puts her arms out and they hug. "You remember him," she says to the woman. "My old writing professor. Philip Seidel. You met at the reception after the diploma ceremony. Jesus. Almost fourteen years ago." She introduces him to her mother and says the child is her sister's son. "I have him for two weeks while she's in China." He says "How you doing, and how's Claude?" and she says "We're in the midst of getting a divorce." "I'm sorry," and she says "Don't be. It's fine. But also don't tell me you thought we were the last couple on earth to ever get divorced." "Why would I? What do I know what's going on between two people, married or not?" "Hey," she says. "I heard from Whitney and Evelyn that the launch event for your new book at the Ivy was a smash." "You mean a debacle." "No, they said you had a big crowd, more people than chairs, and the pieces you read were perfect and the Q and A went well too. I wanted to go but I was teaching that night. I haven't bought the book yet but I will." "Don't bother. You know…sometimes I think my work's only meant to be written, not read. I'd send you a copy, because the publisher did such a beautiful job on it—the looks. I just know they're going to win design awards for it—but I only have two left, one with the corrections to all the typos and the other to keep in pristine shape in my bookcase. I can also imagine how busy you must be with everything and also have lots on your mind. How are your kids?" "They're taking it pretty well." "That's good. Listen," he says, "we should meet for lunch or just for coffee one day." "I'd like that. Let me get your phone number." "First one to pull out his pen gets to call the other," and he takes a pen out of his pants pocket, piece of folded-up paper out of his pants back pocket and says "So give it." She does and then says "After the holidays. I am pretty busy till then." "After. That'd be great. Can't wait. Lunch, so we have enough time to talk." They hug, he says to her mother "Nice to meet you again. And you too, little guy," to her nephew. "What are you going to have for lunch?" and the kid says "Chicken salad sandwich." "Good choice," and he goes back to the table. "Sorry for holding you up," he says to the couple. "She was maybe the best student writer I ever had, and it was such a treat seeing her again. I loved having her in my class and fought off my colleagues to be her advisor. She didn't say anything about Abby. Maybe she was being discreet. Or I have seen her since Abby died, but a while ago. That must be the case. And I think I even remember getting a condolence card from her, none of which I ever thanked the senders for. She looks a lot like Abby, wouldn't you say? Though that's not why I always liked her." The woman says "Abby was gorgeous. This woman's only cute."

He thinks about calling her every day after that. Writes her phone number in his address book, telephone numbers section of his weekly planner and on the medical appointment card fastened to the refrigerator door by a magnet. Dreams about her several times. In one, they're in a kitchen he doesn't recognize. They're saying goodbye. He forgets which one of them is leaving. He leans over to kiss her cheek, but she kisses him on the mouth. "You're surprised, I can see," she says, "but I wanted to know how it felt. Not bad for a first time. Your lips are nice and soft and your breath's sweet and the kiss was quick and satisfying. A good sign. My rule of thumb is if it doesn't feel good the first time, don't try it again. What's yours?" In another—right after the last one, he thinks— Abby and he are in the Roosevelt Memorial Hall in the American Museum of Natural History. He sees Ruth, this woman, walking down the grand staircase in the Great Hall of the Metropolitan Museum of Art. She doesn't notice him staring at her till she gets to the bottom of the stairs, looks his way and waves. "Hello," he mouths silently from about fifty feet away, "how are you? You look terrific. What a pleasure to see you again." Then he turns back to Abby, whom he realizes he stopped talking to midsentence when he saw Ruth at the top of the staircase, but she isn't there. He looks around this huge room but she seems to have disappeared and the staircase is gone too. He makes his way through a crowd to Ruth. It seems to be a party. Everyone's holding a drink and talking about literature and art. "In 1882…" someone he has to maneuver around is saying. She just stands there, smiling at him, waiting for him, it seems. "I lost Abigail," he says when he reaches her.

He Googles Ruth. Not much on her. Nothing about her age or even a clue, like what year she graduated college, to help him estimate it. He guesses she's around forty, forty-two. She's had several short stories in some of the best literary magazines and one in a major magazine, which was then republished in a *Best American Stories* three years ago. He wonders how he can get the book without buying it or going to the library. He didn't know about the stories. He doesn't keep up with any magazine. She probably has a book coming out or one almost finished and an agent to sell it. She's a visiting assistant professor in the English department of a local university. She also has an advanced degree from the Sorbonne.

He fantasizes about her. She's maybe thirty-five years younger than him. He calls her and they meet for lunch. The next time they see each other—he finds it hard to call it a date—they go to a movie, and then dinner out the next time they see each other. All right, a date. He can't think of a better word for it now. But 42, 77. It seems so wrong to use it. Anyway, after dinner she invites him back to her apartment or house. He'd picked her up this time and drove her home. "Why use two cars?" he said on the phone or in an email. The first two dates they each drove to the place they were to meet at. Her kids are with their father that night and won't be back till the next afternoon. They had kissed a few times, but just quick ones on the cheek when they first greeted each other and then when they said goodbye. They finished a good bottle of red wine in the restaurant—he insisted on paying for their lunch and dinner and let her buy the movie tickets and a bag of popcorn at the theater—and have a glass of wine or two at her place. He says "May I sit beside you on the couch? And it's not because my chair's uncomfortable." Or he's on the couch and she's in a chair and he says "Would it be a really dumb thing to say 'Wouldn't you be more comfortable sitting on the couch?' Although maybe the chair's perfect for you." If he's on a chair and she's on the couch, she says "Please, do what you want." He says "What I want, and I hope you don't throw me out of the house and banish me for all time for saying this, is to kiss you. But I can't do it, if you'd let me, while I'm on the chair." He moves to the couch. Or she does. Anyway, they're there together—they could even start off there, she first, or he first, but probably he first while she's out of the room to get the glasses and wine—and he says "May I kiss you now? I know it seems absurd, my repeatedly asking, but it's been so long. I just don't know how to put it." She says "Don't ask. Just do. There can't be any harm to it, and if we don't like it we'll stop," and she holds her arms out the way she did in the restaurant that time she was with her mother and he was with his friends, and they kiss and they kiss and they kiss. He recalls a dream he had before he had this fantasy, of him kissing his wife for three minutes and then opening his eyes, which had been shut during the entire kiss, and finds he's kissing Ruth. He remembers waking up and thinking "Well, I got the best of both worlds with that one. What's it mean? Several things, all of them too easy." In his fantasy, he feels her breast under her shirt, strokes her behind through her panties, and she says "Why don't we move this to the bedroom?" which is almost word for word what Abby said to him before the first time they made love, also in her living room and on a couch. "*Oy.* Look at me," he says. "You can see how nervous I am. A confession. I haven't made love since I last made love to my wife a month or two before she died, and that was nearly five years ago. Confession two. I haven't made love to any other woman—not even a deep kiss like the ones we just had—since I first met my wife. But I should shut up about her. I'm ruining it, I know." "It's all right," she says. "I understand. But you don't have to say anything else about her, at least not tonight. Otherwise, it'd be difficult to contin-ue." He fantasizes more. Their lovemaking goes well, for instance. "Good," he said, "I found out I don't need a pill to help me out. Big relief. I didn't think I would. But after so long, not that I haven't—confession three—been masturbating, you never know." "It would be all right with me if you did have to use something," she says. "But I'm glad it turned out the way you liked." They start seeing each other a few times a week. Two or three. She's teaching, he's retired. They're both writing and getting things accepted. She wants him to read everything she writes soon after she finishes it and he doesn't let her see anything of his till it's published. "That's the way I was with Abby, except when maybe I was having trouble with a line or two or coming up with the right word or phrase." The age difference makes him feel self-conscious sometimes. Like when she takes and holds his hand when they're walking outside, or in a movie theater, even when it's dark. She says, the one time he brings it up, she never thinks about it. He says "You have to," and she says "Honestly, I don't, so leave it at that. But you don't want me to do things like hold your hand when we're around people or kiss you hello when we meet someplace, I won't." "No," he says. "I like both of those, so do them all you want. I'll come around." More fantasy. He asks her to move in with him. "I'll take care of all the expenses, you won't have to contribute anything, so think of all the money you'll save. The house is small but large enough to accommodate you and your kids and mine when they visit, if I get the basement fixed up as a guest bedroom, and you can have Abby's old study all to yourself." She says she'll think about it—"I wouldn't mind getting out of the apartment" or "selling the house"—and eventually she and her kids move in. They go to Maine for the summer. Her kids first stay a month in Switzerland with their grandparents—her husband is Swiss and he remembers her telling him when she was his grad student that she and Claude would spend a month every summer with his parents in Lausanne—and the second summer month with them in Maine. By now she's divorced. He says "Why don't we get married? I'm aware that it can't last for twenty-seven years as Abby's and mine did. But I think I'm good for twenty years, or maybe just fifteen. Still, that's not bad. You'll be almost sixty. And I promise never to get feeble and to make a super extra effort to be healthy and to control the health problems I already have." She says "Let's keep it the way it is. One of us might tire of the other. I don't see it happening. But I didn't see it happening with my husband either. And I don't want, more for the kids' sake than mine, to go through another divorce. Things are perfect now, aren't they, so why fuss with them? Though maybe, for practical reasons,

I'll change my mind." He stays well. Works out at the Y every day, and she often works out with him. He swims, jogs, cuts back on his drinking, watches what he eats, takes long walks and bike rides with her, loses about ten pounds of belly fat, feels healthier than he has in years. At his next physical his doctor takes him off high-blood-pressure pills—"You no longer need them and you were borderline anyway"—and his prostate seems to have shrunk to normal size. "Your hands no longer shake and your balance and reflexes are better than I've ever seen them, so I'll probably end up reducing those pills and possibly taking you off them too. You're a medical miracle man. I want to show you off to some of my patients who are half your age and nowhere near the physical condition you're in." "It's all your doing," he says to Ruth. "What a mess I'd be now without you." They make love about three times a week. Sometimes once at night and then the following morning before they get out of bed. They laugh a lot with each other, never run out of interesting things to do together and talk about. Never have an argument or really any kind of disagreement or row. Her kids think of him as their second father and his daughters look fondly on her kids as their much younger sisters. He writes several stories about his love for her and his life since he first saw her in that restaurant and also his fears he'll suddenly get very sick and from then on she has to take care of him and another that she leaves him for a much younger man, one of her grad students. He tells her what he's writing, still never shows her them till they're published. She tells him he has nothing to worry about, she loves him and would never hook up with another man. If he got that sick, she'd take care of him the best she could, and if there was anything she couldn't do, and she thinks that would be very little, she'd get an aide. "Sure," she says, "we've talked of the likelihood of your dying long before me. Though I could also all of a sudden get very sick and die of a disease months after I was diagnosed. Or my illness could linger on for years, while you remained healthy, and during that period it'd be you who'd take care of me as you did with Abigail. But let's not talk about it or ever again, unless something like one of those did happen. It's too depressing. You're happy, I'm happy, our kids are terrific and happy and we're all healthy, and we're both writing like there's no tomorrow. That's all we need." "You're right, you're right, you're right," he says. "It's terrible of me, I know. But a couple of the things I haven't been able to get rid of or control, though I should have, seeing how happy we've been together—and we are, right?" and she says "Yes. Of course." "Is my predisposition to melancholy and penchant for imagining depressing things and subverting most of the good that's happening," and he gives her a big kiss and after it they laugh.

He calls her and says "Lunch still good with you?" and she says "Sure, I'd love to." They meet at the restaurant where he last saw her—she says it's the closest one to the school she'll have to pick up her older daughter at after lunch—and they talk about a lot of things: books they're reading, what she's teaching, tires she's ruined because of the many times she's driven over curbs, and so on. They laugh so hard at times he feels their laughter might be annoying other diners it's so loud. She's as wonderful as he remembers her—that's what he thinks about while she's talking at length about something and he's listening. Smart, clever, funny. Beautiful, he thinks. He knows he always thought her attractive but he doesn't remember ever thinking she was beautiful. Could it be it's something in him that's changed? That just being so much younger than he is being beautiful? Something like that. And with her relatively young age and natural good looks—well, the two could add up to beauty to him. Who knows? He's all confused. The truth is, just being with her makes him confused. Or maybe he's on to something.

When they start talking about serious things—or when he does and she's just listening—she looks too serious, staring straight at him, hand cupping her chin, that sort of pose as if she doesn't know how to be serious so can only pretend to look it. Is anything wrong with that? He doesn't think so, or not much. She doesn't like to be serious. Or she has enough serious things going on in her life—that could be it and probably is. Divorce, money problems, a car that's falling apart—she brought it in to get it fixed this morning and had to leave it there and borrow a loaner—and she doesn't know if she has enough money to cover it. She'll go to her husband. He got the better car. And just dealing with her husband. And teaching and writing and worried about not getting tenure and nobody to help her the days she has her daughters. Lots of juggling. So what's he saying? He's not sure. No, he doesn't know. Got a little mixed up there again. Maybe she just likes things to be light and funny and unserious and gets depressed when they're not. Especially, he's saying, when she's taking a break from all the other things in her life, some of them troubling, and having what she hoped would be a casual pleasant lunch in a restaurant. But he doesn't know her, at least not since she was his grad student and advisee and a little after when she used to pop into his office with one of her infant daughters for a chat, so what's he making all these assumptions for? The check comes. "On me," he says. She says "Then next time it's on me." "Next time…you like movies, right?" "Love them." "So next time maybe we should go to a movie—a matinee. The Charles or the Senator or a theater like that. A weekend day if you can manage it." "I'd like to," she says, "if you let me buy the tickets." "We'll see." "Stop that," she says. "You're not being fair. You have to let me buy them. And I'm ordering your book online this week. I've been too busy with other things to do it before." "Don't order it," he says. "It's a hardcover and expensive and not worth it. Let me give you my pristine copy. If I need another pristine copy I can buy it at the Ivy." "Not a chance," she says. "Consider it done." "All right. I give in," he says. He walks her to her car. "This was fun," she says. "And I know I got lucky. Whitney told me you never accept invites to dinner or lunch." "Well, you see how true that is. And I invited you, didn't I? And I wouldn't call you lucky. Lunching with me, I mean." "Nonsense." Don't say it, he thinks, but that's usually what Abby said when he said things like that about himself. They kiss each other on the cheek goodbye. He gets an email from her later that day. She must have got his address from Whitney or someone because he doesn't remember giving it to her. "Hi! Thank you for lunch. The sandwich was delicious, the soup divine, the double espresso exactly what I needed to get thoroughly started today, and the cortavo (little C or big?), if that's what it's called and you introduced me to, the perfect end-of-lunch coffee to top it off. As I demonstrated, I love food and I felt great after. We'll talk. Ruth." He thinks: Should he reply right away? He wants to, but give it more time. Don't want to seem too eager: remember? Ah, just do it. No harm if he's careful what he says. "Dear Ruth: No thanks needed, but thanks. I like their food too. But because I know what a mess I can make, I'm never going to order a salad with so many little parts to it. From now on, just solid pieces of food I can eat with a knife and fork. Soup I never have in a restaurant unless I'm alone and facing a wall or only with my daughters. I do everything wrong other than eating it with a fork or lifting the bowl to my mouth and drinking from it. I like the restaurant you chose but have lunched there so much or at one of its branches, that I think I know the menu by heart and have had almost everything on it at least twice. For a change, if we ever do have lunch out again, let me treat us to Petit Louis Bistro. Been there only once for lunch, and the food was good, the setting pleasant, I loved the afternoon light that came through the windows, and because the place is French and the service is so attentive and refined, I'm sure my latent good table manners will kick in and be unimpeachable. Maybe we could even do it the same day we take in a movie, though you'd probably be too busy with other things to spare so much time. Lunch-movie. They go together and in that order, I'd say. Anyway…best, Phil." Did he write too much? And should he read it over a couple of times and change and fix what needs changing and fixing and wait a day or two before he sends it? He reads it. It's harmless, really only there to make her laugh, nothing in it to make him seem eager to see her or that he has anything but friendly feelings toward her, so send it, and he does. After, he thinks: Did he just now make a big mistake? Stop it. You're killing yourself. It's all right what you wrote and all right that you wrote. She emails him the next day. "Hi! Only opened my inbox a minute ago and read your email very quickly and can't reply this moment. Gotta run. Busy busy busy. More later. xx, Ruth." She's still writing him, not taking days to do it and those x's. Kid stuff. Don't make more of it than's there. The rest, all good signs.

He dreams of her that night. Dreams twice of her but only remembers the second. He's cutting across one of the quads of the school he taught at and hears someone behind him say "Hi." He doesn't turn around because he thinks the "hi" was for someone else and he's late at meeting up with her. The person's still behind him and says "Hi." He turns around. It's Ruth, smiling at him and carrying a large canvas boat bag filled with books. "That was me, before, saying hi," she says. "How come you didn't stop?" "I thought it was someone else," he says, and puts his arm around her and pulls her into him and kisses her on the mouth. "Oops, sorry," he says. "I thought you were someone else," and takes his arm away and with his other hand takes the canvas bag from her and holds it. She says "That's all right what you did with your arm there. Put it back," and he puts his arm around her again and they walk that way. "The bag's lighter than I thought it would be." "That's because there's nothing in the books," she says.

He checks his computer's inbox about ten times that day, hoping there'd be something from her. Four days after he gets her last email, he emails her. "Hi. See? I've adopted the prevalent, or what should we call it—or I call it—accepted email greeting? If I knew how to italicize on this machine, I would've italicized 'I.' But I'm saying no more 'dear' heading and the addressee's name. Nor will I, from now on, sign off with 'best' or 'very best' or 'sincerely' or such. Just my first initial or name. Don't want to appear too passé, know what I mean? So tell me, any further thoughts of a movie you'd like to go to, if that's still on? If you get a chance, let me know. If you're too tied up to go to a movie or even get back to me, it's perfectly understandable. I'm the one with all the free time and two daughters out on their own. Very best, Oops, sorry. It'll take a bit of getting used to. Phil." She emails him back the next day. "Hi! Apologies for not getting back to you sooner. As you surmised, I'm tied up in knots and nots. What does she mean by that? She doesn't know. So excuse me for trying to be literary. I invariably fail there. I'm much better at plain speaking and also sticking to the same pronoun. I thought of three movies—it's a specially fruitful period for movies in Baltimore. But I have the kids all week—Claude is out of town at a linguistics conference—so I want to but no can do. Best. Very best. Sincerely. Simply showing my solidarity sibilantly, and another literary failure. xx, Ruth." He checks the computer several times a day the next week to see if there's a message from her. Then he calls, ten days after her last email and she says "Oh, gosh. I was supposed to call you, yes?" "No. You told me to call or write you after about a week." "Good," she says. "I'd hate for you to think I didn't mean it when we talked about going to a movie. But I've been so occupied with schoolwork and mom work and housework and even the girls' homework. Middle school math, for me, is tough." "Not to worry, really," he says. "As I said, I'm the one—" "Hey! I just thought of something. I'm giving a reading from my new novel a week after next. The first public airing of it, and if you'd like to, please come. It's in a new mortar and pretzel bookstore, which has a wine license, so you can drink while you listen. I'd be curious what you think of the part I'll be reading, and you won't have to listen to me long. There are three other readers." "I'm coming. Only my car breaking down could stop me." She gives the name of the bookstore. "If you Google it, you'll get the announcement of the reading on its events calendar and better directions to the store than I could ever give. I always get people lost. And Whitney and Harold are having a small drink party before the reading. I know they'd love for you to come to it." "Not the party," he says. "I don't want to get looped and then drive. I'll have a glass of wine at the store. And the one party I've been to at their house, when Abby was alive, took us half an hour to find it. It was evening and they lived in what looked like woods." "Then give yourself plenty of time getting there and only drink Perrier." "You're so nice," he says, "encouraging me to step out and socialize more—I know what your angle is. And I will, but one event at a time. Something tells me that's what I should do. So I'll see you at the reading, if you're too busy before then to meet me for coffee or lunch." "Till the day of the reading, I am," she says. "A ton of half-theses to read and then discuss with the writers. You know how it is. You did the same with me. And though you told me mine, and later my full thesis, were the easiest to read because of all the brief dialog and half my stories were short-shorts, I know it took a lot of your time. I'm sorry we can't meet sooner. I had a good time that lunch." "I loved our lunch," he says. "Loved it. But there'll be another. "Of course there will," she says.

Next day he buys an illustrated book each on Indian and Greek mythology for her daughters. One an expensive hardcover because the store didn't have the cheaper edition. The salesperson said she could order it but he wanted to mail the books today. Kids love their presents gift-wrapped, and the paper he selected at the store was special for kids. His daughters used to read the same books and also the Nordic and Roman ones, by the same author-illustrator, or he'd read the books to them before they went to sleep. He'd sit in the lit hallway between their bedrooms so they'd both be able to hear, or sometimes would take a chair there. Then he'd shut off their lights and kiss them goodnight. He never read some of the more violent myths if he thought they might have bad dreams from them.

He emails her for her address. "But only if you want to divulge it. I'm serious. You might have reservations about giving it out. This is for some books my daughters loved when they were your daughters' age, and I think yours would too." She write back. "Here's the address of the house I'm renting. Destroy this email after you copy the address down. Just joking. I've nothing to be cautious or anxious about. It was Claude who asked for the divorce, and it's all been sweet, easy and amicable since then. You're so kind to want to send my darlings something. More later. Ruth." No x's, he thinks. Maybe an oversight or she didn't want him to think they meant something they didn't. After he mails the books to her daughters—Priority, as he wants them to get there the next day—and is walking back to his car from the post office, he thinks: Did he do the right thing? There's a strategy to all this. There's a strategy? Yes. And he doesn't want her to think he's trying to worm his way into her life partly through her kids. They have a father, who always seemed like a nice guy. He met him several times, though a while back, at department functions and once for dinner at someone's house, when Abby was alive. He was quiet and modest and a bit reserved, but from what she told him, is very paternal, and probably still is. "He's a good father," she said in his office when she brought her recently born second child for him to see, "just like you." He wants something to happen with her, that he's sure of, but he could be killing it by being too obvious. He's thought this before, but get it ingrained. So that's the strategy: Don't scare her away. Do, and she might never come back. In fact, odds are she won't. But it might be too late. She'll open the Priority envelope with her kids and say "Oh, what beautiful paper," and then "What beautiful books," and think "It was nice of him but it wasn't necessary and it was maybe a little odd," and also the gift is too extravagant—with postage, it came to almost fifty dollars—and she knows what he's getting at, and finally, he's too old.

He has another dream of her that night. They're at her rented house. Seems to be a birthday party going on for one of her girls. Lots of kids the same age; balloons are stuck to the walls. She points to a group of well-dressed people talking in the next room and says "See that man there? Know who he is?" "The one with the gray goatee? Very distinguished. I feel like a tramp in comparison. Your husband, I presume." "That's right," she says. "A sweeter man than he has never lived." Then he's sitting at a card table with her older girl. The girl holds up several paper dolls to show him. "Did you make them yourself?" he says. "No, I cut them out of a paper doll book," she says, "but did all the coloring of their clothes. Don't tell anyone. I want everyone to think I did all of it myself." "I won't, my little sweetheart." "Who are you?" she says. "Philip. An old friend of your mother's." "And my father?" "I don't know him as well, but you can say your father too." Ruth is standing nearby and seems to be mad at him. "I do something wrong?" his expression says. She signals him to follow her. They go into the bedroom of one of her daughters. The little light in it comes from a slight opening of the door. They stand with their backs pressed up against a wall and their heads turned away from each other. Then her face turns slowly around to his, gets very close, their backs still pressed to the wall. He thinks she's going to kiss him for the first time. Just as her lips almost touch his and he can feel her breath on his face, she turns away and walks out of the room and shuts the door. "Close," he says to himself, "but not close enough. She knows I'm dying to kiss her. It'll never happen. Why am I making such a fool of myself?" and he kicks the wall, feels his way to the door and leaves the room.

Next day, he tells his therapist just about everything that happened with Ruth the past week. Then he reads some of his dreams of her, which he typed up for the session so he could remember them better. She says "What do you think the dreams and the abundance of them mean? To me, right down to the gray goatee, they seem quite clear, except for the paper dolls." "No, that's all right," he says. "Then why did you read them to me?" and he says "I thought you'd be interested in them." "Would you like me to give my interpretation of what these newest dreams mean? It just came to me what significance the paper dolls might have." "No, I'm fine," he says; "really." "Okay. Let's go on. Your waking life with Ruth." "Don't I wish I had one." "Yes, yes," she says. "And this business about making yourself into a fool. You're not. Never be ashamed of your emotions. But easy does it, I say. Don't rush into things. You could get hurt. Form a friendship first. It seems that's what she wants too. Let her get to know and appreciate you even more than it sounds like she does now. You have a great deal to offer. For one thing, and very important, she more than likely looks up to you and your writing and that you've stuck it out all these years and written so much and such good work. But don't scare her off." "I know," he says. "Though she's so lovely and I'm so drawn to her—I mean, I can feel it when I get next to her—that it's difficult not to pounce on her. Though I know. And by pouncing, I mean affection-ately. But hearing you say it is good for me. She's not giving me any reason to make a move on her, so I won't. If she never does, I never will. I'll keep how I feel about her quiet and under control. I don't want to confuse and scare her, like you say, and send her fleeing." "Don't even make a move if you think maybe she's giving you signs she wants something more from you than simply lunch and your attendance at her reading. No maybes. Let it be absolutely clear she wants to take the relationship to a deeper level. You're very obser-vant, so you'll know when it happens." "I hope so." "You'll know. And you're still a good catch. The two of you have many things in common. You are much older than her and there are your health issues." "All of what I thought," he says. "But want to know what I think? That I was misdiagnosed for Parkinson's. Look at me. It can't just be the pills, which aren't that strong to begin with. My hands don't shake. My balance is good. I can walk as straight as anyone, and now I'm jogging every morning and sometimes I go at a good speed. Also, my vocal cords are back to normal, or the mus-cles that control them are. And I was so borderline hypertension, that I might not have that too." "I'm glad, if all that's so," she says. "Though don't take chances, Philip. And I don't think you're delud-ing yourself with Ruth. Look at that famous actor—Jeffrey some-one. So famous, I forget his name." "I don't know either." "Mar-ried a woman forty years younger than him when he was eighty, I think, and they had twins." "I don't want twins," he says. "Or to be a father again, and I'm sure two kids is enough for her too. But ev-erything you say is something I already thought." "Then you don't need me anymore," she says. "No, I need you. I have to tell someone how I feel about Ruth. It used to be Abby. I've told you. In thirty years there was never another woman. Now it's Ruth. I feel good that I can feel like that again." "I'm happy for you. You're a very nice person." "Thank you," he says. "One more thing. I had another dream a few days ago that I didn't even type up for you because I didn't think I'd tell you it. And if I then thought I'd tell you, it was so vivid and short, I knew I'd remember it. It's the oddest dream I ever had." "Then I'd like to hear it." "It has penises in it. That'd be all right with you?" "Of course," she says. "Anything." "Okay. I say to Ruth in the dream, 'I'm giving myself away.' Just that opening line is such a giveaway." "Go on, go on." "Ruth says to me 'What do you have to offer?' I say 'Two penises. You can have one.' I pull down my pants. Two semi-erect penises pop out of my boxer shorts. I'm not going too far?" "I told you. No." "One is pink; the other my normal skin color, kind of beige. I think she's going to choose the normal-skin-color one. She reaches down, I cringe because I think this is going to hurt, and she painlessly pulls off the pink one. I think 'Now I'm normal.' That's it. Very quick. Whole thing is over in what seemed like half a minute. It's pretty obvious to me what it means. That I'm revealing my feelings for her too fast and too obviously." "And the now-you're-normal part?" "That I now only have one penis," he says. "If I stayed with two I'd be a freak and she'd never be attracted to me." "So you're saying if she'd chosen the normal-colored one to pull off and left the pink one, it would have been the same." "I guess so," he says. "What?" "There's so much to talk about here," she says. "First of all, why do you think she chose the pink instead of the normal-colored one? And it was a bright painter's or flower's pink?" "Very pink," he says. "Like bubble gum, or what it used to be when I was a kid. But I hadn't thought of it before. Because it's a prettier and flashier color than we'll call beige and she was attracted to it for aesthetic reasons?" "Do you mind if I offer my interpretation as to why she chose it?" she says. "I'll put it this way. Pink is young, youth, new, fresh, a baby. The reason for her choosing it could be the most important part of your dream. It's the age difference again. Perhaps the number one stumbling block to a possible serious relationship with Ruth, so you're worried over it because it isn't something easy to overcome. Again, it's wishful thinking. We've talked about it. Your kissing and hugging her in your dreams, making love to her, pulling her into your shoulder as you walk, her letting you hold her hand. This is what you want to happen, as they do in your dreams. She acts the way you hope she will. And in this instance: she's protective, supportive, considerate, accepting. Age turns out not to matter. She chooses the you you are now over the one you can no longer be. The gap between you has been erased with one single gesture. And everything else being relatively equal between you—your interests, intelligence, you say she's funny, and so forth—it seems you can now get a romance going, which is what you've said you're longing for and want most. It's a positive dream. No pain; her complete acceptance of what you are. Very positive. It may not work out for you this way in real life, but in your dream world it does. It's possible I bungled the last part there. It's all off the top of my head. But did any of the rest of it make any sense to you?" "A lot," he says. "I don't know how I missed it." "It could be other things too," she says. "There's hardly ever one single interpretation for any one part of a dream. But this one sticks out." "No, I like it," he says. "This one will do. It makes me feel good. At least better than before I told you the dream." "I'm glad." "Time's up, right?" he says. She looks at her watch on the side table next to her. "You still have ten minutes." "I think I'll stop now. I got a lot out of it. I want to mull over what you've said and I don't want to get too many things mixed up in it." "Then I'll see you next week." He stands, takes the check out of his wallet and gives it to her. "Off to the Y?" she says. "Your usual schedule?" "Yes. Mind and body. Taking care of both. Thank you for a good session," and he goes.

His sister calls that night and says "So, long time no speak. How are you? Anything new in your life?" "Matter of fact, now that you ask, yes," and he tells her about Ruth. Their bumping into each other at a restaurant after about five years. How happy he was to see her and she seemed happy to see him. Her age, teaching, that she was a former grad student of his fourteen years ago, he thinks it was. Her going through a divorce, has two girls, books he sent them, lunch with her at the same place where they bumped into each other, that she invited him to a reading she's giving and how excited he is to go. That she's a terrific writer—really special; maybe the best he's ever had—and a special person too. "I can't lie about it or in any way be cagey or blasé about it, but I think I'm hooked. First time since Abby I felt this way. That's good, right?" "Want my unasked-for opinion? It can never work, little brother. There's nothing I'd like better to happen to you—nobody deserves it more—but a woman thirty-five years younger than you?" "At most. Maybe it's thirty, or a year or two more than that." "I'd cut it off now," she says. "But I'd love to fall in love with someone again. I almost got dizzy when I was with her. Her presence. Just standing beside her. And you can imagine what it was like for me when we hugged hello and goodbye. It can't be explained—and don't be saying I'm too much the romantic—but there it is. Something—well, I already said it in so many words, but something I almost desperately wanted, and it's finally happened." "What movie have I seen this in?" "Don't play with me," he says. "I'm serious, so you be serious." "Okay," she says. "Serious. You're deluding yourself. Go out with someone much older. Even a woman twenty-five years younger than you is too young. Twenty, but preferably fifteen years younger would be the maximum, I'd think, although twenty might be stretching it too far too. What's her name?" "Ruth." "Is she Jewish?" "No. In fact her mother was an Episcopal minister, or whatever they are in the Episcopal church. High up. Her own congregation. Retired now."

"So her mother's probably around your age. Even younger." "So what?" "Listen," she says. "You're hellbent on hurting yourself and also embarrassing yourself too. But hurt is what you're going to get. I know you. You want more from this woman than she can ever give you and you're going to kill whatever friendly thing you have with her. I'm sure she has no romantic illusions or fantasies about you." "What makes you say that?" "Your age, little brother, your age. The whole idea. Once your star former student, now your potential lovemate? It's not a bad movie it's out of but a bad book." "Is there a difference," he says, "other than one takes one person to do and the other many?" "I don't quite get what you're saying. Anyhow, maybe I've said too much. Maybe I don't know what I'm talking about and something good can come of it, something I didn't see." "You don't believe that," he says. "I don't, but I thought I'd say it anyway." "Ah, you're probably right," he says. "I'm all confused. I don't know what to do." "Don't do anything; that's my advice. But if you have to—if you just can't stop yourself—here's one thing you might try. You say you sent her daughters books?" "Yesterday." "Good," she says. "They haven't got them yet or only got them today. She'll have to email you or call you, thanking you for the books. That'd be the only polite thing to do. If she calls, you have to speak to her. But if she emails, don't respond. Then, if she emails you again after the thank-you one and suggests you meet even before the reading of hers you're going to, then meet. Enjoy your lunch or whatever it is. But don't get lovey or smoochy or confessional as to how you feel to her." "I want to get smoochy. There's nothing I want more." "Don't. Keep it light. Just have fun with her as a friend. That's the only way she'll continue to be with you. If you blow it once, you'll lose her for good. That's guaranteed." "No, what you say's too much like strategy, which I'm against." "Okay," she says. "That's all I'm going to say on the matter. I've warned you. Now, how are my darling nieces?"

Two days later, Ruth emails her thanks to him for the books. "They love them. I love them. It's a wonder how you knew we'd all love them. They didn't know which one they wanted me to read first and then help explain the myths to them. I said I'll read one myth from the Greeks and one from the Indian book. We got on the couch and I read to them that way till each took one of the books to read by herself or just look at those amazing illustrations. Thank you again. You're so thoughtful and generous. Ruth." He doesn't answer her. A week, two. She doesn't email him after that last one. He thought she might, though what would she say? "Haven't heard from you in a while. Everything all right?" That would be like her and nice. He doesn't go to her reading and she doesn't remind him of it. Nor the party before the reading, of course. Why? The day, or maybe it was two, after he spoke to his therapist and sister, he de-cided—"decided"? Felt very strongly that things would never work between them the way he wants them to. He's too old. He looks too old for her. His hair is old; some of his skin is too. His body is most-ly hard and lean but there's flab in places he can't get rid of that only old guys get. He walks like an old man sometimes, but that's because he exercises with weights too much at home and the Y and as a result his back hurts almost every day and is bent because of it. She would never let him kiss her on the mouth and wouldn't like him to hold her hand. Wouldn't like him to put his arm around her. Probably wouldn't even like being in a dark movie theater with him or have dinner in a good restaurant with him where he'd order wine. Wouldn't even want him to pick her up to go to a movie or restau-rant. Certainly no lovemaking. He wants so much to make love to her. From behind, from in front. Hold her from behind in bed and just kiss the top of her head and be kissed back like that. Wants to go to sleep with her and wake up with her and have her say "Oh, it's so wonderful waking up to you." Wants to go to Maine with her in the summer. But first to some hotel on the Eastern Shore, easy car ride back and forth, and go to a bird sanctuary there and seafood places to eat at and walk along the beach with her and so on. So on. He knew if he suggested any of those, he'd look ridiculous to her. So it would never work. It won't work. Get it in your head: not even for a weekend or entire day. It'd just be lunch after lunch, every second or third week. And only maybe a movie—maybe she wouldn't be a little anxious about sitting in a dark movie theater next to him. And maybe dinner out once or twice. But where they'd each drive to the restaurant in their own car, and lots of emails between them and he'd get depressed, but more depressed than he is now, because he'd want to be with her more. But it would have to come from her, but it won't and it never will, and he'd be sad or just glum when he'd see her and because of it she'd say "Maybe our get-togethers aren't good for you anymore, or as much as we've been doing," and he'd say "It's not the way I'd like it to be with you." He'd say it, he knows he would. He's always had a hard time holding in anything like that. "To be honest," he'd also say, "as long as we're talking about it, I'd like to see you a lot more than I've been doing—a lot lot more— but I guess it can never happen. You're going to be annoyed at my saying this," he'd go on. "Or alarmed or put off, or let's just say it'll scare you away from me and you won't want to see me again once I say it. But you know what I'm going to say," and she might say something like "Not exactly. It could be a number of things," and he'd say "Name one," and she'd say "Just say it, although now I'm thinking we should definitely not meet each other, at least for a couple of months if not more." Or she'd say something close to that, but eventually in their conversation—their last one—he'd say "I'm going to say what I've been thinking to. What the hell, by now everything's lost, so it can't make things worse with you than they already are. And it's probably wrong for me to say it and possibly for me even to think it, but I'm in love with you. Deeply, deeply, deeply. And want to be tender and loving and cozy and close and open and everything else like that with you." She'd say "I thought it might be that. But you have to know I like you very much but not that way." Or something. She'd say something that would trounce, or dash, or a better word, his fantasy with her. And if she did, and he has no doubt she will if he does say those things, it'd be something gentle and which she'd think would hurt him the least. He'd then say "Is it the age difference?" and she might say "For the most part, yes." "So when you look at me you see an old man?" and she'd say "I have to admit it, yes." "Oh, no," he'd say, "that's the worst thing I've ever heard." "About yourself?" and he'd say "Yes. It sort of dooms me, not that I didn't see it coming and couldn't foretell almost everything you said." "No it doesn't," she could say. "You need, if you want to love someone, a woman much older than I." Anyway, he didn't email or call her again. She didn't email or call him again, either. Had she ever called him? Once. To say, an hour before their lunch date, that she'd be fifteen minutes late. "How did you get my number?" he said. "I know I didn't give it to you. I took yours, that day we first bumped into each other at the restaurant when I was with my friends, but didn't give you mine." "The phone book," she said. "Like the few people I know who haven't given up their landlines, you're listed."

Just What is Not

They're having lunch in a restaurant, their third time in a month, and he asks her what she's been reading. She gives the titles of two books, "both of which I don't think you'd like or even want to be seen with. They're almost escape fiction, which for the past week I've needed to escape to because of all my work. But they're light and easy to follow and with no big words to look up and they also help me to get through my own writing, when I have time for it. I don't have to stop to understand another writer's complicated entanglements of plot and profundities of thought. What have you been reading?" and he says "Anna Dostoevsky's *Reminiscences*. Also, Joseph Frank's biography of Dostoevsky. The abridged and condensed edition, as the jacket flap copy says, down to around nine hundred and seventy pages from what I think was around three thousand pages in four to five volumes. But I can't part from one chapter in both books, rereading them over and over again because I love that particular time in their lives so much: how Feodor Mikhailovich and Anna Grigoryevna got engaged. Can I tell you it? It's not too late?" She says "I have to pick up the kids in half an hour, but it's only ten minutes away. So if you can give me the condensed-abridged version, I think we'll make it." "Anna was twenty and Feodor was forty-five or -six. He'd hired her—this was in Saint Petersburg, 1866—as a stenographer for his new novel, a short one, *The Gambler*. He'd dictate it and she'd write it down in shorthand and later at home transcribe it in longhand and next day he'd go over it. I think I have that right. No typewriters, then.

You see, if he didn't get it done in a month and turn it in to this very unscrupulous publisher he had a contract with, he could lose the rights to all his past books and maybe *Crime and Punishment* too, which he'd put aside for *The Gambler* and was being published serially and to great success in a magazine. Not his own: *Time*. Did you know he and his older brother Mikhail published a magazine called *Time*?" "No," she says, "but go on. All this other stuff is interesting, but we haven't that much time." "They completed it in a month and turned it in. During that time he'd become more and more enchanted with her—in love, really—but didn't think she'd be interested in marrying an old and sick man. You have to understand that nothing happened between them yet. So, in one of their many tea breaks—they took them between hour-long sessions of dictation—he said to her, and I've read this part so often I can almost quote their exact words—'I have three possible paths to take.' That's Dostoevsky talking. 'One is to go to the East—Jerusalem and Constantinople—and stay there, possible forever. The second is to go aboard to play roulette—a game that mesmerizes me,' he says. 'And the third is to marry again'—he had a very sad first marriage, and his wife died—'and seek joy and happiness in family life. You're a smart girl,' he said. 'Which do you think I should choose?' She said 'Marriage and family happiness is what you need.' Then he said 'Should I try to find a wife, should she be an intelligent or kind one?' and Anna said 'Intelligent.' I forget her reason, and I don't know why she didn't say both. But Dostoevsky said he'd prefer a kind one 'so that she'll take pity on me and love me.' After they completed their work on *The Gambler*, he asked her to stay on and help him with *Crime and Punishment*. And during one of their tea breaks from this book, he said he has an idea for a new novel after *Crime and Punishment* in which the psychology of a young girl plays a crucial part. 'I'm having difficulty working out the ending,'

Dostoevsky told her, 'and again I need your advice. In this novel, a man—an author—meets a girl roughly your age. She's gentle, wise, kind, bubbling with life. The author fails in love with her and becomes tormented whether she could ever possibly respond to his ardent feelings. 'Would you,' he said, 'consider it psychologically plausible for such an exuberant girl to fall in love with a much older man—one my age,' he said, 'and with all my physical ailments?' Anna said 'If she's really in love with him, she will. She'll be happy and regret nothing.' 'Imagine,' he said, 'the artist is me—that I've confessed my love for you and I'm asking you to be my wife. What would your answer be?' and she said 'I would answer that I love you and will love you all my life.' And that's how they got engaged." He starts crying. "I'm sorry, but this happens almost every time I read this passage in both Anna's and Joseph Frank's books. I find it to be one of the most touching stories I've ever read. But what do you think of it? Am I being silly?" and she says "It's a beautiful story. And if you said to me what he said to Anna, I'd probably say the same thing she did. No, I definitely would." "You're not fooling with me, are you? I couldn't take it," and she says "Absolutely not." "Then I've said it to you," he says, "and will say it again as many times as you want. Oh, my sweetheart, my darling Ruth. You can't believe how happy this makes me and how happy I'll be for the rest of my life," and he moves his chair closer to hers, leans across the table and kisses her on the mouth for the first time.

He goes to a reading his former department invited him to. There'll be drinks and dinner at the faculty club after, which he's looking forward to a lot more than he is to the reading. He can't stand readings and hopes this one will be short. He's sitting in the auditorium with about thirty other people, waiting for the reader to be introduced, when someone kisses the top of his head. He turns around;

it's Ruth, smiling at him. "Wow," he says, "what a surprise, seeing you. And what was that thing on the head for?" "That thing was to show how I feel about you," she says. "And how did I know you'd be here? Fiction reading? You a fiction writer? I guessed. I bet you never thought I could be so calculating. And you haven't said if you're glad to see me." "Glad? After what you said and did? Yes. Very. Very. Couldn't be gladder. Here, come around and sit beside me, unless you're with someone." She leaves the row she's been standing in, excuses herself past two people at the end of his row and sits beside him and takes his hand and presses it to her cheek. He's about to say something to her when the chairwoman of the department taps the podium mike a few times, says into it "Can you all hear me in the back?" Someone in the back yells "You're good." She thanks everyone for braving the elements on this cold and blustery night and starts to introduce the reader. He whispers to Ruth "I was about to say I've been invited to dinner after with the writer, but I'm not going to go to it now." "No," she says, "go, and see if you can get me to come with you as your date. They'll do anything for you. It'll be fun and, as usual, I'm starved."

He bumps into Whitney in Whole Foods. "You look like you're in a rush," he says, "but don't go anywhere yet. Freya, my older daughter's here with me somewhere. I want you to see her after so many years." "Haven't got time," she says. "Got to meet Harold. But we have to get together. We can't keep relying on running into each other at these places. Lunch? This Friday? Twelve-fifteen? An odd hour, but it fits in perfectly between my Pilates class and picking up Hannah at school on an early day. New restaurant I love. I'll email you where, and it'll be my treat." "Oh, no," he says. "Always on me." "Don't argue with me," she says. "I've been working out with weights and can't be pushed around as easily as I once was."

She writes down his email address. "Now, big hug," she says, and hugs him and goes to the checkout area with two containers of prepared foods. She's a good friend of Ruth's. Or used to be and probably still is. They were grad students together in his fiction-writing class, or maybe she was a couple of years ahead of Ruth and they became friends when Whitney stayed on a few years to teach expository writing to freshmen. She emails him the directions to the restaurant from his house. They meet, talk about their children, her husband—"Still like two lovebirds," she says. "We got lucky." Their writing—"I'm back at it after an eight-year hiatus," she says. "You, I know, never stop." The fiction writers who graduated with her when it was still a one-year program—"Most have given up," she says. "Larry Myers became a lawyer and is already a partner in a high-toned firm, and Nancy Burnett is a college dean." "I always forget their names once they graduate, unless they publish books that get reviews in the *Times* or they stayed in Baltimore and I keep bumping into them. You still in touch with Emma and Ruth, two whom I remember." "Just Ruth. You know she's getting a divorce." "I do," he says. "We've met a few times. She's also, I think, dating someone in Raleigh, since she drives down there every other weekend. I didn't ask why." "That's over with. It was just casual. I suppose not worth the trip anymore, though he used to come up to see her every other weekend. The guy she really has a crush on, which you must know by now—stop pretending—is our own Philip Seidel." "Come on; what are you talking?" he says. "She's given no signs of it. And to be completely honest with you, though please don't repeat it to her—I don't want to make her feel uncomfortable and stop her from having lunch with me again—it's me who has a crush on her. Imagine; my age and with someone so much younger. It's stupid. Though it's also nice to know I can feel that way about someone again, but that it can never work out has made me miserable." "She thinks you think she's too ditzy, or frantic's more like it—even scatterbrained sometimes and silly. You should try going through a rancorous divorce one time, in addition to everything else she's doing." "No, no," he says. "I don't think any of that about her. I think she's wonderful, capable, smart, the rest of it—everything good. I only have the best feelings for her and I know what she's going through." "Tell her. I'm sure she'd like to hear it. You can even mention the crush you have on her. I know her and I know it won't unsettle her." "Maybe when I get home I can call her and tell her a little bit of it," and she says "What's wrong with now? You don't have your cell phone with you?—because believe me, now would be a good time to call." "I never leave the house with it unless I'm driving to Maine." "Then use mine." She hands him her cell phone—his is about ten years older than hers and was his wife's—tells him how to use it and says if he wants, she'll absent herself for ten minutes or however long he needs. He says "Not necessary. And I forgot her number—I've only spoken with her on the phone twice—and she probably won't be home." "Then she'll have her phone with her. Her number's the oh-four, six-seven one on the phone number scroll." He goes outside and calls. At the end of it he says "This is too too good to be true. Let me pinch myself again. There, I did it, and it still seems real. See you tonight. I'll bring a good bottle of wine—a great one: Chateâuneuf-du-Pape, my favorite—and a beautiful plant to remember this call and which you can replant in your garden. Now, how do I end this talk?" and she says "If you mean turn off Whitney's cell phone, which I can see you're using by the telephone number that came up, just snap it shut."

They're having lunch in a restaurant, she comes back from the restroom and he says "I have something to tell you. It's very serious and I'm willing to take the consequences, which I know will be awful, but I can't hold it in any longer. You probably already know what I'm about to say," and she says "I think so, yes." "I didn't want it to come out. I knew nothing good could come from my saying it. But there you are. I'm sorry." "I'm sorry too," she says, "but you're right. You know yourself that something like that could never work out. For one thing, and it's the main thing—you're really very sweet and smart and generous and I like you, but there's the age difference. For instance, say something did develop between us: when you'd be eighty-two, five years from now, I'd still be a relatively young woman. And in ten years, you'd be eighty-seven and I'd only be entering, or would have entered it a couple of years before, early middle age, but I wouldn't be considered old." "Like me now," he says. "Funny; doesn't feel like it. Maybe you think I'm bullshitting you for argumentative reasons, but I feel young—thirty years younger than I am, and maybe just entering middle age, not that I'm sure when middle age begins, ends, and how many years it is. Anyway, we shouldn't see each other anymore. I know I couldn't. No more lunches and no movies and dinners we talked about going to—Gertrude's for fried oysters; Petit Louis for whatever they got, and so on—terminatively postponed. And don't phone me. No emails either. No communication between us. I want to try to get you out of my head as fast as I can. I'm done with my lunch, by the way. I can't eat anything now." "I can't either," she says. He pays up and they hug outside the restaurant and go to their cars. She emails him about eight months later. Nothing between them since the last time at the restaurant when she ended their friendship or he did. He did. In it she writes that both her daughters are fine and a delight to her. She's officially divorced now and she's okay by it. She thought she'd take it harder. Her writing's going only so-so, and she'll explain why momentarily, though she still managed to publish two stories since the last time she saw him, and if he's interested she'll tell him where he can find them. But more important and why she's writing him: she's been diagnosed with the same disease his wife had. "I'm scared. You told me how horrid it got for her, especially her last five years. They tell me it's a very bad case and that I'm pretty well along with it. Unbelievable as this seems to me, I've even begun using a walker. There I am, shuffling, shuffling. Not the one with wheels, but I guess that comes next. I've had to cut my teaching load in half for next semester, which cuts my billfold in half too, I'll tell you, but what can I do?—I only have so much energy. I've tried to keep my illness a secret from everyone but my mother and chairman and dearest friend, but now it's so obvious—shuffling, shuffling—I can't hide it anymore. I hate hitting you with this bad news. But we got close as friends, so I thought it wrong not to let you know or for you to hear it from somebody else. I also in the future might come to you for advice, since you lived with it with your wife for twenty years, right to the end, you said. So. Maybe we'll talk. Love and hugs. Ruth." He calls her that night. They talk about her illness, what medications she's on and doctors she's seeing and experimental treatment she's participating in, and then he says "Listen. This is all very gloomy and dispiriting, I know, but there could be a positive side to this also. At least for me, and I hope for you too. I thought this over since I got your email, so here it is. I still feel warmly to you. I think I once told you that you're my favorite person on earth, other than for my daughters." "I don't recall that," she says. "Maybe it was in one of my over-the-top emails to you, when I was still stupidly fantasizing a, shall we say, romantic relationship with you, or I just thought of saying or writing you it. But what I'm saying is I can take care of you if you ever need me to and help you out with money too. I have enough, and I have more than enough time to help you." "I wouldn't want your money," she says. "Thank you, and I mean that, but I'll make do." "But how about what I said about taking care of you, if it had to come to that, which it could? And this is not a one-shot offer. I'd do it till I'm too sick and weak to, which I don't see myself becoming." "This is very interesting, what you're saying," she says, "because my greatest fear is that eventually nobody will take care of me except people I pay to, and I'll have little income and savings for that. My mother's too far away and she's getting old and I wouldn't want to burden her. Same with my kids, though too young, and my sister's even farther away than my mother and has her own growing family to attend to. Friends have said they'd help. But other than driving me to places and bringing me food when I'm no longer able to prepare it and things like that, I can't expect much more from them—certainly not the dirty work. Claude, God bless him, has said he'll take on more of the parental duties. But nobody but you has offered to help me the way you said you would, or has the experience to, when things get really bad for me. So, yes, unless I come up with a better solution, and I doubt there's one, I'll take you up on your offer." "See how things work out? You can even, in time, stop renting your house, which'd save you a bundle of money, and move into mine with your daughters. I've plenty of room and will make even more room if I have to. But up till then, and again, only if it comes to that, I'll be here for you any time you want and for as long as you want or need me to. I'll marry you, even. Not 'even.' I'd want to. It's in fact what I'd love to do. And we can share the same bed if you'd let me share it with you, although that doesn't have to be part of the arrangement if you don't want it to. All up to you. But all right. Or have I once again blown it with you by saying too much too early? And forget the bed and marriage part. I don't want to chase you away." "We'll see about all of that," she says. "Tell you the truth, I'm kind of drawn to the idea of that sort of companionship too. So, my dear, while I can still cook, would you like to come for dinner tomorrow night? I'm going to make something Moroccan— my specialty. I think you'll like it." "What do you drink with Moroccan other than tea?" and she says "I like ice-cold beer. But if you prefer wine, a chilled semi-sweet sauterne would be good." "Then I'm there with a couple of bottles and dessert. Is six okay?" "Six is fine." "I also want to say," he says, "that starting tomorrow I'll do everything I can to get you completely well again so you won't have to need me or anybody else." "That'd be appreciated," she says, "and it's nice of you to say it. But you know as well as anyone it's not the kind of disease where that can happen."

She goes to an academic conference in San Diego, comes back and emails him. "Hurray, I'm home," she says. "Too many writers at the conference, but it was still fun. I missed you. I didn't think I would. I didn't even think I'd think of you. But I did, a lot. Why didn't you email me while I was away? I'll be sitting at my computer the next three hours, grading papers I put aside to go to the conference, so take me out of this drudgery and write me soon as you can." He reads her email ten minutes after she sent it and writes back "Why, did I promise to write you? I thought of it, then thought you'd be too busy, and I also didn't think you'd want me to. But call me, please? When you have time. I want to hear with my ears those missed-you words directly from you. Or I'll call you. Are you still there? Over and out." She writes right back: "Let me call you. I started it. Shut off your computer and let's just talk." He shuts off his computer and stares at the phone, which is on the table the computer's on. About three minutes later, she calls. "Hi," she says. "Sorry for the delay. I had to find your number before I could call. So, I'll repeat what you want me to say. Are you listening?" "I'm listening," he says. "But you don't have to repeat it. You might think that too silly and it'll reflect badly on me." "No, I want to. I missed you. I thought of you a lot. I didn't think I would, but I did. I know I never showed it be-fore—affection, I mean, other than a friendly affection…does that phrase make sense?" "Yes." "Is it a phrase?" "I think so," he says. "Some writing teacher I am. But I now think the way I think you think and that's that we have something going here. Do you still think that way, if I'm right about what you think?" "You're abso-lutely right in every way you said," he says. "So when could we next see each other?" "Tomorrow's Saturday," she says. "Claude's got the kids for the weekend. You can pick me up or I'll pick you up and we'll do something. Movie. Dinner. Anything you want." "I can't wait," he says. "Movie and dinner. Why not? Now you'll want to get back to your papers." "Yes, that's very considerate of you to think that. We'll talk tomorrow—by email or phone—to see what time." "Tomorrow," he says. "I really can't wait, but will have to. Oh, I'm so happy now." "I am too," she says. "Happy that you're happy and happy for me. It's exciting. But now drudgery calls. I'm hanging up, okay?" "Okay. Me too."

He can tell by her emails and how she acts and what she says when she's with him that she isn't interested in him the way he is with her. She's funny, dry, conversational, doesn't seem to want to be hugged or touched by him and only offers her cheek to be kissed. But he could never hide his feelings for very long with any woman he was interested in. He's been a good boy, you can say, not letting anything slip out that might reveal how he feels about her. But he's tired of just this friendship and wants more. Real kissing, lovemak-ing, exchanging endearments, that she'd only be seeing him, and so on. He's not going to get any of it, so should he just tell her how he feels and make that the last time they see each other? Or should he not say anything and continue to meet her for lunch every other week or so as they've been doing? He'll say something, get it out, say it all, in fact, and that this should be the last time they meet. "It's been fun," he'll say, "but it's become hard for me to see you when I feel this way and get nothing of the same thing back. Oh, saying hello when we first greet each other at the restaurant isn't so bad. But near the end of the lunch, when I know it's going to be over soon and I won't see you for another two weeks, and definitely when we say goodbye and you head for your car, are very difficult for me to take." That's what he'll say, or something very much like it. So they meet two days later. Another of their lunches. They talk about the books they're reading, movie she saw, what her daughters are doing, her cat, the novel she just turned in to her literary agent, what they should order. "Want to split a sandwich and salad again?" she says. "Or just a side salad and each of us a cup or bowl of soup and the sandwich we'll share." The food comes. "Dig in," she says. "My soup looks good," he says. "Want to try it?" She says "You don't have to ask me twice," and he passes his soup to her, she takes a spoonful, says "Delicious." "Have some more," and she says "One dip's enough. I have a whole bowl to devour. I'm afraid you won't want to taste mine. The shrimp in it." "Right," he says. "I wouldn't want to chance it. I'm a three-time loser." "Wise move, then. Though I've never heard of a four-time loser." "That's good," he says, "good. But look. I have to tell you something. And I hope what I say doesn't disturb you, but I have to get it out." "You didn't like the story I gave you the last time." "Damn," he says, "I forgot to bring it with me. No, I liked it a lot. I'm surprised I didn't already tell you. It's a terrific story, and I'm not just saying so—probably the best of yours I've read. But it's this—and I'll mail you back the magazine first thing tomorrow." "Save it for when we next meet," she says. "There's no hurry." "Okay. We'll see. But listen to me. I've never been one to hide my true feelings. Not that I haven't tried, but I always fail. It's just not me." "What are you trying to say?" She puts her spoon down. She looks serious. "What I'm saying is I'm glad the feelings I have came. I haven't felt this way since Abby died. And it feels good, but also disappointing, because nothing can come of it." "What?" she says. "You must know by now. This will have to be the last time we meet." "I must know that this will have to be the last time we meet? Why? I like our meetings. I look forward to them." "I'm saying because of my feelings for you." "You mean they're more than just friendly? If so, I'm glad. Because if you're about to say you have strong feelings for me in an amorous way, shall I say, and I know this is no joking matter so I'll try to keep the jokes at bay, and also the rhymes. But I have, and I was afraid it might backfire on me so I never expressed it, similar feelings for you. Now, is that what you were going to say? If so, I'm glad. I'm repeating myself, but I am. The big question is why you would have these feelings for me." "Don't be silly," he says. "Sorry. I meant that in a nice way. I could ask the same of you, but sure, I can say. You're beautiful, wonderful, smart, kind, a terrific writer, funny, joyful— all those words. Did I say 'smart'? I did. Exuberant too. More. You make me happy. I think of you almost constantly. I see you in my head most of the time I'm not with you. I feel you're perfect for me. The other way around, I don't know. I want to be with you always, and other things. What about you?" "Well," she says, "I wouldn't go as far as all that with you, but much of it is the same. Do you mind if I take your hand? Hold it, I mean?" He puts his hands on the table and she takes both and kisses one. "Oh, dear," he says, and starts crying. "God, you're such a softie," she says. "Another thing I like about you." "My age doesn't bother you?" "Are you kidding? No more than my age bothers me. Now," she says, putting his hands back on the table, "we should get back to our food. Then we should pay up and leave an extra generous tip—this time you have to let it be my treat entirely. It's not fair, you paying all the time," and he says "This time you get whatever you want." "And then we should go to one of our cars—where did you park?" "In the parking area right out front. Got a good spot." "Then we'll get in my car, since I'm in the enclosed parking area upstairs and it's more private, and seal this with a few big kisses and an enormous hug." "I can't wait," he says. "Neither can I," and she picks up her spoon, he hasn't started yet on his soup, and eats. "I don't think I can eat anything now," he says. She says "Nothing's going to stop me. You know me by now. Always hungry."

They meet for lunch almost every other Wednesday or Friday, the two weekdays she doesn't teach, and always at the same restaurant. It's a five-minute drive from her house and a little more than that from her kids' schools, and after lunch she usually picks up one or both of them. The restaurant became their only one for lunch after the first time they went to it. Good imaginative food and great coffee at moderate prices, not that a more expensive place would bother him. It's a cheerful and attractive place too, always crowded at the hours they go but with a low noise level, and plenty of tables and counter space, so they never have to wait to sit down. He also likes that you seat yourself wherever you want and the service is informal and fast. Almost every Saturday or Sunday for the past two months—if it's a Saturday, he doesn't go Sunday, and the reverse—he goes to the restaurant alone. It's only ten, at the most fifteen minutes from his house by car. He goes there mainly to bump into her. She told him she's often there on weekends, sometimes just to buy bread and muffins at the restaurant's bakery there, most times for lunch with her kids or a friend. When he's there alone, he sits at the long food counter, which has a clear view of the rest of the restaurant, opens a book in front of him or, if it's Sunday, the *Times* book review section, orders a cup of soup and a coffee and looks up every thirty seconds or so to see if she might have come in. If she did, he planned to get her attention by waving at her and then, if she was alone, invite her to join him—at least for a coffee—at a table or the counter if there was an empty stool next to his or two empty stools next to each other somewhere else at the counter. If she was at a table when he came in, he planned to go over to it and say something like "What a nice surprise," or "It seems we can't get enough of this place. Well, it's that good," and if she was alone or with her kids or someone, hope she'd invite him to join them. If it were a guy she was with, he wouldn't sit down with them if asked to. He'd say "No, you're busy, and I've got some things to do too," and go to the counter, order, read, and try not to look up at her again. He probably wouldn't even stay in the restaurant if she was with some guy at a table. He'd just turn around, hope she hadn't seen him, and leave. Anyway, he goes to the restaurant one week-end day a week for two months with what he knows is only a small chance of seeing her there. Then—it had to be a Saturday because he'd brought along a book to read—he's sitting at the counter but-tering the chunk of bread that came with the soup and wishing he'd instead asked for a dish of olive oil he could have got for the bread—and sees her standing on the bakery line. He puts down the knife and bread and waits for her to turn his way—he's about thirty feet from her—and when she does, he waves at her. She doesn't seem to see him, maybe because she's not wearing her glasses, and looks away. He waits for her to look his way again, but she doesn't. He goes over to her, says "Hi. What a surprise." She says "Oh my gosh, it's you. How nice." He stands with her on line. She's here alone, meeting no one; her kids are with their dad. He says "Same with me. Had nothing to do. Been to the gym already and wrote myself out for the time being and decided to take a long break and have some soup. Care to join me? I'm at the counter, but we could get a table." She says she could eat something and the counter's fine with her. Even preferable sometimes. "You can rest your arms on it and there's more room to put your things." She gets an Irish soda bread—"It's great toasted, and Saint Patrick's day is this week. Not that I'm Irish, though my hair might be"—and three cranberry muffins and two croissants. "Did you know they also make brioches?" she says. "Better than any I had in France. I practically lived on them there, and the five kilos I put on showed it—I was the only adult in France to gain weight—but they don't have them today. Boo." She pays up and they go to the counter. A man on the stool next to his, without being asked to, gets up and moves to another stool so they can sit together. "People are so thoughtful in Baltimore," she says. "It's a good city to bring up your kids." She digs into her shoulder bag and gets out her glasses. "Now I can see who I'm talking to. I'm so absentminded. I forgot I took them off and I also don't know why I did. Usually I lose them when I do, unless it's when I put them on my night table when I go to sleep." She looks at the menu, says "Remember. Keep your mitts off my check." "Got you." "I mean it." "I know. But I'm thinking, what a coincidence, seeing you here. What are the chances of that happening?" "With me," she says, "since I come here so often—restaurant, bakery, sushi bar, confectioner's stand, juice and smoothie bar?—it should almost be a given I'd run into you every time you're here." "Truth is," he says, "you once told me you come here a lot, so I was sort of hoping you'd pop in. And I'd say half a minute after I had that thought, there you were, buying bread. I'm glad, of course. It's been a busy day so far, but too quiet. I haven't talked to anyone, and I'm not saying this to get sympathy, since I spoke to my daughters on the phone last night. If I hadn't bumped into you I might not have said anything to anyone all day, except the server here with my yellow lentil soup and coffee and a pad of butter, which they always forget, for my bread. Just writing and exercising. What a dull day sometimes." "The writing part doesn't sound too bad," she says. "I get so little time to." She turns over his book on the counter so she can see the front cover. "Oh, I read this. I think you assigned it to us in class." "Maybe I suggested it, since I never gave the grad students anything to read other than what manuscripts they were critiquing the next week. Did you like it?" and she says "I don't remember a single thing about it. Maybe I didn't read it if you didn't assign it. It was fourteen years ago and we had plenty of other work to do." "This is my third time with it," he says. "Since I hardly ever reread a novel, it's got to be one of the few I really like. And actually, and this might get me in trouble, and it has nothing to do with books, I've been sort of fibbing to you. I left my house hoping you'd be here and thinking, because I figured weekends would be when you come here the most, that I very well might." "Might what?" and he says "You know. Bump into you here." "Oh. Okay. You've got a confession, then I got a confession. While I was driving here I asked myself am I going there to buy baked goods and have a cappuccino to go or stay? Or more to possibly run into you, since you said once that this had become your favorite place for lunch." "Did I?" he says. "I don't remember, but I must have because it's the truth." "Wait. There's more. I also thought that if you were here I'd fib, as you put it, that my running into you was unplanned. Why I took off my glasses when I left the car, I don't know. Absentmindedness again, perhaps. Because how would I be able to run into you if I couldn't see you?" "Maybe you thought I'd see you," he says, "and would go over to you and say 'Hi. What a surprise,' which'd make it seem even more like an accident on your part. But let me get this clear. You're saying that at least part of the reason for your coming here was in the hope of bumping into me? If I got it right, that's infinitely better than anything I ever hoped for today. I'm overwhelmed. I might not sound like it—I know I don't. I know what my voice sounds like—though that might come from my shock at hearing what you said—but I am." "Good," she says. "You're overwhelmed and I'm happy and relieved." "I'm happy too. But for the same reason I also might not sound like it." "Good," she says. "That's what I want you to be. Okay. And now that we got that out, they have my absolute favorite soup today—winter squash with couscous and kale—which seems to be the favorite of half the people who have soup here. So before they scratch it off the menu and replace it with one I like but not nearly as much, let me order it. Then we can really talk, although maybe not here." The server asks if she's ready to order. She says "Bowl of winter squash soup, Portobello mushroom sandwich cut in half—you'll share it with me, I hope," she tells him—"field green side salad and a cappuccino." "I'll take another coffee," he says. "And please make sure the check for my order and his coffee goes to me." "If that's the case," he says, "I'll have a cappuccino too. Only kidding. Just another coffee, please. Regular. No milk."

To hell with it. Call her. Get it over with. Tell her how you feel. You won't be worse off with her than if you don't call. For what could be the worst that could happen? No more meeting her for lunch? Well, that had to happen. So better now than later. Because being with her that hour to an hour and a half every other week has become too much for you. You get more depressed, after, every time you see her. So he calls her. Uses the house phone because the reception's better than on the cell, and picks up the receiver a half-dozen times before he finally dials her. "Hi," she says. "How nice. And how unusual too, a call from you. I like it better than emailing. And you're not going to believe this, because I know people are always saying this on the phone, but I was just about to call you." "Oh, yeah?"

he says. "What about? Because in all the time we've known each other recently, I've received only one call from you and that was for the first time we had lunch. I called you and got your answering machine and you called back." "First tell me why you called. Just to talk?" "More than that," he says. "And I've a feeling you're going to be so put off by what I say that I doubt you'll want to tell me why you were about to call." "What could you say that I'd get so upset about?" "I didn't say 'upset.' I said 'put off.' Though maybe you will get upset. All right. I know we're supposed to meet for lunch next week. But I think that should be the last time, and if you feel uncomfortable after I tell you why I think so, then maybe we shouldn't meet even then. I'd hate to lose our friendship, since I've really enjoyed our lunches...well, up to a point. They've been a little tough on me too, which I'll also tell you about. But the main thing I'm going to say... In other words, what I feel I have to say—" "Come on, out with it. Then, after we talk about what you said, if you want, I'll tell you about my intended call to you. And I mean it. My hand was practically on the receiver, ready to dial. And I seriously doubt our friendship would be compromised by anything you say. Though it could be when you hear what I have to say." "I want our friendship to become deeper," he says. "That's what I called to say. Or a little deeper at first and then much deeper and then as deep as anything could get between two people, or as close as it can be to that. Am I making myself clear? Are you upset, uncomfortable, put off? I don't see how you're not, at least one of them. And I'm saying this over the phone, you understand, because I don't see how I could have said it in person at our lunch next week." "It's so ridiculous," she says. "You're going to think I'm lying. But in my call to you I was essentially going to say the same thing." "That's impossible." "You see?" she says. "But you couldn't have been thinking that. And now I definitely don't know if I should even believe you were about to call me when I called." "Believe me, Philip, believe me. I don't know how it happened, the two of us with the same thoughts about the other and then calling the other, or about to, at almost the exact same time to say it, and probably also the same reason for not wanting to say it face to face. Do you know, if I had picked up my receiver a few seconds earlier to dial you while you were dialing my number, I would have got a busy signal after I was through dialing and you might have too, although I'm not sure how it works. And then both of us might have had, after we put our phones down, second thoughts of calling with what we wanted to say and not called. Isn't that strange?" "We would have said what we felt we had to say, sometime," and she says "I don't know, though I guess so." "I'm sure of it. I at least know I would have. I would have called you right back, hoping you'd just got off the phone, or kept dialing your number no matter how many busy signals I got till I reached you." "Mind if I change the subject a little?" she says. "Would you like to come by later to tell me why you wanted to move our friendship to something resembling more a romance? And I say 'wanted' rather than 'want' because it seems, with just this phone call, it's already moved there. I'd like for you to. The kids will be here, but we can still have a nice quiet talk. If you'd rather do it another time, that's fine with me." "No, tonight. Name the time," and she says "Sevenish? The kids will have had their dinner." "Sevenish it is. God, this has been some day. One hard to believe." "Incidentally, I didn't say it but I'll say it now. I'm very happy you called." "I no longer have to tell you how I feel," he says.

"Did I ever tell you the story how Dostoevsky proposed to his future wife, Anna Grigoryevna Snitkin? Or 'Snitkina,' if you want to do it the Russian way." "You have told me it," she says, "but tell me it again. It's a lovely story, I remember, but I forget most of it.

She was much younger than him, am I right?" and he says "Twenty-five years. He'd hired her as a stenographer—a new profession in Russia—to transcribe his writing and dictation of the novel he was writing, *The Gambler*. He had to finish the book—I think he even started it at their first stenographic session—in a month. All of October, 1866, I believe—or he'd lose the rights to all his previous books published by the publisher he'd signed a contract with for *The Gambler*. The writer was taken advantage of like that then, far worse than anything that goes on today. *The Gambler* wasn't one of Dostoevsky's better books. In fact, if you want my opinion, it's pretty far down the list. Maybe because—" "Just go on with the proposal he made to her. I'd much rather hear about the writer's life than get an analysis of his work. And you yourself have said that's how you usually read bios of writers—skipping the book critiques." "Got ya," he says. "How did I ever end up with such a wonderful woman?" "Is that what Dostoevsky said about her?" "No, that's what I'm saying about you," he says. "Although now that you mention it, he did say something very much like that at their wedding reception, I think to her mother. 'Look what I've married,' he said. 'The dearest girl in the world.'" "He called her a girl?" she says. "Well, he was considerably older than her. And maybe that's how all women then were referred to, no matter what their age, except the babushkas. A different time. As a woman, not one I would have liked to live in. And I remember how difficult it was being Dostoevsky's wife. Their poverty and his gambling and depression and epileptic attacks. But the story. Finish it. Then we have to pick up my kids, if you still want to go with me." "I do, I do."

Missing Out

He first sees her at a party. She's pretty, maybe even beautiful. Blond hair; simply dressed; nice body; animatedly talking to a woman. He can't see from where he is if she has a wedding band on. He goes closer. If she doesn't—even if she does—he'll try to start up a conversation with her. He doesn't know what he'll say. "Hi. I'm Philip Seidel, a friend of Brad's. You know him too or you're a friend of a friend of his?" Not that. But something always comes.

But she's always talking with one or two people. She went from that woman to a couple who seem to belong together. For a few seconds the couple holds hands. Then she's talking to Brad, the host of this annual Christmas party. Then she's standing by herself at the food table, looking as if she's wondering what to put on the plate she's holding. Now's his chance. He starts over to her—is going to say something like "So you're hungry too. Food looks good. He always does a great job on it—" but another guy gets to her first. She doesn't seem to know him. They start talking and get food on their plates and get a glass of wine each and sit in chairs close together and eat and drink and talk. They laugh a few times. This goes on for about half an hour. Then he goes to the bathroom and when he comes back they're no longer in their chairs. He walks through the apartment looking for her, hoping she'd be by herself again, and sees them in the foyer. She takes her coat off a coat hanger in the coat closet there. The guy already has his coat on and helps her out with hers. She must have come early, because when he got here that closet was filled. Maybe they knew each other before. It didn't seem so. They talked and laughed like two people who had just met each other. He never did see if she had a wedding band on. Forgot about it. Anyway, too late to introduce himself to her. If only he had gone over too her sooner. Especially when she was talking to Brad. That would have been the perfect time.

He thinks about her a lot the next week. Then calls Brad. "Hey. Great party once again. Thank you. I'm also calling because there was a woman at your party, very attractive. Blond hair. Average height. Slim. Around thirty. Wearing a navy blue blouse. Not navy. Baby blue. A light blue."

"You must mean Abigail Berman," Brad says. "A doll. A living doll. Someone I knew through school but who quickly became one of my treasured acquaintances. So smart; gentle. Brilliant, I'd say. Post-doc. Russian scholar and translator. You'd like her work and authors. Twentieth century poets, mostly. Pasternak, Mandelstam, Akhmatova, Tsvetayeva, if that's how you pronounce her name."

"You got it right."

"And that face. So spiritual. Standing alongside her is like being in the presence of an Italian Renaissance model for a painting of the blond madonna. Ghirlandaio. Botticelli. You know what I mean. Same with her voice. So soft. I can't rave about her enough. If you're interested, I think you're too late, though you could always give it a try. An old buddy of mine, Mike Seltzer, met her at the party and they left together and Mike called me last night. He's seen her twice since the party and he's got a big date with her this weekend, he says. It seems, if you want my opinion, their relationship is already hot."

"Then I better not call her."

"I wouldn't."

Next time he sees her is at Brad's Christmas party the following year. He didn't speak to Brad about her after that one time and was hoping she'd be here and alone. She comes in with the guy she left the party with last year. The foyer closet is filled and she heads his way to dump their coats in the bedroom, where his is. He smiles and says "Hi" and she smiles and says "Hi" and goes in back. He feels nervous, agitated, something, and has since he first saw her come into the party. To calm himself and get out of her way when she comes back, because he doesn't know what he'll say and do then and he doesn't want to just say and do nothing, he goes into the dining room where the drink table is and makes himself a Bloody Mary, drinks it quickly and makes another, this one not as strong. He doesn't want to get looped. Then he'll sound like an idiot if he does speak to her. He hangs around the same room she's in. Tries not to be looking at her when she turns his way. Then she catches him looking at her—she must have a few times—but this time looks back at him with an expression saying "Do we know each other from some place?" He raises his shoulders and looks away. Why the hell he do that? He had a chance to speak to her. About twenty minutes later—he left the room and came back—she's in a circle with three other women. He decides to wait to talk to her but to definitely talk to her sometime tonight. Why? He doesn't know. Maybe just to speak to her once and see what she sounds and acts like when she's talking to him. When the circle breaks up and for a few moments she's standing alone, holding an empty wine glass, he goes over to her and says "Excuse me. And don't be alarmed at what I'm going to say. But I know you caught me looking at you before. Staring, even, and I apologize. But we do, sort of, know each other. Maybe that's a bit of an exaggeration. Even a huge exaggeration. We were at Brad's Christmas party last year. Oh, my name's Philip Seidel."

"Abigail Berman."

"Very nice to meet you, Abigail. And I remember, at last year's party, I wanted to talk to you— Would you like a refill on that wine?"

"No, thanks," and she puts the glass on a side table.

"But some guy got to you first and before I knew it or could say a word to you, you left the party together."

"That would be Mike. He's somewhere at this party. I met him here that night and I guess we've been a couple ever since."

"Lucky guy."

"Oh, yes? Thank you. But lucky gal too."

"But I mean real luck, too. Because who knows what could have happened if I'd gotten to you first. In other words, got there seconds before I would have, because I was really on my way. Sorry. That was dumb of me. Too much of what I was thinking came out. Parties are good for meeting new people and drinking too much and maybe even saying the wrong thing, and Christmas parties especially, it seems. And I haven't drunk too much. I don't want you to think that. Although I have had some. But enjoy yourself. I don't think I ever acted so foolishly to a woman as I have with you just now. Of course I have, once or twice, but it's not my typical way of behaving. As I said, enjoy yourself. Nice meeting you."

"It's been interesting, but same here, Philip."

She sticks out her hand and he shakes it and walks away.

What must she think of him. A first-class schmuck. He's embarrassed by what he said to her. Almost everything. He should have planned it better, not that anything would have helped him. She's already hooked up. Talking to her made him nervous. Just thinking about talking to her before he actually talked to her, made him nervous. He talked nervously. Not that many women have had that effect on him. He's just dazzled by her, that's all. Was from the time he first saw her last year. So he should have thought of that and been more careful in what he said. Should have talked about her Russian work and authors. Opened it with that. Maybe brought up Babel and Chekhov too. Said Brad told him about her work. That would have been all right to say. Doesn't sound too much like snooping. Or maybe it would have gotten him in deeper. No, just about nothing would have. What he said got him in about as deep as he could go. He gets his coat from the bedroom and starts for the front door. Brad stops him. "Leaving so early?"

"Yeah. Thank you. Got some stuff I gotta get done by noon tomorrow. Once again, great party. And that woman, Abigail. She's really something. I talked with her. Very bright as you said. And still with the same guy she met here last year."

"That's right, I sort of was matchmaker. A real couple. Will probably get married. Mike, her boyfriend, is head over heels for her and, according to him, the feeling's mutual from her."

"Lucky guy."

"Yep, she's a honey. And so everything else: smart, lovely and accomplished. She's not standing behind me or anywhere near us?"

"No."

"Not to say good-looking."

"Good-looking? Beautiful. Gorgeous. You said so yourself when we first talked about her."

"We talked about her?"

"Shortly after your party last year. You called her a blond madonna."

"I said that? What do I know about madonnas? Sure I can't convince you to stay?"

"As I said, too much to do tonight in preparation to finishing it tomorrow. Thanks."

He sees her at Brad's Christmas party two years later. He was invited to last year's party but got the flu and couldn't go. Doesn't think he would have gone anyway. He was still embarrassed by what he said to her and figured she and her boyfriend would be there. She's wearing a maternity dress. Four, five months pregnant; maybe more. She's certainly showing, and not just a little. Sitting on a couch, drinking from a mug with steam coming out of it, so it's probably herbal tea. At least a noncaffeinated tea, or maybe just hot water. He goes over to her. "Mind if I sit on the couch with you? All the chairs are taken and it's been a busy day and I'm a little tired."

"Please. Sit." She moves over to one end of the couch to give him more room.

"I don't know if you remember me."

"You do look familiar. Did we meet here last year at Bradley's party?"

"Actually, it was two Christmas parties ago that we spoke and three years ago when I first saw you here. To refresh your memory, though it's hardly worth remembering. But I was the fellow who said your husband, though he wasn't that then, and I have to assume he is now, since you're wearing a wedding band and I saw him here, beat me out by a few seconds in introducing himself to you. And look what it's come to. Marriage. Baby. Congratulations."

"Now I do remember. You got upset at what you said. I forget what my reaction was."

"You were fine. Seltzer. Do I have the last name right?"

"Mike's you do. Mine is still Berman. Abigail Berman. And thank you for your congratulations."

"You must be very happy."

"Deliriously so. Are you married?"

"No marriage. No children. No prospect for now. But who knows? Well, I don't want to bother you anymore." He makes a move to get up.

"You're not bothering me. Why would you say that?"

"It'd seem I'd have to be bothering you, with that missed-out-by-seconds line. It would bother me if I were you."

"Obviously you're not. So. Nice to meet you again…?"

"Phil Seidel. Philip. Either. Yeah, I better get moving. Unless I can get you something first." She shakes her head. "Then it's really time for me to go."

"As you wish, Philip."

"Of course it isn't important one way or the other for you."

"Why are you talking like that? Be reasonable, Philip. Maybe we should end this conversation. Something doesn't feel right where it's going and I think it can only get worse."

"I'm honestly sorry. Excuse me." He gets up and goes to the coat closet and gets his coat and starts to put it on. He sees Brad, opens the front door, closes it, turns around and goes over to him. "Once again—it's become something of a habit."

"What do you mean?"

"I'm doing the same thing I did at the last Christmas party of yours I went to. Leaving early. You know. It's crazy. But I can't be in the same room with that woman. Abigail Berman. Probably not the same party."

"Why? The gentlest person I know of? What could she have done?"

"It's me. If you must know, I'm absolutely taken with her. If only it had been me who got to speak to her first three years ago here. Haven't I told you? Before Seltzer did. Seconds. Missed out by seconds. And not that he wouldn't have worked his way in there somehow. He's a pushy type, aggressive; I can tell."

"He's not. You don't know him."

"Anyway, there was always a chance something could have worked out between her and me. She was unattached then, am I right?"

"I think so. She was ready, at least. But she ended up with a very nice guy and their marriage is a good one and now the child. Be happy for her."

"I am, I am. Not for her husband, though. He moved in on her too fast. Ah, what am I bitching for? Just jealous. That's all. I see someone I think's perfect for me, and I can't get her out of my head. When it comes to her, I'm always talking silly. Did the last time, did this time. Gotta go, really, and thanks," and he leaves.

He gets a job in California less than a year later. Lives there for five years. Has girlfriends. Almost married one but they weren't right for each other—he wanted someone more brainy and she wanted someone less—and she broke it off a short time before the wedding date. He's not sorry either. Moves back to New York. He missed the city and never felt comfortable in California, and he lived in three different cities there. Next time he goes to Brad's Christmas party is seven years since the last one he went to. Though it's now known as Susan and Brad's party, since they got married and already have three children. He still thinks about Abigail now and then, "the girl of my dreams" he's referred to her a few times to other people, and hopes she's at the party, but there's probably not much chance of that. It's been so long. She and her husband could very likely have moved away too. And not to talk to her—though why not if it comes to that?—but more just to see what she looks like and if she's changed much. He's kidding himself. He wouldn't have come to the party if he didn't think there'd be even a slight chance she'd be there. He's actually anxious about seeing her and his stomach feels a bit queasy because of it when he rings the doorbell. It's a much larger apartment than the one Brad had before, and in the same building on Riverside Drive. This one overlooks the Hudson and New Jersey rather than a sidestreet and airshaft the last one did. Some of the guests brought their kids, even infants. Never did before. And the party started at two in the afternoon instead of six or seven at night. She's there. Her husband too. In different rooms. She's in an easy chair, wheeled walker to the side of it. Her face is the same. Still youthful and beautiful. She's by herself, just observing, it seems, some of the people there. Then she calls out to two young girls who come into the room. He assumes they're her daughters. The older one looks a lot like her. Color and texture of her hair, high forehead, heart-shaped face, and he thinks the eyes too—greenish blue or bluish green. The other girl seems to resemble her husband—dark hair and eyes and small upturned nose. Without asking her, the girls seem to know what she called them over for. They place the walker in front of her, help her out of the chair and make sure her hands are holding the walker, and stay on either side of her till she tells them she's okay, she won't fall. She starts pushing the walker forward, when he goes over to her.

"These beautiful young ladies yours?"

"My daughters, Freya and Miriam."

"How do you do, young ladies. I'm Philip. And if I may say so, you're a great help to your mom." And to her: "I doubt you remember me. It was so long ago. We talked a little at one of these Christmas parties, but in Brad's old apartment. Have you been injured?" touching her walker.

"No, it's for an illness. This is what I've quickly been reduced to."

"Oh, I'm so sorry. And I didn't mean to pry."

"And I didn't mention my illness to elicit sympathy. I'll be fine. I trust life has been good to you since we last spoke, though I have to admit I have no recollection of our conversation."

"No reason you would. Party talk. And I'm much the same. Still not married and no kids. Still writing and teaching and going to Christmas parties and stuff like that."

"Doesn't sound so bad to me, the last part. But I'll have to cut this off, Philip. I'm a little tired." And to her girls: "I know it seems we just got here and you're going to be disappointed, but would you tell Daddy I'm ready to leave? If he wants, he can put me in a cab, though one of you will have to come with me."

"Nice to meet you again. 'Abigail,' it was, right?"

"Your memory's better than mine. Perhaps we'll see each other at next year's party, if there's one, and can talk some more."

"I look forward to it. And I'm sure there'll be a party next year."

The girls have left the room. She starts after them.

"Can I help you in any way?"

"No. This has to be done alone. It's slow but I get there. Thank you."

Half an hour later he sees her and her husband and daughters at the front door, hats and coats on, saying goodbye to some people. He smiles at her when she looks his way, and she smiles back. At least, or so it seems, she doesn't have any bad feelings toward him anymore. Maybe because she actually doesn't remember anything about what he said the last time they talked.

He calls Brad the next day. "Once again, great party. I forgot how much I missed it. Christmas parties weren't the same in California. You need the cold and threat of snow. But tell me, how bad off is Abigail Berman? She sure seemed weak. Though maybe she was just tired, as she said. The holidays and all. It can get to anybody."

"I wish it was that. The worst kind of MS. Went downhill very fast, and still sliding. Exacerbating—something else. Chronic progressive. I forget the medical term. At our party last year she was able to get around with only a cane. The one before, she didn't even need that and showed no signs of it except for her eyes, which were a little off."

"The poor dear. I feel so sorry for her. I only wish I was the one married to her, so I could take care of her."

"That's nutsy, Phil. Don't repeat it to anyone else. And Mike seems to do an excellent job."

"Of course."

He's invited to the next Christmas party, but is out of town and can't go to it. Very much wants to, mainly to see her again and have a real talk. About a year after it—Thanksgiving weekend—he sees her in a movie theater on the East Side. The movie ended a minute ago. He has his ticket and is waiting on line in the lobby to go into the theater and she's in a wheelchair, on the other side of a rope separating them, being wheeled out of the theater into the lobby by her older daughter.

"Abigail. Stop," and he climbs over the rope and goes over to her. "Hi. Philip Seidel. From Brad and Susan's Christmas party."

"Yes. How are you? And I remember you this time."

"I'm fine, thanks. Haven't seen you for a couple of years. Nor your daughters. Hi, kids. Freya and Miriam. I'm almost sure that's right. I hope you're all doing well." And to her: "I don't know what to say. And I usually end up saying the wrong thing, so excuse me beforehand. But this chair. I hope it's only temporary."

"It will be if they come up with a miracle cure for me. And I'm impressed you remembered my daughters' names. As for the Christmas party. We've been invited, as I'm sure you have, and don't embarrass me by telling me you haven't, but I won't be going to it. I've become a traffic problem, being in a wheelchair at a crowded party, people tripping all over me, besides other more personal inconveniences. My daughters will be there if their father takes them. It's become a nice tradition for them, and they've even made friends with some of the other children there. So, if you go, give Susan and Brad a big hello from me. Now we should get home."

"Wait, wait, wait. What are you doing? It's pouring out." The doors in front of the waiting line open and people start going inside. "None of you have raincoats and maybe not even an umbrella."

"We'll manage. My daughters know how to look after me."

"No. I don't want you to. You'll catch cold. The kids too. Here. It's wet, but take my umbrella. It's large enough for all of you." He gives the younger girl his umbrella. "Wait. What am I doing? You stay here and I'll get you a cab. There's a whole fleet of wheel-chair-accessible cabs now running around New York. At least let me try."

"Thank you but we were planning to take a bus. The crosstown here and the number 5 uptown. They're all handicapped accessible now and they let the wheelchairs on first. You're going to miss the beginning of the movie. Are you seeing the same one we saw?"

"I doubt it. One I'm seeing's not for kids. But the hell with the movie. Heck with it, I mean," covering his mouth and smiling. The girls and she laugh. "And I only came to it to get out of the house. Anyway, I'm getting you a cab and paying for it. My idea, so my expense. It's the least I can do."

"What do you mean?"

"Well, to help you and the kids out best as I can. Stay here. I'll signal you when I get one. But I'll take the umbrella till I get a cab and get you into it."

"You're a stubborn man, Philip. Okay. We'll wait here."

"One question, though. If I can't find a cab that can't take a wheelchair any other way but folded up in the trunk, are you able to get out of the chair and into the rear or front passenger seat with a little help?"

"No. Not without the danger of falling. And getting back into the chair from the seat would be even worse."

"I understand." He goes outside, opens the umbrella and stands in the street in front of the theater looking for a cab that can take someone in a wheelchair. He's out there for about fifteen minutes. Several regular cabs slow down or stop but he waves them on. Give up. He's never going to find one. Shouldn't have been so confident. Should have known it'd be tough. Now he has to go back there and tell her, but he knows she won't mind. Not the kind of person to. She might even blame herself. Goddamn rain. If only it wasn't coming down so hard. He goes into the lobby. "Sorry. No luck. Rainy night. I should have known. And now I've wasted your time. Here, let me walk you to the crosstown bus shelter. You three will get under the umbrella. As I said, it's abnormally large, so you can all fit—and I'll hold the umbrella over you."

"Please. You should see your movie. Go. Enjoy it. We'll make do."

"I told you. That's out. I just want you to get home as dry as you can be. I'll even take the crosstown bus with you and then transfer to the number 10 downtown. I live right off Central Park West."

"Okay, if you want. I can't thank you enough. For my daughters and myself."

Should he try to redeem his movie ticket at the box office? That'll just waste more time and he also doesn't want her to think he's petty or cheap. Anyway, no. They walk the block and a half to the bus stop. Her daughters take turns pushing her and he keeps the umbrella over the three of them. Thank God the rain's now only a drizzle. Still, he's soaked, feels chilled, but he'll be all right once he's home. Few seconds after they get to the bus shelter, he sees a cab that can take a wheelchair and runs out into the street and flags it down. The cabby stays in the driver's seat, releases the liftback door, and he pushes the chair up the rear-entry ramp to the one empty place where a seat would be. Then the cabby, without leaving the cab, goes in back to strap the chair down till it can't move. The younger girl sits beside her and the older one is in the front passenger seat.

"I guess I can take my umbrella now. I don't think you'll need it anymore. Actually, keep it. To get into your building from the cab. I've got another just like it. Promotion ones, from a bank," and he folds up the umbrella and puts it on the floor next to her.

"Maybe you can come with us as far as your downtown bus stop."

"I'd love to, but doesn't seem to be room. And I'm getting wet, standing here, even for me. Bye-bye, my friends." He shuts the door. She says something to the driver. Probably their address. Cab starts up. "Wait." He runs around the front of the cab and knocks on the driver's window. Window's lowered, and he gives him a twenty and a ten. "That should take them anyplace in Manhattan. And help them into their building." Cab drives off and she and the kids smile and wave at him. He waves back and gets in the bus shelter. Damn, should have gone with them. Even diverted the cab first to his building, which isn't too far from the Central Park West crosstown bus stop. Made room some way. Just to be with her more. Even with one of the girls on his lap. Nah, she might have minded that and the girl too. But get home fast. He goes into the street and flags down a cab.

He gets a teaching job in Baltimore. Two years later he's in New York for the Christmas holiday and goes to Brad and Susan's party. He hopes she's changed her mind about not going to it, if she's in town, and is there and this time they can really talk. That night it rained and the movie theater and he had so much trouble getting her a cab. Did any of them come down with a cold, after? What's he thinking. She wouldn't remember that. "But how are you? It's so good to see you again. And your kids," if they're there. He gets to the party early, just in case she gets there early and is planning to leave early. Hangs his coat in the coat closet and gets a drink and looks around for her. Easy to spot too, if she's still in a wheelchair.

Even if she's with people or seems deep in a conversation with someone, he's going to go right over to her. He sees her husband. "Mike Seltzer. Phil Seidel. Maybe you remember me. We spoke here a few years ago. You were with your wife and kids. I don't see them. Is she here? How is she?"

"Jesus, another one. I can't believe it. You're number four."

"Four of what? I don't get it."

"The fourth person to come over to me—and how long have I been here? Fifteen minutes?—and ask after my wife and doesn't know she died."

"Oh, my goodness. What a shock. She was such a wonderful person."

"Please don't say anything." He looks like he's about to cry. "I knew I shouldn't have come. Goddamn fucking mistake," and he walks away.

Goes over to Brad. "You didn't tell me Abigail Berman had died."

"I didn't know you knew her that well."

"I didn't. But you knew how I felt about her."

"No. I must have forgot. How did you?"

"Come on. You even criticized me for it. Thought I was acting like a love-sick fool. I was completely taken by her. You're probably the only one I told."

"So something did once happen between you two? Even once snuck in a kiss or something?"

"Nothing. I told you. It was all in my head. Was I in dreamland? You bet. Not that she would have been interested in me. Well, now that I think of the last time I saw her... It was at a movie theater on the East Side. I guess before she really got sick. She was with her kids. I got them a cab because it was pouring out and I was afraid she'd catch a cold and even worse. And she might have. She was in a wheelchair and her kids were pushing her and she said something that seemed to indicate she'd be in that chair the rest of her life. What a loss. I mean, I can't believe it. What I'm saying is…well, I don't know what I'm saying. I'm glad, though, Mike was a good husband to her. Looked after her when she got sick. Couldn't have been easy."

"It wasn't anything like that. He only did so much for her at the beginning and then couldn't take it anymore when she could only get around in a wheelchair and had her first bout with pneumonia. He left her. Probably around the time you saw her at the movie theater. Her teaching days were over, so she became entirely dependent on him. He gave her enough to keep her comfortable. And kept giving it, though he didn't have to for too long, so she could stay in the apartment with the kids and have an aide when she needed one, which eventually became round-the-clock. He quickly got hooked up with someone and got Abigail to agree to a divorce so he could remarry. She's here. Nice woman. Quiet, but accomplished. A pediatrician. Abigail didn't want the divorce, she told Susan. She thought she'd lose some of his benefits, but he took care of that too."

"What a scumbag. Why'd you even invite him to the party?"

"Why wouldn't I? You're an old friend, he's an old friend, and he's always been a terrific dad. What went on between Abigail and him was their business. Who knows what I'd do if I was in the same situation?"

"I would have become even closer to her, if it were me. If I were Mike. If I were married to her and she had got the same disease. Any disease. I could kick myself that I didn't move faster that night."

"What night?"

"The first Christmas party you invited me to. What was it, twelve, fifteen years ago? A long time, when I first saw her at your old apartment. And maybe when I bumped into her at the movie theater, she was already split from him."

"It's possible. Everything went very fast."

"So I could have made a move on her then. She needed someone like me. Got her phone number. Called. Taken her out for lunch. Pushed her in her wheelchair to it. Later, taken care of her. Even married her. Put her on my health plan."

"Don't talk silly. Enjoy the party. There's a woman coming tonight I want to introduce you to. She's divorced, has three young sons, two of them twins. And is quite attractive and smart and considered tops in her field, and with a terrific sense of humor."

"No, thanks. At least not for tonight. And I know I'm usually hustling out of your party early, but I have to go. I feel so bad for her. Abigail. And I don't want to see that prick of a guy's face ever again. I could really kick myself. Kick myself till it hurts. Shit. Thanks for inviting me all these years," and he puts down his glass, gets his coat out of the closet and leaves.

A Different End

'm all confused. What if she hadn't gone to Emergency that last time? She didn't want to go. I told her she had to. "Listen, you're sick. You can't stay at home. We can't chance it. You have what seems like pneumonia again. After four times in two years, I can recognize the signs. You've been talking gibberish. I don't mean to be mean. Not gibberish. Just that at times you don't make any sense. For a few moments you didn't know who I was. Like the last time you went there, they'll move you to ICU and put you on antibiotics and a couple of IVs to keep you hydrated and fed, and you'll be cured in a week. Maybe two. I don't want to lie to you to convince you to go. But no more than two weeks, I'm sure, and this time no post-hospital rehab in some critical-care center."

"I'm not going to the hospital. Don't take me. Don't force me. Don't have the emergency medical people strap me down on a stretcher and drive me there. You have no right. If I'm a patient, I have my rights. I don't sound confused to you now, do I? I can hear myself talking and I don't."

"No, you sound good. But you don't look well, my sweetheart." I put my hand on her forehead. "You have a temperature. That I can tell just by touching you. Your forehead's burning. And your face is red, especially your nose. All those were signs of pneumonia before. An infection in your chest. Your lungs."

"What before? What are you talking about? Am I sick, do you think? Then I have to stay home. The hospital will kill me."

"Even there, see? You're saying things you don't know you're saying. I'm saying, they make little sense. Let me call 911. The EMS, or whatever the fuck its name is—the ambulance truck. They'll come and the paramedics in it will examine you right here in your bed and maybe they'll say you don't need to go to Emergency."

"I'm not going to Emergency. If I have to die, I want to die here, but in my regular bed."

"You're not dying. You're going to be all right. Can I call Marion and have her come over and look at you and speak to you?"

"Why would you call Mary Anne?"

"It's Marion. She was once an Emergency room nurse and she's become your best friend here. You know she'll level with you. If she says you should go to Emergency, will you go? I won't force you. We'll do what you want. You get to make the final decision, but first let Marion have a look at you."

"Call Marion. Call. Call anybody you want. I don't care."

"So I'm going to call."

"Isn't that what I'm saying? Call her. Call my mother, call my father, call the police. But what I'm saying is what I'm saying. Nothing will make me go."

"Even if Marion says you should?"

"You'll just get her to side with you. But we'll see."

"Let's hope she's in." I put my hand on her chest above the breasts. "You're warm here too, and sweaty. More signs. I don't know what I'm going to do if she doesn't answer."

"I hope she doesn't. I want to stay here. If I am sick, I know I'll get better staying home. I at least won't get worse."

"Okay. I'm going into the other room and calling. I'll be right back." I went into our bedroom. Abby was in our older daughter's room, which I had set up like a hospital room. Hospital bed, oxygen if she needed it, other equipment and machines and supplies to take care of her for various things. I dialed Marion's cell phone, her only phone. It wasn't a working number. I went back to Abby. "You okay?" She just stared at me. "Are you feeling all right?" She continued to just stare at me. "I tried calling Marion. Thought I knew her number by heart. Do you remember it?"

"I don't know what you're talking about. I'm fine. Why are you calling Marion? The house is crowded enough."

"It must be in your address book. Are you comfortable? Do you need another pillow behind you? Something to drink?"

"Nothing."

"I'll only be gone a minute." I looked up Marion's phone number in Abby's address book. Dialed. She was in. I told her Abby's very sick again. "I'm almost sure it's pneumonia. All the same signs. Temperature. Confusion. Everything. But she won't let me call 911. I thought if you came over and told her she needs to go to the hospital, she would."

"I'll leave right away."

I went back to Abby's room, pulled a chair up to the bed and held her hand and kissed it and stroked her forehead. "Still warm. But you'll be all right. We've been through this before. We're old hands at it. I love you, my sweetheart. Everything I do is for you. Marion should be here soon."

"Good. I like her. Better than I like you. She doesn't make me do things I don't want to."

"I understand."

Marion came in ten minutes, was in the room with Abby about five minutes, with the door closed. She said she'd be able to reason with Abby more if I wasn't there. "Girls' heart-to-heart, okay?" She came out—"We'll be right back, Abby. I have to give Phil something"—walked me to the living room and said "She doesn't want to go, but she probably should. She's not well. Her temperature feels like a hundred-three. I don't need a thermometer. Disoriented. A little trouble breathing. She should be in intensive care. But we can't force her. It wouldn't be right."

"Even if it might be saving her life?"

"Even that. She might hate it so much and fight everything they try to do for her, it could make her even worse."

"Let's try. Maybe the two of us can get her to agree."

We went into Abby's room. Marion sat on one side of the bed and I the other. I said "Please, my darling Abby; for me and the kids. But for you mostly. Let me get you to a hospital. And by that I mean calling 911 and them taking you to it in a special van. Anytime you want to leave the hospital once you're there, I'll take you home in our van, no questions asked."

"You're lying."

"Believe me, I'm not. If I were lying you'd never trust me on it again."

"What does Marion think? She told me I don't have to go."

"She meant we can't force you."

"No, she meant I'm not sick enough to go. And that if I am a little sick, I'll get better faster by just staying home. That being in my own house with you is the best medicine I can get."

"Marion, what do you think? Be honest. Do you think Abby would be better off staying home?"

"You probably should go to the hospital, Abby. It'll be best for you. You'll get a complete checkup, possibly some medicine to take, and you might not even have to stay overnight. In and out. But we can only do that if you go."

"Do I have to go in the ambulance? I hate them. They hurt my head and back."

"That way they'll be able to deal with you faster at the hospital than if Phil wheels you inside in the chair."

"All right. If you say so. The two of you. You broke my defense.

But when I say I want to come home, I'm coming home, even if it's today."

"That's okay with me," I said. "I want you home. And you're speaking so clearly. Great." I stood up and kissed her forehead. She looked away when I did it. "Okay with you too, Marion?"

"I think it's going to work out. I won't even go with you, and I'll probably see Abby here tomorrow."

"Oh. You're both such fibbers. Anything to get rid of me."

I called 911. The EMR truck, or whatever it's called, was at our house in a few minutes. We heard the siren from far off—"I wonder if it's for us," I said—and then it was turned off when they pulled into our driveway. The paramedics examined her quickly. One said she should be taken to Emergency. "Her lungs sound congested." They got her on a gurney and into the back of the truck. This time they said I couldn't ride with them in the front passenger seat. Some new rules. There was an accident. "We'll see you in the Emergency wing of the new hospital. GBMC good for you? I called in and they have room, not too jammed."

"That's where we've gone before, every single time. It's the closest and I guess as good as any."

Marion said she'd call me tonight. "Or you call me if you've time. I'll be at the hospital first thing tomorrow morning. And you better call your girls. I'd do it for you, but I'm sure they'd rather hear it from you."

"What do you think? She'll make it?"

"Sure she will. She's so strong. Look at those last times. They gave her a one-to-three-percent chance of surviving, and she fooled the experts."

She was in the intensive care unit for five days. Every day she said she wanted to come home and I always said "Give it one more day. The antibiotics haven't kicked in yet."

"They'll never kick in. You've gone from being a bad fibber to an even worse liar. You know it's hopeless. They didn't even put me on a respirator. No need to, thank God. I'm finished. They've given up on me. One thing, though. If by some miracle I come out of this, I'll never let you drag me into a hospital again."

The doctors in ICU said she needed to have a feeding tube put in. It's a simple operation, they said, and the only way she'd get nourishment. She said "No feeding tube. That would be the end of living for me. One tube, the trach, isn't enough? I was told it'd only be a month or two and it's been a year and we all know it's never coming out while I'm alive. And then those other tubes around my waist inside to my back for my baclofen pump. Did I need that too? The MS specialists said I did, but I now think the baclofen pills I was taking would have been enough. Everyone's lied to me. Everyone's a liar except my daughters. And the doctors are the worst liars. Or should I say 'husbands too'?"

"Mommy," one of our daughters said. "Dad's doing the best he can."

"You don't think I know that? Everyone is. What a joke."

The hospital's palliative team is asked by the ICU doctors to examine her. After the exam, what seemed like the head of the team signaled my daughters and me to step outside the room. With the three other members of the team standing around her but not saying anything, she said "We hate to break this to you, but the hospital can no longer help your wife and mother. Nothing more can be done for her, other than making her as comfortable as she can be, and she now needs a different and much less aggressive kind of care."

"Wait a minute. Slow down. She's dying? Nothing more can be done? Everything's been tried? This time, unlike the last four times she was here, the antibiotics failed and the pneumonia can't be cured and you've no other medications or antibiotics or any other means to help her, and you've determined this in just four to five days?"

"That's precisely what we're saying. There's been irreparable damage done to her lungs the last few years. If she goes home now, she'll be back here in a week or two, or even less, and in much worse condition and probably in great pain and discomfort, and again there'd be nothing we could do to reverse it. Everything possible has been tried. What hasn't been tried are medications we know won't help her. As doctors, this isn't easy for us to accept and is very difficult for us to tell the patient's loved ones, but there it is."

"So what now?"

"There's an excellent hospice care facility not too far from here. Gilchrist. Maybe you've seen the entrance to it on Towsontown Boulevard. You should pay it a visit. Just go right in. You don't need an appointment. Tell them you're scouting it out for your wife and mother. And take your time in all this. We're not rushing her out. Make your decision in the next couple of days. I've spoken by phone to her general physician—filled him in—and he agrees that this is the course she should take. If Gilchrist doesn't appeal to you, we'll give you the names of others. They're all much the same, you'll find. The one advantage of Gilchrist, though, isn't only its proximity to the hospital and your home. Mrs. Berman spoke with great delight of her love for your cat. Streak is her name?"

"His. Close. What are you getting at?"

"It permits patients there to bring their pets with them. Just one, or one at a time, and to keep it there so long as the door remains closed. That can be an added asset in keeping the patient's spirits up. Another advantage, although I believe they all do this, is that you and your daughters can stay in her room overnight and they'll provide the cots."

"I'm sure my wife wouldn't like being in a hospice—I know her.

But we'll visit the one you said, just to have something to report back to her and to give her the final choice." And we did—took a tour, as the woman at the hospice's front desk called it—and told Abby about where we'd been the last hour.

"Even if the one you saw were like an Arabian palace and they'd wait on me hand and foot as I slowly expire, I'm not going to it. It sounds like a death camp. The hearses are probably flying out of there several times a day. I also wouldn't want Sleek to experience it, my poor dear cat. Listen, you're wasting what precious little time I have left. Besides making me even more miserable with this repulsive talk. While you were out I came to a decision, and you can't stop me from going ahead with it. I'm coming home. Today, not tomorrow. In the next hour, if it's possible. Don't argue with me about it or I'll scream, I swear it, I'll scream and cry and make you feel even worse than you already do. And once home—and listen carefully; this is part of my decision—I'm not going to eat, drink or take oxygen anymore. And no medications, either, except what you give me to keep away the pain before I fall into a coma. And then when I'm in one if I show pain. Morphine. Make sure there's plenty of it around and you don't run out. They'll give it to you if you're taking care of me at home. Home hospice care will. I've heard. But I want to die at home in my own bed even if it has to be the hospital one at home. Now what do you say? Today!"

"I want you to first let them put in a feeding tube. You have to try it. It's a painless procedure and they say you need it to live. The food will give you strength."

"You awful person. I wanted to say much worse. Why are you acting so despicably to me?"

"Mommy, don't be so hard on Daddy. You know how he feels. And Daddy, you have to do what Mommy wants."

"I don't have to. I want to help her."

"You do have to. And you're hurting her with your demands."

"Let's give it one more day. Please, my darling Abby. If you haven't changed your mind about the feeding tube—"

"I won't."

"I know. But if you haven't by tomorrow morning, we'll take you home. Is that fair? Is that fair?"

"All right. Now all of you leave. I want to be completely alone in my room tonight. Not with you, one of the kids or a private nurse hired for tonight. I just want to think."

"Okay. We'll be here, or only I will, bright and early tomorrow morning. Now will you let me kiss you good night?"

"Of course. Have a good dinner at home. Or all of you go out for dinner. There's still time."

Phone rang very early the next morning. It was still dark out. My first thought was that she had committed suicide, or tried to, in some way. That that was why she wanted nobody to stay overnight with her. Because I would have. I had no intentions of going home. It was the head nurse in ICU. Abby was hysterical, wanted to know where I was. Wanted to be discharged from the hospital right away. "I told her she couldn't be discharged till much later this morning. There were forms, procedures, instructions. The people who took care of that don't come in till nine. We almost had to keep her down with wrist restraints."

"Are you in her room?"

"Yes."

"Can you give her the phone receiver?"

"She doesn't want to speak to you. 'No more malarkey,' is how she put it. I've tried to explain things to her. But she says she only wants you to get here immediately and take her home."

"Tell her to relax. I'm coming. That I just have to wash up and dress. Did she say anything about a feeding tube?"

"That's mainly what she's so hysterical about. It's a no."

After dealing with the paperwork and instructions how to take care of her at home, we left the hospital around ten. She went home by regular ambulance this time, not the big emergency medical truck. The previous time I drove her home. She died in her hospital bed at home fifteen days later. Was conscious the first five days and then slipped into a coma she never came out of. She refused food, drink, medicine and oxygen. The visiting home hospice care nurse, who came every morning for about twenty minutes and, once Abby was comatose, resupplied me with morphine whenever I was almost out of it, was surprised Abby was still alive on the sixth or seventh day of her coma. "No medicines? Nothing to eat or drink or for her breathing since she came home? I thought she'd be gone before I got here today." The only thing she drank the first five days other than ice chips every so often, and I suppose you can call that drinking, was a sip of champagne from a glass held up to her lips. Only foods she ate during that time was a chocolate-covered strawberry—it was around Valentine's Day, so something the bakery at the market I go to had—and a small piece of nova on half a rice cracker that had to be placed in her mouth. Both of these and the champagne on the second day she was home, when we had a little party in her room with our daughters and her best friend and her best friend's husband who came down from New York. She didn't want to see anybody else. "I don't want to scare people with how I look." I don't know whose idea the party was. Maybe it was mine. I remember wanting to lighten the mood in the house, and it seemed to work for an hour or so, at least for her. "My last bite," after she ate the nova and cracker, or part she bit off. "I might throw it up, but oh, it tasted so good. This is one of the foods I'll miss. Nova. Sturgeon. Smoked whitefish. Russian caviar. Raspberries and artichoke hearts. Quite a spread. And the champagne. Such a good one too. Everybody: eat up. So much good food I can't touch. Finish the champagne—it can't keep—and open another bottle for yourselves. Phil, we must have another good bottle of champagne around. What we didn't drink but intended to last New Year's Eve. There's no law saying it has to be chilled."

I haven't got all this down exactly right. I could ask my daughters for help with some of it, but I don't want to bring any of it up to them again. It only makes them sad and me sad and they don't want to be. Me? I don't mind, and the truth is, sometimes it feels good. I don't even know if I got the order right of what happened those last fifteen to sixteen days. But I think this is how it generally went. I didn't take notes or keep a journal. I never do about anything. It's all memory, in my head. If it doesn't come out when I'm thinking of it, it usually comes out sometime later. But to get back to where I started from: I've been wondering if she would have lived longer—and I'm not talking about a few days or weeks but months; years, even, where she still might be alive today—if she hadn't gone to the hospital that last time. Crazy thought? You bet. But possible, I'm saying, possible. A thought just to make myself feel even worse than I already do about her? Maybe that too. But maybe she would have gotten better—recovered completely from the pneumonia, that last time—if she hadn't gone to the hospital. No threat of a feeding tube or of being intubated again, which is the worst thing that can happen to you there, the air tube or whatever it's called forced down your throat into your chest and kept there, with you on your back the whole time, for God knows how long. For Abby, the three times it was done to her, it was more than a week. And the fuss and discomfort and anxiety, too, of being driven to the hospital in that truck and wheeled into the emergency room and then the intensive care unit and tests and x-rays and oxygen mask and IV's and everything else including screams all night from patients in other rooms and nurses and aides waking you up every two to three hours to take your temperature and blood pressure and draw blood and empty your urine bag and maybe change the catheter and check your IV's and ask if you need to use the bed pan or are in pain and give you medicine in liquid or pill form. Maybe it all got too much for her, just as she might have thought it would, once she was in the hospital for a couple of days, and she gave up trying to fight the disease and complications like pneumonia that often go with it, and thought what's the use? She'll only be back here in a few weeks under the same if not worse conditions, the ICU doctors and palliative team giving up on her even faster than they did the last time, and got the idea, or finally settled on one she'd been thinking about awhile, to starve and dehydrate herself to death at home. So what am I getting at? I lost what I was thinking. Then what was I thinking? That maybe I shouldn't have pressured her the way I did to go to the hospital. Not "maybe." I shouldn't have, period. And also not got Marion to urge her to go to the hospital too, which Abby absolutely didn't want to do. She wanted to stay home. She might have got better. I should have done what she wanted, or at the very least thought about it more. No, done what she wanted and not just what I had it in my head she should do. Getting ganged up on the way she was and being so unhappy and frightened in the hospital, and because she'd gone through it a few times in the last two years, weakened her to the point where she couldn't fight me or anything anymore and just wanted to die. I don't know. But I definitely think I did something very wrong. Weeks after Abby died, or months—I forget; could even have been a year, two—Marion so much as told me so. We were having drinks in the living room of my house. Marion, just tea. Her husband was there. Actually, we were sitting in the enclosed porch off the living room, it was the last time they came to the house, alone or together, though I'd invited them for drinks a couple of times after that, and I haven't been to their house since Abby and I had dinner there a few months before she died. I've no idea why. Maybe some things I say depress them, and I cried the last time they were at my house and Marion then started crying too. Or being with me reminds them of Abby and that depresses them; at least it does Marion. I'd put out a plate of different cheeses and a bowl each of hummus I made and crackers and olives and a small dish for the pits. We talked mostly about Abby. How much we all miss her. She's not someone you can ever forget, Marion said. The last book she translated that Patrick was reading and enjoying. "It feels like I'm reading the actual Russian," he said. "I don't know how she did it." That I think of her many times a day and have a dream or two that she's in almost every night. "Sometimes she loves me in them and says so. More times, though, she hates me or is very angry at me and won't let me make up to her." And those last fifteen to sixteen days. How it became, Marion said, more and more difficult for her to drop by for even a few minutes to look in on Abby and listen to her lungs and take her pulse, which she wanted to do daily. "It broke my heart to see her deteriorate so quickly once she went into a coma. Though I thank God she didn't seem to be in any pain. So thank God, also, for morphine. But I want to tell you something, Philip. To get it off my chest, so to speak, or out of it, is more like it. Patrick knows what I'm about to say. I've prepared him. And I don't want to make us feel any sadder than we already do about our Abby. But okay. I'm stalling, so here it is. I think we should have, that last time, since we knew her chances of surviving another round of pneumonia were rapidly decreasing with each hospital stay and that this one could easily be her last one and she'd never come home from it—"

"You don't need to go any further. I've had similar feelings myself sometimes. And don't blame yourself, remember, since I was the one to ask you to come here to help me convince Abby to go to the hospital."

"Thank you. I still feel guilty for my part in it, but what you just said makes me feel a whole lot better."

"I have to say I don't feel any guilt. What I thought then, and I haven't changed my mind about it, was that we had no other choice."

"That might be true too."

So where was I? My tendency is almost always to get off the track. Guilt. Hospital. Abby dying before she had to. I've said to myself the last two nights when I was in bed and trying to go to sleep: "I did something terrible to you at the end." And the first night: "The you is you, of course." And both nights: "I helped keep you alive for years and then I hasten your death and maybe even have caused it." That's what I've been getting to and finally got there. I failed her. I failed her. I should have done what she wanted. Abby. I should have said "You don't want to go to the hospital, you want to stay home and not leave our house and take your chances here, then that's what we'll do. Anything you think is good for you is good for me too." Should have said that. Also: "Anytime you change your mind about it, if you ever do, and it's all up to you, I'll take you to the hospital in our van, not the big EMS truck. The hell with that. Who needs another uncomfortable ride? I won't even call 911. I'll just make sure you're dressed warm enough for the outside, because I don't want you catching a cold on your way to the hospital. Then I'll get you in your wheelchair and wheel you up the ramp in the van, fasten the wheels to the floor, get your seatbelt around you and maybe a little blanket over your lap tucked in at the shoulders, and drive you to the hospital's Emergency entrance. We could even wait, if you want to, for the kids to get here from New York, and we'll all go together in the van. And I'll stay in the room with you every night there if you want me to, or hire an overnight private nurse to stay with you if that's what you'd prefer. And everything will be all right. But we'll only go if you want to, I promise. If you don't ever want to go, and I know I've said this before, that'll be fine with me too."

Holding On

He's almost sure he's done this one before. Or one very much like it, but which definitely included Sibelius's *Fifth Symphony*. He was driving a rented car in Maine. She was asleep in the front passenger seat. Last stretch of the trip from New York to the cottage they rented in Brooklin for two months. Route 175, he thinks it is, or 174. There was also 176 nearby, and 177 or 172 not too far from 174 or 175. They'd started out early that morning, alternated driving every hour and a half or so. She got tired at the wheel last time and had been sleeping for two hours with a towel across her chest and arms to keep the sun off her or because she was cold. He wanted to wake her to make sure he took the right road out of Blue Hill to get to Naskeag Point Road, where the cottage was, but thought it best to let her sleep. That way she'd have more energy to help him get the cats and the groceries and all their things into the cottage and clean and set up the place for the night. And he thought he knew how to get there from all the times they did it last year, their first summer together, when they rented the same cottage for two months. So it's 1980. Second to last week in June. They always, even after they got married and had their first child, liked to get there and settle in before the renters and owners of vacation homes really started populating the area the first week of July. In the fall he'd start teaching in Baltimore and she'd finish up her postdoctorate at Columbia and continue teaching there another year. Two courses the first year, one on Dostoevsky. She had about ten of his books and a couple of biographies and several books of criticism of his works in a carton in the car's trunk.

She woke up, looked at her watch and said "That was a good nap and a much needed one. I didn't get much sleep last night, anxious about getting the car and setting off on time. Oh," she said, looking around, "we're almost there. You remembered the way. Did you notice any changes in Blue Hill?" and he said "It all seemed the same—restaurants, stores, galleries—from last year. Still no bookstore or simple sit-down lunch place like the one in Bucksport, which I was hoping for. I can't stand fancy restaurants up here or ethnic ones. French, German, Thai—anything like that. They all seem out of place. Just give me a plain haddock burger, with lettuce and tomato, and not greasy, and made from today's catch. Or a fresh crab roll and some crispy onion rings and the local cole slaw. And, of course, to share a slice of blueberry or raspberry pie with you." "Well, Blue Hill caters to a fairly ritzy crowd, but give it time. Maybe the economy will flop and you'll get your wish. Mind if I listen to the news? It's almost five." "Could I see what's playing on the Bangor classical music station? I haven't listened to anything for two hours. I didn't want to wake you." "You and music," she said. She turned on the radio and went up and down the dial till she found something. "No, that's the sister station in Portland, I said. It's too faint to be the Bangor one. A little further up or down—I forget the exact numbers, but it's still in the nineties, and it'll be playing the same thing," and she found it. Same music that was on the Portland station, but clearer. An orchestral piece, he thought, early twentieth century, he guessed, and one he didn't think he'd heard before. "It's lovely," he said. "All right if we keep it to the end or until it starts getting too brassy or schmaltzy or loud? If it stays as good, I want to find out who it's by and what orchestra and conductor." "Anything," she said. "The news isn't going away, and they'll just repeat it at five-thirty, if I remember from last year." They let it play till the end. Sibelius's *Fifth*. Lorin Maazel. Vienna Philharmonic. "That final movement was one of the most stirring and luscious things I've ever heard," he said. "And that ending. Chord, silence, chord, silence, etcetera. Really unusual for a finish. Thanks." "Now can we listen to the news?" "You didn't like it? You were just putting up with it for my sake?" "I liked it, I liked it, but obviously not as much as you. I remembered I'd heard it before. But forgot who composed it and what number it was. When I finally realized it was by Sibelius, I was going to guess number seven. So I was off by two. I went to a concert where it was played. Bernstein. My favorite conductor. Same orchestra. In Vienna." "You went alone?" "No. Going to hear Sibelius would never be my idea." "The Russian poet, who I remember you said liked to ski in Austria?" "No. My boyfriend in Paris. We took a trip." "Don't tell me about it. And I've never heard it before. All the music I've heard and some pieces on the radio twenty, thirty times, and never that one? How can it be, a piece that great? I'm going to get it when we get back to New York." "That's a long time," she said. "Think you'll remember?" "Maybe there's a record store in the Ellsworth Mall on High Street." "There is, if it's still there, in the rear of a paperback bookstore, but they don't carry classical music. I've tried. When I had a working record player at the cottage, before we met." "We should have brought mine up, with some records. Yeah, but that's we said we'd do last summer, and look at us, we again forgot. We're stuck with just a radio for good music. If you want, you can switch to the news now. It's coming up." "No, the announcer just said they're going to play my favorite Bernstein piece: *Symphonic Dances from West Side Story*." "What a coincidence," he said. "You and Bernstein and the West Side."

He bought a recording of Sibelius's *Fifth* when they got back to New York, brought it to Baltimore with about fifty other LP's and his old record player, and listened to it a couple of times. They got married a year and a half later, had a baby eight months after that, kept their apartment in New York but lived most of the time in a much larger apartment in Baltimore. The baby slept in a pram in their bedroom her first few months—four or five; six, maybe; he forgets how long. She awoke one night and started crying very loud and, unlike previous times, they couldn't get her to stop. She didn't need to be changed or fed, and he checked and both diaper pins were fully clasped. He thought maybe some music and the motion of the pram being wheeled about the apartment will get her back to sleep. Whenever she was in the car seat in the car and they drove off, she fell asleep almost immediately. He wheeled her into the living room, wanted to put on Rubenstein playing Chopin's Nocturnes, but couldn't find the record in the milk crate he thought it was in. Mahler's *Fifth Symphony* was still on the turntable. He'd played it when he and his wife were having dinner that night. He put on the slow movement, turned off the lights and wheeled her around the apartment in the dark. She continued to cry. He took the Mahler off, put on the second side of Sibelius's Fifth and pushed the pram around. The baby fell asleep in about ten minutes. He lifted the needle off the record, which he was going to do before those final chords came if she hadn't fallen back to sleep by then, and wheeled her back to the bedroom. "Good job," his wife whispered.

A week or so later the baby woke up around 2 a.m. and started crying loudly again without letup. He got out of bed and checked her and everything seemed all right: double diapers dry, safety pins closed, and his wife said she fed her just an hour ago while he was asleep. "We've got to do something," he said. "The neighbors." "Want me to handle it this time?" and he said "No, I like doing it, and you should sleep." He wheeled the baby into the living room, put on side two of Sibelius's *Fifth Symphony*, adjusted the volume till he could only faintly hear it, and pushed the pram around the room, staying pretty close to the speakers. She continued to cry. He picked her up, held her against his chest, her blanket still covering her, and walked around the room with her in the dark, kissing the top of her head every now and then. She fell asleep in a few minutes. He sat on the couch, still holding her close to his chest and kissing the top of her head and her fingers till the record was over and the needle returned to the holder automatically. The volume was set so low that the final chords didn't disturb her. He put her in the pram, felt her diapers—they were dry—and wheeled her to the bedroom. "Everything okay?" his wife said, and he said "Fine, wonderful, couldn't be better. What a doll we got," and he got back into bed and held her from behind and soon fell asleep.

Acknowledgments

Stories in this collection appeared in the following magazines, to which the author and publisher extend their thanks: "Wife in Reverse" in *Matchbook Literary Magazine*; "Another Sad Story," "Vera" and "Therapy" in *Idaho Review*; "Two Women" in *Per Contra*; "The Dead," "The Girl" and "What They'll Find" in Boulevard; "On or Along the Way" and "Alone" in *Berlin Quarterly*; "Cape May" and "Talk" in *The American Reader*; "Go to Sleep" in *Unsaid*; "Cochran," "That First Time" and "Just What is Not" in *New England Review*; "Crazy" in *Okey-Panky*; "One Thing to Another" in *Apology*; "Remember" and "The Dream and the Photograph" in *The Hopkins Review*; "The Vestry" and "Intermezzo" in *Fifth Wednesday*; "Two Parts" in *Harper's*; "Haven't a Clue" in *AGNI*; "Feel Good" in *The Southern Review*; "Flowers" in *Glimmer Train*; "A Different End" in *Story Magazine*, and "Holding On" in *Story Quarterly*.

"Wife in Reverse" also appeared in *Matchbook New And Selected* (Matchbook). "The Dead" also appeared in *Pushcart Prize 38*, 2014 (Pushcart Press) and *The Best of Boulevard* (Boulevard). "Talk" also appeared in *The O. Henry Prize Stories, 2014* (Anchor Books).